e galactic mu

by Sunday Williams

Editor's note:

Thanks to Nicole Titus, Andrew Parker, Brook Swainson, Kelsey Parker, and Cindy Ensley for proofreading the earlier editions. With their help, I've managed to eliminate about 99.99% of the sneaky spelling errors and nigh-invisible grammar missteps for this, the first print edition of *e galactic mu*. The remaining misspellings and unconventional punctuations are intentional. Totally.

You are about to read one of my favorite novels of all time. I've read it cover-to-cover more than a hundred times and it still makes me laugh out loud. If you knew what a horrible curmudgeon I am, you'd be impressed. Just think of the surliest person you know, and multiply that by bad traffic and a splintering headache. Anyway, if it works on me, it should work on you. Enjoy!

Grumpily edited by Michael Peterson.
Glorious cover art by Adam Koford.
Impeccable production design by Katie Benezra.
Published by Michael Peterson and Cuddle Manor.
Available from Amazon.com and other retail outlets.

For Mike, for everything.

"It was reported to Solomon that Adonijah, in his fear of King Solomon, had seized the horn of the altar and said, 'Let King Solomon first swear that he will not kill me, his servant, with the sword.' Solomon answered, 'If he proves himself truthful, not a hair shall fall from his head. But if he is found to be false in his prophecy given to him by the horn, his deceit shall be rewarded with all the wrath that God allows me, which is quite a lot.'"

—The First Book of Kings, 1, 54

"I really believe all the things I say to you, it's just that none of them are true."

—Nomeansno

"But beauty, real beauty, ends where an intellectual expression begins."

—Oscar Wilde

CHAPTER ONE

FOR YOUR CONVENIENCE:

To better serve you and your time, please DO NOT ask the oracles if you qualify for an employment position as an oracle. Please ask a cashier for an application form.

It is a federal violation to solicit re'em from any employee of Espress-Kno™ Industries.

For your own safety, please DO NOT leave the questioning booth or approach the oracle during your session.

Remember to enjoy your prophecy responsibly! Not all prophecies are concise enough to base serious decisions from.

Thank you for choosing Espress-Kno™

1.

The first time Edelweiss visited a re'em oracle she was thirteen and worried about her egg production.

The problem was that her two best friends, Aikiko and Kelli, had already laid tiny, under-formed pubescent egg sacs. Both were bubbling over with self-impressed, self-validating selfness, which was vinegar to Edelweiss' baking soda.

"What was it like?" Edelweiss asked the girls. They were swinging in the neighborhood park, as they had done weekly since they met in the third grade. Aikiko's mother, Bernice, had only recently started letting her daughter dress herself and as a result Aikiko had worn pajamas everywhere for over a month.

Kelli, meanwhile, was licking leftover jam from her fingers. "It looked like a sac of snot," she said.

"It was magical," Aikiko said flippantly.

"Oh," Edelweiss said. She was dragging the tips of her shoes in the pea gravel beneath the swing, leaving long, dark, rain-smell lines. A spring bee began to orbit Kelli and she darted away from it, shrieking in terror.

"It's a pretty big deal, I guess," Aikiko said. She played with the buttons on the front of her pajamas. This set was baby blue, flannel, too large, with small doe-eyed lion cubs printed on them.

"Oh, sure," Edelweiss agreed.

"Don't worry, you'll get yours," Aikiko assured her.

Edelweiss hated her guts.

2.

"What was it like for you when you were my age?" she asked her Nanna Evelyn one day. They sat on the porch at Edelweiss' mother's house, drinking heavily sugared TyPhoo and listening to the bougainvillea rustle in the evening breeze.

"It was awful."

Edelweiss put her hand over the old woman's. Evelyn sighed and pulled hers away. "Sweaty child," she muttered, but Edelweiss didn't hear.

"Oppressive?"

"I had the clap and spent a summer at a Catholic work prison for girls. Then my fiancée died in the war. Then my parents were attacked by bloat-sharks off the coast of Florida. Then I had to marry a man I hardly knew to explain my fertilized egg sac."

"Ah, grandpa," Edelweiss said fondly.

"And then I lost the baby and got the marriage annulled. I don't remember the year they had me in the sanitarium. I recall getting after a nurse with a hatpin, though."

"Those years are over now, Nanna." Edelweiss had tears in her eyes.

"I've had a toothpick lodged in my arm since last spring," Evelyn lifted her arm as proof. There was a dark, shiny bulge that extended an inch on one side. It radiated heat waves. "They lost my husband at the funeral home when he passed. We burned an empty coffin."

"You're right Nanna. We're denied fair health care as women. They think we're placated by that yearly pelvic exam sham."

"The cancer sure is real, tadpole."

"That's just what men want you to think, Nanna."

Nanna Evelyn raspberried. "These things would have landed you a fast seat in the sanitarium," she said, flipping one of Edelweiss' dreadlocks with disgust. "But, Sweet Adelaide, they had these real good vitamin shots. Made all kinda pretty colors everywhere."

Aside from being tall and having a particularly pleasant face, Edelweiss had, even at her young age, carefully managed her personal hair growth. Her eyebrows were tweezed relentlessly by a Russian woman into graceful half ellipses of concern; her armpit, leg and pubic hair were routinely thwarted with hot wax by a woman from Brazil. Edelweiss had slender, even dreadlocks that reached down to her mid-back, strung randomly with massive ethnic-looking beads. She left her hair dark brown except for the ends, which were bleached and dyed the exact color of asparagus. She felt it looked "more natural" that way, but what she meant by that was anyone's guess.

3.

The Espress-Kno™ at the Gaffney mall was substantial. There was a time, just a few years ago, when they consisted only of a stand, a kiosk if you will, and had an air of fabrication about them. Presently, as you are aware, they are the size of multiplex cinemas and radiate something more like the essence of creation itself.

The Gaffney mall Espress-Kno™ was wired into Espress-Kno™ cafes everywhere via live feed, with televisions mounted every ten feet showing young people in Boston, New Delhi and Perth standing in line. Speakers emitted a hip Euro beat, overlaid with syrupy-voiced French rappers and Brazilian yodelers. But by no accident, the first thing that you'd notice when walking down the mall towards the Espress-Kno™ storefront was the storefront.

The façade was tiled with soft, gel filled pockets that looked like a quilted oil slick, alternately gray and rainbow. It was astonishingly appealing. Thugs, grandmothers and nervous businessmen leaned against the soothing surface, quiet and peacefully coexisting.

Neon signs and advertising on every surface implored that you LAUGH! and NOD! at how with-it the products were. And they were, you couldn't deny it.

The new coffee drink for the spring was Tibet-oriented (free Free Tibet! T-shirt with every thirtieth cup) and claimed to have the goodness of yak butter inside.

The advert honchos at Espress-Kno™ had a fine time with that one, in their tiny back rooms of Espress-Kno™ corporate, casting darts and drinking cup after cup of the proposed drink.

"It's… Yaktastic!" one screamed.

"Yaktricious!" hollered another.

Yakuccino was roundly shouted down and the honcho responsible was quite nearly punctured, dart-wise in the shin. Zodi-Yak was underappreciated, sending another into a foul sulk. AphrodesiYak, too. Sidetracks ensued through Tibet-au-Lait, Teabet, Himalayatte, Sherpa Shake, Dali Latte, ChaiYak and Yak-Tacular! before the honchos retired to the floor, clutching at their tummies in gastronomic woe. Word came down from the top floor: one of the VIPs husbands or wives or legal domestic partners had heard the answer in a re'em dream:

"BuddhaFly," the kid from the art department told them.

"That is the stupidest thing I have ever heard!" replied the proud father of Zodi-Yak.

The art kid shrugged, and said, "At least you guys get to go home now. We'll be here all night working on the P.O.P."

"That is the most brilliant thing I've ever heard," the adman amended.

"Is it going to be a LAUGH or a NOD?"

"A WINK-WINK." The art kid slumped away.

And now, a mere three weeks later, a man stands in front of the BuddhaFly point-of-purchase display, scratching his head in contemplation of the relative merits of yak butter and such.

"I don't get it," he mumbles.

WINK-WINK, the sign reminds.

"Oh," he says, moving to the register. "Gimme some of the drink with the butterflies in it."

"For this month only that beverage comes with a complimentary micro-mini re'emination!"

"Okay."

"Would you like to upscale it to a full re'emination at sixty percent of the cost of an Ultrafull re'emination for today only?"

"No?"

"Alright then, enjoy your BuddhaFly!"

The micro-mini re'emination was disposable, mass-produced and thoroughly checked out so as to be of the least possible predictive value. In this case, the word "fudge" was printed on the bottom of the man's cup. When he tipped it to peek at the micro-mini re'eminaton, the lid gave and spilled the goodness of steaming-hot yak butter down the length of his right leg.

"Fuck!" he said, and then looked up sheepishly at a mortified stroller-pusher. "Ah, fudge, I mean."

Delighted at this predicted moment, he licked the BuddhaFly from his hand and walked back into Espress-Kno™.

4.

E. Industries, the Neville Manowicz owned parent company of Espress-Kno™, hired the best advertisers and think tanks they could, and this is what they all concluded: no one is impressed by someone surreptitiously doing their job well. Instead, *decies repetita placebit!* You had to keep reminding the customers, it turned out, that you were doing just as good of a job as the least imaginative contingent expects of you. Neville understood none of this, so he kept to what he did know: Neville could see the future in a tiny way, which would have been unexceptional if this gift was related to re'em use, but it was not. It was an unsolicited blessing.

He felt potential energy like a subsonic noise; could spread his attention as a cat might its cunning whiskers. It was a physical odor, a palpable sound, a scratchable itch, and sometimes a giant, visible luminescent arrow pulsing just outside his peripheral vision. When Neville saw uniform sketches, storefront architecture, fabric samples and bathroom layouts, he tilted his head a little each time. Let the wind catch his spit-dampened finger.

Hearing it.

The almost inaudible buzzing. A faint light cast from somewhere, but illuminating nothing. An imagined warmth.

"We were thinking, Mr. Manowicz, and just hear this out—see this with us: we are thinking stone." A pause. "Can you see it? See it. Can you see it?"

"No."

"You haven't really looked at it. This is Ba'het from the Colonia region of Spain. Very chunky. Very texture. Yes?"

"No."

"Okay. We'll leave it with you to sink in a little."

"No. I'm going with the oil-filled polyurethane."

"Oh, yes Mr. Manowicz! Surprising but very hip, very up, you're an upward thinker, we can work this."

"Sure."

And a million conversations of the same, except sometimes puce, or chartreuse? Neither; salmon! Sometimes tiffany-back chairs or Boston style? Neither; stools! So, at some point, everything goes into production, small scale of course, but soon-to-be-hip and growing like a bloom of algae, unstoppable.

5.

"I am very sorry for the people of Paris, but the Eiffel Tower will fall."

The Region Six Department of Established Patterns Committee Sub-Director fill-in looked up from his clipboard. "What was that? Why didn't you contact someone sooner?"

"It wasn't clear until I saw you."

"Me?"

"Yes, you."

"But I'm the fill-in."

The oracle was named Regina Carey and was distressingly unattractive. Regina at first glance appeared to be a male of the teenage variety, and not in that NAMBLA way. Her short hair was reddish, curly and damp, her skin shining wetly with pure sweated lard, eruptions of bacterial primordial ooze performing fits of meiosis all over her cheeks, temples, and chin. Upon closer inspection the so-called moobs were actually boobs and the faintly lispy, falsetto voice was not an affectation, but a latent genuine femininity.

The Region Six Department of Established Patterns Committee Sub-Director fill-in stared at the rolls of fat that hung down over Regina's unlaced canvas deck shoes.

"Do you have an urgency scale?" he asked. He was panicking a little. Page twelve in the Region Six Department of Established Patterns Handbook was specifically about not panicking. Remain calm, it advised. Hysteria helps no one. What should you not do in a predicted destruction event? If you have to look it up, it goes down on your permanent record.

"I dunno. Pretty urgent?"

"I need a scale, though." His voice was reedy with fear.

"Well, I can't give you one."

On page twenty-seven, the handbook also recommends that in the event that a scale cannot be placed, it defaults to a high priority, or a Scale One Urgency Predicted Destruction Event.

"But that means I'll have to give it a Scale One!"

"Look, do you have my re'em or don't you?"

"What? Jesus, here," the Region Six Department of Established

Patterns Committee Sub-Director fill-in handed the re'em oracle a hologram-sealed, crimped cardboard tube the size and shape of a de-toilet-papered roll. The tube itself contained several of those long mutant cotton balls, which in turn cushioned an aluminum tube with a tight-fitting cap. Inside the aluminum was a plastic-wrapped glass phial with an odd nipple on one end, just above a score line. When gripped tightly and wrenched, the top would snap off cleanly and in a highly satisfying manner.

Regina Carey clutched at the tube and squeezed so hard it almost became a projectile due to the thin, oily film of powdered nacho cheese on her fingers. The Region Six Department of Established Patterns Committee Sub-Director fill-in didn't notice her fumbling and handed her his pen. She needed to sign to receive the re'em, business as usual—but then again, it wasn't. He was trying to act casual about not remembering whom to tell about a Scale One. Was he supposed to register with the Region Six Committee Director, whom he couldn't even recall the gender of, or the Boys in Washington? Who were the Boys in Washington? He was fairly certain he had the Boys in Washington's hotline number somewhere in his clipboard.

"Anything else?" he asked Regina.

"Nope. Well... I got some spooky mass murderer vibes off a client the other day. It may ah, take some more than my allotted," she tapped the cardboard tube and waggled her eyebrows. Scratched at the hologram seal a little. Gave it a shake.

He was unmoving, staring at the orange fingerprints on his clipboard.

Holy shit! The Eiffel Tower! This is big! What did the goddamn manual say? "But, I'm the fill-in," he reminded her.

"Are you going to call the Boys in Washington or what?" Regina asked, getting antsy. She'd wiped her hands cleanish on her stretch pants and left nacho orange Neanderthal cave painting prints behind.

The Region Six Department of Established Patterns Committee Sub-Director fill-in fumbled his phone open, and dialed the Boys in Washington. They answered after he spent thirteen-minutes at a touch tone menu. He told them the news. They assured him he'd done the right thing and then hung up on him.

6.

"Can I get a soy BuddhaFly, quad?"

"Anything else?"

"One of those buckwheat flax scones."

"Spirulina or wheat grass jelly?"

"Are they both good?"

"Yes."

"Spirulina I guess."

"Did you want Femuppliments in your BuddhaFly?"

"What's in that?"

"Non-GMO isolated soy protein, fructose, tricalcium phosphate, potassium citrate, magnesium oxide, psyllium, oat bran, microcrystalline cellulose, spirulina, ethinyl estradiol, carageenan, citric acid, vitamin E acetate, choline bitartrate, anti-freeze, inositol, apple pectin, niacinamide, bee secretions, vitamin A palmitate, zinc oxide, manganese sulfate, ferrous fumarate, calcium pantothenate, acrylamide, lecithin, lemon bioflavinoids, papaya enzyme, bromelain, activated charcoal, chlorophyll, pyridoxine HCL, riboflavin, clay animal litter, thiamine HCL, vitamin B12, vitamin D, folic acid, biotin, potassium iodide, gouda, chromium chloride, sodium selenite and sodium molybdate as a stabilizer."

"Sure, okay."

"Anything else?"

"A re'emination."

"Just one?"

"Yes."

"Full or Ultrafull?"

"Full?"

"Do you want Clarification with that?"

"No thanks."

"You can get a partial Clarification for only fifty-nine cents today only. Would you like to upgrade?"

"No thanks."

"It's regularly a dollar nineteen."

"Well, okay."

"Alright then, your total is twenty-three thirteen. Thank you!"

"Yeah, thanks."

"You're welcome, have a nice day."

"You too."

"Thank you."

"You're welcome."

"Goodbye, now."

"Goodbye."

"Next."

7.

At that point in her life Edelweiss was getting gangly. As is the folly of children (who are frequently incapable of speculating more than five minutes into the future), they often laughed at her for it. They were too inexperienced to know that gangliness was a spring shoot poking through the icy topsoil; beneath the surface was a complex, stunning bulb waiting to grow. Beneath Edelweiss' surface were mostly fatty tissues and stringy musculature, but they too were only biding their time. Just as the warming rays of the sun would lure the bulb into exposure, the warming excretions of Edelweiss' hormones were whispering in tiny ladybug whispers to her very cells. Grow, they suggested. Grow perfectly.

In the meantime she was one-third twiggy legs, one-third torso flat as a board and one-third hair. She was only thirteen, so the clearish down growing on her legs looked white against her olive skin. Her knees and elbows were already as large as they were ever going to be, so it looked as though she had some form of teenage arthritis. Her breasts were barely twin chocolate kisses under her T-shirts. Her teeth were too large. Already men were turning to look at her coast along in her daddy-long-legs stride, and in the next three months she would grow so rapidly that it would cause her physical pain. By the time she was fourteen the baggers at the grocery store would be calling her ma'am.

In the line to speak to the re'em oracle there were seven people. It was the slow part of the day at the slow time of the year on a Tuesday morning.

On Saturday afternoon there would be between thirty and forty. During the holidays, upwards from sixty, opening 'til closing. Edelweiss was last, drinking a Femupplimented BuddhaFly through a straw. Her determined sucking caused several individuals' cloaca to dampen.

Directly in front of Edelweiss was a woman in her early forties, casually snacking on a muffin. She was carrying several shopping bags, each containing one small item. She was a boredom shopper, purchasing things that were cheaper than normal: nylons; a candleholder shaped like a rabbit; a plain pair of silver hoop earrings (in case she lost her other ones). When she thought no one was looking she would forsake her customary nibble to stuff large wads of the muffin into her mouth. Her chewing was almost imperceptible.

"Hey, you're in my pre-algebra class, right? With Mr. Mogen?"

Edelweiss turned and looked down. It was a boy around her age, slender, mousy, freckled and with eyes the precise shade of Payne's Grey watercolor.

"Yeah, you sit next to Aikiko Ellison," he said. He was smiling nervously, the corners of his mouth flitting up and down in time to some internal barometry.

"I don't think I know you," Edelweiss shrugged, and began to turn back around in line. She wanted to see the room where the oracle was, but no one was coming out or going in.

"Yeah, I don't talk much. I don't like math. What's the point, right? I'm not going to be a physicist." He appeared to be amusing himself.

"Oh sure, but I don't see what pre-algebra has to do with physical education," Edelweiss told him in a scholarly tone.

When he began to chuckle uncertainly, she turned to look at him again. He thrust his hand at her. "Kale. Kale Gibson. At your service."

"Oh," she gave his hand a shake. "Isn't kale a weed?"

His expression dropped a centimeter. "A vegetable," he laughed. "A garnish, really."

"Well, that's cool. My name is a flower!" Edelweiss smiled radiantly, inducing in Kale a temporary and minor cardiac anomaly.

"What are you going to ask the prophet?" he asked.

"Nothing."

"Nothing? C'mon, it has to be something."

"Nothing!"

"Oh, I'm sorry," Kale answered quietly, embarrassed at her unexpected volume. "It's not important."

"What are you asking the oracle?" Edelweiss bit into her scone. Spirulina jelly quivered on the corner of her lip and Kale gesticulated at his own.

"What?"

"Your lip, there's some jelly."

Edelweiss' eyes widened and she began to giggle delightedly at the silly concept of gesturing at ones self to demonstrate an event occurring on someone else, which, for a fleeting moment, made sense to her. Kale clasped his hands together in front of his pants.

"Ah, it's a favor for my mother. My grandma is pretty sick, so my mom wanted to know if an experimental medication will help."

"Wow, I'm so sorry."

Kale shrugged and smiled. "I don't know her that well. She's pretty old. Probably for the best if she just died quickly, you know?"

Edelweiss raised her long fingers to her chest in shock. "That's terrible! You should respect people that get that old!"

"Oh, I respect her, I'm just saying that I would at least hope for a quick death when I'm too old to see or hear anything and have to wear a diaper, wouldn't you?"

"She can still be read to, can't she? And have her shoulders rubbed?"

"Again: deaf," he said, and shuddered involuntarily while imagining touching the old woman's liver-spotted shoulders.

"I think you should be happy that your grandmother is alive. Mine were both dead before I was born and I never got to meet them."

"I'm sorry."

"Wait, no. They were alive and then they weren't. Or, one of them is still alive. Oh yeah, Nanna."

Kale pointed past Edelweiss, and she looked around, perplexed. The line had moved. She had missed her chance to look in. Dismayed, she turned back. "Look," she said, furrowing her brow. "I think that old people are the future. I mean, they have been around for a lifetime, and you can't say that about anyone else."

"Uh," Kale said, and the line moved again, so he pointed again.

"Shoot!" Edelweiss stomped her foot. She turned to face the front, determined not to say another word. She wasn't sure she liked this boy. He was one of those weird kids that wore buttons and shirts touting unknown bands. He read a lot at lunchtime and joked around with the theater kids. She began to suspect he was a dork.

Eventually, the line moved the entire rest of the way, but the one time that Edelweiss got a chance to look in, she saw nothing. There was a wall just past the entrance where people had to turn, like public bathrooms with no doors, where you couldn't see in. She stood with her toes hanging over the edge of the line on the floor, her heart beating quickly. At one point she caught a glimpse of Kale behind her staring solemnly at his shoes, but she could hardly be bothered with such things.

The shopping woman came from the entrance beaming. She was rushing off to a sale that she didn't know of until thirty seconds ago. The attendant motioned for Edelweiss.

Don't savor the steps, run! Such is youth.

Now, if there is one thing in this crazy world that you can't deny it's that everyone loves the paranormal. Those that don't believe in it are tickled to dispute it. Those that believe are nearly knocked out with joy at anything that might possibly constitute proof. Those that have never considered it are like children being introduced to ice cream, opinions unformed but overwhelmingly interested. Then why, why do the adjectives always make it sound so immature? Whatever the case, the best words to describe the oracle's room were 'trippy' and 'spooky' and 'moist' (which may have had a little to do with the theatrical machine fog).

Edelweiss rotated in a tight circle, absorbed. The room was dark and smelled faintly of the sea. There was some kind of projection on the ceiling that looked like curdled milk clouds moving in the night sky. Heavy drapes guarded the entrance door from a metal-railed platform—which was the only place to stand. There was some twangy, moody Celtic music swelling from nowhere, or for the less romantic, from flush-mounted ceiling speakers. Edelweiss stepped up to the platform.

"Hello?" she asked. This was so cool! When she was younger she remembered the kiosks in the mall where the oracles sat in the open, pitching little random future tidbits at people, eyes dilated with re'em. It was easy to spot the people who would immediately believe over those who wouldn't: women were the most likely, old people second. Old women were one hundred percent guaranteed.

A soft light appeared directly in front of her. She realized someone was sitting there in the darkness, a face emerging in the accumulating light. Edelweiss nearly fainted with excitement.

"What query have you of beyond the veil?" the speakers bellowed. The voice was lispy and androgynous.

"What?"

"Offer forth your trepidation to the void and it shall be answered."

"I'm sorry?"

"From the swirling oblivion, truth!"

"I have a question, please?"

"What is it?"

"Um," Edelweiss ventured, and was overwhelmed with embarrassment.

"All questions are welcome."

"I'm nervous."

"I've heard them all before."

Edelweiss leaned on the railing and avoided any distant creepy eye contact with the oracle. She wasn't entirely comfortable about not being able to discern the oracle's gender. "Well, it's a girl question."

"Ah yes, the ancient woe, all things of the heart are guarded and strange."

"I don't understand what you're saying."

"You're in love, right?"

"No... it's about, well, all of my friends have had their first egg sacs and I haven't. I was starting to get worried."

"What is your question exactly?"

"Well, am I going to get it?"

There was a pause, and the face in the light lolled about as though possessed. "The depths of the universe are immeasurable, but a pinpoint of light shines for you. I see that yes, you will begin to get egg sacs."

Edelweiss clapped her hands over her mouth, tears springing to get eyes. "Oh, when?"

"In the thirteenth year of your life."

"Yes, but when?"

"I'm sorry, you only ordered a partial Clarification."

"What?"

"You ordered a Full re'emination with the special of a partial Clarification. You received your partial Clarification in the form of the answer, 'In the thirteenth year of your life.'"

"But. All I wanted to know was when."

"Sure, kid, but time is a complicated thing, you got a partial answer for a partial Clarification. 'Kay?"

"Can you at least tell me where I'll get it?"

"Uh, I don't know, in your pants?" There was muffled laughter over the speakers.

"No, I mean, where I will be at?"

"If you had purchased a Des-Cryption I could have told you that."

"Can't you tell me now? I'll pay for it when I get back out there."

"Sorry, you have to pay for your product before you receive it."

"But—"

"Thank you for using Espress-Kno™, please come again."

Then the lights went down around Edelweiss and a spot light centered on the entrance/exit behind her. A green exit sign flashed insistently.

"But I'm not done."

"Espress-Kno™ thanks you for your patronage. There is no limit to how many times you can use Espress-Kno™, so feel free to return to the cashier and upgrade your question. Have an enlightened day!" This time the voice was distinctly male and obviously a recording.

Edelweiss stared at the exit for a few more seconds before she, in a fit of self-conscious theatrics, ran all the way out of Espress-Kno™ and loped to the mall's central courtyard where she promptly felt better.

8.

"How was your day?"

The Region Six Department of Established Patterns Committee Sub-Director fill-in was unbuttoning his shirt, which was white and too large since he had purchased it himself and had no idea what the numbers '18-33' were supposed to denote.

"Well, dear-heart, I may have saved hundreds of lives," he said, without a trace of pride.

His wife was brushing her long, cereal-colored hair at her little powder table. She was wearing a nightgown of some kind, which was sweet, because he was just going to pull it off in a few minutes anyway. It was a little game they played. His wife turned to him slowly, brush in mid-stroke.

"Did I hear you right?"

"Yes ma'am. The man you see before you very well may be a hero." He was mostly joking, but got an electric shiver from the look on his wife's face all the same.

"Oh, Region Six Department of Established Patterns Committee Sub-Director fill-in, you're my hero every single day," she said, sweeping up from the powder table. When her hairbrush settled hard onto the table top it slid sharply to the side, where it knocked over, in a tragic tinkle of breaking porcelain and glass, some of her favorite perfume bottles.

"Oh no!" she said, turning to look.

The Region Six Department of Established Patterns Committee Sub-Director fill-in grabbed her by the shoulder, spun her around into his arms and whispered, "I'll buy you two new ones for every one that is broken."

"Dear, but my sister sent the one back from Paris."

He looked at the floor and his eyes narrowed. Amongst the shattered hearts of glass and leaking crystal phials was a tiny broken figurine shaped like the Eiffel Tower.

"Shit," he said.

CHAPTER TWO

1.

Aikiko's mother, Bernice, was born and raised in a town in southern Japan called Miyazaki, which would later be famous for the world's largest indoor waterpark and its obsession with forest conservation (of which, it should be noted, the waterpark successfully eliminated hundreds of acres). It was also nearly tropical most of the year, which was why when she married her American husband they moved to the most similarly miserably sub-tropical place in North America: South Carolina.

"Kids," she called upstairs. She had an almost impenetrable accent, despite having lived in America nearly as long as she had in Japan.

"We're coming," Aikiko hollered back. She turned back to Edelweiss on the futon. "I'm serious."

Edelweiss was as curious as any other kid, but when it came to actual procurement, she found herself chickening out. She had taken part in the local chapter of Substance Use Compromises Kids just the year before and was still chock full of re'em horror stories.

There's the teenage boy who re'em dreamed he was going to be handicapped in a particularly grisly accident, so he offs himself to avoid the agony. Or the man that shoots his dog because he 'prophesizes' it will bite a child down the street. Or the girl whose boyfriend has a re'emination that she is sterile, so the girl spawns willy nilly, leaving fertilized egg sacs from one end of town to the other, and ends up with eighty-two kids. Edelweiss didn't want to be any of those poor bastards.

"I know you're serious. I'm just not sure, you know?"

"Well, let's go down for breakfast before mom freaks out. Then we'll talk some more."

Edelweiss was wearing a pair of Aikiko's pajamas, cotton ones with the kittens rolling balls of string across a green and yellow tartan. Aikiko had recently taken to a red satin Chinese dragon print with extra long sleeves and knot-buttons that led to a mandarin collar, which could have looked royal against her half-Japanese skin if not for her crazed bed-head.

Downstairs, Bernice had prepared them a small breakfast. It was her habit to prepare something traditionally Japanese for every meal, but for patriotism's sake she made sure there was also something equally American. This morning breakfast was soupy rice with raw egg, a small dish of garlicky seaweed and a stack of blueberry toaster waffles with corn syrup. There was evidence that Aikiko's father had already departed for work.

"Do you have any maple syrup?" Edelweiss asked, reaching for the waffles.

"Maporu sulup vely expensive!"

"Uh," Edelweiss said. She tried to eat the soupy rice without tipping the bowl to her mouth, even though Aikiko and Bernice were demonstrating that very approach, and instead spooned it up a few grains at a time.

"What lou gils planu today?"

"We were going to work on the fort some more. The one way back in the woods," Aikiko answered.

"Ah, shiro-zato, lou calufu, okay? Many danger with hammoru."

"The what?" Edelweiss asked.

"Hammoru!"

"The what?"

"Hammer, the hammer," Aikiko said.

"I didn't know we were working on the fort," Edelweiss turned to Aikiko.

"Yes, Eddy," Aikiko said, widening her eyes. "Like we were talking about upstairs. Earlier."

"Eh?"

Aikiko and her mother began to converse in Japanese during which Edelweiss tried to eat, and watched as the two Ellison women scooped up mouthfuls of seaweed by folding the waffles in half into taco shapes, and then loading up the folded pockets with garlicky sea greens. Edelweiss felt ill.

They cleared the table and Aikiko ran to the front door, stepping into her sandals. "Ready to go?" she asked Edelweiss.

"I'm still in my pajamas."

Aikiko rolled her eyes. "You're a prisoner of society's norms, Eddy."

"That's light," Bernice yelled from the kitchen. "Lou must fight theiru image with lou tlue shelf."

Edelweiss glanced at Bernice in incomprehension before whining, "These pajamas are way too short."

"You're freakishly tall," Aikiko sassed.

"Shiro-zato, evelyone is light sizu."

"Hurry up then," Aikiko spat at Edelweiss. Within minutes they were walking down the long dirt driveway, away from the house. A fantastically verdant and steamy summer day was about to hit its stride in Gaffney; the smell of saw palmetto and a hundred different moss species preceded it.

"Where are we going? The fort is back that way." Edelweiss pointed.

"To the N-E-Time Mart, Eddy. To meet up with Corduroy McBeen."

"What? But he's sixteen!"

"He sells re'em."

"Ha-ha! We made a poem."

2.

Corduroy McBeen was raised in the backwoods of Gaffney, which there were quite a lot of, so it was not the kind of description you gave if you wanted to be found. He grew up in a plank-floor house built directly on top of the soil. In the summer time when the earth baked into flour, any movement across the house caused a choking cloud of dust to rise, covering every dish and table linen.

It was enough to drive his mother insane, and eventually had.

Corduroy's dad worked at the textile mill down the way, and was about as silent as a non-clinically mute person can get. It was unlikely that he even noticed his wife's insanity. Or that his children were alive. Such is life, and the older Corduroy got, the more he appreciated his father's long absences.

Corduroy was an asshole. He was easily misconstrued as a bully, but on the whole he was disinterested in other kids. He beat them to chutney only when they got in his way, and taking their money was never a high priority. In fact, more often than not, it was offered to him outright, before he had thrown a single punch, which baffled him. Money didn't stop him from hitting kids, but sometimes they got away when he was counting it. He didn't really need the money, see, he sold enough re'em to keep his family fed and clothed. His dad gave his mom ten dollars a week for groceries and toiletries, which hadn't been enough to cover the costs in quite a few years, but Corduroy's secret income made up for it. And before you think his generosity was one of altruism, rest assured that laziness was the true motivation. It was just easier to let his mom do the shopping.

Corduroy McBeen had been in the habit of purchasing a packet of salted peanuts and a cola in a glass bottle on his way into town. He would tear open the packet and dump the peanuts into his glass bottle of soda. This would cause it to fizz considerably, and as a side effect, produce a mysteriously tastier drink. When he was done drinking the liquid there were cola-logged peanuts to enjoy.

Corduroy thought he had made this up himself, despite the fact that all southern children do this. That's the bad part about inventing things: most of the time, you ain't. In Corduroy's case it didn't matter: he was his own biggest fan.

In this same school of belief, Corduroy thinks he is one of maybe two people in his county (where the world starts and ends for him) who has a set of shacks way back in the back of the backwoods. These shacks are impressively dilapidated, even for shacks, as a result of their contents, which was nothing less than a dozen unicorns. The unicorns ate everything in their proximity, making it imperative for Corduroy to nail up new pieces of wood and aluminum siding almost every day to keep them contained. It was work, sometimes, but it beat bagging groceries.

Before school ended for the year, Corduroy gave his phone number to a middle-school girl with a Jap name, something he couldn't remember. She had been wearing some Jap duds that looked like pajamas.

"Japamas," he said to himself, and laughed.

She had called him, a few weeks into summer vacation and arranged to get some re'em from him. Whatever. He was happy about going to the N-E-Time Mart because they had chicken taquitos. If there was one thing in this world that hadn't let Corduroy McBeen down, it was chicken taquitos.

3.

Back around the time that chocolate was illegal and shitting was a sin, re'em was also experiencing a crippling blow called, optimistically, "the Temperance Act" (misunderstanding the word in the most Victorian of ways to mean not moderation but illegality). Of course by crippling, I mean the same amount was being consumed–more, possibly–only behind drawn and tied velvet curtains as thick as slices of toast.

Women, after centuries of getting the jagged, infectious, crappy end of the stick, discovered that all of the prohibition nonsense fit in nicely with their already established routines of secrecy. It was quite a gas to have the ladies over for bon-bons crafted from the finest hedonistic chocolate, cups of tea laden with enough cream and sugar to defy saturation physics and cut doses of re'em snorted straight off the Ouiji board.

Edelweiss was unaware that her great great great grandmother Magdelena di Trattidocelli was known to don a scarlet satin turban crowned with a sapphire the size of a titmouse and a giant white ostrich plume, and tell the future. Magdelena would do this after consuming truly Victorian quantities of fine tawny port, hefty slabs of lemon-and-rose-water scented cake and heaping mother-of-pearl spoonfuls of re'em. Consequently great streams of information would flow from her, generally in the form of drunken metaphor, shocking local gossip and a rare peppering of distant prophecy. The distant stuff was dismissed due to its air of witchcraft, as was common at the time. Certainly, the occasional alchemist or philosophist paid heed, but, wisely, they recorded their sooths in the most elaborate of codes.

Although there were other eccentric women who had equally fascinating manners of eating re'em and dropping into trances, the intrepid Magdelena di Trattidocelli was the only one around who was certifiable. When she saw arrogant young Maria's husband awash in a loud sea of red and pounding blows from heaven, as sure as the sun rises he was trampled to death by his own stallion. Magdelena's own grand-daughter, with the malformed hand (quite a scandal she was, often swaddled so tightly to keep her hand from showing that she turned the exact color of an August tomato), grew up to be, after many years, strikingly beautiful, married and happy. Until then, Magdelena's many assurances to the family that the child would be fine were regarded with tired disbelief.

This was all well and good, but what the women wanted to know was what the Parisian women would be wearing in the fall and whether or not they would become too plump. In time Magdelena no longer even warned of the disasters she felt hovering just outside the curtains, because no one did a thing about it. Change it, she told them. The future seems to be made of some heavy, coarse silk that can be unraveled and woven back together however one pleases. This was dense information to digest, the idea that one could directly affect the future. Most chose to ignore it.

After Magdelena died (from a growth in her lungs that she had never prefigured) and after her daughter died (struck across the back of the head with a pewter stein by her husband, as Magdelena had known about for decades but had tucked away into a spot where she pretended she'd never seen it) and right around the time that Edelweiss' great-grandmother (the exotic looker with the broken wing hand) was having her own children, the Temperance Act was repealed. Re'em still had its shadowy side, more than its fair share, but no one had been hung for it in quite some time. Religious reverence for re'em was becoming a novelty. The drug seemed less occult by the day. Governments around the world were even establishing secular foresight agencies outside the church to watch for catastrophic future events that could be avoided.

Unfortunately for Edelweiss, the gift of true re'emination was not inheritable. There was no formula for when the drugged mutterings were useful and when they were merely a conversational mirage. One thing was for sure, though, and that was that everyone, every single person that ate re'em, believed they were the real thing, for a while, anyway. The one-in-a-million.

That's an awful lot of let down people, after a time.

4.

"He'll be here."

"Aikiko, I'm so bored. Really. I want to go home. What do you think your mom is doing?"

"Meditating on the washer, probably. Look, he will be here. We are going to buy drugs, he wouldn't stand us up."

"I'm gonna to go inside and get something to eat."

"Suit yourself."

"I will."

"Will you get me something?"

"Yeah."

Edelweiss stepped into the shaded cool of the N-E-Time Mart and waited for her eyes to adjust. The various soda machines, ice cream cases and bait coolers hummed discordantly against each other, occasionally synching up in a sustained whine, then thrumming back out of harmony again. She walked back to the beckoning red light of the hot foods case, where hotdogs rolled perpetually in a ruddy purgatory.

"Excuse me," Edelweiss asked the man behind the counter. He had been eyeing her, trying out mental variations on the phrase 'she sure looked eighteen.'

"Yep?"

"I was wondering if there were going to be any mini tacos soon."

"Well, I generally don't start a batch of those until eleven."

According to the antique cat clock behind him, whose rigid, bulging gaze rolled back and forth with a click at either side, it was 10:48.

"Okee dokey."

Back outside, Edelweiss squinted, her stomach rumbling. Aikiko was talking quietly with a thick-bodied teenage boy.

"Hi," Edelweiss said.

He said nothing to her, but stared, eyes hesitating at the heavy wads of friendship bracelets around her ankles.

"I'm Edelweiss Santucci."

"You have money?"

"Yes, do you need some?"

Aikiko gave Edelweiss a gentle elbowing. "Eddy," she hissed.

"Ten bucks a dose," Corduroy said.

"What is?"

"This is Corduroy," Aikiko told Edelweiss.

"Look, you guys have money or what?"

Aikiko spoke, her voice pitched an octave lower than normal. Tougher. "Yeah, we got money. Twenty, then, for the two of us?"

"That's the math, genius."

Aikiko pulled a wad of dollar bills from up inside her sleeve and thrust them surreptitiously at him. He took the money, counted it twice, and then pocketed it. He then took two tiny plastic baggies from his pocket, making sure their zippers were tight before handing them over. "Happy hunting," he said with a sneer.

"What's that mean?" Edelweiss asked.

"Good luck, you know. You aren't going to see anything." He sniffed at the air, ears practically perking. Edelweiss caught the odor of fried foods coming from the N-E-Time.

"Are you saying this shit is no good?" Aikiko asked, gesturing with the little bags of re'em.

He settled back on his heels, sized up the girls, his facial muscles twitching into an expression somewhere between contempt and weariness. "No one sees anything," he said. "Everyone is a fucking loser. Get used to it before it's too late. The shit is good. You're not."

"Some drug dealer you are," Aikiko muttered, tucking the little bags up her sleeves.

"What the hell d'you mean by that?"

"Everyone knows it's a one in a million, can't you at least pretend like we might be the next big thing? That way, maybe we'll want to buy it from you again."

Corduroy considered. "Yeah, okay. But you'll see. You don't believe me now, you think you're okay with not being 'the one' now, but just wait."

Aikiko said nothing.

Edelweiss' stomach growled.

5.

Have you ever done re'em? Do you know of the velocity of thought attained?

Imagine or remember an intense moment in your life. I'll pick a car accident, since that's a nice showy comparison. Imagine you have all your regular problems, your average life stuff, everything is normal. Life life life. You need to pick up some toilet paper. You were assigned extra shifts at work. Your significant other is currently not speaking to you and wants you to figure out why. You think you might be putting on some weight. There is a new model of gadget that you like, and if you keep saving, you might be able to afford it. You are driving to a store.

What happens next happens quickly, so you have no ability to observe it from second to second. You experience it as a memory. There is a noise, a shudder. It is more visceral than actual, if that makes any sense. True violence is scary, not something you can fully respect from watching the telly and no matter how old you are, how hard you are, it makes you cry. Not the pain, even, not at first, just the violence. There is something primordially unfair about it.

After it is over, there is a period where your legs are all gelatin and you feel like you're going to vomit, and then you are just immersed in the memory. You put pieces together, you start to see where you may have been able to swerve if only you had been more vigilant, that kind of thing. It takes some time, but you build the whole picture and the result leaves you feeling tired and scared and a little bit grateful to be alive. Colors are brighter. Food tastes better. For a time, anyway.

Aikiko and Edelweiss had eaten their little plastic baggies of re'em, briefly tempted to snort it but getting freaked out at the last minute. They are too inexperienced to worry about being in such close proximity to Bernice at this point, not knowing that the effort it would take for them to maintain in the event that she try to speak to them would be phenomenal. Instead, they sat in Aikiko's room and waited.

"You feel anything?"

"Nope," Edelweiss looked back and forth between two music albums.

"Me neither."

It had only been a few minutes since they ingested their re'em, and not knowing what to expect they had set out comic books for themselves to read and daifuku to snack on.

"You feel anything?" Edelweiss asked her friend.

"No. I guess I feel nervous. My legs feel funny."

Edelweiss had a good laugh over that. A very, very good laugh. "Man, that's funny."

"Uh oh," Aikiko said, smiling.

"What?"

"This is it. I think this is it."

Edelweiss gave a chuckle again, and suddenly stopped. "Whoa, that was weird. Was I laughing for like, five minutes, or not?"

"Not. We're definitely high."

"You're paranoid. I always laugh for a long time. What is that sound?"

"There isn't any sound," Aikiko said uncertainly. "You're tripping."

"But I don't know anything about the future."

"Well, maybe not yet."

"That's weird, I knew you were going to say that."

"No you didn't."

"That too!"

"Stop it."

"Whoa!"

Separately, the girls were having that just-after-the-wreck feeling, but it went on and on, developing speed. They were seeing visions, not entirely external, but distracting nevertheless. They were reeling from it. This is it, they thought. The future. It would have been easy to shrug it off as a drug haze, but consider this: what if it were fact?

Listen. Have you ever woken from a dream and briefly felt like it had been true? Something about it seemed so real, your subconscious couldn't have made it up, you couldn't have imagined it all on your own.

And the feelings it left you with during those thick, ill-lit moments when you first awake, they were real feelings, were they not, even if falsely earned?

Tell yourself it was real. The more you push the feelings, the more solid they become and you are the only one that knows. What do you do? Do you call someone? Keep it to yourself, wait until it happens then lamely claim, 'I knew this was going to happen'?

I understand that this is a difficult concept. But ask yourself one question before you continue: is life worth living just because we aren't sure of what is going to happen, and if you knew of the horrors that were in store, would you bow out now? Is your existence really only interesting because you may or may not get what you want from it?

What a wonderful and repulsive feeling.

6.

"You can have some of this spaghetti, if you want," he said.

"I don't like spaghetti."

"It's a major nutrient source, though, since you're a vegan."

"A what?"

"You don't eat animal products, not even ones from live animals."

Edelweiss considered this. It sounded right. "Okay, I'll have some."

"Do you want garlic bread with it?"

"Is it made with soy margarine?"

"No."

"No thank you," she said. "I am a vegan."

7.

"It's too bad you are going to Seattle."

"Why am I going to Seattle?"

"Because of your important meeting. Because you're late, you're late, for a very important date!"

"I didn't know anything about that," Edelweiss frets.

"Sure you did."

Edelweiss searches her memory for some facts to make this concrete. Eventually, she thinks she finds something. Close enough, anyway. "I'm happy that I am going to Seattle," she said.

"Yes."

"I don't know anything about Seattle, though."

There is no answer, but she is clobbered with images of a restaurant, a beautiful restaurant, with golden lighting fixtures and curtains made from wheat-colored linen. She was being served a silver-edged plate of Belgian endive stuffed with pimento and saffron soy cheese and a garnish of Nicoise black olives imported from France.

"Thank you, this looks great," she says.

8.

"Do you believe in love at first sight?"

"Yes?"

"Yes? Is that a question?"

"I don't know. Yes. Yes, I believe."

"That's nice for you."

"Where am I?"

"You're here," he says, and extends an arm to the horizon. It's a city, unidentifiable, beautiful in its crispness. At night, cities are what they were intended to be: testaments to pack mentality and electrified conductivity.

Edelweiss can feel a hot wind on her face, coming up off the city in starts and gusts. Smells like Indian food and car exhaust and semen and iodine scrubs. She lives here, in the future.

"Hey, I live here, don't I?"

"Rent is reasonable," he says.

9.

an assault, an attack, beaten from every direction, its not fair! it hurts,
    "Eddy!"
    this is totally fucked up, so fucked, dozens of people, hundreds of them,
this is called something, something bad, but what? Somebody should call
CNN immediately—
    "Eddy!"
    "Who?"
    "Eddy, it's not real, relax."

10.

Eyes the color of hackney horses, the ones that step so nicely, like princes.
    Edelweiss is in love.

11.

What is this variant of pizza? It's fucking brilliant, that's what. It's like, how
can you improve on bread with tomato and cheese? You'd think you couldn't,
but this, this is something else.
    "This is great!"
    "It sure is, and it's your very own invention!"
    Warm living room with rusty dead blood walls, a well-used couch and
low lighting. "But what is it?" Edelweiss asks.
    "You should know, you rat."
    "You don't know?"
    "You never let me see what you were doing. Only you can make such a
fantastic meal, and you'll take the recipe to your grave."
    "But I can't remember how to make it."
    "Quit teasing."
    "I'm not teasing, I've never eaten this before."
    "You're a card, Eddy, a real card!"

"I thought I didn't eat cheese, though."
"You do now, I guess."
"No, I don't... Do I? Did I before?"
"Cheese is a product of an oppressive society. Maybe you don't."
"I'm confused."
"Damn, this is good."

12.

"Eddy."

"Who?"

"Edelweiss."

"Aikiko?"

An especially odd intellectual musing of humans is the quandary of where the consciousness is centered. Many grand and ancient cultures believed it was in the chest, which only makes sense, considering the way the pulmonary lace seizes when the brain is sad and the weight of the torso is relieved at the very sight of the ocean waves landing at the shore like sheets of paper.

However, many doctors of medicine and butchers agree that the organ called the brain is responsible, and the sensations in the chest are but the sack of meat running on auto-pilot. Surely the brain is the Holy Grail, the true self. It's where most input is received, it's where the orders are given. The logic is flawless.

But what if there are many points located along one's vertical axis, which can be illustrated through colorful diagrams of individuals in a state of peace, each spot of soul glowing a different color and radiating various lotus-shaped puzzle pieces?

Or, is it that so royal arrangement of tissue between the legs, hotly keeping time? Many will agree to that.

And what of the question: does it matter? Sure, healthy questions all, but to what end? It seems more worrisome that there are those drifting around our cities and neighborhoods and tundra that haven't any consciousness at all.

No matter what the belief, there are times when the body is too separate. When you feel the need to fight it, as though it had an independent agenda from your self. It lets off painful bursts of gas, it burns with internal secretions, it pulses with unexplained rushes of minute quantities of self-concocted tinctures and it sometimes slows and fails when the timing is really, really bad. You catch yourself cursing it as though it were a recalcitrant car or a naughty pet.

"Eddy?"

"Yep?"

"Are you okay, or what?"

Christ and Christ. Edelweiss is coming back to the land of the fleshy, and it takes her quite some time to realize that her eyes are glued shut. Something sticky is holding the eyelids together. When she gets them apart, the light hurts her feelings.

"What time is it?"

"It's after seven. Your mom called, she wants to know when to come pick you up. I told her you had a stomach ache from eating too much candy and you had to take a nap."

"Oh, she is going to be pissed. I'm not supposed to eat too much candy."

"Well, I'll call her back and tell her you took some re'em."

Edelweiss thought it over. "No, that's no better."

"I was joking, douche."

Aikiko was sitting on the bedside next to Edelweiss, and had dark bags under her eyes. They stared at each other in the fading late summer light, a hot breeze shifting Aikiko's cobalt crane-printed curtains. This scene lasted for a long time.

"I feel pretty bad," Edelweiss said eventually. She was thirsty and craving sweets. And something fried, anything at all fried, really, she wasn't feeling particularly picky.

"I know, I feel bad too. All rubbery."

"I saw the future."

Aikiko looked out her window. "Me too."

"Did you see the city, the one with the vegetarian restaurant?" Edelweiss asked eagerly.

"The what? No, it wasn't like that. It was odors and my grandmother telling me stories in Japanese," Aikiko trailed off to a near whisper. "But they were stories that hadn't happened yet."

"No, no, it was a city, at night. I'm pretty sure it was Seattle, the weather was lovely and the city lights were so beautiful."

"I'm sure we saw different things, Eddy."

"We can't both have seen the future if they were different, Aikiko, and mine was so real. I fell in love and something bad happened, something really bad. People got hurt. It was a battle I think."

"No kidding, people are going to get hurt in some kind of war?"

"You saw it too!"

"You're a buffoon."

Bird cries outside seemed to be getting louder as the light faded. There was a distant clatter of dishes in the house, and it lulled the girls into a slumber. Something about someone loudly making dinner, food frying, it was the ultimate safety. The same with water being drawn for a bath or a shower started. Someone brushing their teeth. Cards being shuffled and then slapped to the table. A heartbeat to latch on to.

Edelweiss jerked awake. "I better call my mom."

Aikiko had slumped over and was beginning to snore.

CHAPTER THREE

1.

Ardella Santucci read through the paper every morning like it was assaulting her. It was often this sound that woke Edelweiss up for school. If not that, then the cussing.

"You be careful walking to school today!" Ardella shouted from the kitchen while Edelweiss dragged herself from bed. This was punctuated with the snapping of newsprint.

"Why?"

There was an explosive rustle that sounded like the paper may be winning. "Unicorns! Goddamn sonuvabitches ate part of the library last night! There must be a big pack roaming. Why don't they just shoot them?"

Edelweiss was lighting a small bundle of nag champa at her shrine and rubbing the sleep from her eyes. "Mom, unicorns are native animals. We are the intruders on this land. This is Indian land."

"I think the word 'Indian' may be derogatory, Eddy," her mother called back.

"There is nothing derogatory about those gentle people!" Edelweiss shook her head sadly. There was quite a deluge of smoke rising from her shrine. The people in the movies always lit giant bundles of the stuff, but whenever she did it was like a forest fire in her room.

"Why are you coughing, Eddy? Are you getting sick?"

"No, mom."

"What is that smell?"

"Positive energy."

"Well, it's burning my eyes."

2.

Edelweiss' mom and the Gaffney Daily were not exaggerating the destruction that had occurred the night before. It was a fantastic, stunning, gorgeous fall day when Edelweiss set out for high school. It was her junior year. She was doing poorly in every class with the exception of Anatomy (which she was flunking spectacularly) and Political Science (because her thirty-six-year-old teacher was in love with her).

On the walk to school, she passed by the library and stopped to gawk with all the other rubberneckers. It was quite a sight.

The Gaffney library, like many buildings in the South, was a miniature Parthenon of local granite and less local marble. Massive steps led to equally impressive oak doors towering six feet above even the tallest Gaffnian's head. The message was clear that anything inside would be far over their heads as well.

Equally Southern and grandiose was the obligatory brass statue of some civil war hero astride a rearing stallion, sabre drawn and held high in defense of life, liberty and the pursuit of chitlins.

On one wall of the library, the white-painted wooden window sills had been eaten away almost entirely, revealing the dark wood beneath. Something in the paint must have tasted good. There were test nibbles on the unpainted oak doors, but no real munching had been done.

"They think someone had a breedin' farm that got out!"

Edelweiss turned and looked at an elderly woman standing next to her who was munching languidly on a sweet onion. She was wearing orange polyester shorts and a cotton wife beater. She used a dented aluminum cane to stand.

"No kidding?"

"Yeah, one of them re'em growers. Hooligans."

"Hooligans? What about supporting the expansion of minds do you oppose, exactly?"

A dozen faces turned to look at Edelweiss, rheumy eyes struggling for focus, chigger bites competing for attention. The people of the South, were, if nothing else, up for a good argument.

"What'd she say!" someone at the edge of the crowd yelled, not from anger, but due to a hearing aid with a dying battery.

"You'd better get on to school, now, missy," a kindly-looking man in overalls and little else advised her.

Edelweiss nodded and skipped off, dreadlock beads smacking painfully against her back.

3.

"Edelweiss?"

"Here."

"J.W.?"

"Here."

"Kale?"

"Here. Physically, anyway."

There were giggles all around, and not chummy ones, the noise of a room full of teenagers ganging up on someone.

"Dork," someone said loudly. The teacher stifled a smile.

"Hey," Edelweiss hissed, leaning forward and tapping Kale on his shoulder. He turned slowly, in the same manner that a person drags themself outside for a bar fight. It's gotta be done, but damn is it going to suck. Similarly: laundry.

"Yeah?"

"Why are you always so weird?"

"Why are you always so obtuse?" he said after a long stare.

Edelweiss laughed appreciatively and sat back in her chair.

High school is an easily dismissable thing, for adults. By which I mean, it's often thought lightly of, since, when it's over, it's really over. Not like having children, where the stress of hatching seems like the end of the world until you realize that the child isn't going away. And high school is not like the Holocaust where societal comparisons will dog your grandchildren to their graves; it's just a flash in the pan. A growing pain, a road marker of bigger things yet to come. We all did it, and so will you, Edelweiss' mother told her.

This is the basis of most lies known to man.

High school is the test you are given before you are taught the answers. High school is a pottery class for blind club-fisted epileptics.

People say they 'survived high school' by which they generally mean they are still breathing. This is flawed logic. Some people didn't make it. Some people are casualties of high school, never to be recognized or given a dramatic memorial. They often work at discount stores and/or have legions of babies, which is still considered successful by some standards. Some of them are big players in even bigger companies, tediously trudging towards cirrhosis. An unsurprising number are murderers.

This is a world still mortified because a man gassed millions of living humans and killed them. Made them gone forever. But scarier than the idea that a person could justify this is the fact that hundreds if not thousands of his followers also justified it. It was not a fluke, a rogue madman; it was *common thought* in some part of the world. Millions of people. You are not psychically equipped to comprehend this.

I am trying to draw an analogy to high school, if you'll forgive me.

Kale, for example, is the victim of a crime in progress that the police cannot be called for. Other humans are cruel to him. His often astute arguments are laughed at by his teachers and family. Someone, somewhere decided that he is to be sensible. He signs no one's paycheck and thus he is a farmed cottonwood of usefulness: cheap, soon to be gone and of little consequence. It is not of interest that he is struggling to get through high school alive, it is of interest that this is considered normal.

Edelweiss Santucci was one of the many people who could eventually claim to have 'survived'. Glad that's over, she'll say, and then her memories of it will lose ground to warm goofy memories of a movie she once watched about people in high school.

Kale will flinch when his name is called at the doctor's office and when people holler to him from across the bar. He will expect humiliation, always, forever. This is what he learned in high school.

Edelweiss pulled out her stack of homework, which contained exactly seven correct answers out of forty-eight (two of which were accidentally right) and carefully pencilled in her name at the top. She was tall and naturally proficient at sports that ended in the word 'ball'. Her stomach muscles were shapely and near the surface since she had no real fat to speak of, or none in the wrong places, anyway, and her lengthy excess of limb lent her grace without effort. She intimidated mightily when pulling back her dreadlocks—a regular habit of hers—because of the astounding things it did to the front of her torso. Often times she'd then turn the coifing into a languid, groaning stretch, arms lifted high overhead, stomach exposed and jaws dropping around the room in absolute silence.

Kale was pale and hairy in the wrong places. He was no less fit than the other kids, but no amount of activity would prove that after the suggestion had already set in. They had decided he was a weakling. Luckily, there was a fat kid in the class that drew most of the attention.

"Hey," Edelweiss hissed again, and pushed Kale's back gently. When he didn't respond she rapped on his shoulder blade as though his back were a door he could answer.

"What do you want?"

"Here," she said, and thrust a folded piece of paper at him.

The note reads like so:

> hey cool dood!
> man, you are can't take a joke can u? are u tens or what? mr.
> van huse is a total butt-hole. my friends and I are going to
> look for unicorns tonite do u want to come with us?
> edelweiss

Kale was confused and elated and suspicious and critical and aroused. He wrote on another piece of paper:

> Wouldn't you rather ask J.W. to hang out with you? He
> claims that he goes surfing down at Myrtle Beach. That's
> pretty fucking cool, right?
> Kale
>
> p.s., Mr. Van Huse isn't even a butt hole, he is that useless
> dirty area outside the anus that doesn't have a name.

The teacher noted at the front of the room, Mr. Van Huse, was talking to the class in what he probably thought was a quirky, engaging way, and was indeed making several of the more popular kids laugh and nod at his antics, but mostly the class could detect the whiff of desperation to him that so many 'cool' teachers suffered from. He was holding up a copy of the Gaffney Daily.

"I will assume most of you aren't aware of an event that occurred last night," he bellowed, catching everyone's attention. Even Kale stopped and listened.

"Well," he continued, "there was a pack of unicorns that ravaged the city last night, damaging several local landmarks in their path. I figure as your political science teacher, I should bring this up today. This is contemporary news, kids."

No one said anything. Unicorns are bad, everyone agreed, but fascinating in the same way that prostitutes are bad and still fascinating.

"We know the history and the social implications of re'em, so what does it mean for there to be public damage caused by a creature that has been the center of so much debate?" The Pause. "Kathy?"

"Uh, my Dad this morning was talking about hunting parties. He was saying that even though unicorns are a protected species, like, no one would get into trouble for killing them."

"This is true," Mr. Van Huse agreed. "That was a good observation. Our country has established in its higher courts that killing off a creature that not only has a right to live but offers to us a useful product is wrong. However, this creature in turn is responsible for what some consider to be vandalism. What happens when small communities don't care what the higher courts think? Anyone?"

Kale raised his hand. This is a stupid, stupid thing to do, he thought as he did it. He did that, occasionally, forgot that he was at school and then became engaged in a conversation like that. He dropped his arm, but too slowly.

"I'm sorry, what was your name?"

"We're halfway through this quarter," Kale said quietly.

"I'm sorry, what?"

"You still don't know my name? It's Kale. K-A-L-E."

"Like the vegetable?"

"Yes."

"Your brother named Carrot?"

The room erupted into effervescent laughter, like the tickle of so many piranha about to feed.

"I kid, I kid," Mr. Van Huse laughed, gesturing down like a talk show host falsely begging the crowd to relent. "Please speak up."

"I was just going to say that the idea of a supreme governing system, like the higher courts, is nothing but a show. To pacify those that are afraid of individual voices, or of small societies having to work together to institute locally relevant systems."

The teacher visibly mentally changed from his regular boxing gloves to the ones with the lead weights inside. "Ah, but whats good for the goose is good for the gander, Kale. That is how this country works. Someone you elected as your local judge or mayor makes decisions locally, and they answer to someone higher, and on up. So eventually, it's all local, though it may seem far away."

Kale sighed. "I think it's broken; there is no system conceived that can make a superior court or elected official have any idea of what someone is feeling hundreds of miles away, and thus, why a certain bill or ruling may be detrimental for them. And I think that people who put themselves in the position of judging others are inherently flawed. Cops should be chosen from a pool that doesn't want to be in control."

"Well Heil Herr Karl," the teacher said viciously, then smiled massively, showing off state dental benefits for those who chose to play the game. The class laughed along, even though they weren't sure what was going on. There had been a lot of big words tossed around.

Kale tried to keep his anger from rising, the salty hot ball of hate that struggled in his throat from time to time. He chanted internally over and over again, *it's not worth it, it's not worth it*. He took a large cooling intake of oxygen and trace gasses and though he tried to smile, found he just couldn't. "If the people of Gaffney want to kill unicorns that come into their city or county limits, they should have a right to. If there are people here that don't agree with that—assuming they are the minority, of course—then those people should leave. Find a town where the majority vote is to not kill the unicorns. And my name is Kale, sir, like the vegetable, if you recall."

Mr. Van Huse took a moment to chortle, a dangerous sound. "Well, Mr. Vegetable, do *you* think that unicorns should be killed? How do you feel about the exact nature of the unicorn?"

Kale held his eyes shut for a second and then turned to look around the classroom. Some of the students were nodding, eyes dopey-closed, as though the information that had just lodged in their brains was making their heads physically heavier. Kale experienced a swimmy confusion before he locked on to the idea that what the teacher had just said had made no sense.

Kale cleared his throat slowly. "I think they are pesky, but then so are humans. They should not be shot, because it does not offer any long-term solution. And ah, I am not sure what you meant to say when you said 'the exact nature.'"

"Why are you living here, in Gaffney, then, if you don't think they should be shot? Don't you follow your own line of logic?" Mr. Van Huse then raised his hands to actually encourage the rail of laughter from the classroom. They obliged, obviously, and soon there was the sandy abrasion of sound that Kale had learned to associate with the extremely unfashionable bring-the-guns-to-school line of thought.

Kale rubbed his eye sockets. "I am trying to leave this town. It's a little difficult for a sixteen year old without a high school diploma, though."

"Oh, cry me a tiny violin," the teacher chuckled nastily.

"See, that didn't even make sense," Kale said, and turned to hand his note to Edelweiss. "Where are you going to meet tonight?" he asked, not bothering to lower his voice.

"Mr. Gibson!" The teacher barked after locating a seating chart on his desk. "I will not tolerate any further disruption of my class time."

"Oh," Edelweiss was torn between dissent and answering Kale, whom she was intrigued by, in a sort of kooky, eccentric way. "We are meeting out at the library fountain at eight."

"I will see you there, then. Thank you for inviting me."

"Mr. Gibson, take your seat. Class is not even close to being over."

Kale picked up his backpack and gave Edelweiss a conspiratorial smile. He didn't look around as he left the room, and Mr. Van Huse launched into a less than professional diatribe against the dangers of turning out like the regrettably dorky Mr. Gibson. One of the star varsity players of whatever clapped delightedly.

Edelweiss heard none of it, feeling for the first time an unusual surge of heat in her face and abdomen. She had a fleeting urge to run after Kale, but tossed it away when she thought of how long it would take her to get her things together. She didn't care that some of the girls were whispering and pointing. She unfolded the note and read it, blushing harder.

She had a crush.

4.

The light was weak and as a result everyone looked ethereal and ghastly at the same time. The fountain's dreamy tinkling didn't help with the gothic drama, and the small group of people began to shift nervously in the now-undeniably fall air.

"Everyone, this is Kale. Kale, this is Aikiko," Edelweiss paused with a great flourish.

"We've met," Aikiko said, shaking his hand.

"And Kelli and Billy and Aikiko's neighbor Elizabethe," Edelweiss finished, and there was much handshaking all around. Kale recognized everyone from school but had never actually met them. Billy and Elizabethe were seniors and so never spared a glance at him. Kelli seemed to have some developmental issues he couldn't immediately specify.

"So, what's the plan?" Kale asked after the awkward silence became overwhelming.

Aikiko raised her flashlight. "We have two flashlights. I was thinking that we could split into two groups, go for a quick search to see if we can find any traces of the unicorns, regroup and then search again. If there are traces we search in two groups in that direction. If not, we try again. Sound good?"

Billy nodded. He was tall with a dark pony tail (apparently in lieu of impressive facial hair) and was oddly gangly in spite of bearing some weight. He and Elizabethe were obviously a couple: he kept sidling alongside her and fondling her when he thought no one was looking. Kale was mildly startled at the way that Elizabethe didn't respond at all to Billy's fondling, as though she had confused coyness with docility.

"Sounds like a good plan," Billy said deeply.

Soon the groups were underway, Aikiko, Elizabethe and Billy in one and Kale, Edelweiss and Kelli in the other. They walked down the road that led to the textile mills, where the newspaper had speculated the unicorns would go, sometimes looking for tracks and poop but mostly just gossiping. At a point of possible foliage trauma, Aikiko's group slipped off into the woods, agreeing to meet back in fifteen minutes.

"Billy and Elizabethe are totally doing it," Kelli hissed and shivered with enjoyment.

"Doing what?" Edelweiss asked, roaming off road and into the forest on the opposite side. Kale hung back nervously.

"Spawning, stupid," Kelli giggled.

Edelweiss turned back, interested. "You think so?"

"It's obvious," Kelli said.

Edelweiss looked at Kale. "Is it obvious?"

"I'd say so, sure."

Edelweiss seemed troubled, momentarily. She then waved the other two over to the forest with her. As they followed Kelli began to moan. "I don't like this," Kelli said when they were barely three yards into the brush. "There's bad stuff out here. Water moccasins, spiders..."

"Stop it," Edelweiss said. She was a little frightened herself, but not enough to quit.

"We are making far too much noise to sneak up and scare any sort of creature," Kale said as reassuringly as he could. There was no answer but a vague whimpering in the darkness.

After what seemed like an eon of painful, clumsy exploration through the undergrowth (Kale checked his watch twice and confirmed that only five minutes had passed) Kelli suddenly whined "I want to go back to the road!" in a pitch that triggered Kale's eyes to roll in some kind of auto-nomic response.

"It's okay," Edelweiss said without conviction. There was a eerie cooing from the bushes nearby.

"No way, I'm out of here," Kelli shrieked, and Edelweiss' flashlight barely caught the shaking bushes left in her wake.

"Well," said Kale.

Edelweiss was quiet. "I guess we should go after her."

"The road is fifty feet away. If we walk for half a minute we'd see it, and she went that direction."

"You want to keep looking then?"

"Why not?"

An odd blessing of adulthood is looking back at one's own virginity, or rather, the period of time immediately preceding the loss. If you knew then what you know now, ah, what a riot it would all be. The stress alone that had been granted to even the idea of a kiss! It was like the world hinged on your face, your neck muscles, your sense of timing. Eyes open or closed? Jesus, the tomes that could be written on one's breath and its relative freshness! Occasionally in later life you could repeat the feeling, although dilute and under-appreciated. Never again will the sheer altitude of feeling be that great, never will that certain mix of chemicals lodge in their corresponding neural sockets in that unexpected way again (perhaps that is –was– the real loss of virginity), but at least you had the first time, right? Like a virgin, as the song goes. Glandularly excreted for the very first time.

"I haven't seen anything," Kale said some time later, as the flashlight sweep showed nothing but a green confusion in the swath before him. It was getting harder and harder for his brain to differentiate between normal forest damage and what seemed suspicious.

"I guess it was a bum trail."

"You want to head back?" He asked, reluctantly. He checked his watch. It had only been seven minutes.

"Yeah."

Touched for the very first time.

Simple, but effective.

Their shoulders brushed, sort of, Edelweiss losing her balance and having to lean on Kale's to regain her footing. He put an arm around her to steady her. She put her arm around him, mistaking the gesture. There was no mistaking, however, as she leaned down to kiss him, and he very much meant to kiss her back. The flashlight dropped to the undergrowth and the sound of heavy breathing was covered only by the sound of poisonous creatures calling out murderously in the darkness.

5.

Two weeks later, Edelweiss stood, hands on hips in front of her mother, and said, "I think I am ready to spawn." She had already told Aikiko, who had only just stared critically and responded, "You mean you haven't yet?"

Ardella Santucci snapped her newspaper like a bullwhip and then cracked her forehead against the faux-oak of their kitchen table. She lay there, still for several seconds before Edelweiss put her hand out on mother's back.

"Mom?"

"You're killing me."

"Mom, I thought we could talk about this."

"I am waiting to die."

"Mom, I was wondering where you purchase the Ovo-Bloc spray from."

"Oh, I can hear the angels singing. It's so beautiful."

"Mom, I'm seventeen. I'm a woman."

"I'm so cold, Eddy, so cold."

"I can drive a car, I have the right to spawn."

"I am going toward the light now."

"I'm responsible. I'm an intelligent, healthy woman."

"I can see my body down below, Eddy, like I'm floating."

"Can I have some money to buy Ovo-Bloc with?"

Silence.

"Mom?"

"I've passed, Eddy."

"Mom? I'll just get it from your purse."

6.

"I think I am ready to spawn," Edelweiss told Kale several days later. She said this around a mouthful of plain tofu, which she hadn't yet developed a taste for, nor had she figured out how it could be cooked with other things, to flavor it. When she'd ordered from the waitress, she'd just said "Tofu, please," and when the waitress had asked what kind, Edelweiss had said, "Soy."

"Oh," Kale said softly. For some reason it didn't occur to him that Edelweiss might mean *with him*. "That's your right, I guess."

Her eyes lit up and she squirmed in her spot at the little restaurant booth, nodding at Kale. "That's exactly what I think."

The great and miserable thing about first loves is very simple: it's not that you are feeling something you've never felt before (not entirely—hear me out), and it's not so much that you are young and free and the whole world is your mollusk. *It is that the other person can do no wrong.* Let's elaborate.

Let's say that you are a fifteen-year-old girl.

Quiet down, I know you're not. And you, the one that is, you shouldn't be reading this trash, you should be doing your homework. Anyway, say you're a fifteen-year-old girl and your physically swelling chest is spiritually swelling with what Lord knows is definitely and certainly poke-you-in-the-eye love. Love! It's so easy to say at this age. The object of your affection is some strapping young lad (or lass, you dirty birdy), maybe in one of your classes. He is actually scrawny and smells much too strongly of deodorant (you can never be too sure) but to you he is a golden, mysterious, dark, compelling, brilliant, TigerBeat of a hunk whose river runs still and deep. You will surely burst at the sight of him, guts and snack cakes and curly fries flowing like the holy Ganges, you love him so much. Perhaps you'll marry him! Go ahead, write his last name next to your first name. No, scratch that, you're an enlightened girl, hyphenate it.

Do you think you know where I am going with this? That this is the greatest moment of your life, that things will never be this simple or fantastic ever again? You are wrong. This is the crudest, most street-cut shit you can get. If this were cocaine, it would be almost entirely powdered baby laxatives. This is a training bra, which as you know is utter bullshit that you grew out of years ago (remember: you are a fifteen-year-old girl).

The greatest product of this highly embarrassing time in your life is not even something you get to reap for yourself. It's for him. See, you think that he is the finest assemblage of deoxyribonucleic acid that God or chance or Thor has ever compiled.

He can do no wrong.

He will never do better again. Pure, unmitigated adulation for doing nothing more than showing up to class where you can stare at him.

Now that's good stuff.

Right now Kale's eyes are watering with the effort not to weep at Edelweiss. The way she dresses, with the torn sheets of dirty old lace draped over crushed velvet dresses, her decrepit combat boots, her neck and wrists wrapped with length after length of beaded string and the ratty feathers tied into her dreadlocks. The way that she smells, a painfully compelling elixir of shampoo, patchouli, sweaty clothing, dry leather and that unexpected tang of cat food. She could have told him that she needed his kidneys, both of them, and he would have sat there, willing to hear her out.

She could do no wrong.

"So, I was thinking that the full moon is coming up this weekend, do you think that sounds okay? I think it sounds perfect. The full moon is like the fullness of a woman."

"Whatever you like."

"I read a book—well, Aikiko told me about a part in a book where a girl had this ceremony where she named her flower. She had potions and incense. I thought that sounded really real, you know?"

"Wow, I've never heard of that. That sounds very intense of you."

"What do you think we should drink? I was thinking some sacramental wine."

Kale choked a little. "Sacramental wine?"

"Yes, it's a special wine people use for special occasions."

"Uh, yes. I've heard of it."

"So what do you think?"

"Whatever you want, Edelweiss, it's your night."

That Edelweiss had spoken the word 'we' had yet to catalog itself into Kale's memory banks.

"You're really a sweet boy, Kale."

"Thanks," he said sadly.

"Wait. Are you a virgin?"

"Wh-what?" Kale stopped with chopsticks full of tofu halfway to his mouth.

"You are a virgin too, aren't you?"

"What does it matter? I mean, why do you ask?"

Edelweiss looked hurt, which made Kale's gorge rise, bile-ridden tofu nearly ejected from his mouth. He had to swallow convulsively to keep from redepositing it to his plate. "What's the matter, what did I say?"

"You don't think it matters that we're both virgins?"

"I'm confused, is he a virgin?"

"Is who?"

"The guy you are... going to, ah. Spawn with." He swallowed more bile.

"Oh, you silly," she laughed, "stop messing with me. 'The guy you are... duh...'" she mocked in a low voice. "I don't know, I'll ask him," she said seriously, and then a moment later, "Hey Kale, are you a virgin?"

"Oh my God," he said.

7.

The full moon ached like a full bladder at its zenith. A fog of nag-champa drifted through the trees and the underbrush like a made-for-TV WWI movie.

In the heavy quiet of autumn, there were affected voices calling out pagan commands to the four winds, invocations to arcane gods, and giggles over various wordy stumbles.

Certain potions, elixirs and sacramental wines were engaged.

Eventually there was silence, but not of movement.

8.

When high school was over and everyone still had the timidity of recent parolees, Edelweiss announced she had decided to go to the University of Washington. Kale was impressed and (since he had also procrastinated sending off college applications) he looked into Washington's requirements.

When she called and left a message on his answering machine the next day saying goodbye, he thought she was joking. It was ludicrous. No one went to a college before they were accepted, let alone the day after they decided. It took awhile to set in. When it finally did, the funk that settled around him was like swamp water.

He stepped off the front porch of his house one morning that hot summer and found himself looking at an immobile Aikiko. She wore a light cotton summer bed gown and no shoes.

"How long have you been standing there?" he asked.

"I came to talk to you."

Kale rubbed his swollen eyes and was self-conscious of how slovenly he had become since Edelweiss had skipped town. "What about?"

"You can't be all torn up about her, Kale. She doesn't understand anything about people. She'll leave anyone when they are no longer useful to her."

Kale barked a dry laugh. "Yes, I know. I just wonder if she ever loved me."

"Oh, she loved you." Aikiko had not moved except for shaking her head as she said, "But everything is temporary for her, and she expects it all to be the same for her when she returns. All of us here, just waiting, like she'd never left."

"Well, she's in for a nasty surprise."

Aikiko nodded and said with absolutely certainty, "You're closer to the truth than you know. Besides, you'll be at UC Berkley by the time she returns."

"How—I just sent off my application for that yesterday."

The city bus pulled up at the street corner with a blustery squeal and Aikiko shrugged, turning to run for it. "See you later."

CHAPTER FOUR

1.

The style of the time was like so: everything must be outside the lines. Everything must have dual purposes and multiple cross-over markets. Brand names must be sub-companies and all product must be limited run. Brilliant young admen must come up with a fantastic idea a day and get it into production by that evening, although generally such a schedule made it hard to get good Thai food.

One day, about a dozen years ago, a failed re'em oracle who was bitter beyond words had an idea. I know, I know, you're excited, but wait.

Two dozen years before that, Rexine Manowicz's baby was about to hatch. She'd already named it Gloria Ann Manowicz, after her husband's mother, just to piss him off. He wasn't in the room for the hatching due to its being female stuff.

"It's your thing, schnitzel," he'd said.

"But, it's your baby too, Avi," she'd said.

"How can we be sure?" he'd asked.

"Avi, we're married!" she'd told him.

"Shalom," he said, and raised his cigar.

Rexine decided not to tell him that she'd gone to the old man down the street that claimed to be an oracle and paid thirty dollars to know the sex of her child.

Now, I don't have to tell you any more about the hatching scene except to say this: you've seen it a million times on television already, and what you see on the telly is wrong, for the most part. Mrs. Manowicz kneeled on the floor next to the egg sac, gently loosening the gummy, aged mucus that held it to the wall and part of her bedside table. On the telly they are always so clean and even-looking, lit with pink light and run through a filter to catch that pristine angelic mistiness. The whole family is there—mom, dad, young Bobby and the family dog, weeping and catching the little squirt as it slips out of it's sac in a wash of clean water. This is not our scene.

The miracle of life is hardly a miracle at all, when you get right down to it. The egg sac had developed a pickled odor during its first few weeks, which caused Rexine to run out to the grocery store and purchase Worry Free Hatching, by Dr. David Sulu, straight off the little rotating wire rack next to the register. The odd smell was not unheard of. Neither was a little mildew, depending on the relative humidity. There were suggestions for getting stains out of the carpet.

Nevertheless, Rexine kneeled before it, towels and baby basin of warm water ready to go. It wiggled, as it had done for weeks, and the glistening rupture she'd noticed that morning widened even more. About an hour later, fighting urges to peel into the sac herself, a pink, thrashing little person slid from the sack in a lumpy deluge of greasy secretions flecked with gelatinous opaque fat, and into Rexine's hands.

She cradled the baby in her arms, her bottom lip quivering with joy. "Gloria Ann," she said softly, looking the child over. "Goodness, what is that?" she asked aloud to no one in particular.

"I think that's the protein sac," her husband said, who had come up behind her.

"No, not that."

"Can't remember what the male anatomy looks like, silly woman? Or ain't you ever noticed that your cloaca is a little blue slit and mine is a big red one?"

"Son of a bitch," she said, again to no one.

"Well, Neville, welcome to the family," Mr. Manowicz told his newborn son, and left the room to watch the news.

"Neville?" Rexine asked, dismayed.

I know you've heard this story a thousand times before, but like the story of Michael Jackson or Oedipus Rex, for some reason people just don't tire of hearing it. This nothing-special unexpectedly male kid named

Neville Manowicz grows up slowly, or just about the same rate as everyone else, disappearing into nerd-dom for most of his adolescence. Then, pockmarked, four-eyed and still coming to terms with the gut-stabbing possibility that his very convincing re'em hallucinations were not true, he had an idea.

What if he could find and hire all the re'em oracles that were for sure real? People would pay a fortune for the certainty of it. Throw in a nervous-shopper impulse item like, oh, cars or coffee or something, and he'd be unstoppable.

And he was.

2.

If you are driving, Seattle loomed up suddenly like a time-lapse mushroom documentary. If you are flying, everything looked the same as everything else. Some green. Suburbs like linoleum tile. Swimming pools like mentholated cough drops. What everyone referred to as the 'quilt' of the Americas was generally farmland, but Edelweiss thought it all looked like a quilt, and entertained herself by thinking up social analogies to fabric, stuffing and thread.

When they began the descent a stewardess came out from her hidey-hole and put one of the old-fashioned mics to her mouth, the ones that look like a dinner roll made from black plastic.

"Good evening, ladies and gentlemen, we have begun our descent to SeaTac and will be landing in approximately seven minutes. Before we land we would like to give you a little reminder that Seattle is a coastal city, and therefore subject to bloatsharks. If you are not familiar with the precautions for coastal cities, please stop at the information kiosk on your way through the baggage terminal. Thank you for flying Cascade Air and have a nice day."

Edelweiss fiddled with her beaded bracelet and couldn't help but grin at the ever-enlarging world below.

Seattle.

The future.

3.

The bloatshark kiosk was built out of the same material as the rest of the baggage claim, a pallorous beige plastic with navy and charcoal highlights. The kiosk was circular and had a roof even though it was indoors, an architectural fad that was often meant to be friendly for some forgotten reason. Toned-down artistic renditions of bloatsharks, sailing about in an unthreatening manner, were printed on the walls.

"Can I help you?" A man asked Edelweiss after she had stared at the mural for awhile.

"No thank you. Is there really a big problem with bloatsharks in Seattle?"

"Oh no," he assured her, a touch over-enthusiastically. "Seattle is a very environmentally friendly city and has been dealing with bloatsharks effectively for some time. They are practically under control, and there are barricades just to make sure."

"Yes, I'm from Gaffney. It's the same around there."

"Oh, where's that?"

"Gaffney."

"Yes, sorry, what state is that in?"

"South Carolina," she said, offended. There was an Espress-Kno™ hut a few yards away. It was small, like the original ones were. There was a long line of people with massive luggage trails out beside them like malignant overgrowth.

"Oh yes," the man said, "Big bloatshark problem down there. Not like here."

"Hmm?" She said, turning back to the man. She decided he was a homosexual and that she should behave gently toward him. It was so exciting to finally be somewhere where homosexuals worked and lived! "No, they're no problem in the south."

The man seemed to take this personally. "Seattle isn't a threat at all, really. I mean, down in the south, if it's not the bloatsharks then you've got all kinds of poisonous things to deal with, right? Snakes, bugs, oh, and alligators of course."

"Alligators aren't poisonous," Edelweiss said smugly. She felt like she had done well in biology, right there towards the end of high school, the second time. She walked away when the man went to speak to another curious traveler, changed her mind, turned back, grabbed a few pamphlets and headed back for the baggage claim.

4.

Edelweiss believed that she loved everybody. It was more of a religion than a philosophy. It required faith.

Most religions are like this. They are founded under the pretext that all people are good and special and important, somewhere under all the dirt and drugs and pedophilia. Except for the really bad ones, and they must be killed. Or forgiven, but killed is fine too since God can do the forgiving later. Forgiveness is the mac-n-cheese of every culture; generic, cheap, and after all is said and done, not as nutritious as you'd hoped.

To Edelweiss, people that were violent just had misunderstood causes. Those that were stupid or retarded were infinitely pitiable. The elderly were the key to the past and somehow the future at the same time. Same for the children. Third-world countries are home to the most 'real' and 'honest' people on the planet, with Peruvians topping out the list, followed by Rastafarians. Mothers are saints. Single mothers are Goddesses. Aboriginal peoples, raised on their native soils or not, were more important than displaced Europeans. Inner-city kids were potential energy waiting for positive release.

The exceptions of course were corporate anything, business men, governmental anything including sub-governmental mostly clerical offices, banks, factories, automobile industry anything and the military.

Edelweiss was nineteen and sporting crisp dreadlocks that were washed and dried by an African-American woman down at the Jamaica-Me-Pretti salon in the Central District. Hemp clothing was preferable, although cotton and rayon were acceptable, as was silk and velvet, lace of all kinds, and nothing synthetic unless it had a native pattern of some kind on it.

This was all subject to whatever momentary interpretation was needed.

"And in conclusion," Edelweiss said it her most scholarly tone, "As long as the corporate monster is allowed to rule over the citizens of the world, genetically modified food products and organisms will continue to be a threat to humanity." The tag-board behind Edelweiss that had large drawing of corn and soybeans made a little warp noise and fell from the chalkboard's ledge.

Edelweiss grimly surveyed the classroom.

"Miss Santucci," he professor said after he'd recovered. "I fail to comprehend a single point you've made. Is this satire?"

"Oh, I'm sorry," she said, stepping forward and tapping a paper that she was holding in her hand. "The definitions to the words that I was using are on the paper that I handed out to everyone."

"No, Edelweiss," he said sadly. "It's not words you were using, although why you defined 'genetically-modified' as 'a soul-raped organism' I really can't say. What I was referring to was your frivolous and dramatic use of phrases like 'the corporate monster.' Those terms have no debate value whatsoever, and are scientifically and politically meritless."

There was a mild chuckling in the auditorium, as though the room itself were amused. Edelweiss looked around with hesitance at the students, almost all of whom were shaking their heads at her sadly. Or possibly sympathetically. Yes, they were sad for their dim-witted and dim-hearted professor. "What?"

"Look, I would love to talk to you about this over a private meeting later, if you'd like, but frankly I prefer to deal with it now while our thoughts are still fresh. Environmental politics are often emotional since they deal with the welfare of the whole world and generations to come, but we've talked about this before, Edelweiss. Drama has no place in the educational forum. It doesn't win points. It doesn't intellectually move me. Do you follow me?"

"I guess I don't, Professor. My presentation was factual. Genetic modification is an attempt to take even farming away from working man, and it harms the very essence of organisms in the process. Fact."

"I understand those points from your presentation, but you failed to address several key issues, such as how the government should be dealing with crop shortages. The way that we farm now is antiquated and intended to feed only thousands, not millions and certainly not billions of people. You made no mention of these problems or their possible solutions, and that, Miss Santucci, was your assignment."

"But, it's abhorrent the way they are messing with the DNA of plants to twist them to our desires, that was the focus of my presentation."

"You see, you are doing it again. You also did not address the topic that so-called 'organic' foods are grown from radiation-forced mutation and commonly use powerful bacteria as insect control in ways that would never occur naturally. In addition, you're falling back on an emotional response, which I will continue to call to your attention as an argumentative flaw as long as you do it in my classroom.

"Listen," he continued, "we know these arguments top to bottom, it's what we've been discussing for the last two months. So far you've only proven to me that you are emotionally invested in your opinions."

Edelweiss gaped. "Are you saying that we are all supposed to just change our minds about GMOs because you think it isn't an emotional subject?"

"Of course not, what I am trying to do is get you kids to learn how to know all of the facts and then make sound arguments on your own. As long as your argument is solid, I don't really care what you believe. And before I forget, Miss Santucci, I still don't have you listed on my class roster." He rustled some papers and shrugged. "You'll need to clear this through the administrative center before I can continue to take time away from the rest of my students with you. It's not fair to them."

Edelweiss stared at her professor with dismay. "I had no idea that the corporate monster's tendrils ran so deep," she whispered.

5.

About two dozen years ago, two 'spinsters' walked into an adoption clinic and asked if they could have a child. The woman at the desk, Molly McAfferty, held her hands in the shape of a tent and didn't know what to say.

"I am Leelee Vaughn," one of the women said, thrusting her hand out to be shaken. Her hand was dry and callused, although still feminine in that strange way that women's knuckles are always a little bit more angular than men's.

"Susan Lilly," the other woman said shyly.

"Oh, you've been married?" Molly asked, looking back and forth at them.

The spinsters glanced at each other; both began to speak, and then both stopped. It had been assumed they were sisters, and they had realized that this was unexpectedly to their advantage. Leelee took the initiative. "Yes. I was married but, uh, Jimmy never made through the war."

"God bless him," Susan said briskly and crossed herself.

"Right, bless him. God." Leelee cleared her throat loudly.

"Well, I must be perfectly honest with you two. We've never had sisters, that weren't nuns that is, try to assume care of a child. It isn't specifically against any of our policies, but it still raises the issue of providing a healthy environment for a child. A child needs a father and a mother, fate willing, and we do our best here to give them the best chance they can get," Molly felt her voice trailing off even as she said the words.

The woman Leelee was wearing a pair of thick cotton work slacks that matched a button-up blouse. It appeared to be a uniform of some kind. Her wildly curly hair was severely wound into an ineffective bun at the nape of her neck. She looked to be in her thirties, though already was affecting the sort of dumpiness that it usually took a few more decades years to attain. Widow, Molly reminded herself. The other sister, Susan, was slender and dressed sharply in a floral sundress and starched white gloves. She had lovely long, blonde hair that had been teased into graceful sweeps cascading away from her temples. She seemed terribly nervous.

"Why are you ladies so intent on adopting, if I may ask? You're both young and attractive."

Leelee let out a snort and Susan seemed to be suppressing a smile. Susan spoke this time. "Leelee won't have anyone but Jimmy, ma'am, and I am barren."

"Well, I'm sorry, I..." she trailed off again as she became aware of her fingers playing over the application form seemingly without her consent. These two young women, what luck it would be for a child to be cared for by sisters in a happy household, right? Molly let out a deep sigh, picked up the stack of papers and gestured for the women to scoot closer in their chairs.

"Alright, we must do thorough background checks and financial inquiries, but to start the application process, we can get these forms done now. Just separately state your names here and here, as though you were a couple..."

Approximately two dozen years later, Giovanni Lilly-Vaughn, the adopted son of Leelee and Susan, changed his name permanently to ManPussy. He had really thought his moms would understand, what with their lifestyles and everything, but when he told them, Susan had sighed and left the room and Leelee had made a noise like she was going to be sick.

"That is the most tasteless thing I have ever heard," Leelee snapped, looking out the kitchen window to see if Susan had gone to the garden to sulk as she usually did.

"I told you that I was uncomfortable with the gender class you assigned me to when you named me."

"I still really don't understand what the hell you are talking about, Giovanni. You're a boy."

"Mom, my name is ManPussy."

"Augh, that word again. Are you trying to give me an ulcer?"

"I can't believe you! We've talked and talked about this. I want to give up the gender power that my name gives me. I don't want to come up at a list at some college or on a job application and take the job away from whoever really deserves it. With my new name I am given an artificial disadvantage, to level the playing field."

"I know what we talked about, Giovanni, and it wasn't naming your-self something that I won't even say. And that word! We appreciate that you understand what gender privilege does, but we named you Giovanni because it's a lovely name."

"Is mom really mad?" he asked, looking out to the chrysanthemum beds. Susan was standing with her back to the house, her hands gently touching the massive flowers.

"No, she's not mad. She probably disgusted and wants to kill you, like I do."

"Mom!"

"What? I bought you, I can kill you if I want."

6.

"Edelweiss!" someone called.

Edelweiss was in the line at the cafeteria. She turned and attempted to identify the source. Three students and one elderly professor standing behind her jerked their eyes away from her rear.

"Edelweiss!"

She narrowed her eyes at the person that was waving her down at the end of the line. It was a boy from one of her classes, but she couldn't remember which. She stepped out of line and walked to him.

"Yes? Don't we have a class together?" she asked, smiling compulsively at his glittering blue eyes.

"Nature's Bounty," he nodded, holding up a few books to her. The top one was called *Mother Earth Egg, Father Mushroom Sperm*, and she didn't recognize it.

"What's that book for?"

"It's the main text for Nature's Bounty?" he said.

"Oh right, totally, I didn't buy that one," she laughed, tapping the cover. "I mean, the whole text for class thing is just a money-making machine for the school, you know. Besides, I didn't get the book list."

"They're supposed to mail it to you when you register."

"Yeah, the whole registration thing is an even bigger money-making machine. It makes me sick. Hey, what was your name?"

"Oh," he stuck out his hand. "I'm ManPussy."

"You're ManPussy!" Edelweiss squealed. Whenever the teacher called his name for roll there were snorts of laughter, but she remembered that on the first day he asked to explain himself. He was trying to do something Edelweiss couldn't remember exactly, but it was definitely about feminism. Something about lowering his respectability to that of women. "I love what you're doing by naming yourself that. It's really cool."

"Wow, thanks."

"Hey, you want to get lunch together?" Edelweiss asked suddenly, moving forward in the line with him. They weren't to the vegan section of the buffet yet, so they just salivated freely.

"Sure, wicked. Hey, my flatmates are having a little thing this week-end, you should come. I'm in Whitbey dorm, room 217."

"My name is Edelweiss, but I'd love to come."

"Sorry?"

"You called me 'Wicked'. My name is Edelweiss."

"Right. Got it."

7.

Someone brought a small wooden re'em snifter that was carved into a phallic shape and covered with a vine pattern. It was well-used, worn shiny by the passage of hands and the opening was slightly crusted with calcifi-cations of re'em and damp nostrils. After Edelweiss had been introduced and sufficient time had passed, after drinking expensive microbrews and listening to obscure CDs, she found herself holding the snifter. It seemed too light for what it meant.

"You ever bend spacetime, sister?" someone asked. Edelweiss was a little drunk and trying to match a name to the face.

"Sure I have, lots."

"Yeah? Well, ladies first."

Edelweiss held it to her nose, a little self-conscious. Everyone was smiling at her. "Hi," she said reflexively. She took a delicate sniff and felt a small quantity of re'em hit the back of her throat and carve a scratchy path down her esophagus. It was pretty dirty re'em, probably cut with bone-meal.

"Aw, don't be modest, take a good hit."

"I wanted to make sure there was enough for everyone," Edelweiss said, pointing to the shallow reservoir of opalescent white powder. This was a partially true statement, but also a little bit of a lie. She was strug-gling to not inhale until her lungs were full, to up-end the snifter into her mouth and choke down the entire grimy tablespoon, as she would have done if she were alone.

"There's plenty to go around," ManPussy said from across the room. He was taking a CD out of the stereo and picking up a vinyl.

"Hey, dude, we were digging that," some girl whined. She had been making out with another girl on a dog-hair covered beanbag chair in the hallway.

"Sorry, I'm putting the same album on."

The sycophantic sounds of reggae, this time scratchier, came blasting back out of the speakers. It was the exact same album.

"Oh, smooth," the girl crooned, and went back to what she was doing.

Edelweiss took a large hit off the snifter, smiling at the hoots of encouragement, and passed it to the man sitting on the floor next to her. When he passed it back to her so it could make its way around the room, she saw that no one was looking at her and took another hit, polishing off the reservoir. She was already feeling giddy, but from anticipation.

"So," the guy on the floor said after a minute. "You ever have a score?"

"A what?" Edelweiss was busy following the path of the snifter, watching as someone loaded the reservoir again from a aluminum foil-encased zip-lock baggie, her fingers twitching anxiously when the girls in the hallway had it for too long. She could see them taking deep choking hits and then licking each other's nostrils, and then several sets of their arms doing different things at different stages of a ghostly see-though. The flickery translucent edges of the re'emination were already overlapping her vision. Edelweiss rubbed the palms of her hands on her jeans and sighed.

"You know, have you ever hit the white light? Found your oracle?

"Sure, I've been to Espress-Kno™ lots."

The guy suddenly made a violent face with fractal happy, sad, shocked and orgasm faces multiplying out at the sides of his head. He said, "You go to that place? Fuck that, little sister, fuck that shit. You're feeding the system! You're propagating the industrialization of the human right to dream. Eating re'em is as natural a right as eating and swimming in the ocean. It's our right. You can't keep giving money to the people that make it hard for us to even get hold of the shit. They make it accessible only to the rich, both the re'em and the truth of the re'em."

"You mean, prophecies?"

"Sure, little sister, I am talking about the truth, the whole truth and nothing but it. What right do they have to tell us that we aren't seeing it? Have you ever considered that? Their tests are designed to make you think you aren't seeing the truth, to say no, lowly citizen, you are just some regular poor bastard, so hand us some money and we'll help you out. Fuck that!"

Edelweiss' nose buzzed and her cloaca was warming. The re'em was steadily chugging into its peak phase, which would plateau over the next few hours. The girls across the room were staring, zombie-like, at each other's faces and speaking in hushed tones. Edelweiss looked over to where ManPussy sat, sitting alone next to the stereo looking and album covers. She realized the guy next to her was still talking.

"I don't know if I've seen the white light," she interrupted him. "I guess I have."

"Does it all come true afterwards?"

"I think so."

"Feel it out, find the silver thread and follow it. Feel the vibrations. If they are there, then you'll feel them."

She was already standing up and walking across the room to ManPussy. She stopped and turned back to the guy. "I did know I was coming to Seattle before I did."

"Well, there you go."

And for the first time, it occurred to Edelweiss that she might really, truly be an oracle. Not just the kind that sits around in their friend's bedrooms or hangs out at dorms tripping on slugs crawling on window sills, but a goddamn real live farseer, straight out of the bible. She could hardly believe she hadn't known it before.

A heavenly choir sang.

8.

"Welcome to Espress-Kno™! How may I help you? Today only with the purchase of a StrawBreeze-N-Crème Frapetto or a DutchMaid Chocuccino you can add fifteen minutes to your Espress-Waves Phone Card."

"My what?"

"Your Espress-Waves Phone Card, the exclusive calling card of Espress-Kno™. Imagine the bonuses!"

"No thank you. I'd like an application, please."

"Would you like a re'emination with that?"

Edelweiss hesitated. "No. Yes."

"Full or UltraFull?"

"UltraFull please. With Clarification."

"Any Des-Cryption today?"

"Well, I don't think so. I guess you'd better throw it in, though."

"Better safe than sorry."

"That's right."

"Was the application for employment as a barista, or as an oracle?"

"An oracle."

"There is a minor added charge for that. Did you want anything else?"

"No thank you."

Edelweiss stood in line holding the application. It was thirty six pages long, and the questions weren't numbered so it was hard to say how many there were, but to Edelweiss it looked like a few hundred. Some of the questions asked you to fill in numbers at random, and other questions asked you to answer them on a separate sheet of paper. She looked at the neon sign flashing next to her, in two foot tall letters it said KA-CHUNK!, and below that was a glossy photograph of what could have been rich loamy soil or perhaps a close-up of aged, wet leather. MMM, the sign recommended to her. She looked back at the line and found a small child standing behind her. He was eating something dark brown, whatever it was smeared from ear to ear, across the front of his shirt, across his arms and somehow pasting tufts of hair up on the back of his head.

"Is that good?" she asked.

"Mmm," he said, pointing a miniature brown, shiny little turd finger at the sign next to them.

The Seattle Espress-Kno™s weren't like the ones back in Gaffney, though after almost two years Edelweiss was beginning to get used to them. There was one on every block, and though their prevalence would lead you to believe they were all the same, they weren't. The one near her dorm, on campus, for example, was packed with people all day and night and as a result had a peculiar wet-people smell. Edelweiss did her best to support her local Espress-Kno™ but she still found herself going to ones wherever she happened to be when she had a question. There were seven on Broadway that were always too busy and too grungy, uncountable ones along Pine that were always packed with tourists, several of them around the Pike Place Market and the Space Needle that she was too embarrassed to go to and a few in the International District that confused her. Inevitably, she wound up back in one of the Belltown stores because they were never terribly busy and because they were clearly elite. She stood in that one now, checking her many voluminous heaps of lace she wore as pantaloons for maladjustment.

"Ma'am," a woman behind Edelweiss snapped.

Edelweiss, startled, stepped up, unaware that it was her turn. "Sorry."

"Hippie," the woman growled.

The interior of the oracle's room was the one element that was always exactly the same—the same odors, the same lighting, the same curtains—with the exception of the oracle's voice. Edelweiss had little shivers of excitement through her skin, bumps raising. She'd lost track of how many times she had been in one of these rooms and it was still like this, each and every time. The lights raised and the oracle spoke.

"And with I as the conduit, speak!"

Edelweiss didn't. She had been planning to ask the oracle if she should pursue ManPussy, but suddenly the dangerous questions rose in her mind like a grizzly bear standing.

Many people know very well when they should not push a subject. Better yet, to not even start a subject. Romantic relationships are often made or broken based on the individual's sense to push or not to push. What is the bulk benefit of suspecting your sweet lover's perfidiousness compared to the gravity of actually finding out? Do you really want to know the answers? Will they help you live your life, or will they dangle like a wonky eyelash still attached, never quite useful but too painful to remove?

There are categories of questions that people ask, as stated by the Espress-Kno™ biggedy-wiggedies' Lexicon of Comprehensive Re'em Analyzation Techniques. The tome itself was over two thousand pages thick and bolted together with aluminum screws so that pages could be added and removed at the Revision Department's whims, which were often and complicated. The book was not for leisurely learning, but for searching through mid-argument with your superior/subordinate for some kind of statement that might prove you right and them terribly, dreadfully and hopefully firingly wrong. The book was a disinterested third party.

However, if you flipped to page 794 (and not too sharply or the onionskin pages would tear off in ragged sheets) you would read something vaguely similar to this, assuming of course the Lexicon wasn't updated within the last few hours:

CHAPTER SEVENTEEN-B:
KNOW YOUR PUBLIC

(This had been misspelled 'pubic' in edition 17.426.B, which was a popular favorite among employees)

> *One of the most important tasks of an Espress-Kno™ oracle is the ability to intuit the varieties of questions that may be asked at a specific locale.*

(The above statement is of course a laughable one, since suggesting that an oracle 'intuit' anything is like asking the average person to absorb vitamins from the slush in their bowels)

> *It is vital to know what local customs and practices are employed so that questions are not greeted with misunderstanding. Often times local custom may be strange and abhorrent to you, but you must persevere in your duty to the public, and to Espress-Kno™ Industries, and overlook these issues to provide a public service.*

> *Re'emifications are often the only light in what would otherwise be dim lives, which means that the service is often elicited from lower class individuals.*

(The words "lower class" would, in a later edition, be replaced with the word "disadvantaged", then returned to "lower class", and then in the most recent edition, changed to "rural".)

Regardless of background, all questions can be grouped together into the following categories:

Health
1a. details of death
2a. fertilization
3a. sickness

Work
1b. acquisition of work
2b. promotions
3b. deceit
4b. general success

Family
1c. health of family (note frequency to 1a,2a,3a)
2c. details of family death (note frequency to 1f)

Sex
1d. acquisition
2d. general prowess
3d. infidelity of companion(s)

Speculative world/religious views
1e. the end of the world (note frequency to 2a, 1d)
2e. existence of God (note frequency to 3a, 4b, 2d, 4g)
3e. existence of extraterrestrial life

Money
1f. acquisition (note frequency to 1a, 2a, 3a, 1b, 2b, 3b, 4b, 1c, 2c, 1d, 2d, 2e, 1g, 4g)

Miscellaneous destiny
1g. random future speculation (e.g., 2a)
2g. prophetic capabilities
3g. success in relation to unlawful tendencies or fantasies
4g. power fantasies
5g. long-term capability of sex/life partner

The entire mental acuity of man could, through various sub categories listed later in the chapter, be mapped. In the opposite way that mathematics opened grand doors for people, revealing the infinite complexities of the universe, the Lexicon reduced them all to children's not-so-public television. Humans, it turned out, were largely limited to five or six basic thought patterns. It was an unpleasant discovery and kept from the public at large.

Carmelita Juarez lit a cigarette in the darkness of the Espress-Kno™ oracle room in Belltown, Seattle, and groaned audibly. It was a main category g) Miscellaneous destiny, subcategory 2., prophetic capabilities in the works. They were so common and hated they had glossiolated into the word 'toogee'.

9.

Carmelita Juarez told everyone that she was from Puerto Rico, but that was a lie. Though her parents were both one hundred percent of Puerto Rican heritage, they had both met in Los Angeles when they were teenagers. They didn't even have accents.

Carmelita had two brothers, Hector and Pulga, who disappeared during a family trip (which is what her parents called living from the back of the station wagon for awhile) to San Clemente. All that was found were some fragments of a tennis shoe and a basketball. She couldn't read, so she took no notice of the newspaper headlines panicking about a recent bloat-shark attack. (Two Hispanic boys lost. Recovery unlikely. Blood in the air. WHO WILL BE NEXT?)

O, and the stories she could tell about the great United States of America, not that she had been anywhere else. You could go to any town, any little truck stop or rest station or suburb or alley and score some fucking drugs. Shit was coming out of the gutters there was so much of it. It didn't take a super-genius to walk up to some colored kids, flip them a look at a wad of Jacksons and say, "Find me something, you maggots, and run." It was all a part of the mechanism of humanity, and Carmelita of Puerta Rica was winding the bastard. She could work it.

She could tell by the way the gangs ranged in unicorn-like packs whether blow was going to be plentiful this week or tar. She could smell the dirty Ecstasy sweating off the kids as they ran to catch the bell at their schools, and if that Ecstasy was local. One time a drug counselor in the county jail had tried to tell Carmelita that she was succumbing to an inherent human weakness, one that she didn't have control over, and that she needn't blame herself. She could still get help. Carmelita had laughed and laughed, nearly dislodging a section of corroded lung trying to keep from coughing too badly. "Shit," she'd told the counselor, who was as tired and spent as Carmelita, "Do they really pay you to eat spawn like that?"

And to think that one day, when the babies were screaming and Lester was probably off on some fuck-fest with those white girls down at the pizza parlor, Carmelita got it in her head to do as much re'em as she could fit in her swollen abused face. At twenty-six she had had enough. Fuck it, she thought. The man hits me like I'm some kind of rubber-maid he can pop back into shape and the people are pounding at the door wanting money for the rent, money for the phone bills, money for the crack that Lester borrowed like the moron that he is, and money just because there was a rumor going around that she gave out money.

"Yeah, Chico? Remember me? It's Carmalita, you slit. No, you are. You got any re'em around? Oh yeah? Sure, whatever you want."

And that was that.

Instead of what she thought was going to happen, which involved a whole lotta not being alive anymore, a week later she was filling out a W4 for Espress-Kno™ Industries, holding a plane ticket for Seattle and wondering what her ditched babies were going to look like in ten years.

Only two ways to find out.

10.

There is some quantum theory talk that at every point of existence there is an infinite number of results, of branches that spread off into the final plane so densely packed it's just white light, 360 degrees. This seems untrue, though, because Edelweiss has just been reduced to two possible futures. Ask the question she came to ask, or ask the forbidden question? It wasn't about the money wasted on an inquiry that could possibly be unanswerable, it was about the idea. Questioning things you shouldn't can result in unpleasantries.

"Honey, the universe fathoms no boundaries, but you've got to tune something from the cosmic static, okay? I gotta lotta people to talk to out there."

Edelweiss was momentarily distracted. She had never been spoken to so frankly at an Espress-Kno™ before, and she wasn't sure that she liked it. So she said, "I thought I knew what I wanted to ask, but now I'm not sure."

There was a strange sound over the speakers. Edelweiss would have never guessed that it was the sound of someone smoking, only really loud. "Well," the oracle said, "if you want to know if he the one, just ask, right? Isn't that what you bitches always wanna know?"

"Excuse me?"

"Sorry, girlie," Carmelita said after another long suck on her cigarette. "I just see this day in and day out. What you want from him anyway? What d'you care?"

"You're right," Edelweiss said. "I don't care. My question is: was I supposed to come to Seattle?"

There.

She had said it, just like that. The question. It wasn't so scary, now that she had said it out loud, and she felt like she was sharing something very precious with the oracle, like some secret they had in common.

There was a tisking over the speakers. "Aw, honey, why do you care? You think you toogee, huh? Shit. Give it up."

"What?"

"Alright, Lord forgive me, fine. Was you s'posed to come to Seattle. I ride the cosmic fugue and I hold the tunin' fork of the mind. I see but a light that shines for you, and I see that indeed, you were s'posed to come to Seattle. I see inside the fog of the soul that you have a different reason for coming to Seattle than the reasons have for you, but that is your shit to figure out, not mine. And because I want to make myself very clear to you, which time you mean, Legs?"

"This is the only time I've been to Seattle."

"Sure, sure. But you'll be comin' and driftin' away like scummy foam on the tide, right? Mebbe that should be your question. Why can't you keep your feet still?"

"That's silly, everyone looks for spawning ground. It's human nature."

"Whatever you say, Legs. Seems to me that you find yourself an excuse to stay and you find an excuse to leave if you want. You know I can't answer the question that you mean by what you said; I can't tell you if youse an oracle, Legs."

"I know."

"No you don't know, that's why I work here and you don't." With that she smoked the last of her cigarette in a speedy puff, the way she learned to do when she only had a few seconds to take a drag while the babies were crying, and swiftly crushed it out. "Thank you for using Espress-Kno™, please come again."

"Thanks," Edelweiss whispered.

11.

Manowicz's Espress-Kno™ Industries was a fortress of knowledge. The word 'fortress,' as it is used here, is not a metaphor. It was a reinforced, shuttered, cyclone-fenced, motion-sensored, security guarded, mostly subterranean, crazy guard-dogged, turreted, mounted search-lit building that was largely surplussed from Nazi Germany.

The Department of Personnel was massive and took up almost the entire building above ground. Aside from having rooms of farseers that concentrated on who would be working hard enough for a raise soon and who would be sipping one too many Kountry Molasses Froozies on duty, there was the formidable Application Department. It alone employed two hundred and forty seven people. All they did was go over application scores and try to make the questions harder, by which I mean less logical. They were Lexicon of Comprehensive Re'em Analyzation Technique Department drop-outs. They were directly attached to the Prospective Employee Screening Department. In the NE cubicle, grid B-3, Larry picked up a packet from his stack and narrowed his eyes at the top. It read: Santucci, Edelweiss, B.

The name was supposed to be Last, Middle, First. It was the first test. He took out his red marker and checked the box in the upper right-hand corner that read FOR OFFICE USE ONLY.

It was the rejection box.

CHAPTER FIVE

1.

Since the misty bird-song morn of man, doing things that are considered stupid because of their danger factor has been appealing. Addicting, even. It is difficult to say what aspect of someone's psyche causes this behavior, in the same way that most assholes don't seem to have a legitimate reason for being an asshole. It's chemical, apparently. Possibly karmic. In the wiring.

At some point in the planet's past, a misshapen hairy land animal looked out at an expanse of calm water and marveled at the food that swirled within, just out of reach. This land mammal had perhaps seen other land mammals go into the water, fighting and kicking at something invisible that pulled it down into that place where the hairy land mammal knew it didn't belong. Whatever the case, and it really doesn't matter an iota since this is just an elaborate example, at some moment, one of these creatures (which I really hope you have figured out is supposed to be one of your ancestors, perhaps a recent one) strode into the water. It managed to relax just enough to let its natural buoyancy do its thing, and thus, the swimming hairball got the sushi.

However, before you think that what I am implying is that taking risks results in gaining knowledge, or food, or a bath, I'd like you to remind you of a few things: huffing paint; truck paragliding; sea-creature fast-food. Any time your only plausible explanation when something goes wrong is some permutation of "It seemed like a good idea at the time," well, you've got a problem.

I can hear you yaps out there going off about 'never taking risks' and how that's directly related to 'never taking the incentive to improve' and other locker-room spirit-poster baloney. Well, coach, let me tell you a little something about risk taking: someone else will do it for you. Those circus guys who take a cannon ball to the stomach? They do it only because some blockhead did it first and turned out alright. Laser eye surgery? Some shmuck did it first. I mean, God bless him, of course. Who are these people that take the leaps? Is it *all* done because they didn't know any better, or does the muse Lady Science whisper to some?

In the end the question requires too much. Too many whys, like everything else; why is the sky blue, why do good things happen to bad people, why is my wife a bitch, why isn't beer free. Ad infinitum.

2.

"It's just a few more steps, I promise," ManPussy whispered in Edelweiss' ear. She was waving her arms wildly for balance even though it was even ground.

"ManPussy, I'm not sure how I feel about this," Edelweiss said for the second time that evening. "This seems like some kind of borderline control thing I'm not sure I agree with."

ManPussy smiled and had to turn his attention back to the ground in order to keep from kissing her. "The blindfold is very loose," he told her. "You can take it off any time you like. Just, trust me for a few minutes, okay? I promise you'll love it."

The summer air was a touch chilly at night in the Pacific Northwest, and the eternal dampness of large, cold bodies of water in close proximity. In Seattle, one street could be stagnant and poisonous with car exhaust and urine and the next would be crisp and practically therapeutic with sea salt and pine air.

"ManPussy," she said again.

"Here, here," he guided her around and through torn fencing and then carried her, both of them gasping and giggling, down a gravelly ditch and up the other side. "You have to be quiet now, okay?" he whispered.

"Why?"

"You just do."

"But why? Are we going to get caught?"

"We might. Quiet, now."

He set her down and walked her the rest of the way. He had been by earlier in the day to make sure the area was still clear, and indeed the area was suspiciously clean of garbage and the little can of government issue Ovo-Bloc that remained hidden in the foliage was not trash, but a full can with its seals still intact.

The government stuff didn't have the nice cursive and yet clinical script that the brand name did, but had instead, in a plain black serif on a white field, the words "Sulphera-Furazine HCl" with smaller instructions printed below it: "(1) Hold can twelve inches (12") from sac fluid deposit. (2) Holding nozzle toward deposit, press down nozzle and soak area, starting from the center and spraying in an outward spiral to a distance of five feet, making sure to overlap passes. (3) Take care to spray anywhere any semen or sac fluids have touched, despite an obvious sac deposit not being present. Sac may have torn and eggs will not be visible to the naked eye." And then below the instructions in almost imperceptible fairy font, it said, "Deposit in a proper trash receptacle".

Manpussy had worried over whether it was presumptuous to purchase your own Ovo-Bloc or to let the woman bring her own. In the end he'd called his mothers and gotten the advice, "Jesus, Giovanni, isn't there some outreach center at your college that can deal with that hetero stuff?" He decided to stash a canister just in case, to feel out how it was going before he whipped it out. So to speak.

He slid it out of his messenger bag, removed a thin blanket and laid it underneath a concrete overhang and amongst a dense smattering of rogue salal and blackberry bushes. He tugged a six-pack of extremely expensive, extremely unpleasant-tasting microbrew and set it down with a chime of glass.

"What was that?" Edelweiss asked, cocking her head like a dog.

"You'll see."

"Was that beer bottles?"

"I said you'll see."

"I'd love a beer."

He lifted up two beer bottles and smiled. Action, jackson. With his free hand he guided her shakily down to the blanket, facing out of the overhang, and then went to gently, sensually, tug the blindfold off. Edelweiss, when she felt him start to remove the blindfold scrabbled at it with her fingers, accidentally socking ManPussy with her elbow in the process.

She was absolutely silent.

He held his sore nose.

She turned, her eyes black in the marginal ambient glow of the city's light behind them and blinked. "Where are we?" She looked up at the concrete above them, crawled forward a little, and then looked back to the city. "Oh," she said, going still. "Oh."

"We're outside the bloatshark perimeter. I found a way through."

"This is so wicked!" Edelweiss squealed suddenly and clapped her hands over her mouth. "Holy shit! We're outside the perimeter! It's like, totally natural out here!"

"Shh," he hushed, and glanced around. "Yeah, it's natural. There's another outer sea perimeter, but we could still get caught by cops." ManPussy wasn't afraid of getting caught by cops—there was no fine for being outside of the perimeter, it, in fact, was a near-lawless no man's land—he was terrified of attracting bloatsharks.

"Do you think we'll actually see anything?"

He opened a bottle for her and one for himself. "Hard to say. I figure the best we can do is just chill here and be quiet." He wondered happily what they would do to pass the time, since talking was dangerous.

"Is it safe?" she asked, tensing and looking up. ManPussy let his own eyes flick up, briefly, when she wasn't looking at him.

"Sure," he said, drinking his beer as though deep in thought. "This overhang is really low, people must have been using it to sleep under at night, so it must be safe. Or else there'd be, well, bums that go missing from here. I'm sure we'd hear about it."

"You mean the disadvantaged?" Edelweiss asked sharply.

"Of course, I'm sorry. I can't believe I just said that. Sometimes, you know, social brainwashing has its effect whether I try to fight it or not." He added in a choked voice, "I feel so helpless sometimes."

Edelweiss scooted forward and touched his knee. "We can fight it, brother. If we work together." Her voice was husky.

"Work together, yes," he muttered. He wished the lighting were poorer because Edelweiss' stare was steady and sharp, and it frightened him how she failed to blink for great gulfs of time.

He realized with a flush that their spawning was inevitable.

"You're so... bitchin.'" He had said the words as quietly as he could, but he still sounded like a big dumb animal. He cleared his throat.

Edelweiss took her shirt off.

Edelweiss is taking her shirt off, he said to himself.

His eyes watered with joy.

3.

Sodium lamps are the cheapest of all lamps to run and maintain, and this was why the city of Seattle decided to use them everywhere. The delightful thing about sodium lamps is that they put off a distinctly orange glow, and as a result Edelweiss' breasts were like scoops of sherbet placed upon her torso. ManPussy wasn't even close to being drunk but it was all he could do to keep from giggling at how perfectly lovely it was. Edelweiss' tits were there before him like buffet fruit, their curves geometrically sound and achingly aesthetic.

"I find you to have an attractive femininity to you," Edelweiss said softly while unbuttoning ManPussy's pants. He let out a shuddery sigh.

Some people are very turned on at the idea of clothing. Different clothing means different things, though; a disguise is the implication, to be someone or something else simply by changing one's pants, but it isn't the clothes that are sexy, it's what the clothing pretends: tonight, a police officer, tomorrow, a zoo keeper. But it's the chicken or the egg. Was clothing sexy in the beginning because it hid things, or was it sexy to be naked later because everyone had to wear clothing? Some people prefer the enigmatic, an opaque shift, some back-lighting, the very pressure of not being able to do anything but use your imagination.

There is also a certain methodical faction that enjoys the layers of clothing, the peeling back, revealing and unearthing of secrets under inanimate fabric. It was a puzzle that way, a slow and promising one.

Alternately, many find clothing to be the ultimate in imprisonment, a falsely giving warden of elastic, synthetics, coarse weaves and underwire. Removing it is a gesture of peace.

Any way you shake it the result is alchemy. Bellies are furnace on furnace, hands often so chilly seek out the places that welcome chilliness the least. Legs, a thousand miles away, operate as length after length of rope, binding, pulling and pinning. Feet like ice, a squeal, a jump, an anchor. Side of the neck made for your face. The width of the back more important than the ground beneath your feet. Crash course in plate tectonics. In school, they say, sharks must keep moving in order to stay alive. Stillness is deadly. Keep moving, even if it's hardly at all.

Edelweiss sat up suddenly, looking down at ManPussy, her eyes flashing sodium reflections and her hair standing out like a cannibal's headdress. ManPussy reeled at it, wilting a little. She was fucking perfect. Not a single wrong angle, not a freckle or a scar unless the spot needed it. She was a juggernaut of the bipedal function, fine-tuned and overwhelmingly pheromoned.

ManPussy felt like a maggot lying beneath her. She ran her hands down his front, starting at his shoulders and a little too lightly, so it tickled all the way down. She stared between his legs at the reddish-purple swollen cloaca that pressed up medially beneath his skin. She ran a fingernail over it, causing a brief seizure. She hesitated with her fingernail at the flush slit, down near the bottom. He thought he was going to die. And so be it, as long as she didn't stop.

He wondered suddenly if she'd spawned before. They'd certainly never discussed it. With a deft move she wriggled under him, connecting nuclear fuel rod skin tissue with his own magma-borne flesh and he thought, oh, she has done this before. Her cloaca was slicked a bright ultramarine even in the poor lighting.

Work your mind back to watching the National Geographic reel-to-reels, clicking loudly in the dust laden gloom of your classroom, the blinds drawn against distraction. A middle-aged man would have been speaking fondly of the salmon's spawning habits, which you can see through the greenish muck of Pacific Northwest river water. The male salmon develops a red hump and a beak, while the female remains lithe and stone-colored.

For unknown reasons she knows when to deposit an egg sac, just in time for the male to come up behind her, wriggling sharply, explosively, almost angrily, if you didn't know any better. He, in a brief manner, lets the sperm go, hardly caring where the stuff may fly. It drifts about, fertilizing everything within several yards that shares basic fish DNA.

If you are feeling particularly cynical, you may be able to draw a visual comparison between human spawning and this, the spawning of their ancestors. There is a fair amount of wriggling. The male is definitely uninterested in the trajectory of the semen, and often in fact is gone and blending in with the rest of the males before you can even refocus your camera. The snorkel is less important when observing humans but goggles are still a must.

At least fish had mastered the art of keeping their glowing white butts out of the air whilst they wriggled, and thus maintained at least some dignity.

I am a king, ManPussy thought. I have everything man wants. I'm about ninety seconds from orgasm, which is the best motherfucking place to be in the whole world second only to being mid-orgasm. Dear Ganesh, let me die while fucking. Lord, if you have to take me home, and I know you do, please give me a break and take me now or in a moment very similar to now. My cloaca is a miracle. My God, it's full of stars! There should be awards for doing it this well.

"ManPussy?"

"Sure baby, take it."

My ladies are lucky ladies indeed. I should get paid. Wait, suppose I really could get paid for doing this? Why not? I could do it. What if the woman were totally ugly, though? I could just turn her down, I guess, it's not like I couldn't be in charge of my own business.

"ManPussy, do you hear that?" Edelweiss was more urgent that time.

He paused, breathing heavily and marveling at the masterpiece of her furrowed brows. He lifted away from her, cool air brushing the mucousy dampness of their cloaca. "Hear what?"

"I heard something." She clutched at his back and he sighed, looked around. There was nothing. He momentarily remembered the bloatshark problem, looked up and around, wondered a little at the bravery instilled by being mid coitus and shrugged. "I think we're okay. What did it sound like?"

"Like stones falling," she flicked her eyes toward the concrete overhang. He wasn't getting out of this one with just some reassuring words. Well, shit, he thought. He stood up, first cautiously and then with increasing enthusiasm as a bay breeze tickled and pulled at regions of his body that hadn't see the stars in years. He stepped to the side, and looked up the embankment to where he could see the tops of the perimeter arches, their massive sheets of fencing visible even at night and the tiny spinning red lights at the tops that threatened to mesmerize him. A loose piece of gravel dislodged at a ghost's touch, clattered briefly and then stopped.

"It's nothing."

"Okay," Edelweiss rolled to her side, her cheeks nicely flushed.

Just over her shoulder, toward the other side of the overhang (which in some chapter of Seattle's past had a use, but no longer) there was a flick of movement.

"Huh," ManPussy said, squinting. There was a faint noise. Edelweiss twisted around slowly and most fetchingly and let out a ripping supersonic scream that ramped up from disbelieving to hysterical in just under three seconds. She was up and off, streaking the beach like a naked greyhound before ManPussy could even take his hands off his ears.

In some peculiar Safari Channel moment, Edelweiss' screaming triggered all the unicorns that had been sleeping under the overhang to bray and croon in what had to be the most disturbing cacophony ManPussy had ever heard.

It might have been like someone vomiting, but before the liquid got all the way to the top and fully obscured the vocal cords. It was without a doubt mucousy, like damaged tissue sloughing free, egg sacs ripping; gluten, bile, chyme, and vanilla custard being dumped and sloshed in a ten-gallon bucket and the flappety-blapping of gasses ripping free from bloated corpses.

ManPussy stood frozen and nude, jaw hanging loose. He had never seen a unicorn up close before. The odor hit him and he sucked in compulsively, and unfortunately, through his nose. No amount of exhaling could help him then.

Like a cat's, the unicorn's eyes reflect light. Unlike cats, they couldn't see well at night, just barely better than humans, though it didn't seem to matter since there was no data suggesting they would know what to do with the information. Nevertheless, what seemed like hundreds of red, translucent will-o-the-wisps lit under the overhang, two by two, bobbing menacingly. The more that appeared, the greater the noise became. They began to emerge then, and in irritation. They were the very definition of mangy, their coats shiny in places and not with healthiness, but with mold. They were supposed to be white, but most were either gray or greenish and many had identifiable garbage suspended in their ratty fur. A moving soda can winked out in the sparse light, and a plastic bag crinkled.

ManPussy had become alert, and caught himself inching forward toward his clothes before he realized what he was doing. The seething mass of unicorns moved up a little, a few in the front moving skittishly to the side as though they were being pushed. One of them was eating shit directly out of another's anus, the second one mewling with pain as the other gnawed a bit of living tissue.

ManPussy gagged which forced him to once again inhale through his nose.

They always seemed so small on television, he thought, the size of dogs. Big dogs, he now saw. Big, rancid dogs. He couldn't tear his eyes away from the mutilated, scabby stumps where their horns had been sloppily harvested again and again.

Luckily his clothes were strewn far outside of the overhang and not so luckily Edelweiss' were deep within, colorless in shadow. He glanced to either side to see if she was close enough for him to toss her her clothes, but she was nowhere to be seen. It was for the best, he saw, since the unicorns had already started to eat the sheets of dirty old curtain lace she had been wearing as a skirt. There was a loud bang and increased chaos as one of the unicorns bit into the can of Ovo-Bloc. ManPussy took the opportunity to retreat.

4.

The Witch Doctor's mother did not name him 'The Witch Doctor', and in fact would have been quite put out if she'd lived long enough to know that's what people were calling her little Matty. She'd named him Mathias Andrew, but everyone called him Matty with the exception of young Matty himself.

Matty was one of the worst category of nerds there is. It would not take a terrific amount of effort to map thoroughly the entire caste system of all high school students, from the pinnacle of cheerleader/football queen/king, to the lower of the fat, slow crybabies. The art came in understanding the complexities of the larger groupings: e.g., being fat didn't take you to the bottom rung unless you were also stupid and being athletic didn't take you to the top unless you were also clear-skinned. The stickiest of all was the 'smart' category, for being smart could be especially good or especially bad. Being popular or athletic or attractive or rich was one thing, but if you were any of the above and *smart*, then you were gold. To be fat, ugly, slovenly and poor was a feat in itself, but to be smart on top of that was the guarantee that you'd be beaten within an inch or your life every day after school.

To be a nothing special wallflower middle-class genius is its own curse, but was something that the Witch Doctor fell easily into because mediocrity is the gentlest tide in the ocean of humanity.

The only way the Witch Doctor was special was this: he was the most average re'em dealer in the world.

The Witch Doctor was 5'8", 146 pounds and moderately attractive. More like, not unattractive. His handsomeness depended totally on what you were used to. He had his hair cut for eight dollars at a chain salon, wore seasonal clothing from a chain clothing store and with luck, name brand sneakers from the clothing discount chain store. He was fairly diligent about having new sneakers ready to go before the current ones got too dingy. He began to grow facial hair at the same time everyone else did and purchased a mid-value Japanese two-door before he turned seventeen. He liked 'Mexican' fast food, but also ate whatever his mother made for him, no questions asked. His job at a chain department store ensured that whatever mediocre material desire he might have would be fulfilled in a reasonable amount of time. These desires were limited to food and technology: video games and the systems to run them, sound system upgrades a year after they were all the rage and plenty of music to play on it. He realized that he made enough money to live on his own when he had just turned nineteen.

The Witch Doctor's best friend was a guy named Jon. Jon was mediocre as well, but in a more acceptable manner—Jon's parents were well off and lived in a three story house on Orcas Island. They hardly ever gave Jon anything, but when they did it was something like an entire brand new, top grade speaker set or some kind of mutual fund that didn't make any sense but paid out checks enough for a month's supply of pizza rolls and rent and some bills. Jon was subconsciously aware of his level of safety and tried to order extra pizza for the Witch Doctor whenever he could remember to, but the weed and the re'em made this difficult.

Still, Jon was a good friend to the Witch Doctor and put a touching amount of effort into not making out with girls that could be coerced into making out with the Witch Doctor instead.

Now, many revered works of literature, if not most, are about the lives of men. Oftentimes, these books about men are about adolescent men, like teenagers and sometimes, boys. On a cautionary note, if the book is about the latter two and was written by William Burroughs, William Golding or Michael Peterson (or has similar themes to Chicano shooting galleries, being stranded on a deserted island, nude, with twenty of your peers, or mercurial war-time helicopter pilots) then the books may be for men, by men, if you know what I mean.

Most man books will herald the brotherhood of men: the indestructible bond of loyalties so deep they are a subconscious response. This, on some small level, is true but is by no means worth filling entire libraries about, at least any more than stories about girls developing strong wills against all odds. In fact, one of the greatest secrets of all time is that most friends-till-the-end guys are actually too lazy to notice their incompatibilities. 'The Grand Brotherhood' is a wistful misperception.

However, with that said, I am going to defend myself for a moment. This great and epic mistake is in no way less respectable than if they really did have some core desire to die for each other all the time. Women, for example, are usually conscious of their hatred for one another and participate in saccharine displays of sisterhood anyway, almost as if to spite one another. It's a messy, messy world out there and I for one am doing my best to stay out of it.

All of this relates to the story as such: the Witch Doctor and Jon had lived together for nearly two years, since they graduated from high school, and without so much as an off-color mutter in each other's direction. There were jokes made, of course, about how much they enjoyed each other's company, but that was drastically beside the point. Foremost, the Witch Doctor and Jon were only vaguely aware of the other's basic behaviors, and secondly, they were friends. Thus, when the Witch Doctor, then known as Matty, proposed that the two get into dealing re'em—strictly for financial security—Jon was first suspicious of how much labor would be expected on his part, and then supportive when he was assured that he would have to do no more than withdraw money from the ATM from time to time. Matty shook Jon's hand solemnly, vowing to repay his friend in what is commonly referred to as a Gentlemen's Contract.

Years later, Jon repaid and re'em sales doing beautifully, the two hadn't even considered moving away from their dark, boxy apartment to a nice Queen Anne flat with actual curtains in the windows.

Before the sales were pulling in regular rent and fun money, Matty was still calling himself Matty. In a classic example of the depths of male feelings for each other, Jon cocked his head curiously when he answered the apartment door one day after a giggling gaggle of high school girls had knocked, light and rapid as hummingbirds.

"Matty here?"

Jon said the only thing he could think of. "Can I tell him who's here?"

"Oh we've never met. I'm Alicia, this is Nicole, Emily and PeeDee."

"What kind of name is PeeDee?"

"It's short for Precious Delivery," the girl snarled around an acid green sucker.

Jon nodded and opened the door wide for the girls to come in. He became slowly aware that he was wearing week-old sweatpants and a tank top with salsa stains down the front. He beat a fast retreat to Matty's room.

"What is it?" Matty asked at the knock.

"Some girls here to see you."

"Girls?" Matty's bedroom door opened a few inches and his face appeared in the crack. "My sister?"

"No, dude, *girls*. They said you didn't know them. Look, I'm going to change my clothes and I think you shouldn't deal from here, at the apartment."

"Why are you changing clothes?"

"They're bangin', dude. Put some pants on."

"Okay. I didn't tell anyone where I live, though. They must have found out from someone else."

"At least change your name or something, man. That way when the cops come, we can be like, 'No way dude, this is Matty and I'm Jon' and they'll be like, 'Sorry, dude, we were looking for a dealer named The Hulk', or something."

"Agreed."

5.

"Matty, it's that hot chick again."

The Witch Doctor looked up at his best friend peering through the peep-hole in their door. Why did people always show up to buy drugs when he was neck deep in Gestapo, trying to shoot the SS gesplechmeisters and dodging panzerschrek in the tunnels below Avignon? It was as though they knew.

"Which hot chick?" A few years ago, it wouldn't have mattered to the Witch Doctor which hot chick was at the door, he'd be up like toast to greet her, Award of Honor instantly paused, flack and shrapnel frozen in pixels, but today he asked this in the tired tone of the working class.

"The one with the dreadlocks."

The Witch Doctor got up off the couch, checked his hair in the hall mirror and nervously smoothed his T-shirt. Jon was already sitting in his 'make-it-so chair', as he called it, picking off Nazis where Matty had left off.

"Hey, what's up?" The Witch Doctor drawled, swinging the door open casually.

"Hey, brother, this is Derek. Can we come in?"

The Witch Doctor looked at the two, eyes moving from one to the other in an attempt to determine if they were a couple. He felt a pang of misfortune as he realized that this Derek fellow was not only good-looking, but not nervous about scoring drugs either. The Witch Doctor preferred it when they were nervous. Unbeknownst to him, though, his calculating stare was not taken for what it was, but instead as a scrutiny.

"He's cool, I swear," Edelweiss said.

Neither man knew who she was referring to, so the Witch Doctor opened the door wider and said, "Yeah, okay, come in."

Inside the apartment, the Witch Doctor gestured to Jon. "That's my roommate, Jon."

"What did you say your name was?" Derek asked, thrusting his hand out.

"The Witch Doctor."

Derek began laughing happily and the Witch Doctor blushed. "But his name is Jon?"

"That's right."

"So you changed your name to the Witch Doctor because you're a drug dealer, for secrecy, but your roommate who is here all the time too, didn't?"

"Yeah, what did you say your name was?" The Witch Doctor asked Edelweiss.

"Edelweiss. It's Italian."

"Yeah, Edelweiss, where's the dude you usually ride with? What's his name, HeBoobies?"

"ManPussy?"

"Right, where's our buddy ManPussy?" The Witch Doctor asked nervously. He was really not digging on this Derek fellow, and though he hated ManPussy for being Edelweiss' boy-thing, at least he was polite.

Edelweiss' countenance became hard, then. "You may think you know someone, but I guess you don't really know them until they try to rape you in a cave full of monsters."

"Okee dokey, well, I'm pretty busy, so can I help you with anything?" He refused to look at Derek and found his eyes running over Edelweiss at a frantic rate. Jesus, she was hot. She was so tall and slender and tan in the most spectacularly un-Seattle way. She was looking blankly around the apartment, one arm wrapped around the other shoulder so to scratch the opposite shoulder blade, and the gesture was better than if she had hoisted up her tits and shook them at him. Well, almost.

"Oh yeah," she said. He was having trouble describing her voice to himself, but the words 'clear' and 'round' were what he got stuck on. He could listen to her talk all day. "We were hoping you'd have some re'em around. Like, a forty?"

"Oh, I dunno," he lied. "I have to check. Re'em has been scarce lately."

"Really?" Derek said with sarcastic innocence. "This friend of mine was just telling me about how he could barely unload the stuff there was so much. Something about a good year for unicorn breeding." Derek picked up a baseball in an acrylic case absently and gave it a shake.

"Don't mess with that, it's a collector's item," The Witch Doctor said. "Why didn't you get some re'em from your friend then?"

Derek shrugged. "Edelweiss said she knew a guy that gave her good deals."

Edelweiss. The Witch Doctor hated the way that bastard was saying the name, giving the 'w' such a subtle and eloquent 'v' noise. The Witch Doctor had thought the word sounded familiar the last time she was there so he'd looked it up. A white mountain flower, German in origin. It seemed so wrong, her name should have been Fire Orchid or Tiger Lily. Wait a minute, the Witch Doctor thought, that cheesedick is trying to get me to give them a deal because Edelweiss is a fox! He grumpily dug through the fire safe box in his room, flipping carefully measured and stacked vials of re'em onto his bed. Fucking asshole. Like hell I'm going to give him a deal just because he's bagging some chick that is way too hot for him.

The Witch Doctor returned to the living room and handed Derek a scant forty vial. He saved the short vials for the jack-offs.

"Oh, it's not for me, it's for her. She's paying."

"Very gentlemanly of you, sir," The Witch Doctor told him.

Edelweiss didn't seem to notice the banter and handed him two twenty dollar bills. "Thank you so much," she said, and the Witch Doctor didn't miss the possessive way she clawed the vial back from Derek.

"Uh," he said, holding the money. He was having a brief pang of guilt over the shorted vial, but he mentally chanted his number one rule to himself: don't care about the buyers.

"Later, guys," Edelweiss was already saying, opening their front door. When it slammed shut the Witch Doctor loped to the window and watched Derek put his hand on her ass on the way to their car.

"Asshole," the Witch Doctor sighed.

"Totally," Jon said. Nazis screamed.

6.

Psychedelic at it's most typical: shudder buffet of air, wind, sounds like headphones with no sound coming out of them. Patterns repeat and sink, reemerge and mutate. You'd have to have been there.

"I'm confused," Edelweiss said, but her voice was whipped away in the wind.

"Leave!"

"Leave?" she asked, her voice catching. Even though she hadn't yet considered leaving Seattle, the command struck her as coincidental. Perhaps she had been thinking of leaving, in fact, she probably was, considering how much she had felt out of place there lately. "But how?"

She saw a vertiginous array of faces and unicorn horns and sherpas all whirling like the guts of an industrial dryer.

CHAPTER SIX

1.

It was so infuriating. That shit Derek and some tramp had spent the entire day in the teepee, (a really accurate teepee at that, one with potent chi) and although Edelweiss had been openly mad at first, she reminded herself that it was all good. She was on her way to warming up for the night: a few glasses of someone's homemade loganberry wine; some very strong barley homebrew; plenty of weed (for digestive purposes); a few nips of butterscotch schnapps because she was drunk and couldn't stop herself from consuming refined sugars; a bite of what she thought was a magic mushroom tofu scramble but turned out to just be someone's dinner; a pellet of hash; a handful of some psychedelic-looking leaves she found growing next to a garden gnome.

Her friends were just beginning their nude solstice dance when the feeling hit her. She'd had her eyes closed and was nodding along to the drums (getting a good visual of the spherical infinity or maybe the mother goddess, it was hard to tell which) and then there it was, a shiver, a touch of a sore throat. The more she thought about it, the more she was fairly sure she'd had some funky weed or something.

"Hey brother," she said to the man sitting next to her.

"Fuck you," the woman said, pulling her girlfriend up and moving to the other side of the fire pit.

"Sister, I'm sorry, you're so in touch with your masculine nature. Hey brother," Edelweiss said, leaning to the man on her other side.

"What?"

"You feel funny?"

"Sure, here," he said, passing her a re'em snifter.

"Oh, hey. That's not what I meant," she said, and inhaled the entire contents of the snifter. She sucked so hard that she began to choke.

The man pounded on her back and handed her his wine skin. "Take a drink, there you go. Easy. Your first time?"

"No way, brother, I'm an oracle."

"Aren't we all," he said, and went back to his friends.

Edelweiss shivered with tight little sensitive thrills, and remembered that she was feeling ill. She focused on the sensations, the heat in her cloaca that made it seem like she'd peed herself, the buzziness, the whispering. Whispering? That didn't seem like bad weed. A delighted and somehow operational portion of her mind realized that she had taken some very, very clean re'em; shortly thereafter that portion was beaten senseless by the wine.

The teepee loomed up, a cathedral of salvation, back-lit by the goddess' own luminescent cloaca, beckoning: Edelweiss, daughter of a thousand daughters, come rest yourself.

"Okay," she said.

She pulled the tent flap back and crouched to crawl inside. There was the tiniest of ambient light from the fire pit and the goddess' cloaca coming through the gaps. There was an odd noise. Edelweiss strained to see.

Where was everyone? There appeared to be just piles of something on the ground, maybe pillows, so she put her hands down to steady herself, but it slipped out from under her on something slick. She let out a squeal. Arms snaked around her shoulders and under her skirt, up her legs, and gently but with astounding speed someone found her breasts and tweaked the nipples to attention. Before she could scream, a mouth found hers and then moved to her nostrils, teasing and plumbing the depths with their tongue. For a moment she thought she was being raped, but she wanted to make sure first.

"Hello?"

"Shh!" and then: "No, sister, no voices."

"What's going on here?" Edelweiss asked. An elbow shimmied into her side and she giggled. Something sensuous was going down in her armpit. "Oh!" she said, reaching for her skirt as she felt it drift away on a human tide. Something hot was pressing into the back side of her knee, wriggling slowly. "Pardon me," she said and did her best to sit upright again, but there were too many people around her. Someone was nibbling her hipbone.

"Is this an orgy?" she asked excitedly.

Someone was right up in her face, then, putting a hand softly over her mouth. She saw the wet glitter of eyes close to her own and flinched. "You need to not speak, okay? Not at all. If you are not ready for this, then leave." It was a male voice. She opened her eyes wide, trying to see who it was. It was hard to concentrate, for there was something wet and warm happening to her toes that caused her to gasp adoringly.

The man's eyes were black pits in a pale, pale face, and the irises began to glow softly and rotate almost too slowly to see. She leaned in, fascinated. They were spirals, endless spirals, and gray-purple highlights that looked like words formed. She focused harder and was pleased to see the words become clearer, saying: "The Nose Always Knows!" over and over again.

And so on and so forth until entire epics had laid themselves, shamefully extended for Edelweiss to see, telling shadows of the future's cast and muddled cocktails of cosmic importance.

Later, when the sun rose over the teepee, which was then an upside-down sno-cone of cum and egg sacs, strewn victims of enlightenment and free love lay littered upon the lawn as far as the eyes could see. If the eyes could see only ten yards, anyway.

Edelweiss woke late in the morning in some scratchy foliage outside the teepee, nude and sticky. She dragged herself immediately to the doctor.

2.

"Alright, Ms. Santucci, what seems to be the problem today?"

"I'm really sick."

Dr. Willard Osgood didn't even hear the words that came from his patient. He was having quite a day.

First thing that morning, his wife told him that his daughter and her husband had fertilized again. And again, it was an "accident". They'd had a priest come to narrow the fertilized eggs down to one. Dr. Osgood asked his wife why it was that his child could not afford a goddamn can of Ovo-Bloc. Especially considering the state gave it out for free.

Mila had answered by crying, telling him that the child would be loved. Though he knew that was true, he still didn't understand how it was fair to any of the four kids to have to share attention and praise, let alone toys and food and friends. If the priest could terminate all but one of the fertilized eggs, why couldn't he do them all? Dr. Osgood bit these words back and drove to his office, the summer sun already doing a good job of giving everyone skin cancer at half past nine.

His first patient was a rosy, blonde, two year old girl with a rash on her legs, a smile like a champagne cork going off and lungs like Dizzy. All that screaming because of cheap bubble bath.

The usuals after that, a flu, a mysterious lump, a yearly physical and a woman who had been dropping upwards of five egg sacs at a time. He referred her to a specialist.

Then, a brief nibble on his bagel with lox and cream cheese and red onions. Mila never could understand the concept of a doctor's breath needing to smell fresh when having a nasal speculum moment with a patient. Thus, lox, onions, liberally peppered meatballs and pickled every-thing regularly made its way into his lunch.

Dr. Osgood turned his attention back to the girl, taking in the ripped leggings, the nappy alpaca shawl, and making the usual assumptions (free love, lack of dietary protein, etc.). He would've felt bad about making stereotypes if they weren't so often correct.

The file said she was achy and felt ill. "You feel sick then," he mumbled, reaching for a few instruments. He looked down her throat, into her ears, listened to her lungs. He tapped on her abdomen and checked her pulse.

"I am in severe pain and look," she said, holding her arms out. A faint reddish cast mottled parts of her arms, but to the physician's eye, it looked like a run-in with either a dirty animal or some kind of skin-irritating plant.

"Have you eaten anything unusual lately, taken any sort of medication?" He lowered his voice to a softer tone and asked, "Any recreational drugs?"

"No. Wait... I think this Vietnamese restaurant I ate at sneaked some meat into my food a few days ago."

"Oh, you're a vegetarian?"

"A vegan."

"It is possible that you're having a reaction to meat if you've not eaten it in a long time. How long have you been vegan?"

"Two years."

"Ah, that's not it then."

The girl's eyes bulged ominously. "Meat is poison to my body, doctor. And I meant three years."

"Okay, but your body will still know how to process it, since it's only been two years. Did you have diarrhea or gastrointestinal distress afterward?"

"Three years."

"Mm-hmm. Any tummy trouble?"

"Don't patronize me, doctor."

"Okay then," he said. He looked closely at the red marks and determined they were of minor interest, as they seemed to be going away and caused her no lymph pain. He ordered urine and stool samples and told her the lab would get back to her.

"There is something wrong with me doctor. I have a strange rash," her voice was rising in pitch and he steeled himself for what he figured was coming. For the thousandth time in his career, he wondered why people were so flummoxed at the symptoms of mild illness. It was always the same, a run-down feeling, sometimes nausea or a headache. He hadn't the heart to tell everyone that it was just uncomfortable to be alive.

"Edelweiss, dear, there are a million explanations for what is going on, and all but maybe one of them are benign. Let's treat this like the flu, you know, rest aspirin and plenty of chicken broth—"

"I am a vegan," she snapped. "I am so tired of your persecution over my lifestyle choice. I can't believe you are using this office as a forum for your moral dictatorship!"

Dr. Osgood put his hands up in apology. "I'm sorry, Ms. Santucci, I forgot you said you were vegan. I'm sure your diet will make room for some vegetable broth, yes? As long as it is warm and un-spiced, I don't really care what it is."

"If I told you I was gay, would my sickness be some kind of gay cancer, then?"

"What? Look, Edelweiss, we seem to have gotten off to a bad start, and you are sick and not at your best capacity right now. I never said anything about your sexual preferences and I wouldn't think they were related if you had brought it up. Just get some rest, okay? The lab will call you."

"It's convenient that I have access to a telephone, isn't it?" Edelweiss said while pulling her shawl on. "What'd happen if I didn't? It's all about the doctor, not the patient. Man, western medicine, I tell you. Money money money."

"Okay then, have a nice day," he called as she left the room.

He couldn't believe his daughter had fertilized again.

3.

You have no doubt heard of Jaspar Moputu: in the eighties, he was a pop star among oracles. He had everything that the public loves in an underdog. He was handsome and shy, innocent and terrified at the thought of offending someone. His accent was thick and melodic, and despite being a fairly recent immigrant, his command of the English language was exceptional. Best of all, he adored Americans.

At a time when most American school children were still being taught that other cultures didn't really have oracles, Jaspar's story was fascinating to say the least. The airwaves were being dominated by intercultural anthems like "We Are the World" and "Feed the World," and here comes *a genuine foreigner with a sad story to tell.* It was a self-fulfilling prophecy come true!

What story? Well, back when Moputu was a young ash-colored African lad, all legs in the desiccated safari heat, he was pulled aside and tested for prophetic talent. The elders of the tribe had told the sorcerer to pick his successor, and in the privacy of the old man's hut, he asked Jaspar: is this what you want from your life?

Now, Jaspar knew how becoming a sorcerer worked, so he knew that you weren't *asked* if you wanted it—you just were. If you had the gift, you had to. No one had tested positively for many, many years.

Jaspar also knew what it entailed, everyone did. You were sent away with the old man, to be trained, and you came back and lived as a strange old recluse who, if you were the harbinger of bad fortune, would take the blame for the Gods' ill will. Jaspar remembered the old sorcerer having stones thrown at him in anger and grief, many years before, when he had forecast a strange fever that would and did kill most of the tribe's babies that year.

Is that what he wanted? The question hung in the still and baking heat of the hut. He realized then what the old man was giving him: a choice. Jaspar shook his head no.

Ah, but the old sorcerer had gotten too old, too slow. A neighboring sorcerer came to the tribe, to consult over other matters, and saw Jaspar for what he was. The tribe fought, with screaming and hitting and wailing, lamenting among everyone involved. The visiting sorcerer had also seen that one of the women in the tribe had the gift and had not been flushed out, driven away to die in the wastes as a witch. The old sorcerer had been protecting many, it turned out, and that didn't bode well for him. There would have to be reconciliation, and not in the hugging sense.

That night when everyone's punishments were being determined, Jaspar and the witch made a run for it. Along the way, many weeks into their trek, she left to beg for help and found a tribe where the witches were not driven away or killed. Jaspar continued on to the south until he came across his first big town. There he stayed and worked, sometimes as a sorcerer, sometimes as a laborer. He didn't recall exactly who told him about New York the first time, but one day he just had the memory of it, the desire to go. He saved enough money to be smuggled in, and before he knew it, there he was, in the most hustling, bullshit, wonderful city in the world.

So how does that make someone a huge hit, you ask? Well, that alone doesn't. What does is that one person noticed this handsome young man, and that one person happened to work for the *New York Times*.

Jaspar had been arrested, you see, for buying re'em off an undercover street cop on a crappy side-street in the Bronx where hookers lounged like limp grocery store flowers. A Times reporter happened to be doing an article about a new company called Espress-Kno™ that the government had given a re'em use pardon to. Since the pardon was both revolutionary and dull as hell (the government practically approving a drug? Unheard of! But who wasn't doing every drug—let alone re'em—in the 80's? Yawn.) the reporter was looking for another angle. She was rewarded with this: a jail-cell full of re'em arrests, every single one a confused immigrant. Jaspar spoke English. The rest didn't. There's the story.

Mr. Moputu was suddenly on The Midnight Show, Top O' The Mornin' America, The Bayer Report and every other TV show you can think of. There were articles, book deals and sold-out stadium appearances. All this, not just because Jaspar was handsome, tall and dark like sleep. It was because he told everyone the truth. He explained what an oracle sees, how they worked, and the public slavered over him.

Espress-Kno™ of course was eternally grateful, since they had had the good judgement to hire Jaspar just as the fiasco began. Jaspar told stories to the potential clients that lured them in, fairy tales for a burnt-out America. He explained, as eloquently as he could, that everything came to him as though in a memory. He would see that his client had many memories of a child growing up and know, intuitively, that the child was their own (for who else would have so many memories, from the poopy diapers to the graduation ceremonies?). He made mistakes early on, with American names and western relationships he didn't understand, but it hadn't mattered. He learned quickly and there was certainly no lack of practice.

He told of how difficult it was to keep concepts of the future under control—the past was easy, but the future hadn't happened yet, so the possibilities were like someone tearing open a feather pillow. They swirled about, each the same and different at the same time, each in turn needing to be examined for statistical probability. But even terms like "probability" were misleading, Moputu warned, for that implied that humans had a machine-like ability to calculate events. It was more like smelling something familiar that had no odor.

And not all oracles were the same, he added, so other oracles were being brought in to consult. Some testified to reading text like a book or a newspaper. Some saw images, just like on TV. Others were there as themselves, walking around in another's shoes, searching for another's lost keys or checking on someone's delinquent lover.

By the time the 90's rolled around, Jaspar was nearly forgotten. He had been the voice of the oracles, for America, which struck him as the strangest bit. How could a skinny little ignorant African child come to tell Americans all about themselves? Well, it didn't matter anymore—Moputu was safe and rich and in no danger of losing either of those things for as long as he lived.

4.

"Alright Ms. Santucci, still feeling bad?"

Edelweiss rolled her eyes and then immediately regretted it. It tipped off the headache that had been dogging her for days. She just couldn't seem to shake this sickness, no matter how many cups of reishi tea laced with goldenseal and echinacea she choked down. She'd tried pouring saline down her sinuses while hanging upside down, she'd tried melting waxed paper cones in her ears (that had really hurt), and she'd pressed on pressure points and eaten those tiny little Chinese pills that looked like green-black bb's. She put inside her cloaca, on good advice from a red-eyed woman at the herbal tincture shop, a clove of garlic. She still hadn't felt any better. She seemed to actually be getting sicker. "Yes."

The doctor sat in a chair and said, "Well, your lab results are back and were very interesting."

"What do you mean?"

"Let me tell you what I know first. You have adult erythema infectiosum, which is commonly known as The Fifth Disease. It's a paro virus infection, which is lengthy to explain, but it all boils down to a viral infection."

Edelweiss felt her heart skip suddenly. It began to race, then. Some kind of tropical virus. "How sick am I?"

"Well, I should hope this is the worst of it. I'm a doctor, not an oracle," he laughed.

Hope this is the worst of it? As in pray? Edelweiss caught herself chewing on her tongue, wondering if she should walk out now. She'd heard of these religious freaks; he probably couldn't wait to get her back into his office like this, he would probably start trying to deprogram her any second now.

"What do I do?" she asked, keeping her voice even and conversational.

"We watch and wait. It's all we can do for now. It's a bit of a rare thing, to get the Fifth Disease this late in life, but no one has had permanent side effects."

She tried her hardest to have her life flash before her eyes then, but got stuck each time on Derek's grody orgasm face and on an article she'd read about the healing powers of potting soil. So this is it, she thought. My life has flashed before me and my most intense memory to date will be this, this ugly doctor's office and itchy arms. "What about this?"

"Okay, well, try not to scratch it, scratching will make it worse. But here is the tricky part, you see, I think that the bumps on your arms are not the pruritus from the Fifth Disease, but a reaction to some kind of organic agent. It's hard to say what, exactly, without knowing what you've been into. I recommend an oatmeal bath, maybe some steroidal cream if it gets worse."

Gears ratcheted, levers pulled, steam whistles blew and Edelweiss finally really realized what was going on. This was about her being an oracle. That would at least explain the doctor's mysteriously nervous, apprehensive demeanor. He was going to tell her she had to stay here, take some more tests, or wait—go to the hospital, fill out some paperwork and WHAM—a straight jacket. She decided to beat them at their own game. "Of course I have organic agents in my system, doctor, I am a friend of the environment. Organic stuff does not cause reactions. And how do you even know I have this Fifth Disease?"

"I know you have the disease because the lab confirmed it with an elevated titer of IgM anti-paro virus antibodies in a serum. And as for the organic agents, I'm not talking about the pesticide-free kind," the good doctor hesitated. "I feel like we should talk about the rather massive quantities of monocerous attrius in your urine, Ms. Santucci. It seems possible that you're having a reaction to that."

"When will I get better? And I haven't been into any of your 'mondo-serious aphids' doctor, so there goes that theory." She couldn't hide the smugness from her voice. She was tying his arguments into knots. "I don't put any chemicals into my body."

"You will get better over time, we have to just watch and wait, treat things as they bother you. It's essentially a flu. The overdose levels were of *re'em*, Miss Santucci. Do you want to tell me about anything?"

"I can't believe this," Edelweiss said, running her hands over her face. "I was healthy last week, totally fine. I didn't overdose on anything doctor, I participated in a human expansion, something you wouldn't know anything about."

"Agreed," the doctor said. "I'm not bringing this up to get you into trouble. I just wanted to make you aware that there are programs to help you, when you find that maybe your life is getting complicated, like this."

Edelweiss collected herself, and stared openly at the doctor with the power of her womanhood behind her, her brilliance and her awesome inner strength. "Should I check in with the lab?"

"I'm not sure I follow you."

"I mean, when this chemical flu you are trying to pass off as an 'overdose'," she made little quotations with her fingers, "starts to get worse?"

The doctor nodded. "Certainly, whatever. Come back, we'll fit you right in."

5.

At Espress-Kno™ headquarters, the only thing they monitored more than Espress-Kno™ itself was television.

Television, in particular, talk-shows, had the power to alter the pattern of human existence on Earth more than any other known force. If, for example, Alfie Silverman of the Alfie Silverman Show were to run an expose on the sordid world of the hotdog industry, mothers around the globe listened, and worse yet, they reacted. Hotdog futures would fluctuate wildly on Wall Street, Head Foremen in heavy denim overalls laid off old friends from the line because the company couldn't afford them anymore. Ton upon ton of pig and cow offal sat, unwanted, until some other industry lowballed a bid on it and used it for energy snack bars.

Or, say for example you had a precocious New York Italian talk-show host named Cynthia who was most well-known for her point-blank questions that left interviewees blubbering and snotting on live TV (arguably she was better known as the talk-show host who started the Cynthia's Books on Tape Club, encouraging her viewers to listen to audio renditions of modern bestsellers). Cynthia was legendary at Espress-Kno™ for something entirely different, however, and that was that she didn't take their advice. Ever. No matter how many revised sheets they faxed her, advising her to cant her questions another direction, there she would be, on live fucking television, blowing it.

On this day, Cynthia had done her worst yet: she had asked, quickly and between other innocuous questions, if the oracle she was interviewing had known anything about older oracles being able to prophesize *without first using re'em*.

"How did that question get through? We audited that didn't we? It was prophetically audited, was it not?"

At the Espress-Kno™ headquarters, the debriefing room was red-lit. A klaxon in the hallway silently twirled, warning unwanted attention away like a poisonous frog. A secretary guarded the door, a massive holstered pistol on her slender waist. Inside a room, a table full of people were watching the Cynthia broadcast in instant replay via satellite, clutching copies of the approved script.

The young upstart that had spoken flipped through his stack of papers.

A portly man next to him shook his head. "We did. It cleared as safe. Something must have drastically changed since the last audit. Is this the most recent version of the approved audit?" He shook some papers in his doughy fist.

A woman with a bad dye job popped up in her seat. "Yes, of course it's the most recent. Jesus." She had been in charge of providing everyone with the most recent copy.

The Director frowned deeply. In the futuristic under-lighting he looked almost like Kevin Spacey. "This is really too bad."

"I think that kid she was interviewing did excellently, though," the portly man said, trying to remember the kid's name. His brain was getting snagged up on the subtitle that had flashed at the bottom of the screen under the Kid's name whenever he spoke: Youngest Oracle's Quick Thinking Stopped Serial Killer.

"Oh yes," a gym addict with a falsetto voice said.

"But it's deplorable that Cynthia's editors didn't cut—they've got a five second buffer! Her job is too secure, I think," said the woman with poorly dyed hair.

"Do we threaten to pull our ad spots?" the gym addict asked.

"That's for the Cost Allocation Department," the young upstart said.

The secretary bustled into the room, whispered to the Director and handed him a long scroll of unfurled fax paper. He looked over it and frowned so deeply that he nearly pulled a neck tendon. "Damage Control says the oracles agree that Cynthia was told about re'em accumulation in oracles at the last minute, and appears to have decided to push the subject in further episodes."

The room gasped in surround sound.

"How could she know?" The portly man asked.

"We have a leak!" The young upstart let loose.

"Damage Control is already on it," the Director said. "But we aren't the only country that has oracles. We discussed this as just being a matter of time."

"The public will not understand," the woman with bad dye job said.

"We are aware that is your stance," the young upstart said. "You remind us every single meeting."

"I mean it every single meeting."

"People," the Director commanded. "We've got a job to figure out. Let's get figuring. We must be more diligent. Let's alter these prophetic auditing guidelines to clear thirty seconds or less before a media event, okay? All who approve say 'aye'—ha-ha, just kidding, I make all the decisions here. Meeting adjourned."

CHAPTER SEVEN

1.

Dante Carfagna, as a child, did not want to dabble in genetics. He wanted to be a racecar—as in be a racecar, not drive one—which is why they don't let six year olds make career decisions.

By the time he got to high school, Dante was still thinking very little of genetics. A passing suggestion from a teacher, an offhand remark that the university was near the coast, and the deal was set. Sure, great, genetics sounds lucrative.

And then, the unlikely.

Dante Carfagna loved it. It was like playing with tinker toys, only better. It was like going to church, only fun. It was like drugs, and especially so since the old man baristas gave him a narrow eye every morning when he arrived, pale and unrested, fidgety and distracted, for his espresso. Dante would assure them, "Don't worry, don't worry, I am going to save the world!" and they would nod, sagely, thinking perhaps he would save the world. With a better haircut and a suit, of course.

Everyone at the lab told young Dr. Carfagna that he was going to be rich and famous and (debatably the most important point) known all over as the man that solved the world's garbage crisis. He certainly had the cover of Time magazine in the bag with his square jaw-line and permanent expression of an apologetic little boy. At least that was everyone's viewpoint from the lab, which had no windows and a little sandwich dispenser that a man came and attended to every few days without saying anything but "Bon Giorno." It wasn't the best place to view the world from, and, as a result, they were wrong.

In Milan, with a thousand of the world's top journalists invited, the crowd was treated to a tacky laser show and a hip, grinding soundtrack. The levels of the music were off and there was a breeze, so the machine fog (designed to facilitate the laser) drifted low and fast and useless. Carfagna's Hound, they called it, and they expected such a flurry of press and international gossip that they'd hired a secretarial company for the weeks to come.

On the stage there was some fanfare, some grandstanding, and then the lights went dim. A spotlight. A leggy model in a lab coat a few sizes to small emerged, leading behind her an animal. The crowd compulsively ooh'ed and ahh'ed, cheering for something they had yet to really see or understand.

It was a dog, they saw, a funny-looking dog with an embarrassing potbelly. Its face looked rather like a catfish's, with long tendrils that hung down on either side of its nose, like a mustache. It made with a snuffling and constant mastication as though it were chewing gum. The sounds of its bowels preparing to pressurize could be heard across the auditorium without the aid of a microphone.

There is a specific sound to a thousand people opening press-release folders, it turns out, and Dante heard it. It was the sound of failure. Everyone was skimming their briefs, shuffling through the snazzy letter-heads and the gloss pics of the lab and the workers.

> *Groundbreaking technology that will allow, for the first time in human history, the people of the world to own a creature that has not evolved anywhere on Earth. More importantly, a creature designed specifically to benefit all of mankind for generations to come!*

Everyone looked up at the stage, and then back to their pamphlets.

> *Never before has the world been approached with such a fantastic offer!*

And back at the stage again.

The model pulled a transparent baggie from the pocket of the under-sized lab coat and held it up for the video cameras and the flashbulbs. It appeared to contain cigarette butts and various other gutter flotsam. She shook it to the ground before the dog and stepped away dramatically. Only in the eternal moment before the big bang had there been such a tense silence. The Carfagna's Hound ambled rotundly over to the butts, snuffled loudly for many seconds, and then began emitting a vaguely Hoover-esque noise, a whistley sucking sound punctuated by an occasional *thwup!* Following this, the dog's rate of mastication would begin doing double-time. It took several minutes to sink in: the dog was eating the butts. A wave of pity ran through the crowd. The dog finished and wagged its lumpy little tail, looking up at the model expectantly. A lone pair of hands hesitantly clapped.

"We are so fucked," Dante's lab assistant Lucia whispered to him.

"Absolutely not," Dante told her, and strode up to the stage. The clapping had increased to several people, and gained a few more every second, but confusion was still thick in the air. Dante consulted with the stage manager and then approached the podium.

"Excuse," he said, clearing his throat. The audience stopped clapping. He mustered up his best English. "You are, ah, very lucky people tonight. You are seeing something to change the world, only it has not happened yet! I hope—"

"LADIES AND GENTLEMEN, DR. DANTE CARFAGNA!" A booming voice-over interrupted.

"Jesus!" Dante screamed. "I excuse me, I am meaning, that was loud. I see what I am trying to say is, I know you are confused because you see something not, elegant and not powerful. It is a dog, a living dog that eats and poops and wants to go on walk. But can it survive? Wait, no, what is the word? Yes, survive on plastic, fiberglass, paper, anything! It has poop that is like the environmental equal of three hundred years! Wait, that does not make sense." He leaned over and consulted with someone to his right, outside the spotlight. "Si, yes, I mean to say the hound accelerates biodegredation. Society may be unhappy to give money for a big plant that we trust is process garbage, but everyone likes dogs! Which would you choose, eh?"

And then, as though they had been waiting for a cue, the crowd surged, flashbulbs popping, microphones thrusting and questions hollered ten deep. No one really noticed the dog skittering around behind the model, and the model skittering away from the dog, disgusted. It gave a breathy yip and the odor of sodden cigarettes wafted forth.

2.

Camus wrote that Florence, Italy, was the only worthwhile city in Europe. I'm paraphrasing of course, but that's the gist. The fact is, everything from Europe seems worthwhile compared to America, and if Al had spent any time travelling, you know, to broaden his mind, he may have written that the only cities in the world that weren't worthwhile were in North America. But he was right about one thing, and that is that Florence is a singularly fantastic place.

"Pardon me," Edelweiss asked, breathlessly, of a man standing at the *tabaccheria* outside the Firenze train station. It was mid afternoon, warm, and the street stank of car exhaust. He said nothing.

"Oh, sorry, I mean, ex-que-see? Can you tell me how to find the Alblerbleh Marie Louise de Mechichi? The people at the airport said there were vacancies?"

The man gazed happily at Edelweiss' generous frontside, and looked around to garner further appreciation. *"No Inglese."*

Edelweiss shifted her bags to the other arm and nearly dislodged the loose shoulder strap of her flimsy ivory-colored peasant shirt. Her skin coloration, various moles and other bits showed clearly through the thin fiber. Her loose khaki shorts and expensive boutique running shoes did nothing but flatter her long legs. "What did you say?" she asked.

"Ah, bella donna," the man said.

"Gracias," Edelweiss turned away from the stand and inhaled deeply from the exotic foreign fumes, not noticing the gaggle of lecherous old men that had grouped around to watch her lungs inflate.

"Signora?" someone said, tapping Edelweiss on the shoulder. She opened her eyes.

"Yes?"

"You need help? I speak English." A young man stood before her, shorter than her, but then so was most everyone. He had a head of dark brown hair so thick and healthy it looked like a fur hat, and a sideways lope of a smile. The older men grumbled jealously.

"Oh, that's great! Yes, I am trying to find my room, but I don't have a map or anything." She fumbled about, laying down bags around her feet and fishing for the paper that had the hotel's name on it.

"Oh, signora, no," he gestured to her bags, leaning to put his hands over them. "There are too many thieves, don't do this. Si, si, I'll help you find your room. I'll walk with you." After they had gathered her things and started walking, he asked, "What's your name?"

The sidewalks were narrow and he had to call this over his shoulder.

"Edelweiss Santucci."

"Ah, Italiano? Are you visiting family?"

"No. Just visiting. It was an accident, actually, the plane I was on was supposed to go to Tibet, but now I think I have business here."

"Work, Signora?"

"I am starting to see that I prophesized something here."

There was an interruption as they leapt around speeding scooters and ran across a street. Edelweiss was momentarily intrigued by a perfume shop, and her guide hesitated.

"You Americans and your re'em," he said, though not cruelly, and lit himself a cigarette. He handed the pack to her, but she declined. "It is funny."

"Funny? I know Italians aren't big on re'em, there aren't any Espress-Knos. I noticed that right away."

"It's not that we aren't big on it, as you say, it is the Church. They are very picky about who is telling their followers what to do. None of us," he swept his hand around, indicating the other pedestrians, "could possibly know what God wants, si? Only the men in the wooden boxes inside the churches know that."

"How much do they charge?"

"Charge?" he laughed, looking up at Edelweiss. "It is the Church, Signora, you give a donation. I don't know, three thousand lira? Something like that."

"How much is that?"

"In dollars? Ah, let me see, a dollar and a half? Two dollars, maybe. If you can afford it."

Edelweiss stopped in the middle of the narrow sidewalk. "Holy shit."

"Holy, si."

3.

The young man was named Joseph and had been educated in Canada, as it turned out. He was a painter.

He came by the *albergo* on the first day to see how she was settled in, and then he took her for a walk to see the city. They drifted about, stopping at a *tabaccheria* for Joseph's cigarettes, and he pointed out a magazine with his name on the cover.

Edelweiss found herself reexamining her feelings for him. Indeed, upon further review, she found him irresistibly attractive.

"What kinds of things do you paint?" Edelweiss asked, licking at a green apple gelato. Joseph was eating a Nutella gelato on a brioche roll sliced in half, and smoking at the same time.

"Oh, many things. The beauty of painting, you know? I change my mind almost every day. I did a series that was very good, or at least I sold the series, that were paintings of rich people in eccentric surrounds. And then I sold them for a lot of money to very rich people who hung them in their very eccentric mansions." He gesticulated sharply with his cigarette as he spoke.

"That sounds nice."

"I suppose it was nice," he chuckled. "People just adore pictures of themselves. Especially when they think they are being ironic."

"Si, si, I get it."

"Saint Michelle, she does speak Italian!" he teased, poking at Edelweiss' arm.

Edelweiss giggled at an astounding volume and gave Joseph a shove.

"Why did you stay in Italy if it was not where you were going?" Joseph asked. He had finished his cigarette and was reaching for another.

"Well, I suppose because I am humbled at the way that our futures, although shown to a very rare few like myself," she placed her hand at an angle upon her chest, "are still not simple. This is a complicated event, it must be important."

"You mean the re'em, si? You took the re'em and decided to find what you dreamt?"

"Yes, it's complicated," Edelweiss said defensively. "Have you ever done it?"

"Re'em?"

"Yes."

"No, no. As a child I was terribly afraid of the men in the boxes that took the re'em and then told people about their rights and wrongs all day. They would tell you when the ah, temptation would be bothering you and how you should avoid it. When I was little my mother took me to church and the man there told me I was going to steal one of those little spawning books from the tabaccheria, you know the ones?"

"The what? Did you mean to say spawning?"

"Yes, I show you," he said, craning his neck around, since they had been walking and were far from the last tabaccheria. He spotted a little stand and walked her over to it, looking around the cluttered piles of magazines, clucking his tongue as he went. He rummaged though post cards, plastic rosaries and prayer kits against everything from malaria to bus accidents. The tobacco was kept behind the cardboard-layered counter where the greasy proprietor smoked a cigarillo and gnawed on a massive hard sausage. He leered openly at Edelweiss and she smiled.

"Here," Joseph said, finding a battered stack of nondescript books among the flotsam. He handed one to her. It was subtitled, "Spawn Anal!" in English. Edelweiss flipped it open and gave a little chirp. It was an entire comic book, just drawings, of large breasted women in many varieties of complication and exposure, cloacas and all.

"This is pornography!"

"Yes, I guess so. Who gives a shit, it is a comic book."

"Pornography is degrading to women, Joseph."

"Degrading to what women? They're just drawings."

"It implies that women behave in degrading ways, and they don't."

Edelweiss skipped a few pages and pointed. "See, that. Men are going to think that women do that."

"They do," Joseph gave a sad little laugh and shrugged.

"No."

"Listen, signora, it is not in good taste, okay, but it is not entirely fiction either. Men, they like it because it is at least plausible, if not possible." Joseph seemed to be holding something back and then burst into laughter, pointing at the page that Edelweiss was still dumbly fingering. "Why, I have enjoyed that very thing with a signora."

"Oh."

"Look, I am sorry, I did not mean to make an unpleasant conversation for you. I meant to be telling you about my youth, si?"

"Okay."

"Well, they sell these books everywhere, probably outside the Vatican even, and to anyone old enough to have enough money to buy one."

"To children?" Edelweiss gasped.

"Sure, si. Italians are not so preoccupied with the spawning as you Americans are, even with all of our religion. Same thing with alcohol and smoking. Some things are for people to figure out on their own, right? As a part of growing up. Like knowing not to drive fast. No law will stop a determined fast driver, but he may die or kill someone, and that will be his punishment. I smoke and I know it will kill me, but when it does, I will be sorry for myself and that will be that, si? Why all the fuss over stopping me?"

"I don't know."

"So, the spawning books, they don't stop kids from buying them because if he wants to, he is old enough. God help him if his mother finds out, though, because no one else will."

"Uh."

"So this man at the church, he tells me that I am going to steal a spawning book from a tabaccheria," Joseph nodded at the proprietor, who chewed loudly in return, "and that I must resist the temptation *and* say thirty Hail Marys and a handful of our fathers and help my mother extra hard with the housework that week."

"You hadn't taken it yet, though?"

"Si, exactly, I had not committed a crime yet."

"In America, you can't be tried for something you haven't yet done, but victims can get a restraining order. Did you steal it anyway?"

"Well, that's America for you. No, I had a brief moment of guilt and bought one with my pocket money."

"I don't get it. Did you say your Hail Marys and all that anyway?"

"Si, of course. The next week, I was greatly disappointed to find out that the man at the church 'knew' that I was going to buy the book instead and that stealing it was a temptation he had placed upon me, as a test from God. Then he told me that I really would steal the next one, and punished me accordingly for that one."

"What did you do?"

"I told him I didn't believe him. He told me all would be lies until I could resist temptation without struggle."

"Did you steal it the second time?"

"I didn't. I bought another one."

"What did you do then?"

"Well, the man in the church tried to lure me into doing other things, and I always told him he was a liar. We told each other these bad things until I was old enough not to go any more. The end."

Edelweiss looked down at the book in slight wonderment. "In America, the oracles don't tell you what to do. They answer whatever question you have."

"Si, Canada is very much the same."

Edelweiss went to put the spawn book back and Joseph shook his head at her. She noticed the proprietor holding a fistful of coins, his smile like a greasy smear across cracked porcelain.

"What do you mean?" Edelweiss asked.

"It is yours," Joseph said, holding his hand out to walk away with her.

"Oh no, no, I can't. Really. It's insulting, it's low..."

"What are you afraid of, that it will degrade your thoughts as well?"

"Women are people, not images."

"Then what are you worried about? That images can harm you?"

"I'm talking about the massive psychological damage inflicted upon the most innocent members of society by the pornography monster!"

"By innocent members, you mean adolescent boys and senile old men?"

"Yes. And women. Women around my age."

4.

The following day Joseph was waiting in the American-style espresso shop across the street from the albergo. He meant to run out and meet her, but instead found himself staring.

Perhaps it had something to do with her height, but when she walked, it was as though the world slowed down. Her legs took an eon to go from a gentle lift—the front of her exposed thighs contracting into lovely planes of shadow and light, her kneecaps smoothing—to a long, slow stretch back down; her shoulder dipped slightly as her hip braced and took the transferring weight. Her buttocks shifted so voluminously as she did this that the hem of her short-shorts lifted to reveal the line that distinguished that intoxicating hinterland between leg and butt.

He ran to catch up.

"Buon giorno," he said, plugging the crooked side of his mouth with a cigarette.

"You smoke too much."

"Si, si," he said happily, and lit the cigarette. "What are your plans for the day?"

"I don't know. Well, actually, it's to find some re'em, and then I'll figure it out from there."

Joseph gave a startled look at her and then fell into step with her as well as he could. "I think you aren't in America, anymore, fiore bianco. People go to jail here."

"I know that. But I also know what basic human rights are, and I will take it to the top if I have to. Wouldn't the media love that?"

"You don't understand," Joseph warned. "You will go to jail. Not like America, there is no way around it. It's illegal here."

"I certainly don't expect you to help me. You've been very nice, Joseph, don't feel obligated."

"You do not want me around? I am bothering you, Signora?"

Edelweiss stopped to cross her arms and glower down at Joseph, nearly wiping out a file of pedestrians behind her. "I love your company. I wouldn't have made it here as quickly without you, and I don't want you to feel like you have to get into trouble with me. Although," she stepped closer to him, looking down at his massive black eyes through his permanent smog of cigarette smoke, "If you are ready to ride the silver truth, I can help you."

He stood still, mesmerized by the proximity of her breasts to his face and her flagrant disregard for how awkward such a thing might have been. He shook his head slowly. "Sorry, signora, I am not ready. But I do know where you can ask around. It will have to wait until dark. When the gypsies come out."

"Gypsies? Don't you mean aboriginal Europeans?

5.

Later that evening, after Edelweiss had sickened herself at a rate of one gelato an hour and Joseph had chain smoked his way into the haunted nether-regions of nicotine saturation, they warmed their hands and settled their metabolisms with minestrone.

"Bologna?" Joseph asked, making a move towards a peach-colored chunk spotted with masses of white. Edelweiss hadn't noticed it until Joseph had gone to cut it.

"What is it?" Edelweiss asked. There was a large dark stain spreading out from under it and onto the brown paper-covered table.

"Bologna? Pork? Beef? I am not sure, exactly."

"Baloney?"

"Si, bologna. Tasty fat," he said, digging at the pieces of white.

"God, no, I'm vegan."

"No dairy, no eggs, like that?"

"Yes."

"Ah, then no more gelato for you."

"I've been eating the fruit gelato, Joseph," Edelweiss drank a hefty whallop of wine and smacked her lips.

"Ah yes, sorry." He rolled his eyes.

Two hours later they roamed the streets of Firenze looking for someone of low caliber. In the fresh darkness the streets were suddenly be-spotted with chestnut roasting carts and old women on red cloths. Young Egyptian men chased them with silver and silk shouting, "Lovers? Lovers?"

"What are those women doing?" Edelweiss asked when they walked by an old crone who was shutting her eyes hard, smashing them closed, really, and then opening them wide again. It was a fairly common trait to someone high on re'em, someone out of control. "They look like they're high!"

A row of men dealt cards onto their filthy red rugs as fast as pit bosses, pointing viciously at the card and then at passers by. One suddenly tossed a small handful of bones into the air and then shrieked, "AMERICAN!" at Joseph.

"Ayah, si, stupido," Joseph replied. The man growled, scraping his bones back into a pile.

"Joseph, what are those people doing?"

"Fortune readers. False prophets, to you."

"So they know how to get re'em?"

"Oh si, and the police pay them double to turn in the stupid tourists that try to buy it from them. Very lucrative business for everyone involved. Well, not so much for the tourists."

"Oh."

Edelweiss stopped, Joseph clutching her arm, as a crowd bottle-necked into the mouth of a narrow street. She glanced down a side alley and happened to see among the frail tarot women a hunched over, giant form.

Edelweiss narrowed her eyes and stood tippy-toe, trying to get a better view. A gypsy woman saw her and began to call, "You will die! I save you! You die unless I tell you!" A few of the other women began to cackle in a phlegmatic chorus until the yelling one broke into a toothless grin.

"Joseph, what is that down there? Is that a person?"

"What's that?" Joseph asked, looking down the thin cobbled alley. "Ah-ha! Good eye, signora," he said, and maneuvered her around into the alley.

"What is it?" she asked again as she began to see that it was a person, and that person was easily twice as big as the desiccated gypsy women.

Two immense hands rested clasped, chipped yellow thumbnails the size of clam shells catching the thin streetlight.

"Good evening friend, how are you?" Joseph asked, holding out his pack of cigarettes.

The gargantuan head turned up, thick mottled eyelids wetly opening to reveal bloodshot eyes with bright yellow irises. It took the cigarettes, and, with the delicacy of a surgeon, extracted one with two summer sausage-like fingers.

"Grazie," it rumbled.

"What the hell is that?" Edelweiss asked, whining. An odor of moss and fried meat came wafting off the creature in viscous waves. Edelweiss pulled at Joseph's sleeve after he had lit the thing's smoke and then his own.

"I speak English, chippy," the creature said, his voice like someone mowing gravel. He inhaled from the cigarette and polished it halfway off. "I'm from Hertfordshire. That's in England. England is a country you may have heard of."

"I know where England is," she whispered unconvincingly.

"Perdone, Hewey, this is le bella donna Edelweiss," said Joseph, "Edelweiss, this is my friend Hewey, the pornography monster." The monster blinked. Edelweiss screwed up her face in disgust.

"Well then. Bully for you there aren't trolls in America, ah?" Hewey said. "Or there are, but you call them what, retarded? Send them off to work camps or relegate them to designated land?"

"Trolls? That's a cruel term, we use the term 'developmentally non-human'," she said kindly.

"Oh ha-ha, no," Joseph said, putting his hand over Edelweiss' mouth and shrugging apologetically to the troll. "Edelweiss, they are trolls. You know, they live under bridges, they make bone-meal bread, they run the sanitation industry?"

"Like the Mafia?"

"Watch it, pollywog."

Joseph made a high creening noise somewhere between laughter and a cry for help. "Oh now, you two," and to the troll: "Americans, huh? Poor education, you have to forgive them."

"Poor education?" Edelweiss pulled away from Joseph. "What is that supposed to mean? I've spent the last two years of my life bettering myself, and that's more than lots of people can say."

"Of course, fiore, but in America."

The troll began to laugh then, a disconcerting tectonic rasping. "Where did you find this one?"

Joseph flapped his arms. "Outside the train station."

"Ha ha! Bloody good then," the troll said, sticking his hand out at Edelweiss. Joseph took Edelweiss' arm and placed her hand inside Hewey's palm, allowing her to be shaken violently once, her shoulder socket ratcheted a warning.

"Ow," she said.

Hewey ignored her and poked at Joseph's cigarette pack for another. "What's the game, Joseph? Haven't seen you around lately."

"Ah, you know, I'm famous now."

The two began to laugh together when Edelweiss blurted loudly, "We were looking for some re'em."

"Ah, fuck, keep it down," Hewey grumbled, hunching his shoulders and looking suspiciously at the cackling biddies on the other side of the alley, who had, all that time, never stopped singing an Italian dirge with unmistakable spawning references and horking hotcake sized green-brown loogies onto the cobbles. They hadn't heard anything.

"Look," Hewey said, scratching his arm. Edelweiss noticed then that what she thought was a thin leather jacket or shirt beneath Hewey's vest was, in fact, his skin. "Leave the prophecies for home, huh? Why don't you run off and have a lovely little Italian holiday, drink the vino, eat some cheese, take a bit of a frolic to a Greek island for an anonymous shag. You're much less likely to have the bobbies callin' your mummy and duddy to send you a ticket home that way."

"Have the who now?"

"He's telling you that a holiday is better than having the police send you to jail," Joseph said.

Edelweiss pulled herself up to full height. "No, you look, Hewey. I'm tired of everyone treating me like I'm some stupid helpless girl. I'm an experienced oracle and a woman. Having access to re'em in a inalienable human right. And trolls. An inalienable person right. Are trolls people?" Edelweiss fingered a dreadlock.

After a great long stare with his massive old fried egg eyes, the troll shook his nearly-hairless head and extracted an olive-sized booger from his nostril. "Sure, sure, I don't mind takin' a pound or two off your hands, anyway. But I will say this: we're going to a might howry place, and I won't deal with your squirmin', nancy girliness, got it?"

Edelweiss stared at him.

"Off we go then," Hewey said, and hoisted himself up like a giant redwood in reverse fall.

6.

"I don't like this," Edelweiss said.

Hewey leaned over to look her in the eye. "What'd I tell you?"

Edelweiss craned her neck. "I'm not sure."

"You got to be real hoyden, got it?"

Edelweiss blinked and looked to Joseph for guidance. He shrugged.

"As I was sayin'," Hewey continued. "I rather think the Italian consulate has it all wrong, right? In 1997 it was all about appeasing the northern trade embargo, particularly after that messiness with Germany in April."

"Si, si…" said Joseph.

Edelweiss tuned the men's voices out and focused on staying paranoid. They were walking along some fairly iffy neighborhoods just outside of Florence. The buildings were older, lower, and packed closer together. Gone were the perfumeries and boutiques, giving way to groceries, librerias and unidentifiable stores a mere two yards wide. There was the occasional café, and despite its being nearly two in the morning, they passed a group of grizzled but dapper old men drinking wine and playing checkers. They stared at Edelweiss as she passed and one of them said something.

"Gracias," she said politely, and they all cackled.

"Hey, watch it, okay?" Joseph said to Edelweiss.

"But I—" she began, but he had already gone back to talking with Hewey.

After a few forays down filthy alleys and across a perilous footbridge, the troll and man quieted. After they crossed a darkened park, Hewey led them around the backside of a particularly elderly building. The troll moved with stealth, but the two humans crunched and stumbled along. When they caught up with Hewey's still form, he was rapping gently at a rickety door.

"Si?" said the occupant.

Hewey began to speak softly in Italian, with the unseen occupant responding in kind.

"What are they saying?" Edelweiss whispered.

"Hewey is asking if we may come inside, signora, and the man is not sure. Hewey is assuring him that we are friendly."

"Of course we're friendly," Edelweiss said loudly, for the occupant's benefit.

"Shh!" Joseph hissed, and Hewey turned to glare horrifically in the darkness.

There was a great deal of blaspheming and vulgarity and the clanging of metal before the door swung open a few inches, letting a crack of light illuminate the alley. Edelweiss wouldn't make out much of the face in the crack, but she could see it was staring at her.

"Hewey, mio amico," the man said, and opened the door. He extended a hand and Hewey grasped it gently.

At Joseph's insistence, Edelweiss stepped through the doorway first and then turned around to make sure the others followed.

Hewey's entrance was like a dislocation contortion act. He got down to one knee and leaned through, headfirst and one shoulder at a time, and by leaning slightly to the side he used his back arm to anchor himself by holding the door jam above his head. Scooting the leading leg forward he stood slowly, still twisting, until he was inside. He was bent over at a steep angle. He placed his hands on the ceiling to steady himself as he sat, tucking his legs up under his knees.

Edelweiss turned to look at the rest of the room and screamed.

The Italian stranger, whom she hardly got a look at, smacked her hard across her face.

Edelweiss burst into tears, howling and holding her cheek.

Hewey, gently but with terrifying mobility, placed his giant hand over her mouth leaving her nose and eyes free, and by holding her entire head, muffled the noise. She rolled her tear-filled eyes and shook violently. One of her hands was stuck under his, still holding a stinging cheek and the other clutched ineffectually at his forearm, where the muscles in his arms rolled, slowly, like sleeping dragons.

"I told you now," he whispered, "to be a tough bird. Those are dead, capisci?"

Edelweiss strained her eyes in their sockets to look peripherally at what had made her scream. Dead unicorns lay across great wooden tables stained black with blood and shelves behind them were lined with hundreds of amber bottles. On the walls were a dozen stuffed heads, unicorn heads, though she could hardly believe it. These were angelic, graced with gentle, soft curls of opalescent white hair, like baby lambs. From each of their foreheads crested a practically luminescent golden spiral, a horn, pointed heavenward with a gentle curve.

"I'm gonna let you go, okay?"

"Mmph-hmph."

Hewey slowly took his hand away from her face, letting it hover near her lest she need to be corked again and she gaped, red-cheeked but quietly, at the walls. Edelweiss walked over and touched one of the horns experimentally.

"It's resin," Hewey said.

"No," Edelweiss whispered.

"They're souvenirs. For bloody tourists. Like elephant feet, gorilla hands, fucking whale bloody penises. Snake gall bladders."

"Actually," Joseph interjected cheerfully, "Snake gall bladders are not poached. It's legal."

"Ah, well, there you are. Edelweiss?" Hewey asked. She was still staring at the heads in either depressed horror or ravenous hunger. Hewey never was very good at deciphering women.

"They're dead," she said.

"Clever girl," Hewey nodded toward Joseph.

At the sounds of gurgly splashing, the three looked back to the stranger. He stood at a large basin with his back to them, violently scrubbing something. With housewife efficiency he scrub scrub scrubbed and then lifted high the limp form of an entire boneless dead unicorn. Edelweiss filled her lungs fully and loudly and Hewey dutifully clamped his hand back over her face just as she began the first shrill notes. Her stifled scream sounded like a distant flock of murderous seagulls.

The stranger turned to look. He was older, or perhaps just wrinklier, than his posture alluded, and his hair was the jet of a new motorcycle jacket. He had the most ridiculously piercing eyes only partly due to the eye-liner effect of his thick black lashes.

"You like re'em?" he said in clipped Italian-heavy English.

Edelweiss, still muted, tried to nod.

"You see future?" He laid the corpse across an oversized dish rack.

"Yes," Edelweiss croaked when Hewey let go of her.

The stranger smiled warmly. "God adores idiots and children."

"Oh I don't know," Hewey said. "If God likes children so much, why is he always giving them leukemia?"

"Mio Dio," Joseph laughed.

"What's going on here?" Edelweiss demanded. She didn't like being left out, and in fact, Italy in general was beginning to annoy her. For starters, everyone was always speaking in different languages.

"I give you re'em, signorina," the stranger said. "115,000 lira."

"How much is that?" Edelweiss asked.

"Fifty dollars, just about," said Hewey.

"Oh no, I only wanted a twenty bag for now, but I'll be back for more if it's high quality."

Hewey belched gaseous compounds that, if ignited, could have welded steel. "You don't get to decide, chippy. He wants 115,000 lira. And I need my 40,000 lira."

"For what?"

"Finders fees."

"That's a racket!" Edelweiss whined, and all three men cringed.

"Well, you aren't getting out of this basement just for being a real bonnie lass with more 'an enough tit to go around. I found it for you, I get 40,000. He wasted his time with you," Hewey motioned at the stranger. "He gets the same. Unless you're buying, in which case he gets 115,000, which is sounding more and more like a good deal, right?"

"Why are you such an asshole?" Edelweiss turned on Hewey.

Hewey was at a loss. "I couldn't begin to explain. Trolls are just that way. My grammy used to make the best bone-meal bread; she said she'd killed a real human for the bones, but I always figured she was out to make us lads laugh. She probably just found some dead tramp."

"Hewey!"

Joseph chuckled and lit another cigarette. The stranger sprang forward and snatched it off his face, plunging it into the soapy water and hollering while waving his arms at the supply shelf. Most of the bottles had pictograms of flames on them.

"Scusa, scusa," Joseph begged.

"Buy now, get out!"

"Edelweiss, pesca," Joseph said, "Hewey works, this is his job. You have to pay him. Things are different here, you know how you have to pay to sit at a café, just to sit?"

"Yes," she said grumpily.

"It's like that. No one is trying to screw you, this is not your home country. I wouldn't let them give you a bad deal, would I? I am the only person who gets nothing for being here."

"Alright," she said, dug into her quilted string purse and pulled out a wad of lira the size of a roll of toilet paper. "But I thought America had liberated this country?"

"Mother of Mary, you're a cheeky monkey," Hewey said, and patted her butt.

7.

"This is a ten dollar bag!" Edelweiss was still complaining when they neared her albergo.

"Yes it is," Hewey had resorted to saying, dully, every time she repeated herself, which was frequently.

Joseph coughed and tiredly stopped at a tripe cart for a sandwich, where the vendor was starting to close up after a long evening of steamy intestines. Joseph motioned to Edelweiss to see if she wanted one.

"Vegan!" she shrilled.

"Ah, si," Hewey said and held up his thumb to the vendor who then put a tongfull of hot tripe into his own bare cupped hand, after having looked at Edelweiss' satin-skinned neck and having forgotten about the bun part of the sandwich. Edelweiss didn't notice. She was ranting to, or rather at, Hewey, whose eyes had glazed over with a thin film of tragic boredom.

"What the hell is that?" Edelweiss pointed down an alley. A rigid, older woman, stilted high on three-inch heeled seven-hundred dollar shoes and wearing a nutria fur jacket was walking an animal.

"That's a Carfagna's Hound. Where the bloody hell have you been?"

"I've never heard of such a thing!"

"Queen Mother, I find that hard to believe. It eats butts, they've just made it," Hewey was saying while helping himself to the tripe. The vendor had run to the end of the alley to plunge his blistered hand into a small wall-fountain.

"Oh, you're a jerk," Edelweiss muttered, and pulled her tiny baggie of re'em back out to glare at it.

"What?" Hewey asked, trying out a hurt look. He was dimly aware that it looked like every other face he made, which was a definite ringer for upper gastrointestinal distress.

"Your tasteless British slang, that's what. 'Butt eating', what is that, a homophobic slam?"

Joseph laughed.

"No, I mean butts. You know, from fags," Hewey said.

"Don't you ever stop? Its words like that that perpetuate the torture and death of hundreds of people every day. People that love someone despite what their exterior looks like," Edelweiss said in an emotion-laden tremolo.

Hewey and Joseph stared at each other and separately guffawed so loudly that a young woman in an ivory slip and her hair in a wrap came to a window above them and began to cuss long Italian syllables at them. This provided Hewey and Joseph with enough hilarity for two more minutes of teary, desperate laughter. Luckily, with the greater intensity of the laughter came greater quiet, as anyone who has laughed to the point of suffocation knows. Joseph had actually gotten down on one knee in an attempt to regain oxygen flow.

"I don't know why I put up with you. I don't even know," Edelweiss was saying.

Eventually there came an awkward moment when man and troll began to stop laughing, and with it that moment when one is not sure what was so terribly funny in the first place. Edelweiss stood before them, red-faced, cross and Aphroditean.

"Signora, it eats, the dog eats *cigarette butts*, the filter bit. And in Britain, a cigarette is commonly called a 'fag'. It's no slander."

"The dog eats butts? Can't it be stopped?" she asked, incredulous.

"No, signora. It is an indefatigable butt-eating machine."

"You know," Hewey said, picking a string of steamed tripe from the ground and eating it. "It's a whatty, an environmental dog. Some chap named Carfagna bioengineered it. Bloody bastard, if I ever find him I'll suck his fucking guts out though his asshole!"

"Wait, it was genetically modified to eat garbage? To help with the garbage crisis?" Edelweiss asked.

"Garbage crisis! What bloody hell crisis are you talking about? It's never been better!" Hewey clapped his hands to the sides of his head with a sound like concrete and a side of cow colliding.

"Gene modification is evil," Edelweiss said softly.

"That's exactly right," Hewey pointed at her. "And so is that dog."

"Even if it's for the good of the planet?"

Hewey nodded, "Yes, right, even if it's for the good of the planet. And what about trolls? What about our needs?"

"Maybe the dog is a gesture of peace. Maybe it's the final answer for the line between abusing a technology and embracing it," Edelweiss said, looking down the empty alley where the hound had once been.

"That trash is rightfully mine!" Hewey shouted.

A young woman in a white slip leaned out her window and dumped a refuse can full of snotty tissues and hair wads on all three of them. "Here!" she called in crisp English. "Have mine, then!"

"I must have a Carfagna's Hound!" Edelweiss said, grabbing Joseph by the lapels.

"You've got garbage in your hair," he told her.

CHAPTER EIGHT

1.

Off the coast of Vernazza, a barketta bobbed on the night sea, making quite a racket for something doing nothing. It sloshed and creaked, and generator-fed lights snapped and slid in brittle reflections across the water. Occasionally, the sounds of expensive laughter echoed, carrying the notes of throats coated with caviar and champagne.

"Such a beautiful vessel," a woman moaned, stroking the resin coated rails absently, enjoying having said the word 'vessel' in such an appropriate situation. Her manicured nails tapped as she pulled her hand away. She was wearing a costly windbreaker, opulent dry-cleaned jeans and a pair of brand new boat-deck shoes that had been tailored to fit from a cast of her feet. Her glass of champagne was nearly empty. She narrowed her eyes at the last few ounces, catching a warped glimpse of herself in the glass. It appeared that her hair, which cost more to cut, dye, style and nourish annually than most people's higher educations, had become windblown in an unfetching way.

"Lydia," another woman called from across the deck. "Lydia, do you need more Cristal?"

Lydia nodded her head up and down, then side to side. "No," she said, and then pointed to the hatch she was near. She needed to use the bathroom.

"Claudette," a man was saying, "For the umpteenth time, it's not 'Cristal', it's an incredibly expensive fine Italian sparkling wine we picked up in Rome. Don't you remember anything?"

"But you said Cristal was the best, Louis," Claudette tittered while refilling her glass. "What does it matter what it's called?"

"You silly bitch," he laughed. "Have you been sober at all this holiday?"

"Oh no!" she hiccuped, and screamed with laughter.

The bathroom below was teak and warm but loud, and Lydia had a moment of panic as she imagined each groan and whisper to be the sound of the boat drifting free in the current, or rooms adjacent filling with chill sea water. After pinning her blonde hair into place again, she fingernailed open her cloisonné pillbox and dumped the contents into her mouth. Washing them down with a handful of sink water, she sighed, wiping the drops of water away from her mouth and checking her lipstick.

She let out a strangled yelp.

How many pills had there been in the little pillbox? She had no memory of when she last put pills in it, but it generally contained between two to six. Had it felt like four on her tongue? Two? Six?

Oh, you are an idiot, she told herself, holding her throat and looking around the tiny room. She didn't know what she expected to find, perhaps some emergency glass to break. Anything. She thought of calling an ambulance and then remembered she was not only not in Manhattan, but she was out to sea as well.

"Fucking idiot," she muttered and leaned over the toilet. Popping three of the tranquilizers, when sober, was enough to make the world swimmy. She'd taken two once when drunk and was fairly sure she almost died, but no one at that party had been sober enough to make such a diagnosis, even though most of the party goers had been doctors.

And how many had she just taken, and on top of how much champagne?

Lydia went to stick her finger down her throat and then grimaced. Her hands were terribly filthy, touching the boat rails all evening and god knows what else. She washed them quickly, with cold water, and then kneeled before the toilet again. "Blech," she said, wondering then if overdosing was officially a new low. Of course, there was that time that she'd had to call the family doctor to pump her stomach after she'd changed her mind about killing herself, but her therapist had pointed out the bravery of such a thing. It was almost something to brag about, that. But vomiting because you didn't know how many pills you'd had? Scandalous.

Lydia thrust her finger down her throat, eyes closed, for that easy-peasy, nothing-to-it, stomach reset lever she'd hit a thousand times before at least, not counting college. Naturally, she missed and managed to stab luxuriously cared-for nail into the back of her throat, drawing blood and an agonized gurgle. "Gah!" she barked, and spat crimson into the pristine stainless steel bowl. "Fuck fuck fuck."

It was then that Lydia noticed, over the obscenities, a muted warmth forming about her ears. The tranquilizers had begun to dissolve. Bravo, she thought to them, as normally such diligent dissolving would be a plus. Well, nothing to do but go upstairs and find Richard. Perhaps he could radio for help. Or perhaps, she thought as more of the drug was released into her bloodstream, there was no trouble after all. Just a little extra drugs. It certainly wouldn't kill her to take three or four, would it? When people killed themselves on TV they took entire bottles. Lydia nodded to herself smartly, collected her things, and oozed back up to the top deck.

"Claudette!" she crooned, crawling from the hatch and giggling, having dropped her purse back down the short ladder. She heard Claudette call out in a shrill voice, Louis too, and shimmied back down to get her purse. "Foop," she said, and laughed. She hummed a little tune as she put her lipstick and perfume and pillboxes back into her purse. "I'm coming!" she called when she heard Claudette's cry again. "Coming, coming, coming."

At that moment, just as she began to climb again, a naughty little gas pocket escaped from her bowels, with a sound like a midget saying "Boot!" Lydia clapped her hands over her mouth, letting go of the ladder rails, and her pristine, never-worn-on-land deck shoes slipped on the rung and she dropped two and a half feet back to the deck with a thud. She looked around the tiny empty hall to see if anyone was around. Atrocious! Disgusting! She giggled like a twelve-year old.

"I'm coming!" she sang out, when she'd heard distant voices carried by the wind. They just wouldn't shut up! Louis must have told a scorcher of a joke, Lydia thought, and kicked her purse under the ladder in exhausted lackadaisicalness. She hauled herself up over the rim and sat for a moment, unable to focus. The sea air here was so warm, she thought, even at night. It pulled gently at her hair and cleared her head of some of the tranquilizer's metallic scuzziness.

"Lydia, for god's sake, why aren't you radioing!" Richard wailed at her suddenly, right up on top of her. She turned slowly to him, rolling her eyes.

"Richaaard," she drawled. "It was two pills. Two. 'S hardly danger. Ous. Dangerous."

"YOU STUPID CUNT!" he screamed, attempting to shove her back down the hatch.

"Fuck you, Richard, the therapist told you to stop calling me a cunt. Richard. Richie. Richeroo. Whoop!" she said, sliding back down the hatch, feet first. Her hands made long squeaks on the metal rails as she slid. Richard went running off along the barketta's length, around the deck to the cabin, and Lydia began to giggle explosively. "Claudette! Pull me out!" she gasped between twitters, and looked up imploringly.

It took Lydia both a fraction of a second and many minutes to make sense of what she saw. It wasn't until a glistening length of intestine slid her way when the boat lurched on a swell, bringing it close enough to touch, that she connected the dots. Claudette's brassy blonde hair lay in patches like grass, stuck to strips of scalp here and there, and the remains of her guts had begun to migrate around the deck on a slick of blood. As Lydia watched, a jiggling lump of tissue slid over the side of the boat, taking a whole string of quivery, multi-hued organs with it. It sploshed into the sea water and Lydia turned her head back to Claudette's torso. One arm was reaching skyward somehow, the hand limp at the wrist and dripping dark fluid, the legs back up behind the head on a spine bent in half.

"Claud," Lydia breathed. Some subordinate part of her was aware that she should look away, but the tranquilizers were in control, and they weren't impressed by the gore. She didn't see Louis anywhere, but she thought she identified, in some morbid flash of forensic genius, more than one person's quantity of intestines.

Lydia looked up, then, slowly, but saw nothing beyond the bright spotlights on the masts. "Bloatsharks," she said, and wondered why the warning sirens weren't going off. They had been within the safety buoys, she thought. She had trusted Richard to keep them sailing between them.

Just then the wind died a little and an airborne snippet of klaxons drifted to her ears. They just hadn't heard it, she realized. Oh, how sad.

Lydia slid back down the hatch, exhausted from the drugs and emulating sadness, and went stumbling off to find Richard. On her way she pulled out her hand-held computer and made a note to schedule extra therapy sessions.

2.

"What is that smell?" Edelweiss asked.

The air fizzed with ozone. A darkened figure stood, reaching out to Edelweiss, who in turn reached out with comfort and self-conscious martyrdom. She snatched her hand away suddenly, examining it for blisters. "Ow."

Whomever was in the room with her was burning alive.

"Uh, let me get you some water," Edelweiss said.

"You will name the dog Kundalini."

"That's interesting," she said.

"Edelweiss?"

"Yes?"

"Who are you talking to?"

Edelweiss turned to blink at Joseph's blurring, shuddering figures. "Sometimes it's not always clear, but the information is always good," she answered.

3.

The Beautiful
and Life-Threatening Lives
of the Bloatsharks.
By Edelweiss Santucci
Mrs.Borgman's 3rd grade class

Long ago the sea were ruled by carchariidae tumeo who did not rule the land. The Land was not ruled. Then the sharks spontaneously evolved. And old Greek scientist Euclid noticed when he was eaten that the shark was flying. They discovered the shark had made an important thing called a gas bladder. The shark fills its gas bladder every day with gas that is lighter than air and would then rise from the water so it could eat delishus land food. It did very well. Today bloatsharks are both a big problem and aren't. We

*have many defenses against the bloatsharks but still every
year lot of people get eaten. They are people that did not pay
attention. Fishing is a dangerous work. We have learned to
co-exist with bloatsharks by killing some of them whenever
they eat us.*

*I think bloatsharks are scary but I understand that they are
animals. All animals just want to eat food and that is okay.
Sometimes bloatsharks fly too far from the water or they
don't know what time it was and then they dry out on land.
This happened near my mothers house when she was little
and she said it fucking stank.*

The End

4.

Aikiko Ellison had purchased a talking rat from a pet store in Charlotte that guaranteed it was a smart one. "Smart!" a hand-written note on the tank read. Aikiko didn't care. She had just been walking by and realized that she'd love one whether it could recite Voltaire or not.

"Cheesh," it lisped from a tiny rat-sized misshapen palate. Aikiko smiled; she had a fondness for things with speech impediments.

"What was that?" Ardella Santucci asked. The two women sat on the patio of a small café in Gaffney, sipping iced coffees and wondering secretly why anyone would drink a phlegmy iced coffee when they could have iced tea instead.

"Oh, it was my rat." Aikiko pointed at her handbag. She patted the flap closed, glancing around to see if anyone else had noticed. "Cheesh! Cheesh!" the muffled rat insisted.

"Well!" Ardella said, smiling. "What is it you wanted to talk about?"

Aikiko shrugged and picked lint from the sleeve of her nightgown. The gown was cream-colored flannel with lace trim and a high collar. She may have passed for conservatively dressed if it wasn't for the ratty leather men's slippers, ratty head of hair, nearly ratty leg hair and the rat in the bag.

"I guess I just wondered what you know about re'em. Specifically, re'em use, what it does."

"Oh," Ardella said lamely. She'd read, of course, along with everyone else in the south, that Aikiko had tested positive for re'em foresight at the local Espress-Kno™. She was already being hugged in the grocery stores by blue-haired old biddies and having her hand grudgingly shaken by veterans.

"Don't you have a physician at Espress-Kno™?"

"Oh yeah, yeah, they're real good about keeping me healthy. Vitamins, you know. Encouraging me to eat well, be vegetarian."

"I thought you already were."

"I eat fish."

"I see."

There came a muted angry yammering from Aikiko's purse, so she opened a tiny plastic serving of liquid cream and smuggled it down to the rat. "Cheesh!" came a delighted cry.

"I heard those talking rats are really smart," Ardella said.

"Well, no. They're like birds, they repeat things. Some less than others," she smiled fondly at her purse.

"I have to say, Aikiko, I'm an otolaryngologist. I don't deal with re'em, other than some of the damage it causes. Which is pretty bad, when people use dirty re'em. Holey septums, burnt-out larynxes. Don't they supply you with safe re'em?"

Aikiko absently tried to untangle a mat of her hair and nodded. "Sure, the best. Pure stuff, government regulated. It comes in sealed tubes."

"That's good. As long as it's fully powdered and not cut with sand or bonemeal, it should be fine. Do you know I once saw a kid that snorted re'em cut with *glitter*? Glitter! It was like she'd stuffed a metal file up her goddamn nose."

"Wow," Aikiko said.

"Yeah, I know it. But that's it, as long as it's clean you're good."

"Okay well, thanks anyway."

"Why are you asking me about re'em? Can't your work answer all your questions for you?" She hesitated and said, "Can't you answer everything?"

"It's funny that you say that. Some things are still hard for me to see, I suppose I have a lot of training to do yet. Like, I can't figure this out."

Ardella looked down at the empty plastic cream thimble that was being pushed out of the purse by dinky, knuckley hands. "Cheesh."

"Figure out what exactly?"

"I'm really not supposed to talk about it."

"Okay," Ardella looked around the nearly vacant patio, making sure that no one was within hearing distance. "I won't tell anyone."

"I know you won't, Mrs. Santucci, but they know. Or will," she said, and tapped her head. "In fact, they already know if I will or won't ask you, if they've checked you out. But I figure if they were really worried, they would have already known, and stopped us talking. Or maybe they want to implicate me. You see how it is."

"That's tricky."

"Yep."

"I don't think I know what your question is."

"That's okay. It was just a long shot."

"I'll think about it, though."

"Okay."

"You don't happen to know what my daughter is up to, do you?"

"It's also funny that you should ask that. If you talk to her, tell her to leave wherever she is. I was practicing at work, picking random thoughts and trying to prophesize on them, it's very hard. I think she'll be home soon because something bad happens, but she's fine. She'll be fine. You told me she was going to Tibet, right? I swear my grandmother is describing more... western European statues."

Ardella's eyes widened and she began to fidget. "That's terrible! She did try to go to Tibet, but she got on the wrong flight! She went to Italy instead, oh, why didn't you tell me this sooner?"

"I'm sorry, since she wasn't hurt, it slipped my mind."

"Can't one of your superiors find out exactly what happens and put a stop to it?"

Aikiko looked across the quiet patio and took a deep breath. She didn't know what to call what she was feeling, because it was too volatile a mixture of both dread and deep affection, and she was getting it frequently now when she was in situations like these; people sitting about being sociable and happy, children eating slices of banana bread served with heaps of whipped cream. Looking at Ardella's face so concerned, hands finely and modestly manicured, gray hair sparkling around her temples, Aikiko wanted to weep. "I did report it, Mrs. Santucci, to an Established Patterns Sub-Committee and they said they'd pass it on. Honestly though, I don't see how with all the problems in the world, that they'd care about someone like Edelweiss."

"That's criminal!"

Aikiko nodded. "Yes, it is. But God doesn't have time to take care of everyone, so you're stuck with us."

5.

Every person is in some way a big weepy chicken. A squealing, arm-clutching, chair-climbing schoolgirl. Some people manage to keep it contained, sometimes even from themselves, insisting they are not afraid, but that is a lie. There are men in the world who, twenty years after they hid from Charlie in the jungle, naked, feet rotting and eating worms for sustenance, can still be found beating garden snakes to death with shovels. There are women, who, despite a grisly car accident leaving their jaw shattered in three places and a shard of safety glass lodged halfway through their neck, wince and cry when the dentist goes to give them an injection. That's why the phrase 'abject terror' has the word 'abject' in it.

Now the bummer part (before you think I am making fun of anyone) is this: those people, by which I mean you, are totally and completely justified. At any given point in time you can't count high enough to list all the things you should be afraid of. Things that are worth hiding in the closet from and begging for God to intervene. They are coming to get you and are waiting for you wherever you run to. They are already in your house—hell, they're already in your lungs.

Oddly, it is comforting to know that others fear the same things as yourself. You can commiserate. Swap stories. Hatch schemes to wipe entire races from the human species off the earth, whatever it takes to stop being afraid, right?

Humans invented many entertaining things to keep the fear of the bloatsharks at bay, so to speak. Long pointy poles were often useful and more often resulted in the death of everything living within a few hundred meters or so, but hey, no more bloatshark, right? They invented fogs and gasses to choke the flying beasts to death with, and as a side bonus, all the dratted seagulls and asthmatics as well. Lights worked wonders, and it wasn't unusual for a massive bonfire to keep everyone nearby safe, depending on your definition of the word 'nearby.' And then the magic that is known as the god Electricity.

Shark prods were born, and then the first perimeter nets. Static field generators, electromagnetic pulse towers and arcing energy screens snapped to attention around coastlines all over the civilized world.

But what the bloatsharks understood, despite their being emotionless, conscienceless rocketing toothed meat torpedoes, was that land mammals, all mammals, were rather dim. Some of them would make mistakes. Enough, anyway.

6.

Every child everywhere on Earth knows about bloatsharks. Kids who happen to live on a coastline, they know about bloatsharks before they know about their toes.

Little kids walking along the Ganges carry reed doppelgangers over their heads, hoping that if a shark were to bite, it might carry the fake child away and not them. And, in certain parts of the Ivory Coast children are simply told to never take their eyes off the sky and travel in groups. They know to start to fling sand then, fling it fast and wide into the air, hoping that at the moment that shark make come for them, it get sand in its eyes and change its mind.

In the same way that there are picture books describing what kids around the world do for Christmas, there are classics depicting what other nations do to deter bloatsharks. These nations were spoken of quaintly, at best, since America had fancied itself bloatshark free. Nearly every coastline and major tributary in the entire US was decked with giant concrete and steel sickle-shaped columns strung with fencing and wire, as though the United States were one giant soccer goal. Shortly after this perimeter was introduced by the safety-obsessed presidents of the 1940s, many towns began to fund bloatshark lures that would turn on at dusk; towering metal pillars sunk far, far offshore, safely away from all mankind and emitting faint electrostatic pulses.

Kids around the planet had this image etched into their bedtime eyelids: a dozen massive forms filmed from a remote camera, the bloatsharks circling in irritation around the lures, all twenty terrifying feet of them backlit and dripping with sea water. Some of the sharks would slam against it suddenly, testing it, others lunging with sickening speed and attacking the metal, convinced it was something alive. The lures only worked for so long, but that was definitely time used well. New sharks were freshly fooled all the time, and old sharks freshly forgot.

Of course, each child, in turn, has become familiar with the old-fashioned wood cuts of early fishermen in their dome-roofed boats, harpooning whales from porticos and the occasional accidental bloatshark harpooning, in which the woodcuts would be a mass of explosion lines and immolated stick-figure bodies. For hundreds of years attempts at extermination were made, and for hundreds of years men were blown to smithereens when the shark's various gasses combined and resulted in detonation. In school, the children were taught that mankind had just learned to co-exist with the bloatsharks, even claiming to admire their seemingly impossible evolutionary skills. However, there were those that felt the truth: the bloatshark was and is in every way a species superior to man. What other thing on Earth could breathe both air and water, have enough teeth and muscle to consume any of God's beautiful creatures and could also explode into a hellish ball of heat and meat shrapnel, capable of decimating everything within a hundred meters?

7.

"So, who can help me with a couple of things that are unusual about the *carachiidae tumeo*?"

Mrs. Borgman was squozed from the same instant-teacher tube like so many others before her. She wore a great deal of pastel and was graying, although her hair was cut short and "spunky", relatively speaking. She was in her late fifties but already had the stink of grandmotherlyness to her that seemed ill-fit. Grandmothers pinched and carried cake in their purses. Teachers wanted to have a word with you after class. It caused a confusing comfort clash.

Mrs. Borgman was, however, more toward the good side of grandmotherly teacher. Instead of smelling like wet cats, Mrs. Borgman smelled like laundry soap and was prone to throwing pizza parties.

"Teddy?" she asked, pointing to the kid who was vigorously waving his hand. It was well known that Teddy not only had T-shirts with bloatsharks on them, but lunchboxes, a backpack, a pencil case, tennis shoes, a baseball cap and probably bloatshark underoos as well. He had very thick glasses and succumbed to burping fits when nervous.

"Bloatsharks are the only sharks that have swim bladders."

"Thank you Teddy, right of course. And they are the only animal in the world that has a what?"

"Gas bladder!"

"Yes, thank you Teddy, that's right, but let's let some of the other students have a chance to answer, okay? Anyone else know something about them that is unusual?"

"They hunt at night?"

"That is true, Stacey, but not unusual to the bloatshark. Most sharks hunt at dusk or at night, when their prey has is at a disadvantage. Why do bloatsharks in particular hunt at night, though, Stacey?"

"So they don't dry out?"

"That's correct! And like all sharks they excrete what?" A pause. "Mucus, they excrete mucus from their skin. Other fish use it to glide through the water faster, but the bloatsharks also use it to keep their skin moist for longer periods of time. Yes, Teddy, I can see you raising your hand. It is about bloatsharks?"

"Bloatsharks have the thickest dentide of any shark!"

"Okay, Teddy, when I asked if it was about bloatsharks, I meant that I didn't want you to answer. I'm not worried that you don't know the answers to my questions, you are the resident bloatshark expert."

The class twittered a bit, although Mrs. Borgman spoke kindly. "But now that Teddy has brought up dentide, does anyone other than Teddy know what it is? Edelweiss?"

"Dentide is teeth."

"Okay, not entirely, but okay. Dentide is the particular formation that makes up the little kind of scales on shark skin. Those little scales are called *denticles* and shark skin is sometimes referred to as *shagreen*. They aren't like snake scales, which like your fingernails, aren't alive but just stuck to you. Denticles are like teeth, in that they are made of a bone-like substance and are each individually alive, with a little blood vessel in them, teeny, tiny little ones. As Teddy said, the shagreen of the bloatshark is packed so densely with denticles that if you threw a spear at it, it would bounce right off. And that is a good thing, why?"

"Because they blow up!" Teddy let out in a half-strangled scream of excitement.

"Right, they aren't the only creature blowing up around here. A great defense, right? Who dare kill it!" Mrs. Borgman punctuated this by puffing her cheeks out and opening her arms.

A child near the front of the class gingerly raised his hand. He was skinny, like all of the other third graders, except for the anomalous little round ones, but his skinniness had a slight sallow tone, a sickness. His clothing was faded and out of date as well, leaving him with an aura of malnourished gloom.

"Anthony?"

"My dad says that the bloatsharks can hear you cry. Can they?" he asked in a near-whisper. Immediately those near him began to laugh.

"Crybaby!"

"Of course they can hear you, they hear wussies the best!"

"Even Teddy isn't that dumb, you momma's boy!"

Teddy's laughing faltered, then resumed.

Mrs. Borgman, who silently lamented for this child that still hadn't learned to keep such embarrassments to himself, quickly interjected. "That's an excellent question, Anthony, because a lot of your parents have probably told you that if you behave a certain way, the bloatsharks will get you." She looked patiently around the room. "Sharks of all families are most attracted to noises. They have other heightened senses, like an excellent sense of smell, but we'll get to that later—later Teddy. As you all know they can sense even the tiny amount of electricity put off by living things as small as a shrimp. Lucky for you," she smiled at Anthony, "We have the perimeter system. So no amount of crying or yelling is going to bring a bloatshark to your house." Mrs. Borgman's stomach lurched at her white lie, but Edelweiss interrupted her.

"Mrs. Borgman?"

"Yes."

"What did people do before the perimeter?"

"They were very careful, didn't go out much at night and they didn't live on shores of oceans or deltas or boats. A lot of people have died from bloatsharks in the history of the world. But then, a lot of people died from the flu, too. Life was hard."

"It's wrong to kill them," Edelweiss said suddenly.

"Certainly if unprovoked, Edelweiss, but all creatures have a right to defend themselves."

"What if it was a baby? I bet its mother would cry for it *every day*."

"I don't think that bloatsharks can cry, Edelweiss, sweetie."

"All creatures feel sorrow, Mrs. Borgman."

"That's called anthropomorphism. A mother bloatshark probably doesn't even recognize its own offspring."

"What if it does?"

"I assume it would feel sad, if it did have feelings."

"I knew it!"

"Edelweiss, they are sharks. We kill them if we have to, but most people don't mess with them. End of topic."

Teddy watched the banter with myopic tennis-match interest. "Bloatshark babies eat each other in the womb!" he announced with glee.

Edelweiss ran from the room.

8.

The sales woman at the dealership spoke impeccable English, and with misguided smarminess, was terribly proud of the fact.

Edelweiss had asked around, and, with the help of Joseph and Hewey, had located the shop in a block that housed a desolate-looking Armani store (quite intentionally desolate, for the rich things never seemed so rich when there appeared to be an adequate supply) and a Givenchy perfumery so pungent that walking past it, passers by were left with a patina of musky rose and lily-of-the-valley.

It was summer in northern Italy, and in a city, so the three let out sighs of orgasmic relief when they stepped into the air-conditioned shop. The sales woman stared in distaste. "Buon giorno," she said, in a tone she normally reserved for transients and housewives.

"Buon giorno," said Edelweiss, already looking around the room at the various posters of Carfagna's Hounds. The photographer had tried every trick to get a flattering image of the Hound, including silhouettes and blurry, hand-colored action shots. It was a lost cause.

"Can I help you?" the sales lady asked, without rising from her desk. She had mastered the posture of '*I will not stand in case you are wasting my time, you understand*', because she was used to lookieloos, gawkers and fun-pokers. She had requested to her superiors several times now, even proposing in essay form, that they show Hounds only on appointment. The powers had refused, citing the very moral foundation that the Hound was conceived from; the everyman should have a Hound. A Carfagna's Hound in every home. Bums and prim Englishwomen alike would stand on clean street corners, their hounds sniffing each other's asses and eating each other's discarded butts. Original designs for the store had a Plexiglas box full of shredded newsprint and Carfagna's puppies lining the windows, for sure drawing people in. Who could refuse a puppy? Only someone who you wouldn't want to have one.

What happened instead was that the puppies ate all the newsprint in a matter of minutes, and the stark little dog babies just sat on the white linoleum bottom looking like so many sausages rolled in dryer lint. Their colicky whimpering could be heard through the window, and terrified pedestrians watched as the sales woman poured saucer after saucer of Pepto-Bismol out for the puppies. When they got larger she switched them to chewable antacids so she wouldn't have to wash the saucer all the time. The boxes were finally removed from the frontage.

Edelweiss tapped a framed poster of a Hound loping awkwardly through the grass, its boxy frame just about to tip to one side. The photographer had taken the photo a second before the Hound had lost its balance and tumbled with a yelp directly onto its face. "I want to buy a dog."

The sales woman stood slowly, a dozen or so clanky bracelets falling around her wrists. "Lovely," she sighed. It always went the same; they wanted one, she pitched to them, she'd bring them back to play with the Hounds and they left.

If they'd didn't leave immediately she'd quickly gloss over care, mentioning their need for unbelievable quantities of antacids and digestive enzymes, sunblock and acne creams, and if they didn't leave still, she'd tell them the price. To date she had sold four Hounds, out of approximately a thousand customers.

"Are there some here?" Edelweiss asked, looking around the barren and now aseptic room.

"Yes, we have some here. Are you American?"

"Yep, American. Can I take a dog back to the United States with me? On a plane?"

"Certainly. Are you a college student?"

"I am, thank you for noticing."

"You know, the Carfagna's Hound is the single most responsible thing you can do as a concerned citizen of this planet. No other personal investment benefits the planet and only the planet. No bills to antiquated garbage and recycling monopolies that aren't even trying to solve the problem."

Hewey let out a strangled cough.

"Oh yes, yes! And they can eat dog food if there isn't any garbage around?" Edelweiss asked.

"Of course, they can eat anything. Some things offer the Hound no nutrients, and pass through neutrally, like rocks, but where would you be where there wasn't any garbage?" The sales woman laughed politely.

"In the future, there won't be any more garbage," Edelweiss said with dreamy conviction. She could hear Joseph and Hewey shifting uncomfortably behind her. "So, do I get to bond with a dog?"

"They are here, if that is what you mean," the sales woman said. She was painfully thin and even more painfully tan, her tiny dark ankles disappearing into her over-priced slingbacks. She was a little taken aback; no one had ever been so straightforward before. It was her first impulse buy. "Please come back with me," she said, walking to the door behind the desk. She turned and flung a sharp look at the man and the troll. "The Hounds are very skittish. I think just the lady should observe."

Hewey and Joseph, relieved, went outside for smokes.

"Where did you hear of the Carfagna's Hound?" the woman asked conversationally as they walked down a hallway.

"I saw one in Florence."

The woman stopped and tilted her head. "An advertisement?"

"No, a dog."

"Really?" she seemed confused. "And, you liked it?"

"Yeah, it's a really good idea. I think that tapping into the problems of man via Mother Earth is where we should all be headed. It's like, even though mankind is obviously making this big mistake with the dogs, the Goddess is still there, making things right. You know what I mean, sister?"

The woman stared, mouth open, and then suddenly thrust her hand forth like a shiv. "I am sorry, my name is Francesca. You are?"

"Edelweiss Santucci, American."

From the state of the hallway, it appeared that the Hound dealership shared the back rooms with other businesses; there were bathrooms and doors with locks and inscribed plastic plaques upon them. Francesca rammed a heavy old key home into the lock on one of the doors and shrugged to Edelweiss.

"They are not puppies," she said sadly. "We've had them here for some time. I mean, if you want a puppy I can order you a fresh one. When are you leaving for America?"

"Two weeks."

"Okay, well, you can decide after you see them." They entered the room and Francesca impulsively took a breath, and since Edelweiss didn't, she had to secure a hand over her nose.

"Wow," Edelweiss said. "Something smells like poopy."

"Yes, it is a little ripe," Francesca said nasally, trying to pretend like she wasn't shallowly panting. "It is because they are so pent up in here. We try to walk them and clean up every day, but you know, they are young and the carpet traps the smell."

There was a smallish corral in the corner of the tight room, and wet, airy noises were coming from it. Edelweiss bent over the corral and exclaimed softly. "Ohh! They're so cute!"

Francesca stood back and didn't move. Twice that day she'd already cleaned up garbage-vomit slurry that the little shits had left behind. She hadn't been able to stop them from eating a mass of filthy plastic bags in the alley behind the fishmonger earlier, and they'd been a little queasy ever since. On top of that, even though they hadn't eaten any cigarette butts recently, their vomit still stank of damp, used tobacco. She'd been nauseous each time she'd cleaned it up.

"They are beautiful creatures," Francesca said.

Edelweiss was picking up one of the juvenile dogs and cuddling it to her massive chest. Its eyes rolled about madly in their sockets, stunned and panicked by its sudden ascension. It let out a moist, ear-splitting fart.

Francesca decided to give in to this impossible sale and went into explaining the Carfagna's Hound care to Edelweiss. She rattled on for nearly fifteen minutes about gas reduction, skin care, pink eye, upset stomach and constipation. On cue, one of the dogs attempted to defecate a partially undigested plastic bag, looking sadly about at its fellow Hounds as it did.

After a long interlude of Edelweiss' sitting on the carpet and playing with the dogs in little clapping, gaspy, happy whispers, Francesca asked, "Do, you like him?"

"She's perfect!"

"Good! It's a 'he.'"

Edelweiss didn't respond.

"Now, for the unfortunate facts. These dogs are costly to breed, would you like to pay with credit or debit today?"

"Cash please."

"Cash? Certainly, signora, cash it is."

Francesca looked around the room and grabbed one of the ropes that she had been using to walk them.

"Great."

Out front Edelweiss was still holding and baby-talking the dog. "Whoosaprettygirl?" she said over and over again.

"Ah, that is one point two million lira," Francesca said as quickly and with as much cheer as she could muster.

Edelweiss was still fussing with the dog and digging her money out. She counted a stack of bills for several minutes, and when she not-so-secretly lost track of what she was counting, she hummed while stacking the rest of the bills nicely. She then grabbed the dog and crooned, "Who's mommy's pretty girl?"

"Well," Francesca sighed, counting out the bills and keeping the surplus as a tip. "Have a great time. Here is your care and contact information," she said, handing over a mass of pamphlets. "And it is a boy, signora."

"Okay, thank you," Edelweiss said, stuffing the pamphlets into her purse. "Her name is Kundalini."

"Whatever," Francesca said and lit a cigarette.

9.

"She is an absolute moron," the woman said sternly. Everything she did was stern, or crisp, or rigid, and occasionally snide. Her name was Honey Smee, and everyone in the business feared and despised her.

Special Interests Unit Director Jimmy Galloway rubbed his face with both hands, as though he were washing it. The rasping noise stopped him. Jimmy was a fairly normal guy with a fairly normal job, with the problems you would expect from a guy like that. His wife was frequently dissatisfied, but the couples unit they attended was helping. His lawn was besieged with crabgrass, but the crabgrass' reign was drawing well into its dusk. Jimmy Galloway had one little problem, and that was that he'd reached his limit.

He was officially doing as well as he could ever do, and this was for one specific reason. He knew what this reason was in the same way he knew his shoes were untied without having to look at them. The reason was that God had given Jimmy a permanent five-o'clock shadow and dark circles under his eyes.

If Jimmy Galloway was feeling spry and determined to please, he looked like he'd slept with a fifth of Old Seagull and two ugly Mexican hookers. If Jimmy was a little sick or tired, he looked like he'd swallowed a balloon full of heroin several days earlier, which had burst but did not kill him, followed by a cavities search sans lubricant, four or five cups of FBI instant coffee, seventeen hours of interrogation and news that his mother was dead. If he was happy people thought him insane. If he was angry, they figured him a rapist. Luckily his wife was legally blind.

"Mrs. Smee," Jimmy began.

"MIZ Smee, Mr. Galloway."

"I'm sorry, of course, Miss Smee."

"Why 'of course', Mr. Galloway?"

Jimmy stopped and drank half a cup of tepid water. "Of course I should have remembered from your file, Miss Smee, but I am getting a little tired. Please forgive me. The question, again, is not whether you find our target a moron, but whether or not you will accept the job. We've been here for six hours already discussing the details. Do you feel informed enough to make a decision?"

Miss Smee swiveled her eyes over to Jimmy in a way that only women can. It was like they were calibrating weapons. She was, without question, quite beautiful, and that was one of the reasons she was good at what she did. Her hair was long and straight and glossy like a satin ribbon, just a shade off black-black. It was the color of a predatory cat. She was taller than the other women in the room and had plump, attention-demanding lips. If she was to wear lip gloss, which she most certainly did, people were mesmerized by the way her lips moved as she spoke. The glossier and redder she made them, the deeper they sank. As a child her mother had told her she could be a supermodel, selling billions of magazines by her own airbrushed mug on the cover alone. It occurred to Honey that such power should be hers to benefit from, not anyone else's.

What an odd twist then, years later, to find out that she was capable of re'em foresight. She was unimpressed. Espress-Kno™ and their puny competitor, Jiffy-Re'em, courted her, threatened her, dangled cash and fame and promises of success, threats of failure, unless of course she worked for them. Recoiling, she created her own job.

"Mr. Galloway, I am not a flawless investigator by luck," she said, and it didn't come out sounding like a brag. "Part of what I need to determine is whether or not *you* assholes know you you're doing. I am aware you want, quite desperately, to keep from the media the fact that you've had to solicit help from a renegade oracle. And I also know that behind that wall," she motioned almost violently to her left, "Are about oh, seven oracles is it? All trying to zero in on my every future action. They don't know I'm an oracle, do they?" Her eyes darkened a little, lids lowering, beneath her heavy and tasteful eyeglasses. "Does everyone in this room know your little secret, Galloway?"

"I'm not sure I know what you mean, Miss Smee."

"We all know," Honey whispered suddenly. "It's just a matter of time. People blipping off the radar here and there—don't worry, I'll never tell." A smile bloomed across the lower half of her face, but did not echo in her eyes. "I accept. As you guessed, I'm sure."

Jimmy propped his chin in one of his hands and stared at her. "You're nasty," he said quietly.

10.

Shortly after the meeting, Honey Smee opened the door to a room down the hall. It was unmarked and she had never seen it before, but she knew what lay behind it.

Seven chairs swiveled to her in the ghostly darkness of a television-lit room.

"Hello," she said. She looked at each of them in turn, hardly needing to since they were all poor copies of each other. Each of them was fat, greasy and lifeless as steamed bacon. The body type was mistakenly associated with re'em use, but this was not the case; it was the effect of being undereducated, overworked and overpaid. It was night after night of the Midnight Show, 'Toon Park re-runs and bottomless bags of Xtreme Caesar-flavored Poquitos. It was pride.

"You," one of them said. Honey had trouble determining the gender.

"Me. And you," she said, pulling out a nail file and casually buffing her nails, "Are gonna fuck this all up."

"We've triangulated it twice, bounty hunter, we don't know why they're wasting their money with you."

"Because you're old and messing up, that's why. You think you're smart, holed up here watching a dozen news feeds at once," she snarled, swinging her hand around to the twelve little TV screens. "You're sending someone right now to stop that bloatshark attack, and you're gonna fuck it all up. Don't think I won't tell them."

"What do you propose we do? Allow the attack?"

"What's the matter, having a bout of conscience after all these years? After all the murders and rapes and child beatings you see go by, unaided, every minute of your sorry fucking lives? Fat chance," Honey was laughing now. "Here's my gift to you: if you allow the attack, then she stays another couple of months. A couple of months is too late. And that little proph- esy was without the benefit of re'em, you fat fucks, that was just common sense."

"You can't talk to us like that," one of them whined.

"You shouldn't have come here."

"You should leave!"

"See you kiddies around," Honey trilled, and shut the door behind her.

"What a bitch."

"She's crazy. That's why she can't work for Espress-Kno™."

"She's right, though."

11.

In Florence, or Firenze as Edelweiss was learning to call it, most of the tourists gallivanted about the Arno River and the robust Ponte Vecchio bridge that spanned it. At one time the bridge had been for carriages and newfangled motor cars, but now it was home to merchants hawking 'traditional' goods to fat Germans in tasteful outfits, flocks of darty Japanese schoolgirls and frosty white South Africans.

Joseph, however, was fond of taking Edelweiss to the Boboli Gardens, which were famous for boring people out of their minds. The Gardens were dry, sparse and hot, like most of Italy, and were decidedly mid-Californian; hardly exotic. Joseph never tired of it.

He smiled, smoking, as Edelweiss ran before him chasing butterflies on the paths, kicking at the dusty soil in his old leather boots. He smoked, slowly, savoring it, as Edelweiss had begged him to cut back.

Later, in a tiny café in the middle of the park housed within a stubby stone turret, they rested. He ordered fizzy water with lemon and smoothed the beads of sweat away from her face.

"Do you think Kundalini will be okay?" she asked.

Joseph widened his eyes and laughed. "I can't believe you left him with Hewey," he said, shaking his head. "I think Hewey finds it an abomination."

"I knew it, we should head back!"

"No, no, he will be okay. Hewey pretends to hate you, you know, but he always does what you ask."

"He hates me?" Edelweiss whimpered.

"No, not hate, never mind. Hewey will not eat the dog, he finds it too gross."

"It's a she, you know. And it has a name."

Joseph waited to see if she was joking. The Hound's callused testicles dragged on the ground when it walked. "Yes," he said when she showed no signs of mirth. "Kundalini."

Edelweiss smiled but immediately became distracted, worried, pulling and replacing the jeweled nose stud in her nostril. She straightened her shoulders. "I have to go back to America soon. School, you know. In September. You should come with me." She leaned forward. "It'll be great! Seattle is such an amazing place, it reminds me a lot of this city. So bohemian."

Joseph winced and lit a cigarette. "Of course, school. Edelweiss, that would be lovely but I have no money for things like that. I am an artist.

And with all respect, of course, Seattle cannot compare with my Firenze. Seattle is like comparing Stephen King to Dante. They have separate appeal, yes?"

Edelweiss looked crestfallen, and Joseph scooted his cast iron chair around to her side, creating such a loud ruckus that the waitress came out to check on them. Joseph put his arm around Edelweiss and said, "I knew you had to go back, you were just visiting. I've been thinking about it, and I can easily give you a list of Universities in the area, surely they would compare to your University of Seattle?" At her smile he added, "And, since Hewey wants to get away from the city, we could go to the coast for your last week, how would you like that? A little seaside vacation?"

Edelweiss threw her arms around his neck, smothering him in the liquidy embrace of her loose breasts. He smiled into the sweaty cotton and considered himself a happy man.

12.

As far as Honey Smee was concerned, there should be a class higher than executive class. She waved the stewardess over and pointed at her shrimp cocktail.

"This is entirely awful. Are these shrimp *canned*? Frozen I could understand, but *canned*? Do you give out little tins of smoked clams as well?"

"Oh, I'm sorry Mrs. Smew, no," the stewardess said apologetically.

"Miss Smee. What other appetizers do you have?"

"We have Belgian endive with a fresh mild goat cheese."

"I'll take that instead."

"Yes ma'am."

The passenger next to Honey piped up, "Yes, I will have the goat cheese as well," she said, handing her half-eaten shrimp cocktail over. "But do you have any crackers?"

"I'll go check."

Honey sipped at her vodka gimlet and made a face. She didn't even want to know what brand of nail polish remover it was that they were trying to pass off as vodka.

"It's hardly worth the money, isn't it?" the woman next to Honey said in a sugar-syrup falsetto. Honey turned and gave her the once-over. She was some bit part actress, in a plethora of films but not a single performance good enough for Honey to recall who she was.

"Well, I'm hardly paying for it, and neither are you," Honey said, and opened up her copy of the *New York Times*. The actress blinked rapidly and then flipped through a glossy women's fashion magazine. Honey sniffed.

An article in the Times caught Honey's attention:

BLECH HUND A "PERFECT STORM" OF GENETIC SUPERIORITY, SAY GERMANS

BERLIN, German geneticists responded to Dante Carfagna's astounding Carfagna's Hound with a hound of their own in Berlin this week.

Enthusiastically called the Blech Hund, They have high hopes for their dog. The Blech Hund is considered by many to be a more handsome counterpart to the homely Carfagna's Hound, however it seems that beauty has its price.

The Blech Hund has already received numerous criticisms for its apparent aggressive nature. Rumors are flying about an inter-lab lawsuit from a female lab technician against the Berlin-based Vorkampfer Laboratorium.

Local court and law systems won't reveal the nature of the lawsuit, although several hospital staff have told local papers that the technician has suffered "severe wounds consistent with mammal attacks". This fueled further rumors that the Blech Hund was violent and prone to attacking. Aside from these rumors, the Blech Hund is reported to be a lighter eater than the Carfagna's Hound.

The article was accompanied by a grainy black and white photograph of a sharp-looking dog standing next to a group of lab technicians. In a strange hearken back to photographs from a hundred years ago, no one in the photo was smiling, and the eyes of those with glasses were completely occluded.

"Here you are," the stewardess said to Honey, handing her a plastic tray with the promised endive and a watery mound of goat cheese. "Miss St. Fontaine, I did manage to find some crackers for you instead of the endive," The stewardess handed over a plastic tray with crackers and a mirrored pile of goat cheese.

"Oh thank you, I just can't stand those bitter things," the actress said, smiling apologetically at Honey. In response to Honey's flat stare, the actress scooted as far away in her seat as she was able.

Honey Smee had tried her best to ignore the woman, but she found herself sucked in, paying attention to the depravity of the woman's behavior. Her being was outwardly high maintenance, which was something that Honey found to be a failure of character. Her manicure was thick and garish, her everyday make-up overly colorful. The woman was flying into Milan; she should have looked as sleek and natural as a seal, as anything less (or more) was in poor taste. She was also, to Honey's disgust, carefully spreading thick layers of goat cheese onto her crackers with a butter knife, as though she were attending a wedding buffet. The actress was preoccupied with what side she spread the cheese on, taking care to turn the crackers over to their tops. At one point she began to spread cheese on the wrong side, stopped, scraped off the cheese and then started over again on the proper side. Honey could not hold back a sigh.

"Are you on business in Milan?" the actress asked.

"Yes."

"For the show?"

"No."

"Have I met you before?" the actress squinted her eyes at Honey, wiping her fingers on a paper napkin. Honey couldn't stop staring at a renegade globbet of cheese stuck to one of the woman's fuchsia nails.

"That is unlikely."

"Were you at Bruce Willis' little summer thing a few years back? You remember, yards and yards of coke and no Demi?" the actress asked, taking care to pronounce 'Demi' with the stress on the 'i'.

"No."

"Oh sure, 'wink wink,' me neither," the woman giggled, and took a long drink from her cocktail.

Honey's stomach flipped. The woman was wearing two perfumes as near as Honey could tell: a base layer of something synthetic and cheap with a top coat of Chanel Mademoiselle to simulate richness. It stank. Chanel Mademoiselle was a well-balanced perfume, a decade-maker, inoffensive and never sickly floral, not on anyone. This woman had butchered it.

"I know you," the actress repeated.

"No," Honey said, and opened her paper again, which is the in-person equivalent of hanging up a phone.

CHAPTER NINE

1.

"I don't believe in marriage," Edelweiss said defiantly.

"Neither do I," said Joseph. It was the truth.

"Oh."

The whole ocean lay before them, hissing away at wherever it touched the earth. Joseph was thinking, alternately, about how odd women were and how it was strange that the ocean and the earth were not the same entity, they just shifted, flirted and nervously avoided each other. It was twilight, and far down the length of the beach Hewey's boulder-like silhouette chased Kundalini's turd-like one in what could either be play-fulness or dinner preparation. Edelweiss was having a hard time teaching Kundalini to not eat sand. He'd already eaten two tin cans, part of a plastic buoy and one unidentifiable rotten sea animal, the odor of which he promptly began to emit.

"Marriage is a ridiculous institution. It should have been abolished at the same time as slavery, since they were conceived under the same ideals." Edelweiss ate a cube of cantaloupe while speaking, an action that allowed rivulets of juice to run down her chin.

"Agreed. Let me get that," Joseph licked the juice from her chin, which of course required him to place his hands on her chest for greater stability, which in turn required her to lean forward and sigh.

"Humans are not creatures that mate for life," Edelweiss said, though a degree sadder than she intended.

"Of course not," Joseph muttered into the crook of her shoulder, "but we are not animals. We have a consciousness. We are taught, alternately,

that we have to stay together and that we shouldn't ever expect staying together to work. I think we should be taught to not think about
it so much." He loved her tits, mostly because they were never bound
in anything tighter than a bath towel. They were like ripe fruit, always
ready-to-eat.

"I like that," she said, and neither of them knew if she meant what
he had said or what he was doing with his tongue. "So, you believe that
someone might stay with someone for a long time? Like, for the rest of
their lives?"

He considered this by nibbling on her lower belly. He glanced over in
the failing light to where Hewey had been, and saw that the troll had gone
further down the beach. Perhaps because Hewey had seen what they were
up to. "I believe in mathematical probability. It seems probable that some
people might, yes. I struggle to not weigh my options."

"Well," she said when his tongue found cloaca. "That's cool, I guess."

"And," he paused, "I don't begrudge anyone else marriage. Ritual is
apparent in every aspect of our lives. Funerals, graduations. What item of
clothing you put on first every morning. Marriage is how some people tell
themselves formally to relax. To trust."

"Oh, in an ideal world!"

"Yes, so sad that people get married because they think the act itself
means something tangible. It doesn't. It's like, how money used to be
backed by real gold, and now it is just a promise. Si?"

"I suppose you believe in babies?"

"I've seen them, I know they are real."

"You know what I mean."

He gave her a little nip and smiled at her hiccup of sensation. "I have
had no reason to think about it yet. That is like asking me if I believe in
an experimental surgery for a condition I don't have yet. I don't know.
Maybe. No. Yes. Ask me when it happens, when it's time."

There was a flurry of movement in the sand near them. In the darkness
Edelweiss saw Kundalini's eyes reflecting brightly. "Sweetie!" she said, and
reached out for her eau de tuna perfumed dog. It scrambled up to her in
a furrow of sand and whimpered loudly, slobbering. Joseph clawed sand
from his mouth and glared.

"Whatsa matter, baby?" she asked, squealing and pushing at Kundalini when he tried to burrow up under her legs, kicking ineffectually at Joseph as he went. "Joseph isn't hurting me."

Hewey could be heard down the beach calling for the Hound, whom he just called 'thief' or 'gobhole.' "I guess she missed her mommy," Edelweiss shrugged.

Joseph's eyes winked in the darkness, reflecting street lights far away in firefly flashes. The beach trail was just before them. Hewey would be walking back to them now, looking for the Hound, so Joseph stood. "Edelweiss?"

"Yeah?"

"Do you ever wonder what would be different about the world if there was like, an alternate dimension? Would it be just a few small things, or would it be a lot of things? The color of the sky, the way people's hair grows?"

"God, I don't know. Why?"

"I just had a funny feeling, that's all. Something about this world didn't seem right."

"There's all kinds of shit wrong with the world. For starters..."

"No, that's not what I meant. It was more that, ah, what is the French term Americans use when they have felt something before?"

"Memory?"

"French term."

"Fran-swa?" she pronounced with an unintended mid-west twang.

"Ah, I remember. Déjà vu. Only, the one that I just had was like, I felt that things around me were new, that I had never seen them before. It still seems wrong."

"Like what?"

"Okay, don't take this wrong, si? I thought your sex odd."

"I am from another country. We do things differently."

"No, your body, my body. I am having a difficult time articulating what I mean, I am sorry. Everything seemed terribly unfamiliar."

There was an ominous movement to the air, a pressure change, as though something massive somewhere in the world had shifted, and the Carfagna's Hound rocketed away from them explosively, like some poorly designed sand-spraying speedboat.

2.

Hewey was laying low to the sand, moving stick-bug slow in an attempt to sneak up on and scare the Hound when it had suddenly begun to yip and flinch. Hewey looked around, confused. There was nothing but beach. "Sometimes I feel that way too," he told it, but the Hound scrambled a sloppy U-turn and ran off down the beach. "Moron," he said softly. He hadn't yet admitted to himself that he thought the Hound to be a rare and fantastic friend. He called after it a few times.

He had assumed that the humans didn't know that Hewey was able to see quite well in the dark. At the first sight of Edelweiss and Joseph getting revolting he'd fled with the gobhole. And now, a ways down the beach and surrounded by massive rocks, he was alone.

"A bit of a fag, then," he grinned to himself, and set about packing his new troll pipe full of tobacco. It took him a good two minutes to get it packed. He then patted his pockets one by one for a box of matches. He wedged fat fingers into the pockets, wiggling them about. He had no fire. "Bloody hell," he muttered, and sneaked a look up the beach. Joseph was standing and talking to the girl, so Hewey began to walk back.

In retrospect, when Hewey was asked to describe the course of events, he couldn't remember but a few details. He remembered walking back to the kids and stubbing his toe on a iceberg-like rock hidden in the sand, and he remembered the sudden flurry of the Hound racing vaguely in his direction (it was difficult to tell where the Hound meant to go, what with his wild fish-tailing). He had felt an oddness to the air just before that, as though his ears were going to pop, and then changed their minds. After that, things surfaced as though through sleeping fits, the sounds of distant alarm clocks in the groggy part of the morning.

Hewey had a good clear memory of Edelweiss clutching after the Hound and moving her mouth, but why wasn't she saying anything? Her yap was just flying and her throat was flexing, but nothing was coming out. He remembered then (or reverse remembered if there is such a thing, since the feeling was more like someone had come along and melon-balled the memory right out and then popped it back in), a terrible collision with the back of his head and the top of his shoulders just as the gobhole reached him. He didn't recall falling or kneeling, whichever happened, but his hands were then in the still-warm sand. He looked up in time to see, *to see what?*

He didn't remember, exactly.

Somewhere in his brain, though, operating systems registered a 'go' on recognizing a bloatshark, but he hardly felt a part of such higher brain function, even long after the event.

The gobhole, he remembered, burrowed under him, shrieking piteously just as a stiff fin like a sheet of plywood slammed across his side and then like a cartoon, these *teeth*, white teeth like porcelain teacups his grammy had, filled his vision like a wall.

He did the thing his ancestral brain told him to do then, and upon seeing the side of its head as it turned to bite, he punched it with all his might. Hewey had closed one eye for aim and by luck or skill his fist had landed solidly on the shark's softball-sized puckered eyeball. It felt precisely like a strong helium balloon, he told the officers. The latex kind, not the mylar. Except, neither the latex nor the mylar rubbed the skin off your knuckles when you punched them.

The shark spun away into the darkness, mouth gnashing.

Joseph looked like a wax model of Joseph, and Edelweiss' face was buried deep under her arms as she cowered. Hewey lifted up from the beach and looked under his armpit at the gobhole, who appeared to have fainted half buried in sand.

Hewey remembered then, he told the officers much later, such a sound. Like a very, very large sheet of metal tearing, if mixed with whale song. Maybe the whale song part was misleading, because Hewey, like everyone else, found whale song to be frustratingly ancient and sweet, like the very sea calling. The sound on that night was corrupt. It terrified him.

And then, Joseph was gone.

Hewey knew he saw, but couldn't quite conjure the memory of, the bloatshark's dive at the young man. The shark was the size of a small bus, but it moved like a thought.

Joseph's last startled gasp hung in the air for millennia.

When the police arrived Hewey was sitting in the sand, still in shock, in amazement, and, for the first time in his life, feeling small.

3.

Milan!

So many fantastic things had been said of it, and there were still as many more waiting to be.

Honey Smee rode the sidewalk escalators out of the Milan airport with a look of utter boredom framed behind Jackie-O sunglasses and Clarins SPF 36 moisturizer. Inside she was heaving an immense sigh of relief. Milan! It was like homecoming for Honey, and might as well be as much as anyone knew. In the way images do sometimes, an image formed stealthily in Honey's mind and ambushed her: burnt orange Formica counter tops and flimsy "wooden" cabinets made from compressed paper. Buckling, torn linoleum on the floors. Wood paneling with printed grain so cheap you could see the little color-dots.

Honey snapped the image in two.

Shag carpet, it whispered.

No, she told it. Milan.

"The train station," Honey told the taxi driver, not bothering to speak Italian. They all knew English, they could pretend like they didn't but they did. Honey was irritated by their infantile refusal to admit it. It was one thing to require a person to know the native tongue when using a cash machine or a metro ticket dispenser (something that America didn't even do—every time the ATM asked her if she wanted her transaction in English or Spanish she looked right at the little camera and said, "I must be dreaming, *am I in Mexico right now*?") but everyone in Europe knew plenty of English.

The shops raced by and the taxi driver pulled over and pointed at the meter. Honey paid him and collected herself on the bustling side-walk. The stupid actress on the plane had suckled at the cheap booze the entire flight and had ended up looking like a Gainesville porn starlet after a long tryout. After Honey had ditched the gimlet, guzzled water, and taken twice her regular doses of vitamins, she positively glowed with health.

Sitting at a little street café, she ordered an espresso and took out her compact. She reapplied her lipstick, blotted the beginnings of a sweat and tapped a bit of re'em against her gums after dipping her forefinger into a vial of the powder. After sitting back and sipping her espresso, she sighed.

Edelweiss was on her way back to the states, and she had taken that troll along. Shit. Worse still, the images had been nearly impossible to cull from the ether—Edelweiss was soon to be flying under the radar, so to speak. Double shit.

Honey looked at her wristwatch and surveyed the street. There was an Armani AX (worth looking at), a Donna Karan (snore), a St. John's Gray (maybe when she turned fifty) and a Prada (always a pleasure). She could hit all of them before she had to get back to the airport.

4.

"I've never ridden in troll class before," Edelweiss said. If she pulled her knees up, she could lie down sideways in her seat.

"Delightful," Hewey said lifelessly. He inserted a foil bag of peanuts into his mouth and began to chew.

"Aren't you going to take them out of the bag?"

"No."

To make conversation, Edelweiss said, "You know, I'm really not afraid of flying. I can't understand why some people are. I think negative energy is what brings planes down."

"If by negative energy you mean drunken lorry drivers moonlighting as aero mechanics, then I agree."

"No, planes crash from bad oracles not doing their jobs. Who's Laurie Driver?"

"If by bad oracles you mean mechanics who forgot to check the oil every 300,000 miles, then I agree."

"Hewey, stop it."

"No, oracles can go shag themselves, they're just back-up. Almost every plane crash ever has been because some guy named Lou or Sven left his spanner in the engine or something. The laws of aerodynamics I trust. Humans, never."

Edelweiss had an overpowering déjà-vu, and then remembered it had been something that Joseph had said on the night—well, the night. What was it? Something about 'mathmamatical problemility.' "Why don't you fly in a troll-built plane?"

"That is a trick question. Trolls would never build a plane. They require too much attention, we would have to check every single bolt every single time the plane flew. It would never be cost effective, and therefore, it will never be."

"Is that why there are only four troll seats on each plane?"

"Yeah. I think maybe ten of us have actually traveled by plane."

"And you twice! Adventurous."

"Twice? No, just the once. I took a train to Firenze."

"But you came from England."

"England is connected to Europe by tunnels, bird."

"Tunnels through what?"

5.

"Cheesh."

"Quiet."

Aikiko could barely see her hand in front of her face, but she had been training long enough to know where everything was. There were two big bottles of Espress-Kno™ Hydra-Life Elixir, which was just water (all of the other employees drank Hydra-Life Elixir Plus+, which contained nicotine and caffeine in equal doses), a box of tissues, a whole stack of Espress-Kno™ Nutra-Life Bars (sans the Plus+ flavor as well), which, as near as Aikiko could tell were made entirely from nougat, caramel and 'yogurt' coating, which was white chocolate. Aikiko had requested her Nutra-Life Bars in Mense-Yo!, the flavor for women, but the assistant had forgotten.

Also in the dark, close at hand, was the novella she was encouraged to read as often as possible, which was unnamed and bound in black leather and stamped with the Espress-Kno™ seal. The gold paint on the seal had almost entirely rubbed off in her hands the first time that she had opened the book. As far as Aikiko could tell, no one in the history of man had ever read the novella all the way through, as even her own instructor's book had intact gold paint on the front.

Aikiko had read the novella twice and couldn't find a single useful snippet. At best it offered words of encouragement. At worst, it asserted mankind was doomed. Employees referred to it as 'The Other Gideon'.

"Are you all set?" her assistant asked, coming up Aikiko's right side.

"Yes, thank you."

"Break a leg."

"This isn't Broadway."

"Might as well be," the girl chirped, and scampered away. The sound of the rear door shutting echoed forlornly in the gloom.

Aikiko was alone. The chair was comfortable enough, and it had to be. She was going to sit there for the next six hours, for the next five days, and after a two day weekend, it was a repeat for the rest of her life. The chair, quipped 'The Throne' ("Is everything named?" Aikiko asked her assistant. "The tissues are just called tissues," the girl answered.), had a series of room control buttons on the arm. She knew them by touch. Up near the front was the light for directly on the chair arm, theoretically for in case she needed to look at something, such as The Other Gideon. Next to that were the room lights. Below that the intercom button, to summon the assistant. Next to that, the exit sequence. The assistant was in the control room then, making sure that everyone in line had paid by watching cameras and controlling the stop and go lights. When the light was green outside the room, Aikiko's light flashed red inside.

At first Aikiko had been irritated by all of the drama involved. Quite quickly, though, as she sat in on re'emifications, she began to be bothered by the emerging explanation: the customers *wanted* drama. They ate it up and begged for more, all of the lights and the florid speech. When Aikiko had made a joke about getting a strobe light her manager had eyed her warily. "Those are still in transit, they'll be installed soon enough," he said. Aikiko had to assure him that she wasn't wasting her re'em delving into company business, that she'd just made an offhand comment. He hadn't believed her.

And here she was, her first real day of work. Aikiko startled suddenly when she realized she hadn't taken her dose of re'em as soon as the assistant had left. Aikiko scrambled with her locket, extracted a large dose on her wet finger and licked it off. So strange, she thought, this issued re'em. It was so finely ground that it had a pronounced flavor like over-cooked meat or burnt fat. She took a hard slug of Hydra-Life.

A lot of her training had to do with controlling the re'em, learning not to get lost in it. It sounded both easy and cliched, but it was the most important element. One day when she'd hit the drug peak and caught herself thinking about lunchtime, she'd become unexpectedly sad. Just a year before, whenever she did re'em she could hardly even remember her name, letting herself drift and collide with prophecies like a pinball. It was so beautiful, being able to pick up a walnut and be given images of its life. These things would make her cry with joy, these bright pages of life and the future being moved around her like she was being fanned with infor-mative text books. There was even a time when she went to eat a peach and thinking about it, had seen what her intestinal tract looked like from beginning to end. What a riot! She couldn't poop for days, thinking about all those cilia.

At the core, Grandma. She'd never met her grandmother, but there she was, every time, in navy kimono and matronly gray hair. She would talk and talk to Aikiko, and although Aikiko had a limited mastery of Japanese she understood every word, every whisper and tut of disapproval. After a time, Aikiko adopted it as her internal monologue.

The red light began to flick on and off. The electricity going through it made an audible clicking in the quiet room.

Aikiko smelled chrysanthemum perfume and felt her Grandma near. The door handle turned.

"Fuck!" Aikiko said loudly then, for her grandmother had whispered this: Edelweiss was back, and with a huge man, a monster. There was a flicker of a person, a woman probably, but the flicker was impossible to focus on. *An oracle*, Aikiko's grandmother whispered, and Aikiko shud-dered at the static that represented others with the gift. Through the tawny mist was a dark torpedo of hate and teeth, a bad combination, and a drift of soggy cigarette-butt odor and flatulence. Aikiko had seen all of this on her first inhale. On the exhale came papers, tickertape, Edelweiss again, though fuzzed insanely, itchily, with static. Towers loomed up like a cheap vampire movie and then, *the tunnel that you never look into.* Aikiko jerked her metaphorical head away, clenching her eyes shut. She knew that tunnel, she knew that it would look into things that no one wanted to see; death was a raging flirt, and Aikiko, like all good oracles, took care to never flirt back.

"Hello?" A man's voice, coming from the direction of the platform. Aikiko became aware of a customer in the room with her.

"Just a minute," she said shortly.

"Okay."

"Cheesh?"

"Not now!"

"Uh, okay," the customer said.

"Not you!" Aikiko shouted. She sighed. This was a bad start.

6.

"Lets see. I got a retro confirmation that Nazis were using fluoride to subdue prisoners, how's that excite you?"

"At least they were concerned with dental hygiene."

"They injected it, asshole."

"Let me see here. Would you categorize that under 'Nazi'?"

"I would categorize it under 'Torture: Work environments.'"

"Here we are, it was already confirmed in 1983 by Cara Adrian. It was categorized as 'Nazis: Torture: Fluoride.' Bummer."

"Double confirm it then, write my name down."

"Regina, you haven't had a viable precognition since February."

"Call me Miss Carey."

"You had a false Level One, not so long ago, I see."

Regina scoffed, rolled her eyes, cleared her throat, pointed accusingly and then slouched with affected boredom. "I never declared a level. That asshole fill-in did. Not my problem."

"But you predicted the destruction of Paris. The fill-in was acting within procedure. Lucky for you he figured it out before we evacuated a city with a population of 2,252,000 people, not including all of their goddamn poodles."

"Look, I'm not impressed. It is not my job to deal with your paper-work problems. I never said I saw an evacuation or death or anything. I said I saw the Eiffel Tower fall, it's all in the report, see for yourself. Case closed. Ha."

"Certainly. Just so you know, if you don't start having viable prophe-sies soon you're going to be up for a review."

"Let me ask you this: has anyone ever been discharged? Really? Where are the old prophets?"

"Hey, I have an idea, why don't you see for yourself? Do a little re'eming?"

"Fuck you man, you know I can't."

"I do, sure. And you know to keep your fat hole shut about it. Policy, you know. Can't have people going around being afraid of oracles doing whatever they want, can we? Where do you think the old oracles go? The Old Prophets Home?"

"I think you do something to them. I think maybe you kill them."

"You're wrong about that. Relax Miss Regina, just focus a little and the review will be all routine. Give us a little nibble, okay? Tell me, tell me that the President of Mozambique is pregnant, then we'll be good pals again, just like old times."

"Where is my re'em?"

"Here you go. Mmm, dependency."

"Eat shit. This looks like only three grams, what happened to my five grams?"

"You've been cut until the review, it's all standard."

"Fuck you!"

"Sure, sure, have a good one."

7.

The only two interesting questions death raises are as follows:

1) Why exactly is death scary? Pain is scary, but death? Why would the prospect of not knowing what happens when you die be any more scary than not knowing what is going to happen to you for the rest of your life?

2) If death is officially the scariest thing ever, why has so little been done to stop it? Millions of dollars are invested every year in sun-tan lotion, which is more than is invested in really, really trying to cheat death. Instead of committing one's life work to remaining alive, most people commit their lives to creating an illusion of eternal life, i.e., making babies and writing novels. What if everyone had worked on immortality instead? You'd be free from death right now.

Ah, but questioning is best left to philosophers and teenagers. Housewives, fishermen and astrophysicists don't ponder death, for what would the outcome be? They face death every day in some incarnation, and almost every time take rain checks.

And then there are the oracles.

How many times have you been to an Espress-Kno™ or a Jiffy-Re'em, or to a sorcerer or a gypsy or a neighborhood psychic (who serves tea and watercress sandwiches—sans crust—twice daily at eleven and four)? Have the words ever slipped from your mouth, casually but then held out, lips sucked tight against the teeth to prevent the question from leaking back in? How did you word it? I was wondering how I *was going to die*? When? Will it hurt? Will I go to heaven? Is Fluffy there waiting for me?

If you did ask, then you already know what they tell you: All matters of death and other-worldliness are closed to me, they will say. Sometimes: I see you die a million ways a second, you are dying right now in some way, and in the next moment and in the next. Or: you choose when, my child—you are free to die any time your attention slips, or you stop believing, or you have grown too tired to go on. And rarely: I'd rather not say. Here, have a peppermint. Assume your last day is today, live well, and don't ask me again.

As you know, the painful part is that the future is malleable. Perhaps you die tomorrow, squashed in the prime of your life by a giant anvil falling from the sky. If you had known, you could have cheated, stayed in bed. But you don't know, so it's sealed anyway, in a permanent, horrible way.

If only the oracles could see death, life would have meaning then. Wouldn't it?

8.

Hewey generally found culture shock to be a delicious earthly distraction. Humans in the grand scheme, struck him as strange anyway, but since he was often travelling and rarely saw another troll, he would slowly forget he wasn't human. He would, the longer he traveled, become used to the way everything was too small, as he grew to love the way that children gawked and old French men tipped their pipes to him, remembering the troll-aided battalions of WWII. He was not offended that trolls were forbidden from entering the Vatican—who wasn't forbidden from entering the Vatican?

America, however, blew his mind just a little.

"What are you looking at?" he asked a small crowd of people waiting for their luggage. They shamelessly pointed and he heard the word 'monster.' He hadn't been stared at by an adult for as long as he could remember.

Edelweiss harrumphed. "People in America are very bigoted against other races," she said.

"I'm another species."

"Yeah, it's cool."

A baggage handler pushed a cart forward with an animal box on it. "Sign here," he said. Edelweiss signed. "And here."

"What's this? Is this a bill? I already paid for Kundalini's shipping."

"It's an added charge. Your animal ate one plastic food bowl, one plastic water bowl, one leather work glove, a bungee cord, a stopwatch, four square feet of industrial all-weather carpeting and we think an escaped ferret."

"Kundalini is a *vegetarian*, mister. I won't pay for it."

"We didn't charge for the ferret."

Edelweiss signed, brows furrowed, while the employee hid a sexual flush with excessive coughing.

Edelweiss and Hewey waited outside with their luggage, wishing the Gaffney bus would get a move on. Hewey looked around, getting perverse pleasure from the stares of curiosity and the paranoid glances. He flinched at the giant rotating holograms advertising for Espress-Kno™, at a giant animatronic Donald VonRonald and a television two stories high blaring commercials for TraveLunch, the liquid meal in a tube. A new commercial started with the Many Stars brand top ramen mouse, Mi-Ki, singing his song about instant noodles.

On the bus a teenage girl sat next to Hewey and Edelweiss and immediately clapped her hands with glee. She had a pink spiked topknot of hair, gigantic headphones around her neck and a jumpsuit that was the texture and colors of a beach ball. She oozed optimism.

"Oh, you're a troll! This is great! My name is Emmy!"

Hewey's neck flexed. "Cherry, bird. Names Hewey."

"What? Hey! You totally have to come to this microrave tonight! Everyone will freaking *transcend*!"

Edelweiss' eyes widened happily before she remembered the task at hand. "Emmy, that sounds wicked, but we've got to get back to Gaffney. Peace anyway."

"That's cool! The rave is in the U.S. Rubber building off Adams street. Sucre Vida!" She put up two victory fingers and catapulted herself to the front of the bus where she crawled all over a few other teenage passengers. Hewey sighed deeply and looked to Edelweiss. "We don't have that shit in England. Punk rockers, aye, gyspies, aye. No bloody clowns."

"Clowns? No, that was a Candystriper."

"Like a hospital volunteer?"

"Uh, I don't know if she volunteers for the hospital. Anyway, you know, Candystripers? A Peep? They eat rockcandy, snort candycaine?"

"I have no idea what you're saying."

"They're totally drug addicts," Edelweiss rolled her eyes. "All they do is eat nerve candy and dance and lick each other."

The landscape projected itself by, green green gray green. Hewey was given one of the seats near the back that had no partitions, so though the seat was wide enough, it wasn't deep enough to accommodate his posterior and as a result he had to perch. His legs were cramping. Edelweiss was sound asleep and the Candystripers were singing showtunes and spraying the air with cotton-candy air freshener.

Joseph is gone, he thought. The pang in his chest was physical, stopping his throat up, but when Hewey tried to force himself to remember the bloatshark, to be angry, he just couldn't. He clenched his fists and raged a little at his inability to get angry instead. The really hard part was that Hewey had nothing to show for Joseph, no photographs, no magazine articles, nothing but a rapidly disintegrating set of memories and a whole lot of feeling sorry for himself.

Kindred spirits were hard to come by, for him as well as everyone else, he assumed. Edelweiss was oblivious. The attack had scared her, but she'd just sent Hewey out for more re'em and buzzed out, babbling and insulated. Hewey smoked his pipe and drank wine whenever he could get his hands on it.

This landscape here is lush, he thought to himself, surprised. So green to England's wet wool. It probably never got too foggy to go for walks, here. Edelweiss shifted in her sleep and muttered something about a mother goddess. Hewey shook his head. "So daft," he said softly, and found himself worrying about the gobhole, down in the luggage hatch.

CHAPTER TEN

1.

Riko Takahashi was a sharp-witted, tight-lipped city girl everyone called O-Yuki, or Snowdrift, since it was clear as white snow that her intelligence collected in silent deep drifts, unmarred. She dressed smartly, wore corrective spectacles, studied European literature and smelled of chrysanthemums—never too strongly, but always just enough. Men did not ask her out because of some natural, correct instinct that for the most part, she did not need them.

She was interested in Western culture, in particular their manner of dress and eating. The dress, because it seemed so sensible and the food for its absurdity. When introduced to chewing gum she loved it at once; it served no purpose, rotted your teeth, was always rude and had to be spat back out to be disposed of.

O-Yuki was in fact smoking American-style cigarettes when the newspapers came out with word about the bomb.

The top High-Esteemed Precognition Excellencies all agreed, morbidly and with great weariness: the Americans were going to try to bomb Hiroshima. It was nothing against Hiroshima personally. Even more shocking than the bombing was that it was to be with *atomics*, if you could believe such a thing. Atomics! That technology had been scrapped almost a decade before due to it being so unbelievably inconvenient. They had come out with an atomic car and an atomic train, but once the novelty wore off and the rich grew tired of driving all the way to the Atomic Depot for the tiny plutonium pellets for the engine, they all switched to petrol. And now this.

O-Yuki stared at the paper in dumb bafflement. It said that the two governments were in talks. The Americans of course had denied everything, right down to implying they were about to stop warring with the Japanese anyway, so why bother with a costly bomb? It had a photograph of President Truman shrugging in apparent confusion and pointing blame at an office aide. O-Yuki sighed miserably. They would not let the bombing happen now that all eyes were on Japan. It was a fantastic thing, the Precognition Excellencies. They kept Japan in such tip-top shape. Hardly anyone had died from a tsunami or an earthquake in ages.

Feeling oddly lighthearted about the world in general, a few days later O-Yuki stopped to buy a rice ball with a pickled plum in the middle for work. On a whim she purchased an American fashion magazine as well—generally she didn't waste money on such things, but she felt she had to celebrate feeling as smart as those American gals looked. At work, when she sat at the desk and began to type out the day's copies, her superior approached. O-Yuki stood and bowed deeply.

"Yes?"

He stared at her, a little sweaty around the edges, and picked at a paper in his hands, otherwise unmoving. O-Yuki glanced around and became aware that the other two girls in the newsroom were typing and weeping. "I am very sorry, O-Yuki," he said, and thrust the paper at her.

O-Yuki broke the seal on the note and read through once quickly, and then again three times very slowly. She was being drafted, if she pleased. She was to ship out in two days. The other two girls had papers on their desk as well.

As suggested earlier, O-Yuki was a sensible girl. She was a little confused and a little irritated, but she settled down to work and at the end of the day went to the drafting office and informed them that she had never signed up for any kind of draft. She was unaware that one even existed.

The young man at the counter sifted through piles of documents before finding something. "Riko Takahashi?"

"Yes."

"The High-Esteemed Precognition Excellencies predicted your signing up for a draft as of yet to be announced. Your as of yet offer had been accepted."

"I'm sorry, I don't think that could be right. I have a job, I am to attend University in two months. I would not have volunteered for this."

"You will have done it. We gladly accept your volunteering and wish you great success with protecting our beloved Nippon."

"Ah, no."

"Your country is in need, Ms. Takahashi. Surely you would agree to that?"

"Yes, but me? What will I do, read to the Americans? What about my apartment? My canary? Who will take care of my canary?"

The man watched her without expression, than re-filed his paperwork. "You have until the end of the week to get your personal affairs in order. That is plenty of time to find someone to watch your canary."

2.

The battleship *Ijiwaru* hit typhoon seas around the time that O-Yuki's seasickness had begun to recede. She was in the middle of reading *War and Peace* when the feeling hit her, a slight roll of her inner ear, her eyes not tracking properly. She pulled off her spectacles and scrambled for the sugared ginger she kept in a little waxed paper packet in her bunk. By the time she'd choked a piece down it was already on its way back up.

The girl in the bunk above her was vomiting into her issued government vomit tin as well. "O-Yuki!" she moaned. O-Yuki passed the ginger packet up to her. "O-Yuki, why are we here? Why should I know what it feels like to be in a typhoon on a battleship?" the girl asked. Her name was Junko.

"Because you volunteered. Don't you remember?"

"Ah, that's right," she said. It was a private joke. No one remembered volunteering because it hadn't happened yet, and now wouldn't happen since they had preempted it.

In addition, O-Yuki thought it very convenient that they were sailing through typhoon weather because the girls were already begging to get to wherever it was they were going. In fact it was just at that breaking point when the women were told what their mission was, which would be occurring in the next five hours.

They were informed by a jowly, greasy man that they would be thwarting an invasion of Americans on a small Micronesian island by the name of Truk. They were amidst a great precognition battle, but the Excellencies were sure they had the most recent precog advantage over the Americans. The girls would be given gattling guns, precisely enough ammunition to get the job done, and their two swords, the small tanto and the larger *wakizashi* (which had been issued the day they arrived at the battle camp, to allow the optimum training time). These were largely ceremonial but the use of the two swords together, *dai-sho*, had been considered effective use of the weapons since samurai had roamed.

So then, before you can say *watashi wa shitsubo shimashita*, O-Yuki and all the rest found themselves beached in a squid-ink gale-force dawn, one person already unaccounted for on the beach, guns too heavy for one and sometimes even two of the girls to carry, sand in all the places where there should be silk and minds heavy with the last-second instructions to "Run for the cliffs as fast as you can! The Americans are almost here!"

Several hours later, when Junko was feeding rounds into the gun that O-Yuki was firing through the screaming rain at what she hoped were American soldiers and not Japanese late-comers or native Trukians, her face reverse super-heroed with a gun powder scorch silhouette of her spectacles, O-Yuki had a thought. She stopped firing for a moment and yelled to Junko, "I have read that these terrible events pass like a blur. Are yours?"

"No, I don't think so. Fire!"

Up and down the beach cliffs came the same rhythmic rattle of gunfire, and for so long that it was getting hard to tell through the rain and the wind what was a moving body and what was a still one. The great piles of black that she assumed were soldiers formed a bit of a wall, often around the sides of beach rocks and foliage islands. These dense piles would easily hide a person if they crept slowly enough. She fired a few rounds at the darkness to soothe her consciousness. After a wait she realized that all of the guns had slackened off, and she stopped to pull part of a rice ball from an oiled cotton knapsack and handed Junko the rest.

"This is awful. I hate it," Junko said sourly, rain pouring down her face so heavily that she couldn't see a thing. Junko groped at the rice ball with a flustered sigh. "I don't want this stupid rice ball. It isn't even good, it's hardly stuck together."

"I think it's the rain," O-Yuki said, who was eating hers like soup out of her cupped hands.

"I want to eat udon! I want hot udon with fishcakes! I want to go to the movies with Tetsuo! O-Yuki, if the point of the Precognition Excellencies is to foresee how the war is going, why can't they just see it all the way through to the end and then say, 'Well, the Americans will win, now we know. No need to fight'?"

"It doesn't work that way, Junko. The future can change," she paused. "I don't want to be here either, though."

There was a loud crackle in the forest behind the girls, and Junko went slipping a few meters down the slick hillside in an attempt to pull her swords while O-Yuki tried to swivel the gun all the way around before she realized it didn't. She too reached for her dai-sho in time to see another Japanese woman come scrambling out of the bushes. "Sisters! It's me, Naoko!"

O-Yuki lowered the gun, bile rising in her throat as the unused adrenaline left her system.

"I was over with Miko and Saseko and they ran out of ammunition. Ryoji-san radioed back to the ship and they said we definitely shipped out with enough ammo. We need some of yours, I guess."

Junko, still dizzy from being startled earlier, slowly began to dig through the ammunition cases, separating the empty ones from the full. She looked up to stare at O-Yuki and Naoko. "We only have two cases."

O-Yuki said to Naoko, "The extra must be with someone else. We've hardly got enough either. In fact, Junko should go with you to fetch us some."

Naoko shook her head sharply, as though shooing flies. "No, they have to be here. You're the last of them. I've checked everyone else."

The three searched the surrounding brush for cases that may have escaped. Great gusts of wind buffeted them suddenly and through it came the sounds of gun fire. O-Yuki scrambled over to the cliff edge and squinted out into the dark typhoon. "Another group!" she yelled. Shadow-shapes of men were drifting across the beach, dropping in with the dead bodies and then running again as the girls lost sight of them through the rain. White flashes blinked and the distant *tak tak* of rifles seconds later. O-Yuki settled herself in behind the gun, feet braced. "Junko, get the ammunition ready. Naoko, we don't have the spares, you need to check everyone again, maybe you missed something. Maybe it got left on the beach. Find it."

O-Yuki turned after there was no response and saw Naoko staring into the distance, dazed and unresponsive. "There isn't any more ammo," she said after Junko had begun to load the gun, and then pointed out to sea. There was an odd break in the squall, and through it they saw at least four or five more American rafts, each of them holding four men.

"There's not enough?" Junko asked, looking back and forth between them.

"There is," O-Yuki said firmly. "Naoko, go and find out what is happening, now!"

Within an hour of frugal shooting, the rest of the ammunition was gone. O-Yuki and Junko were on their hands and knees in the miserable light of the afternoon, searching for bullets they had maybe misplaced among their things. They turned to look at each other roughly at the same time, eyes wide. The last of the big guns had ceased firing. "Do you think Naoko is okay?" Junko whispered.

"Why wouldn't she be," O-Yuki challenged, and then scuttled to the edge of the cliff. The last raft had landed and no one was shooting at the Americans.

"Oh no, no," Junko moaned. O-Yuki turned to tell her to pull herself together when she saw Naoko and another girl, Mitsuko, come stumbling through the brush. They were hauling the radio with them.

"Why doesn't Ryoji-san have the radio?" Junko asked dumbly, but O-Yuki just nodded.

"Because he's dead," O-Yuki said, and rushed over to Naoko. Mitsuko was bleeding from the shoulder, where the arm hung limply. "Were you shot?" The girl nodded, eyes wide in the rain. There was no way to tell if any of them were crying.

O-Yuki grabbed the radio and signaled to the ship, forgetting protocol and not using any codes. A cranky Japanese came back, "This is *Cuttlefish*. Not Naoe! *Cuttlefish!*"

"Shut up, Naoe! This is O-Yuki, we are out of ammunition! I repeat, we are stranded on the fucking beach without ammunition!"

Junko looked up from doctoring Mitsuko's arm and frowned. "O-Yuki, such language."

After a long pause the radio cracked, "Why isn't Ryoji-san radioing us?"

"He is dead, Naoe. I told you, we are out of bullets and there are still troops landing. Something has gone terribly wrong!"

After another long pause, "No, you're mistaken. You shipped out with precisely enough ammunition to take the beach. Did you lose it or something?"

"No, damn it, we are really out! There has been some mistake. We definitely don't have enough, we don't have any at all!"

Single rifle shots echoed along the cliff and the four jumped. The radio came back, "Well, you left with enough."

"How can not having *any* be enough, Naoe?"

"Look, this was triple-predicted by the Precognition Excellencies. For maximum savings you took enough ammunition, down to the bullet. You can't mess up, you just shoot."

"Yes, I know how it was supposed to work, but you have to listen to me when I say that something went wrong and now we don't have any and we are being shot at," and indeed, as she said the words, the rocks by her feet pinged threateningly and then a log behind them thudded. O-Yuki turned and stared at the fresh hole in the log a foot or two from her head.

"You'll have to make it work," the radio hissed, "Because that's all you've got. We'll send the pick-up when the beach is secure."

"*Make what work?*" O-Yuki screamed into the radio. "You're leaving us here to die!"

"You have enough! Get to work, Nippon is counting on you!" And then the radio was silent.

O-Yuki stared at the dead electronic box for a moment until more gunfire brought her back to alertness. She became aware of her soggy underwear, her waterlogged feet and the eerie sighs of the jungle in the wind behind her. She crept to the edge of the cliff again and peered down below, where three slow-moving men were scaling the face about three yards below. She crept back and ran to where the other girls lay, sodden and miserable-looking.

O-Yuki drew her swords, both of them, and took a deep breath to tell them to get theirs out as well. Just as she was about to say something, Naoko's eyes shot open wide, and she pointed over O-Yuki shoulder and to the cliff edge. That was fast, O-Yuki thought, and turned to face the Americans.

Except there were no Americans.

Something immense moved through the air with the grace and speed of a sparrow, something that made the sound of a very old bamboo cane bending under great stress, an almost pleasant creak. O-Yuki knew what it was before she had time to blink again.

The three girls quickly dragged the fading Mitsuko around and behind the log where they all crouched, O-Yuki and Junko with their dai-sho held upright, and Naoko's hand held over the unconscious Mitsuko's face to staunch the rainfall.

"Bloatsharks!" Junko hissed, unbelieving, and the three became rock-still. They were Japanese, after all, and you can't be Japanese and not have been taught what to do in case of a bloatshark. They practiced in school so often that one night when O-Yuki was little she had leapt under her kitchen table at the sound of the doorbell. From somewhere the wind brought the sound of a woman screaming horribly, and rifle shots. It was impossible to tell if it was related to the bloatshark or not.

O-Yuki's breath caught as the Americans came over the cliff, guns held before them, eyes blinking through the rain, squinting for the enemy they suspected was there. O-Yuki let her vision stray to a distant cliff-top when a flash of convenient lighting lit up a horrifying sight: a bloatshark, mouth open and thrashing at the tiny figure of a woman, her wakizachi held above her head and one leg forward in a lunge, and the blade came down, just as the shark rocketed towards her too fast to see and—

BOOOOOMMMM

O-Yuki was slammed into the ground with enough force to knock the air completely from her lungs, unaware until she'd landed that she'd been thrown through the air. She gasped feebly, reaching for her dai-sho lying on either side of her and saw that two of the Americans were gone, presumably thrown back over the cliff. The third lay coughing.

O-Yuki sat up in the brush, air coming back into her, and gaped at the mushroom cloud rising from the decimated cliff, fires raging in the super-heated brush steadily doused by the typhoon. She wondered who she had just watched die.

She looked about for the others, eyes resting on something she hadn't wanted to see. Junko had not been so lucky in keeping free from her swords when she'd been thrown. Her friend lay face-down in the foliage, the long bladed wakizachi emerging out from the back of her shoulder, the tanto hidden somewhere under the torso. O-Yuki didn't see Naoko anywhere, oddly, and Mitsuko lay unmoving under a thick layer of debris.

The American was shakily rising to his feet. Without thinking, O-Yuki ran out to him and gave him a gentle shove, frightened, at just the last second, of touching him. He tumbled silently off the edge and into the darkness.

She waited for a minute, half expecting him to come climbing back over, too terrified to look down below for his body, and looked up at the beach. The wind and rain had let up just a little, and in this reprieve she saw an image of hell emerge, something that gave her the most total sense of the willies, something that she never could have imagined on her own.

There were a dozen or more of the black sharks darting and zipping through the rain, many feasting violently on the bodies that lay below, some moving so quickly into the foliage after some hiding person that they gave the illusion of simply disappearing.

O-Yuki slowly backed into the jungle, dai-sho up, eyes roaming the sky for the demons. Once O-Yuki was deep into the jungle, she was too stunned to move. It was quiet in the trees and brush, and not as wet. Her hands clutching the swords before her steamed as though fresh from a wok.

She had no idea what to do.

3.

Records would show that as the typhoon died a few days later, the brave Japanese men that waited patiently for the women to take the beach came in rafts, rifles ready, helmets strapped tight. They weren't prepared for the carnage, although the records would omit that. They mentioned off-hand-edly that the bodies of the American soldiers were stacked three and four high and as wide as fifty feet in some places. The beach was a mess, as one can imagine, between the typhoon offshore and the battle inland, hardly one square foot of beach remained gore-free.

Up beach trails they began to find the women. Each corpse had her dai-sho drawn, although some of the swords were missing. They were found later, as the Americans had taken them for souvenirs, presumably, before they too died. All of the men that made it above the beach, not a mere five rafts that the women thought they'd faced, but nearly a few dozen—all of the men were chopped to death. Many of them were almost or totally decapitated, which was quite a feat. Beheading someone by sword was not easy—neck tendons and spine are solid as wood, so to sheer a head clean off required such brute strength that did not seem to be at the women's disposal. Nevertheless, the sea of heads, entrails and random butchered meat the Japanese men came wading through was enough to shame dozens into demure vomiting. It became clear that there may be no survivors.

Hours into the day they heard a scream. The soldiers rushed forward and found a wild-eyed Sgt. Bunko holding up his arm neatly severed at the wrist, pumping great bloody gouts. Between the sights of eight rifles, sixteen eyes realized what they were staring at.

A woman, so caked with blood that she seemed to have been dipped, crouched, rigid, wakazashi and tanto crossed over each other over her chest. She was ready to spring.

"Identify yourself, soldier!" One of the men commanded.

The woman snarled, silently, teeth like sugar-cubes against her brick-red face. With aching care, she seemed to relax a little, and then laid the tanto down on the rock next to her. With her free hand she wiped a film of blood from her spectacles and pushed them back up her nose. After she'd picked the tanto back up, causing eight rifle barrels to bob nervously, she said, in a hoarse crackle, "O-Yuki, sir."

Success! they told her, patting her on the back through the wool blanket they'd draped over her. Albeit bloody, but a success. Another victory for the Precognition Excellencies.

Staring at the receding shore, the sky a lurid cerulean, she whispered, "But Junko, Naoko, Mitsuko, Saseko, Miko, Ryoji-san, Nami, Eiko, Mayu, all of them, all of them, they're all dead."

"Very sad, so sad, but is there an American left breathing? No! Quite a feat, O-Yuki-san! A sign of the might of Nippon."

Ms. Riko "O-Yuki" Takahashi was on the cover of every newspaper in Japan, and was greeted with respect every where she went for the next year. Old men took her hand and patted it and old women wished her a thousand blessings. They all praised the Precognition Excellencies and she nodded, deaf to it, for the rest of her life.

4.

"Hey, does that tattoo say something in Japanese?" the kid asked. He was six feet tall, the combined weight of two wet medium-sized dogs (or one large and one small wet dog, or possibly an entire laundry-basket of those little tea-cup Chihuahuas, also wet), blonde, and profusely zitted.

Aikiko looked down at her arm in surprise. She just had the one tattoo and even though it had been there for years, she still generally forgot she had it.

"Oh, yes."

"What does it say?" he asked, taking the movies from her.

"Roppongi," she said. "It's where my grandmother lived, in Tokyo. Electronics district."

"You know," his voice cracked, "Ahem, you know, I asked my friend Blaze if he would manage my band," his voice cracked again, and he smiled all-knowingly. "But he was like, 'no way dude, electronics are scary!'"

"Uh?" Aikiko wondered if she was supposed to know the kid from somewhere.

"Yeah, I know! So I'm like, 'what, you're crazy!' and he's like, 'man, when I see that electronics stuff, I get all rage against the machine on it and I want to smash it!' and I was like, 'no, dude, that's my mixer!'"

Aikiko waited for him to finish.

"Hey, you're Aikiko Ellison, aren't you?"

"Yep. I'm sorry, what's the total for the movies?"

"Whoa, no way! Wait, can't you tell what the total is? Oh man, this is so *cool*!"

"I don't see the future when I'm not at work."

"Oh, c'mon, just try! Hey Stu! *Stuart*! Check it out, it's Aikiko Ellison!" the kid screamed at someone in the store, pointing down at Aikiko's head.

"No way! What's she renting?" Stuart called back.

"Dude, *kung fu movies*!"

"Righteous!"

"Hey pizzaface, tell me what the fucking total is," Aikiko snarled and then stepped back. What the hell was that? Her heart was racing and she grew nervously light-headed. "Oh, I'm sorry," she lamely offered at his shocked silence. "I am really tired, I'm sorry, and it gets so old when people are always asking you questions when all you want to do it watch Kung Fu movies and eat an entire box of GrapeRocks by yourself."

The kid's adam's apple quivered and he remained shocked.

"I'm sorry," she said firmly, "It's just that I have to actually eat the drug, the re'em, in order to prophesize, you can understand that, right?"

"Sure." He looked like he was being held up.

"I'm terrible at math, I can't even make an educated guess what the total is," Aikiko waved her hand over the stack of videos. "Ah, twelve sixty-three."

"Ohmygod, you *are* Aikiko Ellison!" the kid shrieked joyously.

Aikiko's face fell and she moaned out, "Don't tell me that was the total?"

"Oh sure, I believe you, you're like, 'I don't do that when I'm not at work' and I'm like, 'sure, I believe you'!" He bagged her movies and handed them to her. "The movies are on the house, Miss Ellison."

"No, please, if that was the total, I was guessing. I wasn't seeing anything. It was coincidence."

"I'm taking statistics in school right now, Miss Ellison, and I know that the chances of you guessing that is *low*!" He grinned. "It is so cool to meet a real oracle."

Aikiko lifted the bag, sighing, and headed for the door. What a bizarre thing, she thought, guessing a number like that. Must still be high.

Perhaps the most frustrating quality about experiencing the event known as déjà-vu is that right around the fraction of a second that you realize what is happening, it has already begun to fade. Within five seconds of identification, the feeling is often gone entirely, leaving the victim feeling dazed, worried about things like God, and generally creeped-out. This too passes before the next blink.

So then, dear reader, imagine this: as Aikiko Ellison passed through the safety glass and aluminum door of BERSERKER VIDEO!, she felt what at first she mistook for a change in air pressure. It tickled around the tiny wisps of hair that lived in front of her ears; it caused her breath to catch. It intensified. And Aikiko got a very strong feeling that she was *going to have déjà-vu very soon*. The afternoon warmth of early fall was suddenly oppressive, and she had a seat, dropping the videos to the ground.

"Are you alright?" someone asked.

"Yes!" Aikiko said hoarsely. It was riding around the edges of her memory in a fashion that she was fearful to describe as mocking. "What what what?" she breathed at the air, and felt it dip in slowly, a memory she never had, first person.

It begins with a young Japanese girl, one with a penchant for American things even though it is WWII...

And it unfolds, real time, the girl being drafted, the storming of the beach, the subsonic moan of a dozen bloatsharks moving like meat cleavers slamming over and over and over—

"Hey lady, are you okay?"

"No! No, there aren't any more bullets! There's been some mistake!"

Aikiko blinked, her breath gone ragged in her chest. It was dark out. She was chilled to the bone, her clothing soaked through with sweat. "What time is it?"

It was one of the video store clerks. He glanced at his wristwatch. "It's nearly midnight. Hey, aren't you—"

Aikiko was up and running, her leather men's slippers slapping at the pavement with loud pops, her pink nightgown snapping in the wind. The smell of chrysanthemums ghosted along with her.

CHAPTER ELEVEN

1.

"Excuse me? Excuse me?" Honey Smee rang the little counter-bell twice. "Yes, could you tell me where there is a hotel in Gaffney?"

That morning in Milan, Honey had washed her hair with human keratin and hydrolyzed caviar shampoo with no sodium laureth sulfate in it because sodium laureth sulfate's only objective was to foam madly and had a nasty habit of drying hair into a parched, desert wasteland—but at least the shampoo had a nice thick lather, right? Honey Smee was not so easily fooled. She'd then rubbed in a Russian clay silt hair masque to exfoliate her scalp, letting it sit longer that the recommended three minutes so the kelp extractives could penetrate. With that rinsed, she'd carefully applied a dense layer of one of the most expensive conditioners in the world, which was made from a tiny Brazilian orchid shown to harbor a molecular compound known as collotin-3, which was proven to hydrate so well that forensic scientists used to it extract microscopic portions of DNA from bone tissue that was in previous years thought to be too desiccated to be of any use. While that sat, she started on her face. She washed quickly with a triple-milled glycerin and olive oil soap, rinsed, and then rubbed papaya enzyme and apricot seed exfoliator with pineapple hydriants, careful to linger in her t-zone, and then rinsed. With that done she washed the conditioner out and tipped a small puddle of her own concoction she'd made fresh, into her hand: three parts extra extra virgin olive oil (from the Umbra region only, where the soil was less acidic) and one part mashed Haas avocado. This she smeared on and waited. Meanwhile she began to exfoliate her entire body with a fresh sea salt and coconut oil scrub. She carefully razored the stubble from her armpits. Her legs, feet and arms were waxed by a woman name Josette back in the states. Honey sat precariously at the edge of the tub and applied a thick layer of an exfoliating foot masque to one foot, waited for it to dry, than began the tiring process of rubbing the dried masque and skin back off her foot. When she was done she started on the other foot. While sitting, she picked out the grime from under her toenails and tisked at the flaking polish. She had fallen for the advertising on a polish that claimed to contain Teflon, but it had lasted for only a day or two, compared to her regular drug store variety that contained lots of formaldehyde and alcohol. She rinsed the olive oil and avocado from her hair, washed her body quickly again with a lightly perfumed milk-based soap to remove the olive oil, and then turned the water to it's coldest setting to close the hair shafts' scales and the pores on her face. She gasped and turned the water off.

Honey Smee patted her skin dry with sponging motions and lightly squeezed her hair dry, careful not to pull or twist the hair in its fragile wet state. Quickly, while her skin was still fresh, she spritzed every inch with distilled artesian rosewater. After that she used a chamomile and agave body moisturizer that employed colloidal oatmeal instead of commercial greases, the colloidal oatmeal being the miracle product that created a hydrostatic bond with cells and water molecules, this actually forcing each cell to intake two hydrogen atoms and one oxygen instead of coating the skin with petroleum and sealing in a film of moisture (which created the illusion of hydration). Her feet got a thick layer of peppermint extract lotion that did have heavy greases in it because feet weren't as sensitive on the moisture issue.

She selected a pure unbleached cotton ball from her things and wiped briskly at her face with grapefruit oil and green tea toner. She switched every other day between that toner and one that had a small quantity of tea tree oil in it, which controlled bacteria but was too strong for daily use. She then moisturized her face with an oil-free, wax-free, alcohol-free lotion made from seventeen different distilled alpine herbs and berries. Honey dipped her finger into water and then into plain table sugar and rubbed vigorously at her lips, rubbing free the night's collection of dead skin from them. She applied to her under eyes a refrigerated mint-colored aloe-based gel that contained a small quantity each of caffeine, Methylparaben USP, and Benzalkonium Chloride USP, also known as the active ingredients in hemorrhoidal creams which also constricted the tiny blood vessels around the eyes with quartz crystal reliability. She applied it by starting in near her nose and sharply, painfully, smacking the skin out to the outside corners of her eyes. Satisfied, she applied a red clay and sage underarm stick to her pits, scarlet satin panties to her pelvis and a custom-fitted cotton-lined silk demi-cup bra to her chest. Over this she buttoned a classic light gray silk buttoned blouse (no pleats for god's sake, she wasn't a pirate) and left the collar and the top two buttons open. She slid on a pair of charcoal bias-cut linen slacks with a bit of a nap to them. They fit snugly in the hips, buttocks and thigh, but fell straight-legged to the cuffs, which provided a masculine counterpoint to the blouse and the girl and was, Honey knew, attention getting. She tucked in the blouse and put on a three-inch wide leather belt that did not go through the belt loops (there were none) but sat asymmetrically on her hips.

Nearly finished, Honey began her make-up. She spot-applied an organic oil-free concealer to her under-eyes with a dense professional make-up sponge so as not to encourage bacterial growth. She used a plum-tinted gel dye on the apples of her cheeks, patting it slowly in circles for an even effect. She then used a wax cake of dark brown to brush in and shape her eyebrows, which did not need plucking as she had done it the night before so that the skin would have a chance to heal and unswell during the night. Then, with a rounded sable brush she applied a heliotrope band of eye shadow to the crease of her eyelid and a lighter mulberry one to the lid itself. Honey Smee did not feel that excessive make-up was attractive on anyone, so she lightly powdered her face with talc-free powder, painted around her lips with a wax-based product designed to stop lip gloss from feathering, penciled in her lips with a lip liner that was almost the same shade as her skin, and then used another sable brush to paint in scarlet lip gloss with the finish of NASA mirror glass.

Honey pinned her hair up in a loose bun that took less than thirty seconds to achieve, put on a gold necklace with a pendant of pure tooled platinum and gold oval that had her initials on it (she'd purchased it herself; she did not wear gifts), put on two gold and coral rings, a stiff-banded gold watch with a tiny face and then sprayed herself with a ridiculously expensive perfume by spraying the air in front of her and then walking into the resulting cloud.

After stepping into a new pair of Prada low-heeled boots and putting on a floor-length wine-colored wool coat, Honey retrieved her black lambskin purse and stepped out of the hotel room, snapping her fingers at the bellhop standing in wait at the end of her hall.

"Fuck," she'd said when she realized she'd forgotten to brush her teeth.

"I'm sorry, what was that honey?" the little old woman at the desk asked, squinting at Honey like she was glowing brightly.

If there was one thing that Honey hated most about the South it was that everyone called her 'honey', which gave her the willies every single time.

"I said, can you tell me where there is a *hotel*, please?"

"Oh, well, we have many vacancies right now, and there is the Gaffney Carriage House down Columbia Road that surely has rooms, and—"

"No, ma'am, those are all *mo*-tels. I want a *ho*-tel. Something with auto-flushing toilets and mints on the pillows."

"Ah, a special night, is it? Well, there's a little bed and breakfast run by Esther and her husband that is the sweetest little chunk of Heaven that God allowed to fall to earth, if you have a taste for Esther's homemade fudge, that is," the woman winked conspiratorially.

"What is the name of the town I flew into?"

"Oh, the city?"

Honey suppressed a shudder at the idea of the place that she had just taken a taxi from being called a city and nodded.

"Why, I think you're thinking of Spartanburg, honey."

"Yes, that's it. Could you call me a taxi, I think I'll try Spartanburg tonight."

"Oh, well, as you like. Have business here in Gaffney, then?"

"Yes."

"What kind of business?"

Honey Smee tapped a Nat Sherman on the surface of the front desk and held it before herself critically. She hated nosy people. She hated old people and their good-natured rudeness. "I guess you could call it kidnapping," Honey said, and stepped outside to wait for her taxi.

2.

Ardella Santucci, for whatever reason, fell into an immediate and platonic love with the troll. When the travel-worn pair arrived at her doorstep, Edelweiss weepy and Hewey bleary and irritable, it was Hewey that she embraced with tears, not her daughter.

"Mom," Edelweiss was sobbing, clinging to Ardella's shoulder. "Mom, I'm home."

"Eddy, munchkin, don't think you're moving in here, you have to get back to school soon. Son, what is your name?"

Hewey leaned over to get a better look at Ardella. No one had called him 'son' in a long time, and a human had never said it with kindness. "Hewey, Ma'am, yourself?"

"Oh, it's Ardella," she moaned happily, hugging his hip and burying her face into the fecund folds of his leather vest. "You have a British accent, that's so handsome," she crooned, muffled.

Later, over tea, the three shared stories, Ardella telling of the now-famous Aikiko Ellison, Gaffney's own oracle, the first in forty years.

Edelweiss was devastated. "Aikiko? My Aikiko. The girl I grew up with, Japanese-looking?"

"Eddy, dumpling, what is the problem? Yes, Aikiko. It's not such a leap, you know, she's always been so... odd. Like it was meant to be."

"No, she never had any *precognition*. She just had conversations with her grandmother. There's been some mistake—Aikiko Ellison?"

"Don't you think she's rather pretty, Hewey?" Ardella asked suddenly, twirling one of Edelweiss' dreadlocks in her fingers. She seemed too dreamy for a sober and apparently functional person.

Hewey, however, looked like someone had stabbed him through the hand with a corn holder. "Well, M'Lady, although I appreciate her height, I find her, well, no. It's inappropriate for me to say."

"Hewey, we're all family here, what is it?" her voice was polite, but Ardella's eyes glittered in connivance.

Edelweiss was holding a daisy from the garden and touching her tongue to it experimentally.

Hewey sighed, a rumbly affair. "Alright. She's a bit unhealthily thin; I am used to women who," he gestured as though to a bus, "are substantial. Your daughter is a porcelain teacup. I prefer a beer stein. Also, she's daft as a sod brick."

"Hewey!" Edelweiss howled.

Ardella put her head to the patio table in laugh-agony, slamming her fist hard enough to rattle the teacups in their saucers. "It's true!" she gasped.

"You're both terrible!" Edelweiss stalked into the house, a waft of patchouli, mold, falafel and something like insecticide trailing behind her.

"Can I get you a real drink?" Ardella asked when she had recovered. She wiped at the little rivulets of tears that remained, sniffing and sighing.

"No thanks, right? I need some shut-eye. It's been long."

"Of course, it was rude of me not to offer," Ardella said, scrambling up. She cast about the room furtively, looking for something. "I don't know where I'll put you, though. The couch isn't big enough. I can't put you on the floor."

"The floor sounds grand, really. I'm used to it."

"No and no. You'll just have to take my bed, that's all. It's only a queen size, but you can lie diagonally. I'll move the bed diagonally so it doesn't feel weird when you're looking at the ceiling." She sprinted from the room with squirrel-like agility.

Hewey laid his face into his baseball glove hands and sighed.

In the morning, Hewey woke to birds chirping. It took him a few minutes to realize that the sound of a door slamming in the house had woken him, along with the smell of coffee. He rolled carefully from the bed and stepped on something ragged and pointy.

"Blast," he said, reaching to the floor. He picked up a flattened rose, still dewy, and removed the bits still stuck to the bottom of his foot. There was a note stuck there also, and he lifted it between thumb and forefinger up to his eye. It would have been a tiny note even to a human.

It said, in a delicate scrawl that he feared at first was not English:

Darling Hewey,
Please help yourself to anything in the house, okay?
There is fresh coffee and I got you some English Muffins in

case you are Homesick. They are fork split, which I've heard
is English Style, although I don't know what that means.
Eddy will be up late, if she is still the same daughter I had a
few years ago. If there are any problems call me at my work,
the numbers are posted above the telephone in the kitchen.
Have a beautiful day in Gaffney.
Love, Ms. Santucci

The note smelled fetchingly of carnations and cardamom.

Hewey went downstairs, tip-toeing for no particular reason (Edelweiss was not an alert person, even when awake) and came upon the kitchen table. Kundalini sat near the table, eyeing its unreachable heights with a certain longing hatred.

"Bloody hell," Hewey said, and lifted the gobhole to a dining table chair before seating himself. The table was laid generously with a carafe of coffee, a pitcher of cream, sugar, marmalade, currant jelly, sweet butter, honey, molasses, a pitcher of orange juice, a basket of English muffins, a bowl of bananas and fresh strawberries, a dish of lemon curd, a bowl of hardboiled eggs, a small plate with thinly sliced cold steak, salt and pepper shakers and a tiny bowl of breath mints. Hewey yawned and worked his way through it, taking care to give the gobhole the banana skins, egg shells, and butter wrappers as a treat.

Several hours later Edelweiss came down, disheveled, sweaty, musty-smelling and swollen-faced. "Morning," she said.

"It's one o'clock."

"God, it's early. Maybe I should have slept in."

"Which way to town, then?" Hewey asked, giving his head a nod toward the front of the house as a guess. The dog belched a semi-tropical sulfurous cloud.

"You're right, we should go get some re'em. I need to find out if we're going to Seattle or what. Oh!" she became suddenly wakeful. "Shit! I've gotta find Aikiko today. Shit shit shit." She darted back upstairs.

"I ate all the food," Hewey called to her.

"That's okay," Edelweiss said, returned and dressed. "Breakfast is a scam."

"Sorry?"

"Oh yeah, the Food and Drug Administration wants you to eat and eat and get fat and sickly. The Native Americans haven't eaten breakfast in thousands of years and they are healthy and prospering."

3.

"Do you want something to eat?" Edelweiss asked Hewey when they had gotten to town and to Hewey's dismay, had veered toward the mall.

"Uh. Maybe that'd do good, bird. Any tripe carts?"

"Hewey, this is America. Fuck, I can't believe they wouldn't let Kundalini in," Edelweiss looked back at the way they had come. The Hound was tethered outside in the shade behind the garbage Dumpster, and in his rapture, he'd not noticed their departure. Hewey and Edelweiss were uncomfortable leaving him there, but the security guard had held her ground, pointing resolutely at the pictogram of a dog with a 'no' slash over it.

"The gobhole will be okay."

"But she needs me, Hewey. What if someone tries to steal her?"

"I can't imagine anyone that stupid." He looked at Edelweiss. "Or I couldn't until recently, anyway."

"Yay!" Edelweiss pointed. "They have a Sushi-Go! here now. You want to share some sushi with me?"

"Is it tripe sushi?"

Edelweiss glared. "Okay then, how about a wrap? They have a Thatsa-Wrap! here, too."

"What is a wrap?"

"It's like a tortilla, with like, lettuce or spinach and cheese and some-times other vegetables, spreads, things like that."

"That sounds an awful lot like a salad. What else is there?"

"Salad-Nation!, they have good stuff."

"Look, is there any food here that has any gravy or potatoes served with it? Something with custard? Tripe?" Hewey was getting perturbed and each time he reached for his cigarettes Edelweiss would frown and shake her head at him.

"No tripe, Hewey, no one wants to eat intestines here. They are disgusting and provincial. I am going to have a tofu Mighty-Weenie! and you can have whatever you want. They have regular Mighty-Weenie!, too."

"What is 'regular' made from?" Hewey feared couscous, or worse.

"It says," she squinted, scanning the menu board. "'Made from real meats'."

"It'll have to do."

Edelweiss fidgeted through their meal, picking nervously at the organic kholrabi-kraut on her dog and drawing on her tray with the squirt bottle of Brugg's Nutrient Pulpal 'ketchup'.

Hewey had ordered his Mighty-Weenie! with Alabama-style Pork Chutney and was only mildly interested in it. He gave in. "What's the bloody problem?"

"Huh?" she jerked. She took an audibly squeaky bite of her dog.

"If you can't de-hummingbird I am going to leave you. You're bothering me." Hewey didn't admit he wanted to check on the gobhole.

"I haven't seen Aikiko in a few years, you know? And she's an oracle now, Hewey! That's too crazy for me. We used to talk about being oracles when we were little kids. Everyone did." She drifted wistfully away.

"It's pretty fucking brilliant that one of you actually is one, though, right? If I am not mistaken, it's rare. You are lucky to know her even, am I correct?"

Edelweiss brooded. "It was almost me. I missed it by half a second. What am I saying?" she moaned then, dropping her Mighty-Weenie! and holding her face. "Who says I am not an oracle? Espress-Kno™? My mom? You? I see things!" she shouted. The Food Pavilion of the mall hushed momentarily, heads swiveled.

"I see things," she said quieter, and Hewey only nodded.

4.

Honey Smee was having the dream again. She had a furrowed brow, a thin film of sweat formed about her lips, and her feet twitched like a dreaming puppy.

Horror movies didn't bother Honey. Suspense movies were often a chore. Psychodramas tested her patience. It was comedies and romances that captivated her as though she were physically clamped into her seat before the screen with an iron rod against her spine. She would only see movies when she was absolutely positive there was no one she knew there or would ever know, for one reason: she was prone to braying. Laughter emerged from her not as an effervescent drift but of a boil being lanced. It burst and spilled.

There was one type of movie, though, that Honey would gladly cut through a crowd with her switchblade to escape, and that was the quaint country drama, a sub-genre that occurred with surprising frequency. Anything resembling a trailer park or a run down little cabin made her tremble and gag. Women dressing or acting shabbily because they had no other options in life caused a terror to wrack her like a blow to the head.

Once, when an acquaintance asked her to go see the latest blockbuster romantic comedy, Honey had actually accepted, something neither party had expected. Twenty seconds into the opening credits the camera drifted over a lonely, lovely little farmhouse and to the houses far beyond. They were shingle-sided and dilapidated. The camera swept low, a joyful country song playing, and swept past a dirty little girl playing with a naked, half blinking doll. Honey left the theater so fast that she was to her car before she realized she was holding her friend's popcorn. She threw it to the ground and drove to the nearest spa, ordered the Empress treatment and took a Valium.

And so, in the theater of her dreamworld, Honey was not lucid and thus, stuck. The dreams didn't make much sense, but they didn't have to. Her mother was there in her flowered muumuu, holding an iced tea nearly clear with peppermint schnapps. In the dream Honey was hungry, though it was still morning, and her mother was slurring at her to get to school. Honey couldn't go to school because her dress wasn't mended. There was a long tear up one side, exposing her little girl chest, and dogs fought over a captive rabbit in the side yard.

Orange linoleum. Pressboard cabinetry. Potato chips. Saltines with condensed milk for desert. In Honey's room there was a rotten part in the floor near her mattress where she could press her fingers through to the crawlspace. At night, mice scrambled through it.

Honey woke up with an intake of breath and held it. One hand slowly felt the other hand for the gold and coral ring, her amulet. It was there. She exhaled.

She removed her night mask and blinked rapidly in the light. The hotel clock said it was a little past noon. Honey rose from the bed.

5.

To most Gaffneyites, the Gaffney Mall Espress-Kno™ was the closest thing to a cathedral they would ever get.

Many things that are not designed to be holy end up being more so. That lack of intent provides modesty, or divine purpose. And Neville Manowicz, in all his nerdy billionaire glory, was mortally careful of one thing: he would never allow pop influences to mar his image. There had never been and never would be an Espress-Kno™ television commercial, magazine ad, radio spot or billboard. There were no cross-over products. There was no outside merchandise. Espress-Kno™ was not a vision that could be traded or sold, it was its own belief, its own modest and personal thing. Better yet, it was from one day to the next exciting, different than everything else, and somehow just the same as the day before.

When Edelweiss Santucci and her troll companion approached the Gaffney Mall Espress-Kno™, even Hewey, who was suspicious of his own toenails, was impressed.

The first thing you'd notice was the glow. In the best part of the morning, before the sun is too high and after the sun is too low, the light underwater in the reef coves of Australia mirror the colors of the sky, only warmer and more diffuse. It is a touch teal and just a smidgen lemon chiffon. That was the light coming from the entrance of the Espress-Kno™, and it even flickered a little, as though a warm breeze was barely disturbing the surface of the water. This effect was greatly lessened by the hive-like comings and goings of customers, but that was okay. It wasn't supposed to be an underwater scene exactly.

Nearly every texture and architectural structure of the Espress-Kno™ was forgettable, and why not? Nothing to go out of style that way. Even so it was constantly updated, advertisements and displays being moved daily, sometimes thrice, in a subtle and calculated attempt to avoid pop culture. The spring season fad everywhere in the States was a fresh-faced cleanliness? All of the employees of Espress-Kno™ were instructed to show up to work slightly manicured and doll-like. The summer rage is coconut everything? Espress-Kno™ didn't even have to push pomegranate as a new flavor—everyone craved it before they knew they craved it. The popular Chikin-Shak! serves fat-free fried chicken now? Espress-Kno™ launched its controversial *Indulge Yourself* campaign, featuring tiny drinks so high in fat that when they cooled, they congealed.

What Hewey didn't know was that several major "family" restaurants were on the warpath, spending truly Fort Knoxian amounts of money on ads that encouraged family time and extended five-course meals that took three hours to serve. To aid this bonding experience, the wait staff were trained to share with you tiny bits of personal information over the course of the meals, so that by the time you leave you've realized that your daughter went to school with them and that they are saving for a student trip to Poland to research the tragic paths of WWII Jews. This was why Espress-Kno™ was pushing the JET-Fuel Pack, 'Your Personal Dietary ReBoost'. The staff at Espress-Kno™ personally determined your nutritional deficiencies with a tiny painless sampling of your blood, which was to be kept on record on an international database so that you could be mixed a personal cocktail of supplements and nutrients in a handy squeeze bag that easily attached to your waist. From here you could uncoil a length of tube to suck from at any moment that you needed to absorb some custom-made goodness. After the initial set-up, getting the Pack took exactly twenty-eight seconds, and though every magazine claimed the extended family dinners were in, Espress-Kno™ was making a killing giving people excuses not to participate.

Hewey was flabbergasted. In Europe, there hadn't been a revolution in food since the refrigerator, and even that hadn't entirely caught on.

Edelweiss hadn't been to what she thought was a decent Espress-Kno™ in almost six months, and as such, the Gaffney Mall Espress-Kno™, keeper of stored teenage memories, early sanitarium and yes, religious mecca, loomed up before her as a gift-dispensing many-armed heathen god. Would she be treated to poison, or to sugar? She blinked her tears away and shrugged back a heap of dreadlocks.

And then, the slap: a three foot tall, full color, filtered smoky image of Aikiko Ellison posted in the front entrance next to two other faces. The difference between them was immediate, as no amount of filter could hide the others' greasy, flabby zittiness. Aikiko remained as ever, brown, straight-nosed, squinty and bored.

"Wow," Edelweiss said.

"Whassat?" Hewey grumbled.

"That's Aikiko, my best friend. She looks the same. See how they tried to get a shot of her without showing her pajamas?"

"They're all head shots, not just her. What does it bloody matter what she's wearing?"

"Oh sure, but they must have known that a head shot wouldn't show her pajamas, right? Very clever, those photographers," Edelweiss shook her head from side to side, her face twisted into a look of either respect or suspicion, Hewey couldn't tell which.

Hewey said, "Do you think it is possible for people to suddenly blow out some important neural bits from intense lack of surprise?"

"Anything is possible, Hewey," Edelweiss said solemnly, and stepped into the Espress-Kno™.

6.

Certain light waves carry emotion, as every photon-sensitive neurological bundle knows. Show me the heart that swelleth not with the rising sun. I dare you to identify anything pleasant about the nearly imperceptible strobing of fluorescent lights. And, as even Edelweiss knows, there is something hollow and solitary about the blue cast of a dark room lit only by television's necrotic glow.

So then in a room behind an unmarked door, inside the Espress-Kno™ headquarters, sat seven individuals lit in a ghastly perpetual TV twilight.

They were so similar-looking that they occasionally mistook each other for one of themselves, despite the fact they greeted each other every morning, sat together all day and night, and bade farewell only when sleep utterly overwhelmed them.

They required a small support crew. Odd that the seven found this empowering, something like King Henry the VIII demanding to be served only the top crusts of his scones and biscuits. They had become too obtuse and overspecialized to see that if someone didn't bring them their bags of Super Squidy Snax and refill, with hidden faery magic, the paper towel dispenser, then they would, eventually, expire. They would wilt off and die like so many ill-potted houseplants, and that was the only thing that brought the caretakers joy, that and an impressive bi-monthly paycheck.

Frustrated, around a mouthful of artificially flavored X-Treem Dairy Tube-O-Puddin', one of them said, "Oh, I am losing clarity now. This can't get worse, can it? Seriously?"

Another: "I've been losing clarity for days now. The hippie bitch has definitely crossed the event horizon. Don't fucking bogart that jar of whipped marshmallow, asshole!"

The Keeper of the Whipped Marshmallow let off a whistley nasal sigh. "You two aren't focusing. Maybe you would focus on that Kyoto earthquake lead you both had. That sounded showy."

"No, I've been losing clarity on her as well. She's passed the event horizon, there's no doubt. I thought there were more pretzels."

"I used them to eat the nacho powder with. Tough luck."

"How did you eat dry nacho powder with pretzels?"

"Licked and dipped."

"Aw, Christ! Can you spell c-o-o-t-i-e-s?"

"I don't have to, you just did."

"Hey! I need a formal count for this. Who's lost clarity on Edelweiss?"
Five hands raised.

"I would be more angry that *someone* keeps eating the ranch dip with their fingers."

"Alright everyone, here's the deal. I am going to call in a definite loss of clarity on Edelweiss. We're going to catch shit for not reporting this sooner, just so you know."

A chorus of groans.

"Also, no double-dipping any food item, with a utensil or otherwise."

"That's patently ridiculous!"

"Agreed. I say we start getting separate containers of things and keep out of each other's business."

"Fine."

"I am also getting repeat hits on that troll. Anyone else?"

"You just have a crush."

"Eat shit, butt eater."

"That's redundant."

CHAPTER TWELVE

1.

Edelweiss went slowly glassy-eyed at the inside of the stall. Like any mall bathroom, it had a thick frosting odor of sugary disinfectant that covered several spongy under-layers of feces and cheap perfume. Scrawled on the inside of the door was the passage:

here I sit all broken-hearted, tried to shit and only farted.

Edelweiss took a pen from her purse and carefully scrawled:

it is irrespectible to others who need this space 4 natural businiss to mock what everyone does. defecations r healthy!

She had been sitting on the toilet for nearly fifteen minutes while she'd wept, wet and loud, into her shirtsleeve. When the shirtsleeve had gotten too damp to be of any use she'd used the toilet seat protectors. When the toilet seat protectors were used up she finished her crying.

Now, Edelweiss Santucci was, in theory, a smart girl. The cells were there. Important neurochannels were there and the endometrium was intact. Her crimes, at most, were that she was unobservant and thankless for just about everything that she garnered freely from the earth, and alternately, she was grateful for things that were figments of her imagination. She appreciated freedom, for example, but was never clear if she meant her own or others. She scorned her own beauty. She didn't acknowledge a thing about being a young, privileged white American with a parent backed by solid mutual funds.

When Edelweiss was in high school, she happened upon a civil rights march. She'd joined immediately, assuming that hesitation was practically an assent to lynching. The demonstrators had been so overwhelmed and frightened by Edelweiss' screaming, weeping and displays of solidarity that they had eventually insisted that racism really wasn't that big of a deal, lately. They broke the whole thing off and offered to buy her a cup of coffee, if she'd just leave. When a women's rights issue arose, Edelweiss frothed at the mouth and was prone to faint with rage. She'd become so well known among the organized activists in town and nearby burgs that they had all disbanded, from the Armenian Women's Small Business Owners Lodge #402 to the Zephyr Preservation Society. Her mere sympathetic presence was both insulting and belittling to them. Nothing blew a rally like Edelweiss Santucci.

On this same pre-programmed route, Edelweiss had marched into Aikiko's hometown Espress-Kno™ and used every chapter of the Dissenter's Jargon Handbook. She'd practically levitated with self-impressed smugness at articulating the variety of ways that Espress-Kno™ enslaved their staff and misinformed their public. The sheer volume of rights that were being violated within a pico-second of entering the store was enough to form a thin film of spittle around the edges of her mouth.

More importantly, Edelweiss clearly thought she was an oracle, a fact of life that Espress-Kno™ still insisted on ignoring, day after day, week after week.

When she was finished, her best friend from elementary school, her oldest cohort, her holder of secret secrets, had laughed without hesitation right in her face. Edelweiss couldn't even remember what Aikiko had actually said after that, through the static of her rage.

The audacity! The heartlessness! The brainwashing! One thing though, one thing didn't make any sense. It had stuck in Edelweiss memory because it had been so insane, so ridiculous.

Aikiko had said something about how she could hardly blame the Espress-Kno™ corporation when it was the oracles that were evil. When Edelweiss had tried to clarify for her, you mean, when the company is so evil, you shouldn't blame the oracles, Aikiko had just shaken her head. Slowly, as though hearing something in stereo, eyes fixed on Edelweiss', she said, "You heard me right. You heard me."

Edelweiss sniffed in her bathroom stall, confused, sad and a little burpy. Needing a drink of water, Edelweiss finally stood, composed her skirts and opened the stall door. A line of urine-filled women glared at her.

"There isn't any toilet paper," Edelweiss kindly informed the woman that darted for her stall.

"Go to hell," the woman snapped, and, using her leather purse as a bumper, shoved by.

2.

"Ms. Ellison, do you watch a lot of television?"

Aikiko was wearing her current favorite nightgown, a little shapeless gray thing with tiny flowers and a long, limp gray satin ribbon at the neck. Shifting her handbag, and thereby, her rat, she frowned. "What does television have to do with this, Mr. Hymen?"

The man that stared back at her was her regional manager, Nigel. He insisted on being called Nigel, just Nigel, possibly because his last name was Hymen, and since Aikiko was fairly sure that was why, she took care to use it whenever possible.

"Well, I assume you watch a little too much TV because you've given us this," he shook a paper, smiling tightly, as though it were a poorly done illustration of a couple engaged in salacious acts. "This 'resignation', as you term it."

"Mr. Hymen, you still haven't told me what this has to do with television."

Nigel glared. "Call me Nigel. So now you think that since you are threatening to break your contract with Espress-Kno™ Industries, that I am going to beg, please, oh gosh golly, please stay, if you stay I'll give you a raise, right? Now am I right?"

"Or course not, Mr. Hymen. I am quitting. No negotiations."

He closed his eyes as though that would fend back the looming heart attack. "I don't have time to do the hardball thing, so your little plan has worked. Just tell me what you want and we'll discuss it."

"I'm sorry, Mr. Hymen—"

"Call me Nigel!"

"I'm sorry, Mr. Nigel Hymen, but I am not playing hardball. I'm quitting. I mean it."

"It is not going to be degrading for me to make you an offer, if that's what you think. It's my job. I'll make an offer. Thirty percent bump, plus your regular benefits and we'll discuss the increased holiday bonus later. And that's it. No games."

Aikiko shifted her bag again. The rat slid around inside, muttering. It was really rather bothersome to keep him at times, but Aikiko appreciated him nevertheless. When she was back at her apartment, alone, exhausted from the re'em and starving even though she had just eaten, the rat was the only thing that could distract her. That and hot Hong Kong action. "Mr. Hymen, I'm sorry, Nigel, I am going to be leaving now. Please relax. I am not playing any mind games with you. I quit. I can't do this any longer, you people," she looked around the room. It was sparse, richly decorated, but sparse—each of the decorations was impersonal, expensive-looking things that Nigel had obviously not chosen for himself. She hesitated on a misty photograph of Neville Manowicz and his family; a gorgeous empty-eyed blond and two kids that were a terrifying mix of both of their folks. "You make me ill," she finished. She looked back at Nigel.

"You have signed a contract, Ms. Ellison!" he screamed under his breath. "If you break it, you get nothing! *Nothing!* No health plan, no dental, no optometrist, nothing! And you'll never work for Espress-Kno™ for as long as you live!"

"Right, say, do you know where all the old oracles go?"

"The what?"

"Where are they? Where are all the prophets over the age of forty-five?"

"They've retired to the Bahamas, you slacker!"

"Prove it. Prove to me they haven't all died young from hypertension and heart disease. Prove they aren't all wasting away in front of televisions because *they don't even know how to have a life anymore.*"

"You're insane!" A vein in his temple began to pulse erratically. His glasses fogged. "There's no conspiracy here, Ms. Ellison. You're fired!"

"Okay," Aikiko said politely, picked up her handbag, and left the office.

3.

"Seattle, first class."

"Certainly, Mrs...?"

"Miss Smee."

"When were you interested in traveling to Seattle?"

"Right now, I'm standing in the goddamn airport."

"We have a flight available at six seventeen. That's the earliest first class. You can be paged in the airport if you'd like to be on standby, however."

"Standby will be fine. Where's the pilot's lounge?"

"I'm sorry, Miss Smee, the Sky Lounge is for VIPs only."

Honey removed from her wallet a small and powerfully important looking card. It didn't have to say anything on it, it only need bear the logo of the greatest and most pertinent of American corporations, Espress-Kno™. The cards were so rare they required encoded retinal scans and toll-free numbers to verify their presence. "I ride under the good grace of God himself, you bottom feeder. Point in the general direction of the lounge."

The flight checker blanched and tremulously pointed. "H-have a nice day."

"I will."

4.

There was, statistically anyway, a possibility that Kundalini was the greatest dog ever to exist in the history of the world. Such a difficult declaration would require immense debate and copious categorizations. For instance, if majesty or grace were heavily weighed, Kundalini would rank below dogs that had lost certain limbs to grain threshers or raging cows. Based on sheer pluck and verve, Kundalini would be just below a blind de-barked and neutered dachshund. For displays of intelligence, he would rank just under a dog that ran into sliding glass doors on a regular basis, despite the thick smears of dog-snot and canine eye-boogers that had rendered it opaque. It was up for discussion. The most difficult to measure category might be the ephemeral 'understanding humans,' or 'behaving uncannily like a self-aware individual.' Here, Kundalini stood out. Here, Hewey and the dog bonded.

"Gobhole."

Two milky, bloodshot eyes swiveled around to Hewey.

"I am going to have to go back to England, soon."

Kundalini shifted his eyes away as though he hadn't heard. An elongated wheezing fart escaped him.

"I'm going to try to get that daft sod Eddy to let you come with me."

The eyes slowly tracked back to Hewey, the head unmoving.

"Or, we don't have to ask her at all."

The dog's eyes widened and a half-chewed cigarette butt fell from his voluminous lips with a plop.

5.

When Ashleigh Moore slid from her egg membrane on a sunny, warm summer morning, the gathered family gasped in awe. She was perfectly rosy, had the beginning wisps of what would be naturally blonde hair, and long tapered interlaced fingers as though wrapped in prayer. She opened her eyelids to reveal sightless ultramarine eyes of such luminescence and depth that they appeared to be viewing portals for a glimpse of an unmarked soul. When the surrounding mucus and curded secretions were scraped away she let out a sing-song wail that ended in a toothless smile.

As a young child she had literally stopped traffic by skipping perfectly along a sidewalk in a daffodil-colored Sunday dress and white mary-janes. Within the traffic was a gaping, mesmerized modeling agent. Soon, Ashleigh Moore's blonde ringlets were emblazoned across a thousand billboards representing everything from Pearly Soap to Frosty-sip Fruit-like Drinks. She grew as almost no children do, gliding effortlessly through what others referred to as that awkward stage where a kid has some of the attributes of an adult, but not enough. Instead she simply elongated just a touch and the ringlets turned into waves. The eyes remained the same, but the lashes grew darker and longer. The lips remained quivering, perfect cupid's bows but got pinker and held within them larger, whiter teeth. It was very much as though one day she was a tiny well behaved Aryan angel and the next she was the Queen of Cheerleaders, an American Vision of Loveliness, a flawless, lightly tanned girl next door that no one lived next door to because she lived in a smallish mansion set back on a gated property guarded by attack dogs, motion sensors and armed butlers.

At nineteen, on the set of a commercial for a toothpaste Ashleigh had never heard of, the film crew grew hushed. She had been leaning over the catering table, picking with irritation at the grapes and fat-free cream cheese she had demanded they serve. She nibbled at a grape, made a sour face, then set it back down to try another one.

"Testing the grapes for poison?" someone asked near her. She whirled around.

"I'm sorry?" she asked. The man before her was perhaps an inch shorter than she, nerdy, bespectacled, and topped with an unruly mop of dull colorless hair.

"I said, are you testing the grapes for poison?"

Ashleigh gaped. "I don't know what poison tastes like."

The man chuckled. "Of course not. I'm sorry, I'm being very rude. My name is Neville."

"Hello, Neville," she said, and looked around at the crew. They all seemed to think something was up. Should she know who this man was? "Are you with the agency?"

"No, I'm just a fan."

Ashleigh frowned. It was totally not cool for them to let a fan in, especially such a dweeb, but she shrugged and set her plate down. "What would you like me to sign?"

"If all goes well, our marriage license."

Ashleigh fidgeted in confusion. "Uh, I don't really see fans…" she looked up at the crew and attempted to gesture surreptitiously. When she turned back to Neville, she rolled her eyes. "Look, hey you!" she snapped at a gaffer. He froze. "Can you help this guy off the stage? I've got only another half hour of lunch break and I haven't eaten yet." She looked back to Neville. "Sorry."

The man tiptoed over as though there were booby traps.

"Do you know who I am?" Neville prompted gently.

"Sure, Neville, please feel free to buy a signed photo from one of my people on your way out. Thanks so much for all your support!" she cooed in a practiced and insincere tone.

The gaffer hung back, wringing his hands. Neville stepped closer to Ashleigh. "My name is Neville Manowicz. I am a big fan of yours. Please let me buy you an espresso."

A very, very vague recognition dawned on Ashleigh. She had definitely heard that name somewhere. Unfortunately, she was getting weirded out and was afraid this guy was one of her dad's associates again or something. She'd be on a nice family outing with them and the next thing she knew "uncle" somebody would be slobbering all over her and trying to shove his face up her skirt.

Her make-up girl suddenly marched over. "Ashleigh. This is Neville Manowicz. He is the CEO of Espress-Kno™ Incorporated. Maybe you two want to get a drink and talk about stuff?"

Ashleigh grinned. "Espress-Kno™! I love that place! What's a CEO?"

And the rest is history, if, that is, you take your history from the covers of magazines or nightly entertainment reports. A massive secret wedding that somehow everyone in the world got photographs of was just the beginning of it all. Wasp-waisted champagne glasses, each with semi-precious stones swimming at the bottom, graced the cover of *Decadence Monthly* magazine. The fabricated tidal grotto with real dolphins and actors dressed as mer-people throwing orchids at guests was featured in *Beau Monde Quarterly*. The galleries that showcased photographs of tropical birds alighting on ice sculptures and waiters walking around with golden trays of paper-thin slices of blowfish arranged into plum-blossoms were instantly famous.

So then, eight years later, our little love story replete with castles, galas, speed yachts and 3am caviar sandwiches becomes a family story.

Neville Manowicz was participating in just this story when the in-house secretary emerged unto the lawns, blinking against the sunlight, her free hand forming an ineffective visor. As per Ashleigh's orders the secretary was practically elderly, supernaturally ugly and a minority. Neville had to send away to the Philippines to acquire someone matching the description. She tottered across the verdant, immaculate green sward in heeled pumps, still clutching the muted telephone to her chest. After a timid pause she heard the bird cries of children and carefully set out toward them.

"Mister Manowiss!" she called, barely able to raise her voice due to never having done so before. She tried again when she got closer.

"Maria?" Neville asked, confused. He could not remember having seen this secretary outside before. Her skin was like an aged morel mushroom, owing to a brief encounter with Hansen's Disease during WWII.

"Mister Manowiss," she whispered again, still doing her best with the lawn. "A telephone call for you. Very important."

"Oh, Maria," Neville sighed, attempting to disadhese himself from his wailing, bloodsucking spawn. Failing that, he dragged them over to Maria with him. "If I wanted to be answering telephones I wouldn't have hired you to take messages for me."

Maria bobbed her head uncertainly. "Yes sir, so sorry Mister Manowiss, what you say is most important code for telephone call?"

Neville froze, reflecting briefly on his mysterious enjoyment of the way she mispronounced his name a little. At her still-startled expression he continued. "It was 'White Flower', Maria. Please write it down to remind yourself."

"Yes, that right! White Flower!" she said, extending the receiver to him. He narrowed his eyes at her.

"Daddy, daddy, what does the zombie woman want?" one of his tow-headed children asked him, he wasn't sure which one.

Taking the phone from her, he said, "She is telling me that Edelweiss has become prophetic and will likely soon alert the world to the fact that anyone can become an oracle if they want to," he said absently, with the comfort of a man who knows he is surrounded by idiots.

6.

"I've got an intense feeling about this," Edelweiss said, in a glutinous tone of self-importance.

"Oh, me too," Hewey said. He was reading a copy of *Snowshoers Weekly* while they waited for their plane. He was doing his best to distract himself from the memory of the baggage kid's look of disgust as they had registered stowage for the gobhole. Hewey had practically called the whole trip off when he had seen the kid rolling the dog away, off to some indeterminate luggage future, the gobhole gazing balefully back at Hewey through the crate slats. He was almost sure the gobhole had nodded at him assuringly. Hewey forced the sight from his mind.

"I mean it, Hewey," Edelweiss whined. He set the magazine down. "It's like this fluttery feeling, I had it since my last re'emination. It was powerful. I feel..." she drifted off, her eyes unfocusing. "I feel something."

"Maybe it's fleas."

"That's our flight!" Edelweiss said as something calmly incoherent was announced over the loudspeakers. She leaned over, heaving at her carry-on, her opulently full tits struggling to get free from her crepe peasant shirt. Hewey briefly understood why so many people in the room were uncomfortably adjusting their pants, but then grossed himself out so badly that he had to close his eyes.

As they waited in line, Edelweiss asked a strange woman, "Do I know you?"

Hewey turned to look. The woman was very attractive by human standards; long jet hair, an immaculately tailored suit, sort of predatory-looking black leather gloves, though she was much more exotic than Edelweiss' filthy Amazonian look. The woman was giving Edelweiss a synthetic polite blankness. He turned back around.

"I don't think we've met," the woman responded. "I would have remembered, I'm sure."

Hewey's ears burned at the tone he had just heard. It was unmistakably Sapphic, so calculatedly so, in fact, that he could not resist turning to look. Humans were unappealing to him, but two female humans enjoying one another was a lure even trolls were susceptible to.

"Yeah, I guess I would have, too," Edelweiss purred, and Hewey was delighted to catch them ogling each other's racks. He gave his ticket to the stewardess at the gate and boarded the plane.

Once they had been seated, Edelweiss a hue more flushy than normal, Hewey attempted to elbow her knowingly.

"Ow!" Edelweiss cried, clutching at her shoulder. Hewey heard a distant wooden cracking as she rotated it.

"Sorry," he shrugged.

"Why did you do that?"

"Ah, well, I was going for a sort of nudge, nudge, right? Ask you what was up with that bird in line." He craned around, but failed to see the stranger's distinctive hair over the heads of the other passengers. "Where'd she go?"

"She said she was riding in first class," Edelweiss sighed. "But she asked if we would meet her for a drink in Seattle when we got there. She's never been there, so I told her about this cool bar called The Oubliette. She said she'd like to go. So."

"'So' is right."

Edelweiss rolled her eyes. "Hewey, please. I don't think of women like that."

"Like hell you don't, I saw you check out her knockers."

Edelweiss looked suddenly as though she was either re-living the checking out of the knockers, or calculating the severity of her reaction to having heard the word 'knockers.' Hewey assumed correctly that it was a combination of the two thought processes, and was confirmed in this line of reasoning when Edelweiss spontaneously dozed off. He had seen her do this before, as a survival mechanism to prevent overtaxing her delicate brain.

Hewey smiled, or grimaced, or showed his teeth (they were all the same to any curious onlooker) at Edelweiss' sleeping, furrowed brow. The plane thundered and popped and groaned in its general way, lulling some and torturing others.

Hewey picked up a discarded newspaper and perused the lurid world of human dramas. He found himself reading the following article:

MILAN, ITALY. The scientific community reeled today as the Ethics Committee announcement was revealed. Carfagna Industries Carfagna's Hound was given a cease and desist order on all new Hounds. This ruling comes after a long battle with animal rights groups and scientific communities.

This follows the shocking finding that the Carfagna's Hound is a genetic cocktail containing the genes of the common unicorn.

Dr. Dante Carfagna declined comment on his potentially disastrous evolutionary creation. It is still in question whether existing animals will be destroyed. Certain scientific groups have warned that the Carfagna's Hound, if allowed to inter-breed with other, unaltered dogs, could give life to creatures even more bothersome than the unicorn.

The Carfagna Laboratories released a statement that, "...suppressing this technology and this animal is reactionary and, in the long run, a backstep for mankind."

On another note, a Brazilian laboratory has announced its effort to cosmetically alter regular dogs to achieve a Carfagna's-like effect. This cosmetic surgery has been met with wild partying in Brazil, which has already caused several festivity-related deaths.

Across the Pacific, a Tokyo-based lab has announced it's intent to market a dog "attachment," a mechanical device that upgrades a common house pet into a Carfagna's-like garbage eater.

Hewey moaned, foghorn-like, loud enough to turn most of the heads in coach.

7.

"Gawl, that is one ugly dog," the baggage kid said, covering his nose even though nothing smelled. The man operating the conveyor belt chuckled. The kid leaned down close to the cage and gave it a solid rattle.

Kundalini yelled pitiously and then reined it back to a supersonic whisper. A tiny squeaky fart provided a momentary pitch-perfect harmony.

The kid turned back to the conveyor operator and guffawed. "You hear that! Haw!"

Kundalini yodeled in neither anger nor fear, then. The kid turned back and smacked the cage again. After the dog calmed, he again yodeled softly, then stood awkwardly in the tiny crate and smashed his nose against the slats.

"What is it, Lassie?" the kid asked, and then nearly busted a gut laughing. "Timmy's banging the neighbor girl in the barn? Let's go watch!" Right then the kid whipped around to garner appreciation for his fine comedic taste when a poorly stacked tower of luggage slipped from the hold and clobbered him into a temporary star-filled void. As the crew swarmed about, moving luggage and calling for an ambulance, the conveyor operator watched the Carfagna's hound with wary respect.

"What's up with the dog?" Someone asked the operator, jostling him as they carted the kid off on a stretcher.

"What's that supposed to mean?" he blurted.

"You've been staring at it for ten minutes. So, what's up with the dog?"

The operator noticed the EMT uniform on the man and swallowed. "Well, it was kinda odd, see. The dog, well, I think it was trying to warn the kid." He swallowed again. "It was whinin', like."

The EMT began looking at the operator's head as though looking for signs of damage. "Okay, sure. I've heard dogs whine before."

"No, it was different. It was whining regular-like when the kid was messing with it, and then when he went to walk away the dog would— look, I know it sounds kooky, but it was practically talking. You know how dogs do that sometimes? Like a really slow bark? Never mind."

"You okay man? You feel okay?" And then, more gently, "Can you tell me what day it is today? What your name is?"

"Yes, I'm okay, I said never mind!"

The EMT whistled. "Say, isn't that one of those unicorn dogs I heard about? Some kind of abomination? You didn't tell me it was one of them." The EMT walked to the crate and leaned over it, sticking his hand up to the slats slowly, as though the Hound might be able to collapse its cranial structure lightening fast and then squeeze through to bite him. Instead Kundalini belched ecstatically and wagged his sausagey tail. "Maybe it did talk. Who the fuck knows that these things can do."

The operator gulped and nodded quickly. "Yep. See you around."

"Sure, sure," the EMT said, still smiling at Kundalini.

CHAPTER THIRTEEN

1.

Hewey selected his words carefully. "I can't stand crazy people," he said.

He was leaving a bagel shop in downtown Seattle with Edelweiss and was secretly grumpy for having to check the gobhole into the hotel's pet spa. He sidestepped a homeless person trying to sell him news about homeless people and sighed. Hewey had been in Seattle for a few hours, but it had yet to impress. Sure, he thought, the view west was lovely with the trees and the ferries and the trees and the other crap. He still preferred the Queen's country.

"What did you say?" Edelweiss asked, distracted from her attempt to eat, walk and listen at the same time. She looked offended, but Hewey had come to recognize this as her fall-back expression for when she wasn't sure how to look.

He gestured back at the bagel shop. "You see those blokes?" he asked. A couple sat in the window. He had been staring at them the entire time they had been inside the shop, feeling a mysterious compulsion to continue, as though they were hired entertainment.

The young man was demure, quiet, small of frame and cleanly dressed, although a touch shabbily. On the table next to him was a pile of books, each bearing a heavy, and yet, ambiguous political title, such as: *Tofu Bullets: Fighting a Corrupted System (While Still Eating Delicious High Protein Meals)*, or another: *Why We Will Actually Save the World When No One Else Has Been Able To.*

But the girl the young man was sitting with, the girl made Hewey ill. She was masculine in stature and in dress, and instead of bearing this element casually, or even with pride, she threw her shoulders around, spoke in an affected low tone and pounded the table top with her balled fists. When she belched she would immediately laugh, shrilly, in an effort to draw attention to it.

She smacked at her bagel, mouth open, but only when her friend was looking at her. Her hair was cut in a shag around her ears in what Hewey observed was supposed to be an attempt at being crude, but it was ruined by its obvious meticulousness. She wore a large half-moon shaped piece of black jewelry through her septum that jiggled when she spoke and occasionally snagged on her bagel.

Hewey was rarely offended by people. More to the point, Hewey never expected anything from anyone but shit and idiocy, so when he was given otherwise he was pleasantly surprised. He did have ground rules, and they were as follows:

> *Denying the body's function to one's self or others is an insult to the maker.*

(It was nigh a Holy Quest to clear his ear canals/sinuses/bowels etc., when the need arose, and without acknowledging restrictive social mores).

> *There is no harm in trying.*

> *It is pointless to try if the odds are not in your favor.*

> *Animals are sinless, good souls, and food.*

> *Evil exists and, by nature, will prevail unless specifically countered.*

(This was not to say that Hewey believed that good triumphed over evil as pure universal algebra—on the contrary, he had never been presented with any evidence that the process wasn't random. It was just that, in the same way that he could point out evil with a huge knurled finger, he knew he was good, for better or for worse.)

No harm shall befall any cheese. This includes decay and mastication by an unrefined palate.

People should not behave outside their natures.

(Agreeing that this was a flimsy cage, Hewey was open to mutations of the rule, but on principal he despised cruel people even when they behaved generously, crude people even when they had flashes of brilliance, timid people even in their rash moments, et cetera and et cetera.)

And so, according to this last and most important rule, Hewey made the statement, "I can't stand crazy people," which brings us up to speed. "That girl," he announced, pointing at the revolting bagel shop patron, "Is insane. Not in any medical sense. In a character sense. She is askew." He made the appropriate hand gesture, his pointer finger swirling around his ear.

Still Edelweiss stared, again employing her powers of wounded incomprehension. "I don't think you should hate her for something she doesn't mean to do. Or be. Whatever."

"That is my point, my golden lass," he poked a cigarette at her general direction, which was down. "She *does* mean to be that way."

"How do you know?"

A vomit-filled teenager decompressed close to Edelweiss and so Hewey, still talking, lifted her clear one-handed. When he set her down she was already checking her pant leg and overskirt for splatters.

"Eddy, bird, it's like this. Crazy people, I mean people whose hardwiring is crossed, right? People who've had something jostled or took ten hits too many, they aren't lookin' to advertise," he shoved a gaggle of business men from his path and planted them both at the street corner waiting for a crossing light. He waited for Edelweiss to decipher the British inflection on the word 'advertise'. When her eyes finally registered, he continued. "It's difficult to explain, seeings how so many crazy blokes are inadvertently showing their skivvies. You follow, being bloody loud, not paying attention to social rules, right, right. So when I see this cur who is obviously not yet done telling the world to fuck off because she doesn't know who the hell she is, I have to assume she's crazy. Pretend crazy, that is." Hewey and Edelweiss crossed the street, a pedestrian just behind them getting plucked off by a Ford Conqueror taking an illegal left. "Where's the damn pub we're going to?"

"This way," Edelweiss said, walking. "But, everything you said totally denies her rights. I mean, no one wants to be insane! It's her right to be that way if she wants. I mean, if she can't help it. Not that there's anything wrong with that. Ogh!" Edelweiss angrily huffed.

"That may well be, dearest, but plenty of people want to appear insane that aren't. It's a thing they do to guarantee attention. And therein lies my disgust."

"You're assuming, Hewey, that how she was behaving was wrong, which I personally don't believe is possible. I mean, she must have gone through points in her life that give her reasons we don't know, so how are you to say that she doesn't deserve attention for that?" Edelweiss was drawing focus to herself with her tone.

Her voice, as you may know from high school anatomy, emanated from a gristly organ playfully coined her 'voicebox'. This unit is installed in the neck of the human female, which in this example is long, slender, tan, and has a little ditch at the front where sweat collects during spawning. As her voice raised and as the sound waves met and vibrated the eardrums of passersby, they were compelled to look at the origin of the sound. What they found was this thing, this beautiful impossible neck, like a cocaine-dusted sugarplum hung before them in a midwinter fever. Men tripped over curbs, boys shot their skateboards off into traffic and women swallowed their cough drops. Edelweiss was a warm, soft wrecking ball on Seattle's populace.

Hewey horked a loogey off the overpass and ignored the blood-curdling scream that followed. "It's a fairly interesting point you make, lass, but it's irrelevant. See, no social contract says you have to allow for someone's past. An old-lady killing psychopath gets the chair whether or not he was spanked with his mother's dildo as a child, right? It's the law of the jungle."

"That's not fair!" Edelweiss moaned in the twilight. "We're not talking about murder, we're talking about lesbians."

Hewey stopped on the sidewalk and narrowed his eyes at her. He began to laugh loudly. "No one said she was a lesbian."

"Yes, you did. You said."

"No, I just gave a description. You saw her. That could have easily been her boyfriend she was sitting with. That would be the obvious deduction, in fact."

"No, you said!" Edelweiss seemed to be faced with some great personal nightmare. "I didn't stereotype, you did. You said she was heterosexual." Edelweiss relaxed, seemingly free from whatever personal demon had just chased her.

"Bloody hell."

"I don't need your lecture, Hewey," Edelweiss snarled. "I know who I am. I am—" Edelweiss stopped, looking off to the side. "Wait a minute, I forgot what I was going to say."

Hewey pointedly looked above her head. "You said we were going to the Oubliette?"

"Yeah, it's just up ahead, I'm sure of it."

He rotated her by her shoulders. "Oh," she said. "Yes, this is it."

2.

What then makes bars so ultra-real?

It is tempting to lay it on the obvious, the whiskey and the gin, the candied cherries and the pickled eggs. There is a precious kiss of cocaine, re'em, nasty swamp weed and powdered baby laxatives being passed around the bathrooms, but that's not it.

And oh, the pageantry!

Such beautiful men and mysterious women that exist in that moment before you hear them speak. Alas, this is not the source either.

After running a dozen fantasy permutations of the game through various and varied simulations, only one factor remains:

In low lighting, all things vaporous become real.

3.

Hewey had been required to attend public school, since his family was poor in human money, and the only local public schools were human and the troll private schools were far away in deep central Europe. He was oft required in the course of school recitals, to play the roll of the Large Rock, the Wizened Tree, and once, the Barrel of Treacle.

As he got older, he became interested in (and blessedly good at) prop and lighting design, thus retiring him from the world of the stage and into the shadows behind it. Although the teachers each heaved a great sigh of relief, no one was happier than Hewey.

And then, during the choppy chimney-sweep version of West Side Story, it happened. Distracted, Hewey failed to note a curtain lift. A hand on the other side of the stage lifted it, leaving Hewey carving a melon-rind of skin off a callused palm with his pocket knife. Noticing that a prop cart on the other side of the stage was in danger of being seen, he decided to lope across and move it before the scenic curtain was pulled up. Except, the curtain had been pulled up. Expecting a large painting of a London alley to be in between him and the audience, off he strode. Onto center stage. Into a pod of Jets. In front of several hundred humans.

Hewey never grasped the concept of humiliation well, it being an emotion with the prerequisite of fearing someone else might be better than you. The audience of hilarity-wracked humans, clutching their bellies at his folly, could have been an audience of applauding Japanese tourists for all his emotional response. Maria began to desperately hiss at him to get off the stage. He walked off, making a bow of apology.

It was afterward that things changed. Suddenly he was The Oaf, and occasionally Bone-Eater. An instructor that had affectionately called him Grand Chap all year began calling him, as though in insult, just Hewey. Despite Hewey's excellent marks in logic, world politics and natural sciences, he was now openly chided for even the slightest of mistakes. It seemed to him that the merest suggestion of idiocy was all they needed to run with.

He let it go, eventually, left them all to drift off to seed, paunchy, salmon-colored lipstick seed. He traveled. He met a mysterious Turkish troll of the decidedly female variety and lost a few years of his life in her and her bottomless supply of hashish.

As you know, trolls live for a very long time. As you may not know, they have excellent memories. So what Hewey never forgot over the long years, was this: humiliation and embarrassment were nothing to him, but false judgement, that was something which he relished laying the smack down upon.

The foyer of the Oubliette was, in design as well as intention, a stage entrance, an element that did not go unnoticed. Hewey prepared himself, as a ninja might before a roof-top race through the dim of the new moon, by cracking his knuckles and sucking the contents of his sinuses back into his throat.

Action.

4.

In compliance with the local ordinance, the interior of the Oubliette was blood red, poorly lit, smoky, loud, and quirky-vintage. Upon closer inspection Hewey noticed it was all 40's French liquor ads. This could have been tasteful, say, in France.

As usual, Edelweiss created a soundproof pocket as she walked, words thrust aside on the prow of her crested mammaries and left to pool loudly in her wake. "Don't you love it?" she called back.

"No!" he nodded enthusiastically. She couldn't hear him and so she continued beaming.

Hewey noted with certain dismay that the bar had left no cliché unraped. Booths were cumbersome, mirrors on far walls made dizzying vistas of liquor bottles and in the center of the room there was a large pit fenced in wrought iron. When he leaned over he was treated to the rather embarrassing view of several poorly clad young handsome things writhing to characterless beat music. He blew smoke from his pipe at them.

"What do you want?" the bartender managed to scream flirtatiously at Edelweiss. The bartender then noticed the troll, paled, retreated, considered his life in brief, advanced, and then puffed his chest and eyed Hewey challengingly.

Hewey lifted his arm and casually freed a damp hair-and-lint construct the size of an almond from his pit and placed it on the countertop.

The bartender gagged. Edelweiss yelled, "I'll have an organic micro-brew. Extra micro, please."

"Uh, I've got an organic Hefeweizen brewed by bisexual Unitarians or an organic porter out of Alaska brewed in igloos by mentally disabled Inuits."

"Mentally disabled?"

"Under supervision."

"I'll take the Hefeweizen, please," Edelweiss shrieked.

"Eleven dollars," he bellowed.

"Wow," Edelweiss hollered, fumbling with her flimsy silk purse. "Beer got expensive while I was in Italy."

The bartender flexed his muscles, straining at a T-shirt too small for him. It was so small, in fact, that there was no way that he had reasonably thought it might fit him. "Italy, huh?" He set the beer on the bar. "That's hot! It's so expensive because all proceeds go to the Isla Lesbos Unitarian Universalist's Retreat Camp for Lower-Percentile Youth. It's a good cause."

"Oh totally! Hewey?"

"I guess, who cares."

"What?"

"What?"

Edelweiss laughed. "What do you want to drink?"

"Right, a black 'n' tan, please." Hewey enunciated at a decibel that is generally noted on graphs by the words "Inside a Jet Engine."

"A what?"

"Fuck it, give me some rye."

"What's that?"

"Bloody mash, you feckless Yankee sponge! Whisky? Scotch! Do you have firewater, comrade?"

"Oh, yeah! We've got Firewater!" The bartender screamed with relief. He returned with a martini glass of something red.

"What the fucking mouse cunt is that?"

"Firewater!"

Hewey looked imploringly at Edelweiss, which is a lot like looking hungrily at a slab of tire rubber. It's not clear what you expect to have happen. Also, Edelweiss was yet unable to tell any difference from one of Hewey's emotions to another. Still, in those same brief moments when your socks create an electrical charge, Edelweiss had a stroke of understanding. "Firewater is the name of a liquor we have here," she yelled. "It's spicy!"

Hewey swallowed the contents of the glass by putting his face very close to it, positioning his thumb and forefinger as though he were making an incredibly careful 'okay' sign, and moving in slowly. When the fragile glass stem was between his fingers, he pinched. It wobbled warningly. He thrust it at his face, swallowed, and after smacking his lips, he nodded. "Okay, I'll have one of those," he said, reaching behind the counter to select a pint glass.

"Look, there's Honey!" Edelweiss told Hewey, and bounded off.

Indeed, in the same manner that one eagerly awaits for a snarly, feral zoo creature to emerge from the cover of artificial foliage, tension filled the Oubliette. Heads turned slowly, as though to look at a frightening sound. Eyes stilled, flicked away, and returned.

This was all nothing new, as I am certain you know. There have always been those that illicit the side-long glances that become font-long before long. Whomever tries to convince that the soft-spoken wallflower has a secret allure on her side is a liar. It is the flame walker and the star thrower. It is and shall ever be the girl that can walk in heels and wear angora-any-thing. Or the guy.

It is always the one who said she had been "such an ugly little girl" that had become the swan (hint: the true "ugly little girls" will *never* make a reference to their past). Beautiful women who had been beautiful little girls will swear to their friends and lovers: they had been intolerable to look at, practically lepers. They will console each other. No, I was such an unattractive child. Everyone hated me.

Honey Smee, falsely demure and sincerely brooding, stepped long on heeled buckskin boots and greeted Edelweiss with a fierce hug. This is how women greet each other when they have a lot of points to make.

Hewey observed all of this from somewhere between educated suspicion and standard paranoia. Honey and Edelweiss were two distinct calibers of women, and if there were only one thing he could claim to have learned in his lifetime, it was that different calibers of women absolutely did not mix. Ever. Like the way two different species of predator did not chill out together, it was as simple as Wild Kingdom.

5.

For some people, the smoking of cigarettes was not so much a drug habit as much as it was an affectation that could be of either trashy or high order. Like wearing false nails, if you're not following me. As it were, Honey had fabulously false nails of a most tasteful sort, the kind that were indistinguishable from real ones (except they were superior), and hardly ever took a drag from her cigarette.

Because of this, Edelweiss could not remove her focus from the visage before her: the slender hands with their precariously balanced cigarette like a parlor trick, the way she placed the nail of the thumb and forefinger together while smoking and clicked them in moments otherwise still. The way that she would raise the filter to her lustrous lips, part them before the butt in an exclamation point and then change her mind and lower it. If Edelweiss had been granted the gift of perception, she would recall the fine and fragile way that geisha poured tea, the very form of localized perfection.

The two women had located a booth where the sound was somehow confused; it was occasionally loud, in random bursts, but most often it was muddled and soft.

Honey offered a cigarette from an ivory case.

"Those will kill you," Edelweiss chirped and then felt unexpectedly nerdy.

Honey raised her eyebrows conspiratorially, two conductor's batons raising in a mirror. She sipped her cocktail.

"So," Honey said, as though they had just then seen each other. "I feel as though I know you from somewhere." Cocktail punctuation.

"I feel the same way, but I can't remember where we've met."

Honey paused as though in reflection. "Did we discuss something about the Himalayas once?"

"Oh my god, I love the Himalayas! They're my favorite mountain range!"

"Well, that must be it, then. They're mine too. The most beautiful place I've ever been."

"You've been there?"

"Sure I have, I thought that's what we talked about. Like I always say, you have not lived until you've shared a mug of salted yak milk tea with your sherpa."

Edelweiss' eyes twinkled in awe.

Honey stroked an eyebrow in reverie. "I was sure that was where I met you. You wern't there on behalf of the Dalai Lama?"

"Me? Shit, no, I've never met him."

"Hmm. Wait, were you at the Smoldering Woman Festival?"

Edelweiss slapped her palm down hard on the table. "No! Have you been there too?"

Honey lit a fresh cigarette in two fingers arched like the Pope's benediction and nodded.

"Wow! What was it like, was it great? I bet it's the most wicked great thing ever!"

"It's, oh, difficult to describe," Honey narrowed her eyes, trying to recall the image from a news special she watched years before. "I mean, what isn't great about the whole desert full of muddy, shirtless," she gagged a little and took a drink, "green-dreadlocked anarchists on enough re'em to decimate the entire North American unicorn population?"

"Ha ha! I knew it. I am going to go next year. Hey, maybe we could go together!"

"Oh," Honey took another gulp of her gimlet and nodded, wincing. "Yes, maybe we haven't met. Maybe we are just two pure spirits who still remember the same star-filled void." She finished her drink.

Edelweiss became very still.

Now, have you ever accidentally said something *too* meaningful? Think carefully, as this question often has an underestimated gravity. It happens rarely and is recognized even less. More importantly, it is often just a brief query, a 'simple' statement, something launched without a target in mind. It is precisely these missiles, my friend, that cause the most damage.

Honey Smee is an observant person, for a human. This is why when the words left her mouth never again to return, she braced herself, internally clutching her alcohol molecules in a death grip. She said something too meaningful to someone she despised. Now there would be no end to how friendly she would need to be in order to maintain her cover.

Edelweiss whispered, but some malevolent force allowed the words to find Honey's ear despite the peripheral roar: "I have never felt this understood before."

"'Nother drink?" Honey asked, standing. "Alright, me too."

When Honey returned she headed off Edelweiss' ensuing commentary by asking, "So, tell me about yourself."

Over the next half-hour, as Edelweiss unknowingly and semi-knowingly lied through her life story ("I did the college thing, and honestly, I was immature enough then for it to evolve me, to allow me to grow," and, "Oh, I love Europe. I feel at home there, really at home."), Honey prepared herself. She was very good at auto-piloting through conversations and only occasionally dropped back in to catch words like 'communocentric,' 'hypercooperative' and 'psychedelic spawning teepee.' All the while she reviewed her life. This was how Honey meditated.

She didn't become nostalgic or ruminate on life. It was more of a complicated catalog. She mentally culled her music collection for anything that might be considered too "last year." She used her imagination to compare outfits and ferret out anything either too unusual or too homogenized. The beret, for example, was working, but the burnt orange shawl was definitely beginning to distract. She tried to recall how old her mascara was and momentarily panicked when the information could not be dredged. The thought of it being rancid made her try to flinch away from her own eyelashes. But ah! That's right, she had just picked it up last week.

All of these things settled, Lego-like, into Honey's impenetrable wall of self. When she finished her martini and savored the lone olive like a single, grand orb of caviar, she interrupted.

Edelweiss had been saying, "... must have been protesting outside that nuclear power plant for hours. We probably got saturated with radiation. Did you know that miso soup actually counteracts radiation in the body?"

"That's lovely, look, Edelweiss, I'll just come out and say this. I need your help."

Edelweiss froze. "Okay."

"Just, 'okay'?" Honey had a speech prepared.

"Sure."

"Don't you want to know what for?"

"Okay."

Honey Smee flared her nostrils, smiling. "So, the reason I am in Seattle," she reached into her purse and pulled out her little genius, her three-hours-at-CopyTown-masterpiece, her coup de grace of profound scheming.

"What is it?"

"I just set it down in front of you."

"I see, but what is it for?" Edelweiss was fascinated by the pamphlet and touched an edge.

"It's a pamphlet, Edelweiss. You read it."

The front was an image of a small, happy girl admiring a perfect specimen of puppyhood through a window. "What does it say?"

Honey reeled at what she hadn't even begun to imagine as being a problem. Anger swelled in her like gas. She asked, as kindly as she could manage, "Do you have reading problems, sweetie?"

"No, why?"

"Will you read it, please?" Honey commanded and Edelweiss flinched.

The pamphlet itself was large and arranged like a strip comic, four colors and everything. It read: *ALL NEW AND IMPROVED HYPOALLERGENIC PUP'N-A-TUBE.*

The first frame was a 50's style housewife fussing with a shovel. A pipe-smoking neighbor was leaning over a short fence, concerned. His speech bubble said, *"Hiya, Muriel, whatcha doing?"*

The next frame was the woman leaning back, sweaty. She said, *"Oh, just these pesky puppy corpses."*

In the next frame, she said, *"What a nuisance! You know, Harv, the kids lose interest in them the moment they stop being puppies. Then they either starve to death or I have to drown them in the tub. As if a woman didn't have enough to do, what with all the cooking and cleaning and eggsac maintenance!"*

Harv, still smoking, said: *"I am so glad I am a man."*

Edelweiss looked up. "What is this? Is this some pro-life propaganda? Oh, I have had just about enough of this anti-ovo-blocking bullshit."

"Edelweiss, keep reading."

The woman, while still in the exact same position, said: *"Oh, the inconvenience!"*

And the man, as if suddenly having a notion, said: *"I have a notion! This may solve all your puppy problems!"*

The woman, still unmoving, said: *"What is it? A magic puppy?"*

The man's bubble said: *"Ha! You said it, Muriel! Now, have you ever heard of Pup'n-a-Tube?"*

The woman put her hand to her mouth, puzzled, and said: *"Why no, Harv, that sounds incredible."*

The man, still smiling without defined teeth lines, said: *"It is. Imagine the fun your Timmy and Harriet could have with a new puppy and then multiply it by ten."*

The woman said: *"That sounds like a lot!"*

The man, righting himself and coming around the fence, said: *"All of the cuteness of a traditional puppy, but without all the muss. Pup'n-a-Tube is hypoallergenic, clean, self-contained fun for the whole family. Pup'n-a-Tube arrives in a hermetically-sealed polyvinyl plastic environment, ready for play. In the safety of its polymer shield, Pup'n-a-Tube can survive trips to school, trips to space, heck, even a trip to the pool!"*

The woman replied cheerily: *"I bet puppy would get a kick out of that!"*

The man: *"Who wouldn't? Best of all, Pup'n-a-Tube is packaged for easy disposal, so when kids get tired of him, simply toss him in the trash."*

The woman looked wistful. Her talk-bubble said: *"That sounds like heaven. I bet it's costly."*

The man, pointing his pipe at her, said: *"Why, no! Not when you compare it to the cost of kibble and general damage to your valuables your pet is bound to cause."*

Woman: *"And how!"*

Man: *"You said it!"*

The woman, again concerned, said: *"But Harv, you know my kids. They have such terrible Attention Deficit Disorder, I am not sure that even Pup'n-a-Tube would entertain them."*

"But that is the beauty of Pup'n-a-Tube, Muriel," the man said, moving still closer to her. *"Pup'n-a-Tube is always changing! It comes with nothing in it, it seems, so you just plug in the tube and watch the magic happen! The fetus gestates before your eyes, now isn't that educational?"*

The woman claps and said, *"For me as well! I know nothing about fertilization."*

The man, laughing, said, *"Who does? So Timmy and Harriet won't fight over our pal Pup'n-a-Tube, get two and customize them."*

The woman frowned. *"How would I customize them, Harv?"*

"Well Muriel, they thought of everything. Before you plug Pup'n-a-Tube in and start the process, just screw one of the patented FairyDust™ injectors in and introduce one of the many varieties of gene replacement therapy viruses."

The woman threw her hands up, saying, *"I didn't understand a word you just said, smarty!"*

"Of course you don't, and don't worry your little head over the details. All they do is mutate the fetus from conception to anything you want. For example, there is a FairyDust™ booster for Flattest Puppy in the Land, and I tell you, nothing is funnier than a boneless puppy! Also, there is Pretty Puppy, which the girls adore with its long eyelashes and custom tinting you can choose."

"I think I'd like that one!" the woman's bubble exclaimed.

"Well, my favorite is Shaky Puppy, Quaky Puppy. Boy, when they get to tremorin', it's nothing but laughs!"

The woman threw her arms around the man, saying: *"Oh Harv, will men ever stop making my life easier?"*

He patted her on the back, saying: *"Maybe someday Muriel, but not anytime soon."*

Edelweiss read over the pamphlet twice more to be sure that she was reading it right. Every time she read something awful that angered her, she got a delicious shiver up her legs and back, but the print was so small that she was starting to get a headache.

Honey waited, drink perched halfway between rest and imbibement. Her look could only and should only be described as villainous. This is because that is what she was, and to document it otherwise would be an injustice to the reader. This pause was borne from Honey Smee's delightedly anxious desire to see her plan unfurl before her like a dry-cleaned 380-threadcount sheet in Saffron.

Obligingly, horror claimed Edelweiss' features as poison paralyzes the newly insured husband. She panted a little. She went rigid, then slack, then rigid again. She opened her hands imploringly to Honey, begging for her assistance.

"We have to do something," Honey said, and laughed lightly. To anyone but Edelweiss, the laugh would have been obviously mocking, but Edelweiss was in her own stew composed of almost entirely rage, confusion and a case of the munchies.

"We do," Edelweiss hissed, and rolled her eyes wildly as a frightened donkey might. "But what? Oh! Do you know how to make explosions?"

Honey sniggered and waved her hand in negation. "A bomb? No, there is going to be a big protest up in Shorebeach Cove, at the headquarters of Pet'n-a-Tube. It's tomorrow. That's where I'll be."

"That's perfect! But where is Shorebeach Cove? Are there buses going?"

"Sure, sure. Why, are you interested?"

"Hell yeah!"

"That's fantastic," Honey beamed. "Say, here's an idea. Why don't you ride in my car? I have a rental."

Edelweiss bounced in her seat. "Yeah, great. Oh, but I am travelling with a troll." She frowned. "He can't fit into cars."

A snarl crossed Honey's fine face. "Oh, too bad. I guess you can't go then."

Edelweiss fiddled with a strand of beads and bones tied around her wrist. She was sure she should be at the protest, but she had brought Hewey to Seattle show him America—it seemed... something... to leave him behind. Unable to summon the correct feeling from her subconscious, Edelweiss said, "That's okay, Hewey wouldn't even be interested. When do we go?"

Honey smiled wide enough to hurt herself.

6.

After one drink at the Oubliette failed to make Hewey's view on life any better, he decided to leave. He wanted a beer. In a public house with a wooden floor, a fireplace and ideally cranky patrons. The Firewater had been good, actually, but it was giving him heartburn and besides, he knew from experience that sugary liquor did things to your bowels that would make a seasoned sea captain shudder.

He left the bar after locating Edelweiss and waving at the back of her head. He made eye contact with the woman she was sitting with and for a short moment, ever so fleetingly, he was fairly sure that she flipped him off. He shrugged, stepped outside and admired the steady red lights of the bloatshark net protecting the sleeping retarded babe, Seattle. It was a lovely evening, the fall air ripe with smells and gently cold. Hewey then squatted, popped his knees and made for the hotel at troll speed, which, as very few humans are aware, is disconcertingly fast. Hewey figured it as an evolutionary step for chasing rabbits across the moors. As Hewey rocketed past cars honking through city traffic, the sea air whistled in his ears and in a mere fraction of the time it had taken Edelweiss and Hewey to get to the bar, he had returned.

He checked the gobhole out of the pet spa where the hapless groomers had been attempting to attach pink bows to the top of his head. Hewey asked them to point which way to the nearest park and they were off.

Hewey had never had the misfortune of watching music videos and was totally unaware of how he was re-enacting one.

It is, admittedly, a stretch of the imagination to turn a leather-clad troll attempting to frolic with a furry sack of manure into a music video, but have some faith. As for the type of music, it becomes a tad complicated. One might accurately emote this by playing a loud phonographic version of "Best Friend" by Queen. Or possibly, "Me and Julio Down by the Schoolyard" by mister Paul Simon. Or, at certain moments, "I Think We're Alone Now," but as covered by Tiffany. They, and many more, are each in turn too irreverent for words. Not counting the lyrics, I mean. Or my trying to explain it.

7.

Caty Jowl was a good girl, and that's why she was walking through Freeway Park at night. She was known to tell people that she was a feminist first and foremost. Just like that. "I am a feminist, first and foremost."

Because it sounded better than, "I am just your average white girl in that I enjoy having convictions."

That very night over vegetarian sushi, Caty's friend Sarah discussed some finer points of feminism. "Yes, but if you walk through there, you are asking to get raped," Sarah was saying.

Caty shook her head. "As long as women believe that, they will continue to accept what is happening to them."

"It's not an agreement, Caty, it's a fact of life. Like cancer, if you smoke two packs a day for most of your life, you will get lung cancer and die. Cancer and rape happen despite what women *believe*."

Caty struggled to bite a piece of sushi in half which resulted in a tiny shower of cucumber and rice. "I can't help it," she said. "I am a feminist, first and foremost."

So she found herself walking near the park later that evening and about to avoid it. It was a pleasant early fall evening, clear as a glass-bottom boat. She watched the park sadly. What kind of person would she be if she didn't go in after smugly implying that all women should? So Caty stormed it, practically running inside, thinking suddenly of mom's knitted afghans, old Rusty on his rug being cancerous and only generally dog-shaped, and photos of herself, age nine, sans a couple of teeth. It was a very small portion of her life flashing before her eyes prematurely.

And, just as the anxiety began to fade, as the crickets sang and she passed an older couple walking who has smiled at her, she was attacked.

Or, oddly, someone dove at her feet, throwing her viciously to the concrete path. Initially she was quite angry, as anyone would be, but when she heard the grunting and the zipper being pulled (or was that flatulence? Her already post-traumatic stressed mind was fast at work scrambling the details) she began to scream.

Caty wasted no time composing a detailed, slightly detached and mostly tear-filled account of her horrors with an unassigned portion of her brain. She was enrolled at the University of Washington studying the human noggin and had begun to develop certain theories regarding her own corpus collosum, which as you know is the hidden, shy, puffy-taco shape in the brain that is responsible for helping the right and left lobes communicate. It is the desperate child living between two perpetually codependent, non-communicative parents. Ms. Jowl was suspicious that her own corpus collosum was allowing independent activities to develop in her brain, or, to revisit an already stale metaphor, allowing her thought-halves to retire to separate bedrooms. What she didn't know was that *everyone* who studied the brain developed paranoid diagnosis for themselves, and moreso, that diagnosis was almost always accurate. The difference between the average man and the brain surgeon is that the brain surgeon has a better idea of how, exactly, he's fucked in the head.

Unaware that she was constructing a shareware version of her experiences (even as they happened), Caty was thus unaware that her observations were wrong. Eventually, though, the two components caught up with each other and she went real-time.

"Help!" Caty shrieked in a rather girly fashion, embarrassing herself. She had thought she heard someone calling out to her. She hollered again, this time with more aplomb. She had begun to realize that she was lying on her back, on a damp sidewalk, with no one else around. The stars demurely twinked through the orange leaves above. She rolled some wet gravel between her fingers and sighed. She lifted her head.

"Hello?" she called, her voice cracking.

Out of the darkness, a hand descended. The palm was the size of her face, and it beckoned to her, so she grasped it. She squealed as she went from a rather casual sprawl to standing upright in one swift whip.

"You took quite a spill, bird," a voice said. It was the sound of several large, rusted gears misaligning and then turning anyway.

She found herself gaping up at a seven and a half foot troll, yellow eyes lit oh-so-faintly from within. He was holding a moldy sack under one arm.

"Oh," she whispered. "I was attacked."

A match struck above her leaving behind a red tracer. "No, no, he doesn't attack. The gobhole can't even see in the dark, and he was running. Good thing he can't run very quickly, huh?"

Caty looked left to right. "Excuse me," she ventured. "Who is 'he'?"

The troll pushed forth with his mildewey bundle and Caty recoiled from the odor. Was he insane? Had she just been saved from rape or death or some other embarrassment by a cracked-up troll? It was then that the bundle blinked wetly at her and whuffed softly in the way that polite dogs have.

"Oh, hello," she said nasally, for her nose was automatically forced to cease function. The odor of the dog combined with the troll's barely tanned leather vest was enough to cause her brain to short out olfactory centers prophylactically. Caty gave the head a scratch and it groaned, gassed off its lower quadrant and sighed. The farting noise struck a memory.

"Sorry, did you see someone run?" she asked, pointing past the troll.

"'Fraid not. You were entirely alone."

"But I was knocked to the ground," she turned and flung her hand limply. "Right there."

The troll squatted and Caty started at the sound of a tree roughly ripping from rocky soil. "Was that your knee?" she whispered.

"Oh, aye, it's been cracking good lately," Hewey rumbled happily, flattered at the attention. "My dog knocked you over. I am very sorry," Hewey then raised his hand to the dim park. "I get the feeling this isn't a chipper place for chippies, am I right?"

"I have no idea."

Hewey pointed to a group of laughing, well-dressed men coming through the park, but even the ocherous light and the echoing laughter could not ease the oppressive sensation of a concrete-walled park, loud with waterfall white noise. "How about I walk you out of this place, right behind those fellas, so if I'm a predator they'll save you and if they are I'll save you."

Caty looked around the park, the inky interior of the rhododendrons and the narrow, blind staircases. "Okay."

Hewey put the Hound down and, as they walked, Caty watched the various and random crashes the Hound suffered, the asymmetric gait that resulted in painful, prolonged wipeouts, not to mention the gargantuan amounts of trash he ingested along the way. At one point, when he found a large piece of discarded cigar butt, the Hound swooned momentarily like a silent screen starlet, before gobbling it down.

"Mister, is he going to be okay after eating all this trash?"

"Well, I will have to give him some newsprint and plastic when we get back to the hotel, you know how it is. They have such loose doody unless they get some roughage in them."

"Eh?"

"And some antacids, maybe some milk of magnesia."

"Um."

They reached the edge of the park, the city beyond not much safer. The troll and the girl shook hands and parted ways.

"People are okay," Hewey said to the gobhole. He lit a smoke. "A little nervy, but okay. I've been hanging out with Eddy-bird too long." The dog gazed intently at the burning cigarette. "Don't beg."

8.

If you choose to consider some emotional reactions embarrassing, than you must admit they all are. The body responds to everything, even when the brain doesn't. Happiness, if not infectious, is embarrassing. You've seen that woman at the café, squealing like a game show contestant at her friend's joke, clapping a little like a toddler, and throwing her head back in such a way that makes her neck fat constrict and gather. You have to cringe. And the man in the line at the bank, getting red and sputtering at the wait. He is in a hurry, and rightfully so—his blood sugar is low, he's had a long day at work—but there he is, puffing like a pimple, fidgeting and dropping his briefcase and *you hate him for it.*

The nervous child at the pool? Irritating.

The confused older gentleman at the library checkout? Horrific.

The flirtatious bartender? Loathsome.

It is not that they are doing anything wrong, not in the least. In fact they are being authentic human beings, reacting internally to the external, functioning properly for the most part. It is their bodies that you hate. Why? It's all too fucking complex, that's why, it reminds us that we are loosely contained tubes of meat and fat and juice and who-the-hell-knows what else. Do you want to be reminded of that?

Nevertheless, that is how the system works. File a complaint.

Hewey smuggled the gobhole up to the hotel room by stuffing him into a black plastic bag found lying next to an alley Dumpster. By the time Hewey was in the elevator, the dog had suckled a hole through the bag and slid heavily to the floor. Hewey walked casually to the room, unlocked the door and entered, re-securing it with the stealth of a troll before spreading out prone on the carpet.

Early in the morning, Hewey heard a note slide under the door. It read, in sealed hotel stationary:

> *Hoowy,*
> *i am so fucking mad! i feel my soul be taken litle by litle, totally? their making puppys in NONRECYCLYBLE con-taners. how fucked is that? we r going to stop it. i know you don't protest (u r a man after all) but if u want join it is in shorebeach cove. honey sez it is up to woman to fight for the earth. right on!!! Edelweiss*

Hewey's uncontrollable physical response was this: his veins and arteries swelled, flushing his skin. His apocrine glands excreted sweat, which is an important observation since they are the glands responsible for emotional perspiration, unlike the eccrine glands which respond to external heat. His arrector pili muscles constricted, raising every little hair up along his arms and the back of his neck, and his salivary glands went temporarily AWOL.

Hewey was as capable of extrasensory perception as the next troll, in that he occasionally had foreboding sensations, but they were almost always overreactions. He sometimes had the feeling that the phone was going to ring before it did. Once he had a nightmare that a friend had faded into a dense brown fog, and that friend in the waking life soon after revealed a near-crippling but utterly secret dependency on opiates. He often had the feeling that someone was behind him when no one ever was. He bet ravenously on football and lost more often than not. But reading the note from Edelweiss, now that was interesting.

Hewey flung the door open and stuck his head into the hallway, catching the bellhop just as he was about to enter the elevator. "Hey chap?"

"Yeah?"

"Where'd this note come from? A lass?"

"Uh, I dunno, I was just sent to deliver it."

"Ah, so she might still be downstairs."

The bellhop looked uncomfortable. "Uh, no, I was supposed to bring it up here before my break, and that was like, a few hours ago."

Hewey nodded thanks and flipped a quarter to the bellhop hard enough to put a welt on the kid's temple.

Hewey shut the door and leaned back against it. Something was wrong.

He looked to the gobhole who in turn took the opportunity to whine at a supersonic level.

"Me too," Hewey sighed angrily. He knew what he had to do even as he attempted to convince himself not to. When the goodness in him grappled to a superior position, Hewey began to pack Edelweiss' bags for her, and when he was done he called down for a rental van with super-wide seats and extra headroom.

9.

"Where is Shorebeach Cove?" He asked the girl at the car rental desk.

The woman took out a large book of maps and trudged through it for a few minutes before Hewey said, "How 'bout that index, huh?"

The girl glared at Hewey and placed a delicate fingertip over the gap where Shorebeach Cove would have been in the alphabetical order and then grinned triumphantly. "You sure that town was in Washington State?"

Hewey scratched his scalp and rained down confetti-sized pieces of sebum on the countertop. "I suppose I'm not sure. I was pretty damn sure, though. Some kind of factory up there, something like that?"

Another worker at the car rental counter stepped forward then, a demure, hovering man of about forty. "There's a factory up there," he said, pushed his glasses up his nose and tenderly picked up the map. He hauled it over to an elderly copier while the counter girl watched with mild interest.

When the man came back with the copy he drew a highlighter path up the state and left it there, the hesitant tipped pen leaving a neon bloom. "Well, I think it's around there. I don't know exactly. But you can ask around, I'm sure that the locals can tell you."

Hewey grinned back at the counter girl in mock-delight. "Well, fantastic, chap, thanks." Hewey handed the credit card to her.

"Edelweiss Santucci?" she inquired, narrowing her eyes.

"Yes?" Hewey asked.

"That's a pretty name for a..."

"For a troll? Yes, it is, it's a traditional name." He nodded and teepeed his hands in front of his chest.

"Of course. Sign here."

It was still early morning when Hewey set out, eating a bagel with one hand and smoking with the other. The gobhole was belted into the seat across from him eating the bagel bag and an empty Styrofoam coffee cup. The road ahead was foggy and ethereal, trees looming like guardians, sun nowhere specific and the little orange bar on the speedometer flirting with the 75 mph mark.

"Why do I care? Nothing is wrong. I don't even like her," Hewey said to the gobhole who belched and then spontaneously began chewing something. "I got bloody bad feelings about some tart she meets at a bar. I am a piece of work, gobhole, a full-blown sucker."

Hewey chewed a fingernail and let the curl clatter to the floor of the van. The gobhole whimpered. Hewey nodded and said in a low voice, "I know."

And the two propelled themselves steadily toward something gone wrong that they didn't feel like fixing. But Hewey knew that curiosity was always worth indulging in, as were doughnuts and packets of something called corned nuts, which were neither corned nor nuts as near as he could tell, but nevertheless thoroughly enjoyable. He felt bad that the gobhole seemed to have trouble digesting them, but the Hound didn't seem to mind.

CHAPTER FOURTEEN

1.

I would hazard to guess, if I were forced to, and I say this with the utmost reservation and I mean *maybe*, if no other factors are taken into account and I could alter this statement any time and on my prerogative, that humans are simple creatures.

Which isn't to say easy. Sometimes those bothersome steel ring mind teasers only require three twists of the ring to free them, but damned if you aren't at it with a hacksaw, cursing its sinister origins and vowing eternal vengeance on it before five minutes are up. Things both wrecking and splendid orbit on such modest little paths.

For example, the fate of the Americas, and thus, major portions of the world by proxy, rest in the grimy palms of seven people. Instinct would tell you to know these people, to pin down some facts on them, like gender and race. Did they have kind faces, or did they seem hard and guarded? Did you trust them? Were they attractive, aged, wise or greedy looking?

You don't know.

They were, in fact, sitting together in a room as they have done for most of their prevailing memory. Sometimes they leave to sleep. They share a bathroom down the hall. They are like queen's larvae; pale, plump, helpless, and potentially great.

"Get ahold of Mr. Galloway."

Several of them looked up. "Why?"

"Have you got something?"

"Are you confirming my New Zealand cyclone lead?"

"No, no cyclone. Look, that lead is almost 48 hours old, it isn't going to be confirmed. Let it go."

"It was clear as fucking crystal."

"You said that about the rat plague last week, too."

"No, that was me."

"Right, sorry."

"Listen, cheesedicks, here's the shit. Tortillos Corn Chips are going to discontinue the Rajun Cajun flavor. Like, soon, next week maybe, a woman with reddish hair, she's axing it. She's saying something about it being corporate, but she loves undermining the younger exec who pushed the idea. Fuck that!"

"Hey, I've got confirmation on that. Anorexic-looking broad?"

"Yeah, that's her. Call Galloway, this is ridiculous. Have him call the company that makes Tortillos. Fuck, I cannot work under these conditions. I am too goddamn busy trying to keep the world from falling into a sick low-fat regime to focus on my work."

"I don't care for that flavor."

"Yes, and that's why we told you to stop eating them, remember? Since you like the Saucy Aussie flavor so much, you can have them all."

"Is there even any such thing as 'Australian flavor'? Is there a cuisine of Australia?"

"Sure there is, every culture has a cuisine."

"So what is it?"

"Let me see," there was some crunching noises from the back of the room. "Spicy. And sort of... shrimpy? Fishy? Maybe it's ranch dressing. Is ranch its own flavor, or is it something else?"

"Ranch is buttermilk and pepper, dumbass."

"Hey!"

"What?"

"I've got something strange here, but I can't concentrate with you microcephaloids yammering. Is it just me, or is it a bad idea that we sent out another oracle to bring back the White Flower? We can't get any triangulation on them at all, now."

"Well, we didn't send her. Galloway did."

A hushed contemplation sank like a fog. Someone tried to whistle low, but it came out as a reedy off-key squeak. "There sure is no way to get a triangulation. Oh, how nasty. I don't like her."

"Which one?"

"The bounty hunter, she thinks she's better than us."

"Yeah, that's why she's out there tracking down shit like a dog. She can be a scent hound all she wants, we've got the control."

"The troll is with them."

"Don't start with that shit again, no one else sees the troll with them. You're stuck in some subspace eddy."

"Maybe they're separate? Like, one comes later. It's too foggy to tell with the White Flower and that bounty hunter together."

"It's true, we're not going to get clarity on him, but my guess is that he's not with them or we'd be able to triangulate them. Until we've got something better, I don't want to hear it."

"But I've got clarity."

"The fuck you do, fucknut. You have been saying that for days and there has not been a single vague confirmation. Are you cracking up?"

The room went quiet, with the exception of someone loudly chugging soda. Regret hung like flatus. The challenge was too much like threatening to strike a match inside a propane tanker—if one of them was crazy, or even losing prophetic accuracy, there was a good chance they all were. They were now organs inside the same organism, separately crucial and equally dependent.

"I'm not cracking up. I wish you would give me some validation when I tell you I've got clarity."

"Alright, fine, I'll tell Galloway."

"No, you're right, it's no good yet. Just don't call me a fucknut, okay?"

"Does that mean nymphomaniacal or is it like a cashew?"

"I think like a cashew."

There was a sudden scramble for one of the cabinets. "Yeah, hand me one of those cans of peanuts, too. No, honey roasted."

"Give me the salted."

"I thought we had some kind of Cajun flavor?"

"Oh for god's sake, get a Cajun flavored salt lick or something. Not everything needs to be Cajun flavored!"

"Dude, what about Cajun pretzels? That would rock!"

"Totally."

2.

By some fey stroke of luck Edelweiss had found a progressive folk rock station somewhere in the valleyed, radio-resistant wastes north of Seattle. Edelweiss had slept through much of the morning, leaving Honey Smee to a reflective (both internal and externally mist-glinty) dawn. There were few cars on the highway, but most drivers were orchestrating complicated espresso cradling acts. Honey looked down at her own Heirloom Harvest Latte, in Cardamom-Hubbard Squash flavor. It was perilously close to Edelweiss' NutriBloom Hot Fruit Soothie cup lid. Honey was fairly certain that germs were unable to make the short leap from the one cup lid to the other, but to be sure she rotated her tiny drinking hole 180 away from Edelweiss'.

Honey was smug, then, with her prize drooling into the rental car's leather seats. The girl had, at first, been disapproving of going to the pro-test (Honey openly laughed every time the girl mentioned it, delighting in the ridiculousity of her plan and the voracious manner in which it had been believed) in a luxury vehicle, but after Honey's half-hearted insis-tence that it'd been the only rental available, Edelweiss had made short work of turning on the electric seat warmers and optimizing the passen-ger-side climate control. Edelweiss had made sure the negative ion switch was toggled to 'on' before hunkering down with her rather expensive breakfast drink. In moments she had passed out.

Honey was left to calibrate her thoughts. The girl was going to fetch top dollar, but Honey's pride was based on something deeper than that. It was a job well-done, a particularly grueling job. Honey grimaced as the heater drew out a mildewy, catty funk from the girl, invisible tendrils of noxious waft slowly filling the well-sealed car interior. Honey fished from her purse a small atomizer of eau de parfum and doused the girl. It was small help.

An hour later, the girl sat up. "Oh my, what time is it?"

"It's almost nine."

"Shit!" Edelweiss said happily. "I haven't been up this early in years." She leaned her forehead on the window to look outside and when she sat back up there was a translucent smear left behind. "It's so beautiful here."

Honey made a vague noise. It was the best she could muster. It was mile upon mile of future toilet paper as far as she was concerned. No, not even. She was more fond of the cotton toilet paper they were making now. Better yet, something that she had never told anyone was that she had started using baby-wipes. The only flaw with the baby-wipes was that they became surreally cold during the night, so when she used the toilet first thing in the morning and went to wipe, she had to brace herself.

"Eeeeee!" Edelweiss screeched. Honey reflexively slammed the brakes, slowing them down to fifty. *"What?"*

Edelweiss was pointing wildly at something ahead of the car. "Oh my god! There! Do you see that?"

Through the mist, Honey caught a sight of something writhing and thrashing in the undergrowth. For a fraction of a moment she thought it was a group of people and she squinted in fascination. When she realized what it was she let out a hissy sigh of disgust.

It was a small pack of unicorns, not unusual for this part of the Northwest. Though generally the American unicorn made its habitat in the city, where there was an overabundance of garbage for them to eat, the climate in the surrounding forests seemed to agree with them as well. As near as she could tell, the whole lot of them were mounting each other in a rise-n-shine orgy. Sometimes they were stacked three or four deep, and only a few were missing their horns.

Edelweiss was cooing something about the free creatures of the world.

"Those things are horrendous. I can't believe they're a protected species," Honey said. She felt a racy delight in pissing the girl off while simultaneously kidnapping her.

"Oh, how can you say that? They were here long before we were and pure, living things in their own right. We just use them and use them and never stop complaining about how much we hate them. I'm sick of it!" Edelweiss had such an earnest look on her face that Honey smiled. It was the same look that children get when they are trying to lie, that sort of backless concern that had all the right components: the wrinkled brow, the higher tone of voice, the rambling speech, but it lacked a specific sincerity. Honey thought perhaps it had something to do with being a degree *overly* convincing. A mild desperation. And Honey was smiling because it didn't seem to matter to Edelweiss how Honey responded to anything—Edelweiss was too dim to link reaction to action.

"Well," Honey drawled. "I see what you mean. They are a living thing, one that we take for granted. But we should farm them, like we do cows."

Edelweiss shifted. "No, no, don't you see? That's like saying that we should farm the birds that fly free in the sky for their feathers or something!"

"You mean, like geese?"

"Right," Edelweiss smiled. "Like geese. Could you imagine imprisoning such a noble creature?"

"Alas, I cannot."

Honey considered their conversation for a moment and surprised herself by saying, "I suppose it's rather lucky for the unicorns that their horns grow back and that we need them, isn't it? Otherwise we would've killed them all by now, the filthy little shits."

Edelweiss swooned tragically. "It's true, the unicorn is such a noble creature, protected and saved by its own nobility."

Honey turned the radio off. At Edelweiss' hurt look she said, "I'm getting a headache."

Edelweiss made a reaching motion for Honey Smee's face. Honey jerked away, teeth bared, tires riding on the divider bumps, and an overly loud and long-pressed horn went screaming by in the form of an SUV. Edelweiss sat back, startled. Honey panted. "What were you doing?" she hissed at the girl.

"I was going to give you a Brazilian Highlands de-pressurizing rub. I learned it in my homeopathy class."

"I'd rather you didn't touch my face. Or me. I'd rather you didn't touch me."

"Why? Has something happened to you? That you want to talk about?" Edelweiss became distinctly rapturous. "Maybe you can allow my old soul to show your old soul a better path?"

"God, no. I mean, I have an allergy. To skin. Oils. Other people's skin oils." Honey internally scolded herself for the low believability of her lie.

"I've never heard of such a thing."

Honey cringed. "It's new. It's popping up with people who have allergies to ambient chemicals, you know, soaps and deodorants and fragrances. Those people—we—get all kinds of insane allergies on the side."

"I've heard of that! Oh, that sounds bad, but it's great you know, when your body is trying to reverse the damage that mankind was wrought?" Edelweiss became still and whispered, "How do you experience romance?"

"I don't. Very sad."

Edelweiss stared in horror and fascination. "You must pleasure yourself, then, right?"

Honey Smee gagged twice and then powered her window down. An image hit her as though from behind, a limbic sucker punch that cracked her square in her emotional teeth. In the image she was in a field, back home, the creak of crickets in the hot summer sun like the earth itself were stressing and cracking. She was kicking the shit out of a little boy her own age, nailing him several times in his cloaca. Leaving him screaming soundlessly, she stomped back to her own house. That'd teach him. Kiss her without asking. Ludicrous.

When Honey's attention came back they had traveled nearly fifteen miles. She hadn't blacked out, exactly, just bifurcated into two consciousnesses, one driving, and one reliving a personal hell. Honey looked over to the girl, able to contain her impulse to throttle her by gripping the hell out of the memory-foam steering wheel cover. Edelweiss was snoring.

"Fuck this job," Honey said aloud, and mashed the accelerator down.

3.

"Mamas don't let your babies grow up to be cowboys, yow be do doop be dum dum blah blah, somethin' somethin', aw, fuck it."

Kundalini threw his pendulously skin-covered head back and howled an oddly endearing, dry-sounding howl.

Hewey bared his teeth and smacked thunderously at the steering wheel. He was feeling an unfamiliar and pointless happiness, something he normally dismissed as folly. Sure, he was pleased often enough, sometimes more than pleased, but he always knew exactly why: a thick slab of bel paese on ciabatta, or a proper trällern-Krug of dark ale. More recently, the sight of the gobhole's tail wagging, like someone swinging a mangy pork loin about, had been bringing a lift to his step.

He marveled at the way that happiness often strikes at moments when it seemed least likely to fit, but he didn't marvel too much. Happiness responds to attention like an ice cube responds to sun.

Instead, Hewey ruminated on something safer, which at that moment was the surprisingly relaxing effect of driving. Driving in traffic was an excellent example of the malodorously cesspoolean lows mankind was capable of, but freeway driving, real freeway driving, now there was a special thing.

Hewey knew a German troll of deep Black Forest descent, that had crafted himself a motorcycle. Being a troll motorcycle, it was an unquestionable beast capable of cruising smoothly at 180 kph, resulting in its possession of the title "der ZeitSpalten," *the time-splitter*. The Black Forest troll had frankly explained that when he set out on the der ZeitSpalten, the area localized to the motorcycle itself *slowed down*, leaving the exterior world to progress at its frantic, clumsy rate. Conversely, the rider became calm and mentally tidier.

Hewey had been awed. It was like someone had explained the changing of the seasons to him, some fixed neutral force finally revealed.

Of course, riding der ZeitSpalten on the Autobahn and driving a rusty, pinging, windy cargo van on I-5 were hardly comparable, but Hewey was in good spirits.

After another hour or so of driving he careened off the freeway and made for a smallish diner parking lot, marked with a towering neon sign that blinked "Virgil's." Hewey extracted the copied map that the car rental fellow had given him and frowned. He hadn't seen any signs designating a Shorebeach Cove turn off, and he had driven to the end of the highlighter line. He spoke to the gobhole.

"Sit tight."

The Hound blinked.

"I'll get you something to eat."

A gelatinous globbet of saliva made a quiet, stringy descent from the gobhole's secluded mouth. It appeared to contain gravel.

The interior of the diner was monochrome burnt umber, as though an early seventies infection had stained even the ceiling tiles. Several cracked Naughahyde booths cradled equally run-down, plasticky, senior citizens the same shade of burnt umber.

Hewey sidled up next to the only patron that was under seventy, an angry overweight logger, and nodded. The logger made a startled, disgruntled noise and slurped at his coffee.

Hewey smiled at the old waitress. She was wearing glasses with lenses thick enough to give her that fetching, giant watery-eyed anime look. "Jus a minit," she called, and set about running a pot of coffee through a soggy, threadbare filter.

"Lovely afternoon," she lied, struggling to look at Hewey. She slowly leaned in to him, squinting, until her face was only a foot away from his chest.

"What's your special?" Hewey asked, and the waitress, name tagged "FLO", jerked her head away. She didn't seem to be aware that Hewey's head was not located on his chest.

An elderly coughing fit behind Hewey made him turn. The fit had clearly contained the word 'limey' and less clearly a phrase that sounded like 'crumpet humper.' Hewey turned back to Flo.

"The special is creamed beef on cholesterol free egg noodles."

"Brilliant. Give me three orders in separate containers, lass, with plastic silver to go and I'd be eternally grateful."

"Okay," Flo said suspiciously.

"And gizzards if ye've got them."

"What kina gizzards?" Flo asked, while writing his order onto the countertop next to her pad of paper.

Hewey shrugged. "I guess just fried up, like, whatever you want."

"I mean, *what kina* gizzard? Swine? Beef?"

Hewey looked over to the logger who was slowly closing his eyes and taking a deep breath. "I'd like chicken gizzards, please," Hewey told the waitress gently.

"Shore, shore," Flo cackled. "Everyone's favorite. I like swine, myself." She scribbled more onto the countertop. "Comin' right up," she said in a tone that implied otherwise. Hewey watched her hand the blank tab to the cook, who paused while adjusting his oxygen tubes in order to take it. The cook didn't look at the tab, but stabbed it on a skewer of similarly blank tabs.

"Say, chap, you know if I'm on the right path to Shorebeach Cove?"

The logger went rigid, sloshing his coffee-colored water down his knuckles. He matched a hateful glare to Hewey's own.

"I shoulda guessed you was headed over there," the logger said.

"Oh?" Hewey raised his eyebrows with a rustling noise. "Because of the protest?"

The logger absently scratched at his front tooth, his black fingernail coming away with a heavy load of pale yellow plaque. He inspected it for a moment and then wiped it across the chest of his flannel. "Haven't heard nothin' about a protest, but I don't claim to keep accounts of that horse-shit scam they got runnin' up there."

"Bill!" Flo scolded. "Watcher langege."

"Yes'm, sorry," the logger said.

A wizened, toilet paper thin voice behind them croaked, "There ain' nothin' unnatural about oracles, now, Bill Johnson. They carry the weight of God, you know that." Bill and Hewey turned in their chairs to see who was speaking. A tiny withered apple of an old woman sat clutching a fork-ful of Salisbury steak. Her dentures clacked threateningly.

Bill removed his STIHL baseball hat to reveal a shiny paste-like blonde cap of hair and grease. "Gladys, please. I said 'scam', you know, takin' advantage by all us folks with their hirin' up of all the oracles. They left us with no neighborhood farseers. Why, I remember when I was a boy old mister Peterson had farsight, and he was way the hell out in Wickersham. But we all drove to see him, dint we? And he ain't want nothin' but some canned goods mama put up for pay. Once my pap took him a side of fatback and the old man damn dear had an episode he was so happy. But whatever goes on in Shorebeach Cove I can't say nothin' good about."

"Mm, well," Gladys said and stuffed the business-card sized piece of Salisbury steak into her horsetoothed maw.

Hewey turned to see the cook reading the order off the countertop. The cook then wiped off the ballpoint pen with a ballpoint pen-stained rag and wheeled his oxygen cart back to the grill.

"I hate to be nosy, but what does Shorebeach Cove have to do with oracles?"

Bill stared at Hewey for so long that Hewey began to fear the logger was having a stroke. Bill said then, with something akin to awe, "Why, that's the Espress-Kno™ headquarters. Everybody knows that."

Hewey closed his eyes and nodded slowly in the fashion of someone beginning to get the big picture. "Yes, well, I'm not from around here," he said.

"Dang straight," Flo said brightly. The cook slammed a tinny bell and Flo hopped up to grab the boxes of creamed beef. Hewey pawed over his cash and addressed the logger. "Pardon me," Hewey swung a box of creamed beef toward the freeway. "So this road out here, it goes to Shorebeach Cove?"

"Oh no, you gotta take the 542 East."

"Thanks, mate," Hewey nodded, and headed for the door. He paused. "Beg your pardon, the 542 East you said?"

"Ayup."

"But, East is inland. Shouldn't Shorebeach Cove be on the coast?"

"Hell no, son, it's northeast of Maple Falls, right under the Canadian border. That's bear country, you know," Bill shook his head in disbelief. "On the coast," he jeered. "For'ner."

Hewey walked thoughtfully to the van. He opened the passenger side door and scooped the contents of two boxes into the third. He tore up the other two Styrofoam boxes, still steaming with creamed beef, and set them down on the seat with the gobhole. While the Hound set about eating the boxes in his deliberate, almost sensual manner, Hewey told him what he had learned.

"I don't like it," Hewey finished, carefully placing the plastic spork he'd been eating with into the last empty Styrofoam container. "But then, I said that about unsalted licorice and that turned out to be alright."

4.

If there were a technology that could, for a brief and forever frozen moment, take a still photograph of someone's mind, then Edelweiss' would be the cover of a Jehovah's Witness' newsletter. There would be an ideal, improbable environment both tropical and snow-capped, where panda bears, lions, bloatsharks and children of every genetic persuasion frolicked together in a butterfly–flecked dream. It would be in flagrant denial of every natural law: geographical necessities ignored, habitats confused, and most importantly, the idea that a homogenized culture would retain examples of race and individual tradition. Edelweiss would think that her soundtrack would involve some dorm-room feminist folk rock, but the reality is Casio Disco Beat #7.

They turned off the main freeway and threaded their way, without hesitation, down a series of unmarked roads. The surrounding forest was a deep and murky cathedral of old growth, and each successive road more moss-edged and ancient looking. Roadside ferns shivered and whipped in their wake.

Edelweiss was without concern.

As a matter of fact, right up until the moment that the twelve-foot cyclone fencing came into view, Edelweiss had been struggling to remember how to begin a game of cat's cradle. She had gotten as far as tying a piece of string to itself.

"Oh, wicked!" she exclaimed when she saw the fence. At the point where the fence and the road intersected was a guard booth flanked gate. "This place is serious!"

"Very," Honey said.

Edelweiss froze when two guards approached the car. "Identification?" one of them asked. She had the metallic ozone air of a dominatrix. Her dangling nametag, laminated and lashed to her chest pocket with glossy black leather lanyard, read "DEB."

Honey handed her a card. Edelweiss hissed at a volume louder than speaking, "We're fucked!" Edelweiss then drew in a sharp gasp when she realized that the other guard was leaning down at her window to stare at her. His nametag read "BRYAN", and he moved with the nervous twitchiness of someone who had been the guest of honor at Uncle V.C.'s Private Camp for Fallen Flyboys and then treated to seven years of electroshock therapy.

Guard Deb took the card to her booth. She could be seen through her Venetian blinds speaking into a red telephone and squinting to read some small print on Honey's card.

"Are you okay?" Edelweiss asked Guard Bryan.

"Charlie," he whispered, inching his hand along his belt toward his pistol.

"Who's Charlie?" Edelweiss whispered back, interested. She was looking around through the windows nervously.

Honey massaged the bridge of her nose and sighed.

"Pull through," said Deb, suddenly back at the window, "to underground Lot G, Miss Smee. You're expected."

"Of course I am," Honey said biliously.

As they passed through the opening gate, Edelweiss, incredulous, asked, "How did you get that card?"

"They gave it to me."

"Far out! But why would Pet'n-a-Tube give you that?"

"This is not Pet'n-a-Tube," Honey said, cheered again. "This is Espresso-Kno™ Grand Central. Some other names for it could be The End of the Line, The Unhappiest Place on Earth, maybe just The Beginning of the End. I sort of like that."

"Oh wow!" Edelweiss managed to kneel in her seat and bounce excitedly, all without removing her seatbelt. "We're gonna protest Espress-Kno™? Shit, that is so cool, I wish we could've brought that guy whose name I can't remember."

Honey turned to glare. "You don't seem to understand, shockingly enough. There is no protest. If we weren't supposed to be here, we would have been shot long before now."

"Shot?" Edelweiss scoffed.

"Well, there's a good chance, anyway. There's also a pretty good chance we'd be encased in military grade immobilization foam—you wouldn't believe how into that shit Neville is. I swear he hires people to break in here so he can use it on them. It takes a team of people hours to extract you from that crap. Crazy bastard. I'd rather be shot, personally."

They came up on a massive building. It was the kind of building that just appears one day, so simple and cubist in construction and so without any defining features that it could be assembled by the most talentless of laborers, despite its hulking size. Honey Smee pulled the car around through a few narrow concrete posts and then down sharply into an underground lot. Edelweiss, who was only slightly distracted by the many stories of concrete and black, mirrored windows and then the dip into a poorly lit subterranean maze, asked, "Then why are we able to be here?"

Their car passed several narrow guard posts where gun-toting men and women in gray jumpsuits gave approving nods. Honey, as though she had done it a thousand times, whipped the sedan around into an awkward parking stall and shut off the engine. She said, "You get one guess as to why we're not dead or encased in foam right now."

Edelweiss held her breath. "Your dad works here?"

Honey sagged. "No."

"You made a fake I.D. card."

"You only got one guess, and no. Get out of the car."

Outside the vehicle, across the car's rooftop Edelweiss said, "Don't tell me—this isn't really Espress-Kno™, is it?"

"Of course it is. Stop guessing."

The two women walked toward a ramp that led to heavy double steel doors with no handles. It was bookended by armed men.

"Duh!" Edelweiss exclaimed, smacking her forehead with the heel of her hand. "I'm such a moron. This is a peaceful protest, of course they agreed to let us in."

"If you don't shut up I will order them to shoot you."

"Is the foam like that foam they use at foam parties? Because that stuff smells like pina-coladas, and that's not so bad, really."

They reached the armed men at the steel doors. To either side of the doors in human-sized, orange paint was the letter 'G', with a racy stripe coming off each side and extending out a few meters. Honey waited for the guards to enter a code into a keypad in the wall, and then the four of them waited in silence, unmoving.

Eventually Edelweiss whispered, "Why are we standing here?"

The bookend replied, "We're being scanned." Both bookends were noticeably flush.

"For what?" Edelweiss yelped, stepping backwards.

"Your internal organ's shape and heat are being scanned and compared to previous copies that we have. When they are determined to be similar, the doors will open," a bookend said, and, as though they were listening, the doors dinged pleasantly and sighed open.

5.

Hewey let the van idle.

Being a troll, Hewey had seen some things in his time that could easily be classified under a bulk heading of 'scary'. He had seen things in alleys and abandoned warehouses that certain formulaic horror authors would beg and plead to be able to borrow for bestsellers. Dead bodies were nothing compared to the old things whose presence we would not wish to summon.

But the one thing that had always baffled Hewey about humans was their fear of forests. Every time he watched the telly or opened a book it was about something evil down in so-and-so's forest or the people that don't come back from such-and-such woods. Fairies in England, ghosts in China, zombies in Haiti and aliens in America. Hewey would always nod and politely tell people that the most terrifying thing he had ever to assail him from the foggy, chilled depths of the forests outside Manchester was his own mother.

Forests were, as every little troll knows, a benevolent organism. Once understood they were a lifelong ally, a safe haven, a cool friend and a source of tasty snacks. Densely forested coastal regions were haven from bloatsharks. And so, Hewey came across the moss-covered concrete sign that read "E. Industries", sitting alone on an old forest road. To humans, he would guess, this was probably foreboding. Luckily Hewey was not human, but unluckily the drive that branched from the main road and behind the sign forked again a ten meters down the way.

The Carfagna's Hound, which until this moment had been crunching distractedly on a plastic spoon once lost in the seat crack and now relocated, became alert. He sniffed at the air pointedly, producing a mucousy, bubbling goose call, and then barked without provocation to the left.

"Are you sure?" Hewey asked.

A lone poot.

"Good enough for me."

As the van drove triumphantly forward, the greater dilemma soon presented itself. It wasn't that the road forked just the once, it forked many times down each road, becoming exponentially more complicated. Hewey was sure that the roads did not all lead to where he wanted to go, and even the black power cables overhead crossed themselves here and there, playing sneaky wee games of Marco Polo in the sky.

Again, the Hound barked insistently to the left, and again, Hewey barreled the immense van along the road at the dog's suggestion. Kundalini brayed to the right and then upchucked. Hewey didn't question this method of travel any more than he questioned the miracle of the Hound, and instead did his best to commit the route to memory. This labyrinth, he reminded himself, was not to keep people out entirely; it was meant to discourage the not-totally-serious. Only the stout of heart would persevere, and a quick escape was awarded only to those with a decent memory.

After nearly twenty minutes of forward trekking (marred by one overshot, which required the frightfully wobbly backing up of the cargo van on the one-lane road) Hewey spotted the webby undulation of cyclone fencing through the pine trees. As he rounded a bend in the road, Hewey tisked warningly to himself. A guarded gate. The gobhole quieted abruptly.

Hewey's hackles rose. He didn't need to look to confirm that he was being watched from the undergrowth to the sides of the road, he could just feel it. The forest was silent.

"Cut your engine," a female voice said over a loudspeaker. Deb the guard stepped from a booth, her hand resting on a hip holster.

As Hewey leaned forward to remove his key from the ignition, he glanced to his left. He was definitely surrounded, but, as he reminded himself, by humans. Humans were certainly frisky with their shooting of handguns, but Hewey still feared trolls worse. Human bullets were problematic, certainly, but rarely a death warrant. With a more direct look at the undergrowth, Hewey's heart skipped a little. There were people there, all right, but in camouflaged biohazard suits and supporting large hoses aimed in his general direction. Hewey didn't like new things.

Another guard emerged from the opposite booth and made a hand motion at the woman. The woman approached the van cautiously.

Hewey began to formulate a plan.

"Identification?" Deb asked. A distant phone ringing sent the other guard back to his booth. As Hewey patted his pockets for his passport, knowing full well that it was in an inside vest pocket, the male guard stepped back outside the booth, phone in hand, a baffled look on his face. The female guard became hesitant at the interruption and reached for her gun again, nervous.

"Ah. It's for him," Bryan, pointing at Hewey.

"What?" The woman shook her head.

"Code O."

Hewey stepped out of the van, hands up in placation, rising slowly to his full height (he knew about the human height inferiority thing) and walked over to the man. Hewey took the phone gently between two fingers and said, "Thanks," eyeing the man's nametag, "Bryan."

The guards helplessly caressed their guns.

"'Allo?" Hewey said into the phone.

"Is this Hewey?" A young female voice came. She sounded sleepy.

"Indeed?"

"My name is Aikiko Ellison. Do you know who I am?"

6.

Before we can continue we should first go back. Life, you see, is far less linear than is convenient for most.

Aikiko Ellison had not employed even an axon in worry over her lost career. And why should she? She was quite concerned instead with applying a triangular, molded piece of beige plastic to the poorly designed back corner of her shower stall. It was as if those that were responsible for designing the shower were unaware that there was to be water involved with the final product. Her caulk gun ratcheted rhythmically away the hours instead of a time clock.

She had also been attempting, once every three days, to make paella, which if you don't already know, is the spaceflight equivalent of making dinner. She had purchased the necessary special, foolishly large pan and made a checklist of ingredients, which at her last count had clocked in at forty-seven. As it was an undertaking she felt worthy of her attention, she didn't mind it's three-hour prep time.

One afternoon after what she felt was her best paella attempt yet, she found herself lying, abdominally distended, on her hand-me-down floral sofa in Gaffney, South Carolina. A particularly vegetal fall breeze disturbed her curtains and the lace edging on her nightgown's wide shell collar. She belched prawn.

It disturbed her that the only way to know if you had fallen asleep was to wake. It occurred to her, over and over again, that it wasn't the sleeping that was important, it was the waking. This often led her to thoughts of death and she feared, ultimately, that she would be unaware, perhaps as everyone ever has been, when she was dead. That she might be denied experiencing the most important thing that had happened to her since she was born was very upsetting.

This was probably why, when she was woken sometime later, she was initially unresponsive. I could have died, she thought with distaste, and I would have missed it. It wasn't a depressed thought, it was more of an observation, like someone who had discovered a small but irreversible flaw in a favorite piece of clothing.

"Aichiko," a distant plea repeated, reminding Aikiko that she had woken. She felt her thumb, which was on her hand, which was dangling over the side of the couch, being moved by an unseen force.

"Hello?" she asked, looking around her living room. She lived alone. She was sure that she had heard someone say her name at least once. This had never happened to her before. Aikiko rolled over forty-five degrees to look at the floor near her hand.

Her rat blinked at her, brown and sleek.

"There ish a problem," the rat said, its whiskers vibrating.

After a pause, Aikiko said, "I wasn't aware you understood English." A part of her brain scolded herself for using the term 'English' to describe any human speech.

"Yesh," it said, dipping its head in either modesty or shame.

"Can all of the talking rats understand humans?"

"Shome, I think," its tiny palate lisped. It briefly and vigorously cleaned a patch of clean-looking hair above its eye.

"Okay," Aikiko finally said, thinking of nothing else to say. She shifted around so she could bring her head closer to the rat. "So, wow. Uh. Is everything okay with you? I mean, do I treat you okay?"

"Yesh. I would like more cheesh."

"I'm not too sure that you should have more cheese."

The rat went still, its black eyes focusing on an indeterminate point. It seemed to be thinking.

Aikiko felt like a total asshole then. "I'll get you some more cheese," she said, "I just thought, you know, I had read somewhere it wasn't good for you. I wanted you to be healthy."

"Okay," it said, slowly righting itself on its hind legs like a grizzly bear. It bobbed there for awhile, nose and whiskers blurry with sensory reception. "Maybe... not more cheesh, but other cheesh. Are there many kinds?"

"Oh yes, many."

"I would like to try them, pleesh."

"But there are hundreds of kinds, hundreds!"

"Good, yesh," it pulled its tail around to clean.

Aikiko found herself searching back through her memory for ever having said anything rude to the rat, assuming wrongly that it wouldn't understand her.

"There ish a problem," it repeated. "Lift me up."

Aikiko let the rat crawl onto her hand, slightly embarrassed about her dishevelment and bad breath. She lifted him to her chest and leaned back. "What is it?"

"I have been knowing a mind," it began slowly, and seemed to concentrate. "I don't know how to tell you."

"You have a very good vocabulary," Aikiko assured him.

"Yesh. What do you call shpeaking to another wish no wordsh? Or, wish no mouth?"

"Oh, well. I don't know, telepathy maybe?"

"What ish that?"

"It's communicating with another person with your mind only."

"Yesh, that. Telepathy. I know a friend who I shpeak to wish telepathy." He sounded out his words slowly, thickly.

"Who is he?"

"Kundalini."

"I don't know anyone named that."

"He ish like a dog, but not. He ish a closh friend of Hewey, who ish trying to find Edelweiss."

"Edelweiss?" Aikiko blurted, sitting up a tad. "That's strange."

"Yesh. I told Kundalini you'd help them."

Neither of them spoke. Aikiko sucked in a breath slowly, the tiny rat rising like a cork on a wave, and she held her breath. After she'd let it out she said, "You told them I'd help them?"

"Yesh."

"How will I do that?"

"You will eat we'em."

Aikiko shook her head no, sadly. She hadn't taken any re'em since she'd quit her job, and that had been the least satisfying thing she'd ever had to do. She'd bullied herself into pretending it didn't dog her every move, and although she knew it was not physically addicting, it had comprised so much of her young life that she'd found herself feeling absent. Like she had forgotten a major task she'd been in the middle of. She would be standing in her house, still, for god knows how long, and then snap to, like waking up. A panicky sensation would hover, a feeling that she *had nothing to do*, and then she'd start to recall chores she needed to do or movies she wanted to see, and she would be alright again. But now, for the first time, she wondered if she had really cracked.

"Am I hallucinating you?" she asked the rat.

"Are you?" he asked, concerned.

"Only one way to find out," she sighed. Her fingers could already feel the small glass phial in the back of the junk drawer in the kitchen, the last of her pilfered stash she'd kept to prove she didn't need it. "Triple milled for purity!" the paper label called to her.

"If I am hallucinating you, you get no cheesh."

The rat tensed. "I am your friend," he whispered, which was like a violet sighing.

"Oh, of course," Aikiko told him fondly, and then, "I never knew what to call you."

"Emmett."

"Alright, Emmett, let's get this future sorted."

7.

And so, because the gobhole had a bad feeling when he saw the concrete "E. Industries" sign, complete with bad images and a terrible, sticky darkness and the sound of his friend Hewey struggling for air, the phone in the guard booth rang barely in time.

"My name is Aikiko Ellison. Do you know who I am?" Aikiko asked.

Hewey, at that moment, was terribly suspicious. This Aikiko bird was an employee of a certain future-seeing evil empire whom he was currently staring down the barrel of. "I believe I do. You're Edelweiss' mate."

"Yes. Do you know why I am calling?"

"Is it because I am about to receive a mandatory hosing of some kind?"

"In part, Hewey. The guards have a kind of foam that hardens after contact with air. It remains liquid against the skin, which is supposed to keep you from suffocating entirely, but I am afraid that is not how it generally works. You will not escape it, and if you follow with your current plan, you will suffer in one of a dozen ways, I am afraid. I'll not share them with you."

"Thank you." Hewey looked at the two guards wondering how long their itchy trigger fingers would hold out.

"I have an alternative for you."

"Is that a bribe or an ultimatum?"

"Neither, Hewey. I don't work for Espress-Kno™ anymore. I quit. I realize you have reasons not to trust me, but I was asked to help you by your friend."

"Who? What friend?" Hewey said, even as troll intuition was taking over.

"The one who wants another gizzard."

Hewey looked back into the van. The gobhole sat on the dash, stock still, bracing himself steadily by minutely adjusting his lumpy tail. It was an astounding display of balance for the hound.

"Kundalini is a bit of an oracle in his own right," said Aikiko. "Did you know that?"

Hewey made sure his face betrayed none of the wonder he felt. "No."

"Then you have a choice. Believe me and I will tell you how to free Edelweiss—and they are going to do terrible things with her, Hewey. I think you know how humans can be."

Hewey said nothing, but drew in a tired breath.

"Whatever the case, you will be allowed to leave without confrontation. I lifted an active security code." Hewey was certain he heard the chatter of a distant cartoon from her end of the line. "Oh, one more thing," Aikiko said.

"Yes?"

"Kundalini wants you to free Edelweiss. He says it is the right thing to do."

"I guess that's that then."

"I guess so."

Hewey listened carefully as Aikiko told him what to do, and then gave the phone back to the guards. "She wants to talk to you."

Bryan put the phone to his ear, nodding between twitches, and sneaking narrow-eyed glances at the forest. "Yes ma'am," he said, and turned the phone off. "You've been given clearance to leave the area," he said. "I'll have an escort lead you out."

"I found my way in, didn't I?"

Bryan shrugged and, with a great deal of pissiness, retreated to his booth. After Hewey had decided that this was all the dismissing he was going to get, he got back into the van, patted the gobhole on the head, fastened their seatbelts, and then looked up just in time to see the hose-wielding bushmen disappear into the forest, not a branch disturbed in their passing.

When they had found their way back out to the main road, Hewey finally addressed the gobhole. "I can't believe I am doing this for you."

The gobhole wagged his gristle.

8.

The sign on the glass door to Le Framagerie said "NO SHOES, NO SHIRT, NO SERVICE" and someone had hand-written "NO PETS" in under "NO SHOES", which technically meant that if you didn't have a pet, you wouldn't be served, but everyone understood. Nevertheless, since the sullen, fat Frenchwoman behind the counter didn't see Emmett under the loose shawl draped over Aikiko's head, all was well.

The woman was, however, enraged to the point of producing tiny, acrid burps at the Asian girl that was her customer. The girl would read the cheese descriptions out loud, pause, and then order just an ounce or two of at least two dozen cheeses.

"Do you have anymore information on this 'Cheese of the Month' club?" the Asian girl asked, lifting up the pamphlet that was displayed on the counter.

"Eet ees a cheese a month, and eet gets sent," the woman said.

"One kind of cheese, every month?"

"Oui."

"Oh, no, I'd rather come in myself every week," the girl smiled, and the woman stomped on her own foot in anger.

CHAPTER FIFTEEN

1.

The Captain Reverend was sometimes called the Reverend Captain, and although this seemed to be an important distinction (the lead Reverend or his holiness, the Captain?) the issue was never discussed.

Boating culture is a fairly nasty place, if truth be told, wedged somewhere between golfing culture and sommelier culture. Everyone wanted it to be pink-cheeked, outdoor oyster roasts, spotless deck shoes and scalpel-sharp sailboats in cyan weather. That's what was on the cover of the guidebooks, anyway. If everyone wanted it to be wild-haired beardy men in galoshes, an odor that can ultimately only be described as "low tide," the pitter-patter of seagull shit and dockside sewage pumps, than that would have been on an ad-book. But it wasn't, despite the fact that on any given day, (nine and a half times out of ten definitely not cyan) if you took a brisk walk down Dock 7 of the Birch Bay Yacht Club, that's precisely what you'd find.

The Captain Reverend, though, was a king among salted, ancient mariners, even though no one could remember him ever having sailed, or even floated, as such. He was the proud owner of the dingiest, most en-barnacled, least bloatshark-protected floating coffin of them all, docked at the most distant slip at the end of the pier.

Now, everyone knows that the bloatshark towers had never failed around Birch Bay, and that the pier itself had electro-static wire thatching, but no one wanted to be at the end of that pier. No one wants to be the one that sits at the very front of the plane, either: out of some optimistic fantasy that if the plane were to crash, the tail end would remain intact.

The Captain Reverend seemed to think that it was all a part of his lot in life, even though he could move his boat at any time. Anyone who had been on the pier longer than a few days knew the Captain's motto: "Better to be eaten by bloatsharks than have to socialize with you goddamn Mongoloid assholes."

And yet, day after day, the crusty old bastard emerged, his antique woolen trousers straining the stitches apart at the hips with their over-laden pockets. He'd grimace and cuss, run a hand over his four-day stub-ble, and saunter up to the little wharf convenience store for a cheap cup of coffee in a Styrofoam cup.

"Good afternoon, Captain Reverend," said the girl who worked the counter on Mondays, Wednesdays, Thursdays and Fridays.

"You fucking wish."

"Sorry, Captain."

"Reverend!" He barked, and sloshed a little of the self-help coffee onto the stained linoleum countertop. The girl looked back at the coffee counter and sighed. The Captain Reverend had spilled nearly the entire contents of seven creamer cups onto the counter, left the plastic cups adrift, and emptied seventeen sugar packets (though honestly, it was diffi-cult to tell how much had made it into his cup and how much had mixed with the spilled creamer. It seemed about fifty-fifty). Every day the girl experienced this at least twice.

The other girl that worked at the ShantyShak told her that one time, they decided to tell the Captain Reverend that he could no longer have coffee, since they had calculated once and for all that they were losing money on him. In the end, the sheer volume of whining and sighing made it clear to all that the loss on the coffee was worth keeping the Captain Reverend happy. Or caffeinated, anyway.

"Forty-two cents," the girl said after the Captain Reverend stared at her for a few seconds.

"Jesus fucking Christ," the Captain Reverend moaned, and began to dig through his pockets.

The convenience girl picked up a copy of *SOPHISTICATION* mag-azine and began to read. She tried to ignore the Captain Reverend as he dropped packets of rubber bands, torn halves of paperback books (entire pages blacked out with marker), and allen wrench sets; all the while glaring at her as though she were triggering an air horn. Every day, at least twice a day, this happened, and the price of the coffee had not gone up in seven years.

When the Captain Reverend had gotten his coffee (after the ShantyShak girl had let him have it for forty cents and demanded that he leave while he torturously searched his pockets for another two pennies), he stepped out onto the concrete landing and lit a cigarette.

"Captain Reverend," a man said, dipping the bill of his baseball hat.

"Goddamn freezing out here," the Captain Reverend whined in reply. The man leaving picked up his pace. "I'll probably die from the cold tonight!" he hollered after the retreating figure.

"Captain Reverend?"

The mariner turned and scowled murderously as a tendril of smoke drifted back to his eyes. "What?" He then looked up.

"My name is Hewey. Do you have a moment to chat?"

The Captain Reverend was delighted for the first time in as long as anyone could remember, least of all himself. "A troll!"

"Sure, bloke, can we have a bit of a chat then?"

The old man was dancing about, his ratty boots slapping double-time as their loose soles hit the pavement a fraction of a second before his feet did. "Wait, wait," he said, breathless. "Come into the ShantyShak with me. I gotta see that little vixen's face when she sees you! But you gotta growl at her or something, right? Scare her up!"

Hewey looked up to the late afternoon horizon, plucking the lit cigarette from the old man's fingers and taking a drag that polished it off. The distant islands were entirely occluded due to old and new anti-bloatshark technologies. The last few sailboat stragglers were racing into their shelters before the bloatsharks really got going. "Sorry, bloke, but we don't have much time. We're going to chat now."

"Sure, I hear you," the Captain Reverend said. "Say, that your dog?"

Hewey turned to look at the gobhole, whom in the fading light looked to be carved from used, solidified fry shortening. "Right, that's mine."

"Beautiful creature, ain't 'e?" the Captain Reverend asked, patting the Hound's head.

"No."

"Ah ha-ha!" the Captain Reverend laughed joyously.

2.

Bernie Hutchins had referred to himself as 'Flash' since he had been a point guard on the high school basketball team, the Lewiston Compromisin' Natives, seven years before. He had been a decent ball player. No one called him Flash, though.

His junior year, Bernie had sent away the order form for his letter jacket with the request that the name that was embroidered on the left lapel was 'Flash.' At the factory there was a mix-up, and when the jacket arrived, packed in tissue and cardboard as though it were breakable, no one seemed surprised that the name embroidered was 'Bernie.' Even still, he was a little hurt when he called his own mother, greeting her with his usual, "Hey Ma, it's me, Flash," only to hear her say, "Who?"

Honey Smee did not know this when she approached Bernie Hutchins' guard desk deep into the beige hallways of the Espress-Kno™ headquarters. Regardless, Honey didn't miss the wince when she inspected his I.D. tag and then said, "Hello there, Bernie. Give me my delivery slip to sign."

Edelweiss peered around, doing a poor job of acting casual as she tried to read the paperwork on Bernie's desk. Bernie ignored Edelweiss, handed the clipboard over to Honey, and then tore off the bottom after she'd signed. Honey inspected her copy, committing everything on it to memory. She was going to check and see that the sum had been transferred to her account immediately. If it was a nickel short she was going to sue their brains out.

Bernie "Flash" Hutchins stood and tried to surreptitiously draw his handcuffs from his belt, but they clanged against something else metal on his belt with the insistence of a car alarm.

"She's voluntary," Honey told him, pausing while folding the carbon copy to look him up and down. He had the look of a sincere ex-high-school jock trying to make it in the world. Honey snarled in disgust.

Bernie looked back at his clipboard. "Sorry, ma'am, my paperwork says that she's a bounty turn-in."

"That's correct." Honey checked her lipstick with her pocket mirror. She could see an infinite number of herselves, multiplied in scarlet down into eternity.

Bernie shifted his weight and began to whisper. "Pardon me, but don't you think she will try to fight? I am taking her into a locked, windowless room."

Honey gestured elegantly around herself to the mostly locked, windowless hallway they stood in. "No. She doesn't know where she is."

Bernie did the silent, open-mouthed acknowledgement of someone who thinks he is in the know on something he doesn't understand. He watched then, as Honey Smee walked away, her heels striking the waxed floor with painfully loud ratatats. He was pulled between feeling sorely horny and shivering as though from a harmless car wreck. He turned back to the prisoner. She was halfway down another hall, trying to see into a painted-over glass door by cupping her hands to it and looking closely. "Ms. Santucci?"

"Yep?"

Bernie closed his eyes firmly and took a deep breath. Was god torturing him or rewarding him? The Supreme Being was without a doubt doing one of two things: parading before him the two hottest women Bernie had ever seen without any chance of redemption, or he was being given a twofold treat of sugar for the eyes and a chance of sugar for the wick, if you catch my drift, which I am sure you do.

"Will you follow me, Ms. Santucci?"

"Oh sure, where's Honey?"

"She went to the ladies room," he assured her, holding his arm out to gently guide her in the right direction. She smiled and followed as though they had known each other forever and did nothing but stroll through expansive English gardens at their leisure.

"Where are we going?"

"I am supposed to take you to a waiting area. Someone will be along to speak with you shortly. I apologize for the secrecy, but you know how these things are." His mind raced, wondering how much she knew of her surroundings.

"Oh yes, it's for my own safety," she assured him, a mighty collection of eco-unfriendly white teeth burning a tunnel straight to his cloaca.

"Yes," he rasped. When they reached the room, he set her in a plastic chair and apologized profusely for having to secure the door behind himself as he left.

"Thank you, Flash," she said as the door swung to. It snapped back open.

"What?" Bernie asked after a pause.

"I said, 'Thank you.'"

"You said something else. After that." Only his head was inserted in the room but his tenseness was palpable.

Edelweiss chuckled deeply and sensuously. "I don't remember."

"You did. You called me Flash." He realized he had been holding his breath and exhaled with a hoot.

"That's your name, isn't it?"

"I didn't tell you my name."

Edelweiss smiled knowingly. It was as if a glade-green aura formed around her and the twittering of distant birds could be heard. She was sitting precariously on the chair in the lotus position, her hands linked across her lap. "There are many things about our world that do not make sense, Flash, and I am one of those things."

3.

Neville Manowicz found himself wondering what poor people were worrying about right at that moment. Laundry detergent? He tried to think back to the last time he compared prices of toilet paper or the freshness of carrots. Must have been before Ashleigh and the Royal Progeny at least. Then: did Ashleigh deal with the kid's nutrition, or did he pay someone to? Oh, he scolded himself, that's a stupid question.

"Melissa?" He asked, touching the spectacularly innovative and unnecessarily aerodynamic intercom that had been custom recessed into his desktop.

"Yes sir?"

"Who deals with my children's food?"

There was a vacuum silence. "Can you be more specific, sir? Do you mean, ah, your wife?"

"Well bless you for saying that, Melissa, but do you think my wife is capable of that?"

"Nuh... no... sir?" The secretary's voice quavered with uncertain loyalty.

"That's right. You're an astute girl. What I meant was, does my cook just make them food, or do I have a nutritionist? The children don't eat our food, do they?" Neville asked, horrified, thinking back to the crepes and four-hundred dollar tin of caviar that he'd had for dinner the night before.

"Hold please, sir."

He clicked his pen a few times and then scratched at a well-anchored ball of lint on his pants.

"Mr. Manowicz?"

"Yes?"

"You have a nutritionist that meets with your cooks three times weekly. Her name is Miss Harris. She does advise the cooks on your children, who are usually prepared different meals than you. You are also paying Miss Harris to work at your children's school, to oversee their meals there."

"Oh, I remember, the school claimed they couldn't afford to keep a nutritionist on staff. And the kids always want 'a hot lunch at school," he mimicked in falsetto. "So I have to oversee the entire damn school's nutrition." He sighed. "Small price to pay, I guess. Those kids will be the only non-obese people in the world when they grow up."

"Yes sir. And your wife sir, she has issued orders to the kitchen staff that her meal choices superceded any orders you give. Concerning herself only, I mean."

"Seedless grapes, blueberry bagels with fat-free cream cheese and skinless chicken breast with sauce béchamel, am I right?"

A laugh came back over the intercom. "Mostly, sir."

"You want to know the best part, Melissa?"

"Yes sir?"

"She doesn't know that sauce béchamel is made from cream, and no one is going to tell her."

The intercom was silent, but Neville was pretty sure he heard laughing from outside his office door. The secretary was clearing her throat when the intercom came back on. "You forgot peach iced tea with artificial sweetener, sir."

"Ah, you're right. That's why I pay you, though, to catch what I miss."

"Thank you, sir."

"You're welcome."

Neville looked back down to the message he had been sent via pneumatic tube some fifteen minutes before. It had a particularly crisp, important quality to it that he had, of course, hand-selected both by paper weight and color. It read:

> TO: COWBOY
> FROM: STAFF LEVEL G
> RE: WHITE FLOWER
> PACKAGE DELIVERED TO OFFICE COMPLEX
> LEVEL G. BALANCE
> FORWARDED BY ACCOUNTING. THERE WERE
> NO PROBLEMS WITH THE ACQUISITION.
> EAGERLY AWAITING YOUR INSTRUCTION.
> MSG SENT BY: B. HUTCHINS, SECURITY

"Doot-do-da-doo!," he chimed in his best approximation of a video-game power-up noise, and checked an item off his daily planner "To Do" list.

4.

It was immediately clear to Hewey that he would not be boarding the *Wind Gravy*, which the Captain Reverend claimed to own. As the Captain struggled aboard, the boat dipped unevenly in the black rainbow-surfaced water, a certain ominous groan coming from parts of the boat that should not have been affected by the burden of a human form.

In the midst of his wonderment, Hewey realized that such carnage could actually be seaworthy because the barnacles encrusted on the hull were structural.

"Aye, bloke, I'll not be getting in, right?"

The Captain's grizzled head reemerged from the pilothouse. "Huh? Yeah, come in. I'll make you some tea. You like tea, limey? 'Course you do!"

"Well brother, it's like this. I weigh 31 stones. Your girl here, she can barely handle your ten and I've got a lot to say, so you just sit tight for a bloody minute and shut up, okay?"

"Eh?"

"I need a bloatshark, alive, and I need it inland. I haven't got much time, or rather, none. If you help me hook it I'll pay well."

Anyone who has ever been in the vicinity of a human baby for very long soon learns one very important thing: feeding a baby something unpleasant-tasting is pure, priceless entertainment. Just a bit of lemon or pickle will do, and they will make the same imploded, defeated and recoiling face over and over again. This was the exact response that the Captain Reverend had at that moment. "God, no! What're you, a fucking circus? They don't live outside of the sea, boy, surely they teach you that in your own goddamn country. It's been tried."

"What's been tried?"

"Keeping the bastards captive! Can't be done! You're either gonna spend a fortune to have rotten shark meat in a week or you're gonna be responsible for the deaths of yourself, your friends, prolly some nice sweet animals like your dog there or a nice little circus pony, whatever kinda girlfriend you got, and maybe if you're lucky a little mess of chilrens. Oh, and you know how much shark defusers charge?"

"How much whats charge?"

"Defusers! A fucking goddamn fortune! But what're you gonna do if you got a dead bloatshark on your hands? Let it detonate on accident? Nope. You're gonna pay the bastard everything you got n' then some to defuse it so you don't die! Gods, what a racket. I should've gotten into that."

"I'm not going to keep it. I want it to blow up."

The Captain Reverend darkened. "It doesn't have a button, my friend. You can shoot them with a gun fifteen times and nothing, just a ragin', flyin' torpedo of teeth still comin' for you. And a' course, sometimes you'll cough near it and pow, three city blocks, Krakatowa." The Captain Reverend shrugged and looked introspective. "For some reason I like barbecued chicken just fine, but not barbecued ribs."

Hewey lowered himself to the edge of the dock and dangled his bare feet into the frigid water. A school of tiny fishlets fled then regrouped. As a variety of skin bits and what looked to be granola drifted away from his feet the minnows became frenzied.

Hewey, for the uncountedth time that day, felt a tickling, shivery sense of dread. He was troubled by the sensation of a massive abrasive object, all ire and soulessness, streaking through the night sky. He rubbed his knuckles. The bloatshark's sole purpose was to make all other species lesser. Just then, the gobhole sidled up next to him and sighed. Hewey nodded and patted the dog's head. He then smelled putricine and realized it hadn't been a sigh, exactly.

"Well, look," Hewey said. "I appreciate your efforts to spare my life, but I figure you're going to help me anyway."

"Oh yeah? Why's that?"

"Well, for one, it's in the interest of good. Honest goodness, which I think we both don't generally pay our dues to. And second, what other plans have you?"

The Captain Reverend angrily scoffed and set about as though to coil a moss-encased rope piled on the deck of the Wind Gravy. When the Reverend and a family of rats inside the rope startled each other, he snapped, "I got lots to do! The fucking work on this boat is never ending. My whole life is: get up, wash the dishes, sweep up the cat hair—"

"You've got a cat on this thing?"

"No! Filthy! As I was sayin', sweep up the cat hair, do my laundry, get coffee, try to find my goddamn government check, wash the dishes—"

"Captain."

"And there's usually some bird shit to wash off the deck, and tourists that slow me down so bad so's that I can't even get these ropes coiled and—"

Hewey stood and put one foot down on the gunnel. The boat dipped sharply, flooding the deck a little; the Captain Reverend braced himself with a gust of profanities, and shouted, "What's this now! Harassing an old man!"

"Coming or going?" Hewey said. On more than one occasion this same tone had made children and domesticated animals void their bowels.

"Coming," the Captain Reverend said firmly, and belched. "But I don't have any gas money and I'm outta rootbeer schnapps."

"Noted," Hewey said, and patted then crusty seafarer on the head.

The Captain Reverend giggled.

5.

"What's she doing?" one of the security guards whispered.

Special Interests Unit Director Jimmy Galloway, who was observing Edelweiss via the black and white closed circuit television, sighed. She was perched uncomfortably on the plastic chair in the middle of the room. Her legs were pulled up, feet tucked beneath knees and hands out in limp "okay" signs. Her eyes were closed and her mouth hung open, and every so often she would seize violently, a soundless paroxysm that would nearly knock her to the floor.

"She's meditating," Galloway said, and turned to the guards. "The sneezing is not a part of it."

The guards nodded, quickly, as they were company men that had already spent their upcoming Christmas bonuses.

"How long has she been here?"

One of the guards, the one whose lapel pin read 'HUTCHINS', cleared his throat. "Only two hours, sir. She began meditating, oh, I'd say about twenty minutes ago."

"Oh, ten," the other guard said with a disproportionately cheery grin.

Hutchins flicked his eyes at his co-worker. "Twenty minutes, sir," he repeated.

"I'll be right back," Galloway said, and the three of them left the observation room. "And then I'll want to see her. You can give her a magazine or something, Hutchins, if you've got one."

"Oh, I doubt she'll be interested in Bernie's copies of 'Hot Lady Chum'!" the other guard snorted, giving his giant buck teeth a romp.

"It's Flash."

"Never heard of 'Flash'," Galloway said, beginning to walk away. "That a tittie mag or one of those 'erotic story' books?"

"It's my name sir."

"Sure, Hutchins," Galloway said, already several yards down the hall.

When Bernie turned back around, the other guard was still grinning, his two, massive, yellow, hateful front teeth hanging over his lower lip like an awning. "Sure, Hutchins," he mimicked, and then nearly puked from mockery-born joy.

6.

Galloway got around the corner in the hallway and then slumped miserably. He dragged his black dress shoes along the corridor in fit-pitching dread. It was something he considered in a distant outpost of his consciousness, viewing himself remotely and trying to decide if it would be horrible for other staff to see him in that state. What would he care if a co-worker saw him, a stunningly haggard man in a decent suit, face crumpled in tearless agony, shoes leaving long black streaks on the floor?

"Fuckers," he muttered, and indulged himself in continuing to behave like a child. Why shouldn't I? he thought. I'm the one that has always been stuck with the seven, and I don't work for the seven! I work for Espress-Kno™, and for a long goddamn time. He nodded to himself. I've got seniority. I should be working with those foxy broads down in marketing, not wiping the asses of prophetic redundancy department weaklings. He then considered his salary and stood up straight.

Galloway checked his way through two security posts. He, to his horror, shuddered to a full stop as he reached the door, hand out and touching the surface of the door instead of the handle, as though checking for heat. He had to suppress a little gagging shudder as the combined effluvient beyond the door assaulted his olfactory centers prematurely. He wanted to steel himself against it, but already he was visualizing the smell, breaking it down to its base components. And ah, the way his nerve shattered. It would be many times more potent inside: the gamey MSG-laden corn chip funk; the tartness of elderly dairy-based chip dips, cracked and tiled in their age like mudflats; and the specific, almost pleasant woolen-odored mold that was exclusive to corn-syrup heavy soda pop dregs.

He had made the mistake once of drifting too near the microwave nook and its surrounding cabinets of cellophane-wrapped foods, a malodorous fetor unlike any other. The microwave operated like some alchemal demi-demon, combining the smells of Magma Tube brand microwave burritos, mini pizzas, Tuna Sammich Pockets and Butter Nuke microwavable popcorn in Bubble Gum flavor. The resulting atmospheric abortion had nearly moved him to tears. He had been torn, though, between standing near this miasma or venturing into the spaces more frequently occupied by the seven themselves.

Perhaps it had to do with their inexplicable hairlessness (beads of sweat shone through their silk-fine hair on scalps pinkened and visible in the humidity) or more likely, their lab-rat diet superdoses of manmade inorganic compounds, but the seven had the most stomach-churning personal odor Galloway had ever experienced. He had visited a sick niece once at the hospital and the smell there, among the cancer-ridden hot little bodies, had been so familiar he'd run away. It was sugary and yet somehow cabbagey, both deodorized and rottenly sulfurous. It was the putrefaction of tissue that was still alive, still renewing itself, but only just fast enough to keep the main organism from dying. In the seven, he could practically hear the red #40 pushing out through their pores.

Galloway refocused when he felt the guards staring at him. He cleared his throat, fought the urge to defend himself to these underpaid idiot muscles, and opened the door.

He waited for his eyes to adjust to the gloom, making sure to give the door a double spastic wave before he shut it (internally satisfied to hear the guards coughing) and sucked in one last partly-clean breath. He couldn't tell if it was better or worse to let the smell in slowly, through panting snatches, or to just inhale and get it over with.

"Good evening," he said finally, as the bulky silhouettes resolved against the television screens.

"Interesting politics in Africa right now," one of them said. The voice was thick and lardy.

"Yes, we have Beta on that," Galloway said between inhales.

"Uh, Beta Team doesn't handle assassinations, we do." There was a note of hurt in the voice. It was getting more and more difficult for Galloway to ascertain if a new voice was speaking or not.

Galloway said, "It's a very minor assassination."

"That's for us to judge." He was fairly certain the voice had come from a different part of the room.

"Of course, but we need you for more important things right now," he assured them, and then experienced a momentary elevation of heart rate. They can't read your mind, he told himself firmly. They won't know you're lying unless you give them a reason to drag their lazy minds far enough into the future to tell.

Three chairs swiveled. "We already told you, she's an oracle now. We can't see her. No one can."

"Uh," Galloway said.

"You want to pull us from redundancy to put us in your screwball experiments," another said, and there were grunts of agreement around the room.

"Oh yes—" one blurted, and then, "No, no, we are agreeing to this," and also, "There is something else out there, what is it—" before the speech devolved into creepy parrot chatter.

Galloway became angry. "You've been warned about sighting my private work conversations. And I hate to remind you, but your performance is way, way down. Beta Team is weeks ahead of you. Weeks. And Beta Team," he paused in delight, "goes jogging."

There were gasps.

"So you've established now that you *will* in fact, be transferring to the very, very important project with Miss Santucci, whom will be joining us shortly."

"If it is so important, why not put Beta Team on it?" Someone called out in a piteous rage.

"Figure it out yourself," Galloway sneered, and strode from the room. Because I don't give a shit if you're permanently fried from here on out, he thought to himself rather viciously, and then felt the hairs on the back of his neck stand up as seven warped and powerful minds tuned in on him simultaneously.

7.

Down, down darkly, there is the opposite of everything that you know. Where there would be atmosphere to breathe there is something else. It is also invisible, it is also oxygen-laden, but one breath would kill you. Where there would be leggy, precious photons from the sun, from the stars, there is nothing, though it is yet above the Earth's surface, and nothing mankind will ever do can change it. And, since there is no corresponding radiation-heavy reach, there is also no warmth. Oh, occasionally a violent blast or two, but if you're near enough to notice, you're near enough to be poached. This is your home planet, mind you, and you're not welcome here. There are men floating a hundred thousand miles above here, eating gelled Russian vodka from little aluminum tubes—men that will stay that way for a year at a time—but we have yet to put a man down here for very long. Except to his grave, that is.

It is difficult for mankind to imagine a world without him, but that doesn't stop the world from doing just that. Massive, ancient communities thrive, die off, migrate and mutate daily, and all without our help. To make matters worse, these deep worlds are so independent, we aren't even close to understanding some of the basics. There are common chemical compounds occurring that are unlike anything we need or know what to do with. There are body shapes and masses that don't make sense, efficiency wise, but there they go, undulating, flapping, squirting along. There are things with brains bigger than ours, containing as many or more neural connections as us, and yet we can't be entirely sure if they have speech, communities, arguments or nightmares.

Oh now, wait a minute. Whales have speech. It's beautiful, it's pretty enough to record ambient trance to and then dub over some ceremonial pygmy ululations. They have communities as well, families, and I heard a story once that a dolphin saved some surfers from a confused and hungry Great White, didn't you? Why would a dolphin do that? So, what if they did have feelings, just what if? A little mind experiment for shits and giggles, right? That means that some must be flawed, is that a safe extrapolation? Some must have chemical imbalances.

What if some of them, sort of as an evolutionary imbalance, if you will, are insane? Like people are all starting to be insane now? What if some of them are just mean?

What if they were mean, could fly, had predatory teeth, large stomachs, and a defense mechanism that made them essentially unstoppable?

Why, that'd be terrible.

8.

The girls at the ShantyShak closed up at 10 o'clock. Seeing that this was a less arduous activity when stoned entirely out of one's mind, they passed a joint between them and each ate a preparatory Whitey-Cake Snacky Cake. It was a middle school ethics question: would you rather get done faster but experience the terrible, dragging misery of closing-time at blunt force, or take longer and filter it through a snug, funny and fattening haze? Weed generally won.

Sometime around ten-thirty the girls stopped laughing at the repulsive drum of used fryer vat oil long enough to dump it and barely clean it, when one of them stopped.

"Did you hear that?"

If you don't already know anything about weed, this is one of the most vital questions to ask at some point, to ensure having something to laugh at for at least ten or twenty minutes. A few minutes into the laughter, the other one trailed off uncertainly.

"Do you mean what sounds like the perimeter alarm?"

They gaped at each other, started to crack up, and then thought better of it. One swallowed three times dryly, eyes large and startled. She said: "Turn off the lights!" in a tremulous whisper, and the two made for the breaker box. They clutched each other, suddenly not finding anything very funny (well, maybe, one thought, as she caught a glimpse of the other's bunny-print panties), and scrambled to the Shak's grimy front windows.

Neither of them noted out loud that it had been, indeed, the perimeter klaxons sounding up and down the docks, and neither needed to point out that, far off into the night, one of the static fencing towers had a twirling red light atop, not nearly as quaint as a lighthouse, but communicating the same message. *Stay away.* Closer to the shore, another tower began to go. Finally, one of the girls broke the spell.

"What the hell is that?"

"We gotta call somebody! There's a bloatshark after that boat!"

"No, I mean, *what the hell is on top of that's boats' mast?*"

There was an awful, klaxon-punctuated pause.

"Is it... a dog?"

CHAPTER SIXTEEN

1.

Neville Manowicz was an easy-going guy, for the most part, which is an interesting psychology if you consider the other examples of the deliriously rich. Money causes a mutant strain of Aespoean laws of behavior to occur; their stories end with suicides and lost loves, stories bristling with moral considerations. Tales of strange people with none of the same fears but most of the same desires as the average Joe.

Neville had most of the same worries as someone with a thousandth of his salary; he fretted about his children, he occasionally expressed concern for his wife and was tormented daily by the feeling that he wasn't experiencing all that he should be. That all he had done had been a mistake. Everything else he was sure that money could fix, including any lack of money he may conceivably ever have. He was fond of delegating tasks, and although this technique sometimes failed him, it worked more often than not, and those were good odds.

Bearing this in mind, it is not surprising that he had not been down to his Level G office in more years than he could remember. Someone must have been, for there was no dust present and a hot cup of coffee waiting for him. He sat down at the leather chair and adjusted the framed photograph of his family. It had been updated, he noticed.

His intercom chimed.

"Yes?"

"Mr. Manowicz, sir, Jim Galloway is present to speak with you."

"Melissa, did you come down to Level G just to tell me that?"

"No sir, I am up at your office antechamber still. The secretary on

Level G notified me and I notified you, sir."

"Oh. Well, send him in. Or, tell her to send him in. However that works."

"Yes sir."

The door to his office immediately opened, and Galloway slunk in, eyes lowered. "Mr. Manowicz sir, thank you for taking time out of your schedule to come down to Level G."

"It's nothing, Jimmy, I had the school reschedule the play."

Galloway looked up, horrified, only to see that indeed, it was nothing for Neville Manowicz to reschedule his children's play that evening. The billionaire's face was as relaxed as a drunken baby's.

"Well, Edelweiss Santucci has been questioned for the last hour or so and seems to be more willing than we could have hoped for. I thought it may be a trap of some kind, at first, but now I don't know."

"How do you mean?"

"I am not sure if going ahead with the plan will offer us any information. She seems to be, uh, operating at a lowered mental capacity, sir."

"Exhausted? We have as much time as we need, she's in our hands now. Set her up with a cot."

"No sir, I mean she isn't very smart. We've just received her high school transcripts and more importantly, we sent for her college transcripts and they weren't available. No Edelweiss Santucci has attended the University of Washington. Or rather, she was never officially enrolled."

"She attended but wasn't enrolled?"

"Yes."

Neville flipped through the paperwork in the file placed before him, skimming teacher's comments and list of explanations for incomplete grades given. There were also lodged complaints for the attendance of Edelweiss, when the professors discovered she wasn't actually paying to go to their university, nor was she of sufficient cognitive prowess. "Strange. Well, it doesn't matter. This may be to our benefit, however. You said she seems willing to proceed?"

"Yes, and if you can believe it, she thinks she is here of her own choosing."

"How's that?"

"She still doesn't understand that Miss Smee was a bounty hunter, sir.

Edelweiss is concerned for Smee's welfare, she thinks we may have 'done something' with her."

The two men thought about this together, Neville creaking in his expensive leather chair, Galloway squeaking in his patent leather shoes as he shifted his weight from foot to foot. Galloway cleared his throat, and said, "If I may, sir, I think we can use this to our advantage. We can treat Miss Smee like a hostage, use her as coercion for when Edelweiss begins to balk. Not let her see Smee until she is done with the experiments."

Neville, who had only been pretending to think about the problem while he waited for Galloway to come up with an answer, nodded. "Precisely what I was thinking. Have we contacted Smee to maybe play-act this role a little?"

"She is not answering her line or returning our calls."

"Keep trying. Oh, and Galloway?"

"Sir?"

"Don't refer to them as 'experiments,' please. It sounds so sinister. It's 'the research.'"

"Of course, I'm sorry, sir."

"That's alright, Jimmy. I take it the seven have been relocated to the research rooms and are comfortable?"

Galloway's breath caught in his chest, and he nodded in what he hoped desperately was a reassuring manner until he blurted, "Not yet, we've been dealing with Edelweiss and the seven and, okay, the seven aren't the most agreeable people in the world. You know. Sir."

"I don't know, Jimmy, but I'll take your word for it. Let's get this thing rolling. We are going to find out once and for all some of the greatest questions of humanity. Aren't you excited?"

"Yes sir, very exciting times. Super-dosing has always been a big question of mine, anyway." He wondered if he was taking his yes-manship too far.

Neville didn't seem to notice. "It's not just super-dosing, though, we're ruling out factors of far-future-sight here. Why is it that no prophet can get any sort of clarity on anything after a year or two? They get glimpses of fifty, eighty years from now, but no peer confirmation. Shit, we're always riding the crest of a crashing wave, and no one knows why, Jimmy! All that quantum physics bullshit everyone has on why oracles can't see each other, it doesn't make any sense, it's all 'de Sitter solutions of field equations of general relativity' this and 'p-brane models' that. God, what I would give to know what my oracles are doing, all the time," Manowicz drifted away, face going slack. "So you'll take care of this research business for me, Jimmy? I should really get home to the fam."

"Yes sir," Galloway tried to push the image of his tired, angry wife out of his mind. He made the secretary call his house several times to apologize for his not being home in eighteen hours, but it didn't seem to be doing any good. The secretary was even starting to give him disappointed looks.

Neville Manowicz stood, took a sip of coffee, had a look around the room to see if he'd forgotten anything, and then took his private elevator back up to the fifth floor.

Galloway was rooted in the same spot outside the office door for some minutes without moving, without even blinking all the way. Somehow, he mused, he was heading up an illegal 'research' project he could not leave until it was finished, and by having done nothing more than show up for his shitty management job. He was entirely unsure whether to be happy or depressed, so he chose the latter from habit.

2.

Emmett, although he had no whites around his pupils, seemed to be look-ing at Aikiko from the corner of his eye, so Aikiko raised her own eyebrow in question. He didn't appear to recognize the gesture.

"What's going on now?"

"Itsh the shame."

"Everyone is okay?"

"Sho far."

Aikiko stared back into her full, room-temperature yogurt cup. It had been almost a half an hour since Emmett had informed her that the dog, the troll and the elderly sea Captain had attracted the attentions of a bloatshark, and although the rat was getting play-by-play messages from the dog, they were becoming more garbled as time passed. Emmett had referred to them as obliquely as 'getting on,' but Aikiko understood what he meant. It was dangerous for them all to be doing what they were doing, and though they were in some definitions succeeding, it was too early to use such optimism. To top it off, Aikiko's own re'em had worn off long ago, and she found herself fretting over people that she didn't know, getting second-hand information from a talking rat (who had an irksome habit of editing down action to mousy shrieks and depositing little slick, brown pellets on the countertops).

"They can do this," she repeated. "I saw it."

"I know. They can."

Aikiko blinked back the water in her eyes. "It's not worth it for them to get hurt for Edelweiss, I mean, maybe there is another way."

"They chosh to do thish. They wanted to—ah!" the rat peeped, lifting up on his back legs a little, eyes bulging. His whiskers became a haze around his face, vibrating with paranormal transmission. "Sho closh, sho closh," he whispered so faintly that Aikiko could hardly hear him for the sound of blood rushing in her own ears. "Kundalini ish down, he ish shafe, but the men, they are shtruggling to get to the van—" the rat swayed as though woozy, and Aikiko lifted her hand to cushion him should he move too close to the table's edge. "Sho nervous," Emmett said, his slowed whiskers picking up RPMs again, "They have shucsheeded in making the beasht sho angry, a hook wash not needed." The rat, who had been staring off into the darkness of the room, facing northwest, until this point, crawled back over to Aikiko's hand and curled there, tense and rapid with rodent fear. "I can almosht shee the beasht. It ish truly bad..." Emmett heaved a great sigh. "They cannot shtop what they have shtarted."

3.

The conference room that had been chosen to be the 'research' room was, for starters, too bright. It took Galloway nearly an hour to get someone to get a hold of a janitor with Level G clearance. It took another team of three to get the refreshments required by the seven moved down from the cafeteria and set up on folding buffet tables, and then another two, including one very sleepy superior of Galloway's, to get clearance for the several ounces of re'em to start the show. The remaining estimated pound or so needed would require even more seniority. There were the usual channels he could go through in order to procure a pound and a half of re'em, but the usual channels would have taken him three weeks and a sheaf of paperwork completed in triplicate. There was no time for such nonsense. Luckily, like any good corporation, E. Industries was fond of a secret currency called 'favors.'

Galloway stared down at the Espress-Kno™ handbook given to him, all thousand-odd dog-eared, coffee-stained, broken-spined pages of it. He flipped the book open at random and read:

> *"...attributing these caking issues to relative humidity at the time of the ampoules sealing, the relative humidity at the time of the ampoules being opened, the relative latent humidity of the re'em itself (correlated strongly with the region of origin), the possibility of seal compromise of the ampoule..."*

Galloway skipped down to the bottom of the page and read:

> *"... we at Espress-Kno™ have the utmost concerns for the environment and its associated organisms; the ampoules are never to be cleared for recycling at any public recycling organizations. The ampoule, in the event that it needs to be discarded and an Espress-Kno™ recycling station is not available, falls into the possession of any senior staff in charge for disposal at a later date. The senior staff takes all responsibility for legal matters that ensue as a result of possession of heretofore mentioned ampoules..."*

Galloway rubbed his eyes furiously and then sucked in air as a patch of his facial hair nearly abraded the skin off his palm.

And suddenly, the open-handed slap of inspiration struck Galloway across the backside. A deluge of emotional matter flooded him, joy at the freedom granted with his idea, and great sorrow and self-loathing at not having thought of it earlier. He was fairly sure he saw the grand and golden opal pathway of righteousness open before him.

"Hutchins!" he shrieked.

"Yessir?"

"I need you to move the Special Interests Unit to this conference room immediately!"

Bernie looked uncomfortable. "The entire department?"

"There are only seven people, just go tell them and lead them up here."

Bernie seemed to be consulting some inner directive. "I'm sorry, Mr. Galloway, I don't think I know where the Special Interests Department is."

"Unit, they're a Unit. And you wouldn't know where they are, it's a secret. Go to Level E, tell the secretary there you need to have access to the Special Interests reference files regarding," he blinked suddenly, trying to recall the day's code. He became suddenly frightened that the code had been rolled over already, but after looking at his watch and counting on two hands, he nodded. "Pancetta. Tell her it's regarding 'pancetta.' She'll tell you which hall to take, and give the guards this," he pulled his identification tag from his chest pocket.

"I don't look anything like you, Mr. Galloway, that won't work."

"It'll work, Hutchins. They don't get paid to stop people, just to look at their identification cards."

"Do they get paid more than me?"

"Much. Oh, and Hutchins?" Galloway asked as Bernie began to walk to the elevators.

"Yeah?"

"Do a good job and we'll talk about promoting you to my team, the Special Interests Unit. I'm the Director, and I think I'll be needing an Assistant Director before the year is out."

"Sure!" the kid said happily, and Galloway bit his knuckles to keep from cheering shrilly. His eyes went blurry. He began to speed walk to where Edelweiss was being held and pumped his arms with vigorous elation. When he arrived at her holding room, he motioned to the buck-toothed guard to stay put and then let himself inside.

Galloway grinned down at her, and was, not for the first time that night, both compelled and repulsed by the girl's appearance. "How are we doing?"

Her attempt to stare him coolly down resulted in her having a squinty bleariness, like a puppy introduced to a bright room. "I am fine, but I don't want to have to tell you again, Mr. Galloway, that my friend Honey and I are a force to be reckoned with. It would be best if you let me see her."

"Certainly, right this way," he swung the door wide and motioned for the guard to sit down. The guard began to bray nervously at the sight of Edelweiss' chest.

"That's more like it," Edelweiss told Galloway as she smoothed her skirts and drifted out to the hallway, waiting for Galloway to show her the way.

As they began their passage, Galloway slowed his pace and sighed happily. "Now, I have heard that you have the gift of re'em dreaming, but have never had the opportunity to test with Espress-Kno™, is this true?"

"Oh no, I sent in an application and I never got a response back. I don't understand, I was under the impression you hired anyone with future sight."

"Yes, but we are at heart a small family business, Edelweiss, and sometimes things even as important as an oracle recruitment will slip past us. I am sorry to hear that no one got back to you, especially in light of what I hear is a fantastic talent you have."

"Thank you, Mr.—"

"Galloway."

"But I must tell you that I find this corporation's pessimism and unwillingness to acknowledge non-employees as oracles is deplorable. Are you aware that you have almost entirely destroyed the community oracle culture in America?"

Galloway looked shocked. "I'm afraid that's untrue! The goal all along was to use these community resources in a manner that made the oracles successful and made the practice safer. We have been granted a full Federal pardon on the distribution of re'em to our employees. That is something no other country has done for anyone."

Edelweiss obviously chewed on the new information, and her butterfly-leg fine eyebrows flexed and churned under the heat of conjugation. "I never thought of it like that."

"This culture, as you call it so accurately, needs protection, Edelweiss, even from itself. It needs guidance and control, and those are not bad things. Think of a powerful jet that flies people around the world. What fantastic freedom, our generation has, able to fly wherever we please, but can you imagine what would happen to that without guidance and control?"

"No?"

"It would crash. People would suffer. With Espress-Kno™, there is no threat of police involvement, there is no threat that the customers are going to be led by false prophets, and the oracles themselves have full dental. Now, did our grandparent's oracles have full dental?"

"Yes?"

"No, Edelweiss, they didn't. They often were not even paid, but traded unneeded goods. They struggled to survive. I am sorry that you find our business deplorable."

"Right, I just meant that, like, why don't they tell you that in the stores?"

"Did you know that ninety-four percent of all waste we generated in the last year was recycled?"

"That sounds like a lot."

"It is. It's really too bad you have to go with Honey right away, we were just about to start a very, very important meeting you'd probably be interested in." Galloway stopped before a door he knew led to an empty employee break room. "Well, here we are," he fumbled with his keys to buy some time and smothered a big, dopey grin he felt coming on, thinking about how, less than an hour ago, lying like that would have given him diarrhea. Instead, he felt a potent sense of control, the kind of achievement that one feels after fixing a VCR.

"A meeting? You mean the protest?"

Galloway stared blankly at her before remembering that Honey had apparently told her they were attending a protest (he privately applauded the evil bitch Smee a second time, and then imagined her legs getting crushed under a bus). He nodded. "Yep, it's an interesting one, too. There is going to be a meeting of oracles and the public is invited to join. You know, so everyone can work out the future together."

Edelweiss began to make a faint peeping noise. The girl was squeezing her eyes shut and emitting sounds like a baby chicken. "Edelweiss? Are you alright?"

"Oh yes. I am very alright." Her condition did not alter.

For a fleeting, withering moment Galloway thought she was totally insane. Too insane to work with, and all was for naught. He reached a hand to her, hoping maybe he could get her away from the prank door and to another locked room. "Can I get you a soda or something?"

"Do you know how meaningful what you are doing is? How long the world has waited for you to do what you are doing?"

"Oh, more than you know."

"Every war, every time someone has been shot or raped, they have been waiting for this, for your Council of Hopes, Mr. Galloway."

"I'm sorry, are you hiccuping?"

"This is my release of sorrow."

Galloway inspected her dry face and flinched away when she opened her eyes quite unexpectedly. "You said Honey is in there?"

"Ah, yes, she had a meeting earlier, with some of our representatives, and she's napping now in hopes that she can continue in the morning, but we can just go wake her up, snap her out of her restful, soothing nap, okay?" He tried to insert a random key into the lock and frowned when it slipped right in. He mimed struggling with it and flashed Edelweiss an apologetic smile.

"Wait," Edelweiss put her hand on his back. The odor of stale patchouli, hummus and compost drifted up from her hand. "We should let her sleep, I think. I mean, I could just attend this council, the protest, and then her and I could meet up in the morning, couldn't we?"

Galloway pretended to find this suggested unappealing, and then over-acted changing his mind and finding it acceptable. "Alright. I can take you there now, it's just about to begin."

"Great. See, I told my grandmother that everything works out if you have the right attitude."

"It sure does," Galloway said. "Your grandmother was smart to listen."

"She didn't listen. She was in such a negative energy space from the colon cancer."

"Goodness, I'm sorry to hear that. Is she alright?"

"Now that you mention it, I'm not sure what happened to her. Mother's always going to a park to leave flowers for her. I guess they're not talking."

"Uh," Galloway said, and sped up his pace.

4.

The only thing that was keeping Hewey from falling completely apart was that he was aware that he was doing the most terrifying thing he or anyone he had ever known had done—and he was not weeping, shitting himself or screaming like a school-boy losing at cricket. He had thought someone else had been chanting, "Right mate, doing well, doing well," but it turned out it was him.

The van itself, as mentioned previously, was oversized, was once the color white, and shuddered and pinged like a wounded submarine. The inside was metal, every surface, with the exception of the fabric seats and plastic steering wheel. Each of the metal surfaces was pocked with factory-made holes, probably designed for restraining cargo, but now served as starters for a respectable rust farm. It was with these holes that Hewey had intended to tie himself so that he could safely leave the rear doors of the van open while angling the bloatshark, but such a task had not been possible. In fact, the very moment the subsonic booming and the windy passage of the bloatshark could be heard coming from the sea beyond the static tower, Hewey had known his plan was flawed.

And as he held fast to the dock, watching the deteriorated, ruinous form of the Wind Gravy coming in, the Gobhole howling a dirge for himself and the blue-black smoke of the Wind Gravy's auxiliary engines parting in the careful sideways dart of an airborne predator at work, the image of the cargo hold flashed into Hewey's mind. There would simply be no time, he saw that now. More importantly, he had intended to tie the Hound into the back of the van, relatively far from danger, but without an extra set of hands, that too was an impossibility.

The walkie-talkie crackled loudly, causing him to start.

"Aye-uh, that's a fucking gigantic motherfucker we got there, fuck damn it!" the Captain Reverend screamed so loud into the staticky radio that Hewey heard his faint call come from the boat real-time as an echo. "You ready, limey?"

Hewey freed a hand to depress the tiny button on the side of the walkie-talkie. "Ready."

Too tense to take his eyes off the bobbing, racing boat for long (he closed his eyes firmly then, trying to blot out the image of the low-flying,

Teflon-black gargantua) Hewey's vision had flicked to the docks next to him, looking for something, he just didn't know what. Then, obvious as the ocean itself, laying at his feet in a great mouldering pile tossed aside to lighten the weight of the Wind Gravy, was a fishing net.

It had been close. The monster dived for him, ignoring the bait as Hewey backpedaled, and if the hooked turkey carcass (that Hewey had prised from the Captain Reverends tenacious grip; so great was his love of the roasted fowl that he was sentimental even towards it's carcass) had not hit the shark directly in its eye on Hewey's second cast... well. The bloat-shark simply would have gotten Hewey instead of a hand-length steel hook.

More disturbing was the fact that his last minute solution, wrapping the Hound in a fishing net and wearing it like a backpack, would have also consigned the dog to death.

Since necessity was the cesspool of invention, when Hewey had dived into the back of the van (which was already moving, for the Captain Reverend in all his necrotic gangliness, had skittered around to the drivers seat after beaching his boat) he knocked one of the doors shut accidentally with the Gobhole's head. No time to check the dog for damage. He pulled his legs up to his chest as the bloatshark slammed, headfirst, into the closed door, leaving a foot-deep shark-nosed dent in the door.

The van peeled away, pulling the fishing line hard enough to make Hewey's arm's shake. "Gobhole?" he called into his shoulder. Something like a reassuring whine came in reply, but he couldn't be sure.

Later still, tense and cramped solid already, the real fear set in. An almost sad moaning deep and subsonic, yet clear even over the engine's stressed wail. The troll hadn't got around to wondering what would happen if the shark managed a burst of speed and got around the front of the van, but the occasional shoulder-ripping snap as it thrashed on the line caused Hewey to cry out in desperation. If the line broke (which sounded possible, since the titanium line screamed like a violin as the air flew across the tension) or if Hewey finally couldn't keep his strength up, Operation Liberate Edelweiss would fail. There was a guilty hope in this, that the shark would fade away like a hangover and the three of them could share a bottle of rootbeer schnapps in memory of dear ol' Eddy, Girl Wonder. The shivery hot body of the Hound on his back brought Hewey out of this reverie.

"Why am I doing this?" Hewey bellowed into the man-eating darkness beyond the van's back door, his feet the only real thing visible, braced on either side of the door opening. He thought he saw the red-brake-light flash of beady, protruding eyes in the chiaroscuro nothingness behind the van.

"Yeah, lutefisk's alright," the Captain Reverend called back. "How you doin'!"

"Fine, drive! How much longer!"

"Dunno, never been where we're going!"

Hewey dug the butt of the fishing rod deeper into his already-bruised belly and settled in.

5.

Several of the seven wanted desperately to tell someone, anyone, about an impending anxiety. Unfortunately, there are at least three communal societies in the world in which individuals are expected to permanently bond and yet can trust each other with nothing: the teenage educational systems, incarceration facilities and the workplace.

In each of these systems a shared secret is likely to become a well-crafted, vicious, personal weapon within seconds. Imagine, for example, telling anyone in any of these three groups that it turns out you are attracted to a member of your same sex after all. Imagine telling anyone in any of these three groups that you have a super-secret crush on someone who absolutely cannot, under any circumstances, be told. Mention the strange lump growing on your left ass-cheek. The up-side is that you can make a game out of timing how long it takes someone to shiv you in a dark hallway afterwards. Keep score.

While we are on the subject, I feel that I should clarify a common misnomer. Most people are unaware, when calling some aggressively nasty asshole a 'psychopath', that the term 'sociopath' is more appropriate. And as with all name calling, a little bit of accuracy goes a long way.

So several of the seven were feeling this intense, overpowering and unspeakable burden: they were terrified to meet someone in person that they have watched, prophetically. One of them, the one that is generally identified by some gray-brown 'friendship' bracelets garnered from a vending machine years previous, was in fact methodically peeling microscopic layers of fingernail from their blunt, red, almost nail-less fingers, purely in anticipation. Another was gouging a small trough into the poly-wood surface of the cafeteria table with the retracted tip of a ballpoint pen. Several were experiencing a complex medical condition normally associated with currency traders which included, but was not limited to: esophageal hernias, acute colonitis, spleenic reflux and spastic pancreatitis. This could not be observed externally, of course, unless you counted sweating, which you really shouldn't, since the seven were constantly sweating. Needless to say, it would have been an interesting experiment to have the seven attached to a variety of medical peeping-toms, observing the stages of vascular constriction, heart rate increase, colonic seizure, oxygen desaturation and of course, dopamine production. You know, just to see everything take ninety-degree jags when Edelweiss Santucci entered the room, which was what was happening right then.

"Hello—oh!" Edelweiss said, stepping into the conference room and then covering her mouth.

Galloway looked around the room, hoping to just whisk away whatever offending deli tray was guilty of bothering Edelweiss so they could get straight to work. He failed to locate anything specifically offensive. "Everything okay?"

Edelweiss was already walking to one of the catered tables, and lifted a bag of chips with theatric distaste. "Do you know how many grams of saturated fat a serving of this crap has?"

When no one answered, Edelweiss squinted at the label, her mouth moving as she read to herself. Solemnly, she announced, "Fifteen chips per serving."

"Okay, so if you'd like to have a seat, we're already a little behind—"

"Mr. Galloway?"

"Yes, Edelweiss?"

"A vegetable selection, maybe? Organic and washed with a dechemical scrub?"

Galloway pursed his lips and nodded for several seconds until the urge to shout had begun to pass. "Sure. So, if you'd like to have a seat here," he patted the orange molded plastic, "then the seven will bring you up to speed."

Edelweiss sat, after selecting a bottle of water and a large tub of fruit salad coated with artificial whipped cream. She began to painstakingly wipe the fruit clean, grape by grape, diced peach by diced peach. Just before Galloway escaped, she called to him.

"Yes?"

"So, if this is Espress-Kno™ headquarters or whatever, is there any coffee?"

"Sure, cream and sugar?"

Edelweiss frowned. "Cream and sugar?"

"For the coffee?"

"Could I get a LocoCocoa Cappiccio?"

"A what?"

"It's the LateSummer Signature Expression. You know, a company called Espress-Kno™ makes them?" Edelweiss chuckled chummily and winked at Galloway. Or so he thought, it was difficult to determine what she was doing since whatever it was involved her entire face scrunching up and then opening crazily.

Galloway was already trying to determine who he could make go down to the lobby café and make something, other than himself, and could not suppress a surprised grin. "I'll get someone to do that," he enunciated on his own behalf, and left.

Edelweiss turned back to her pile of mashed, slimy fruit vittles and then looked up. "Anyone hungry? I got 'em all cleaned up."

One of the seven stood, employing a long-forgotten fight or flight mechanism. Their atrophied legs quivered as they got up the willingness to dart for the door.

"Sit down!" another hissed.

"I won't walk it over to you, for your own good," Edelweiss advised.

"Edelweiss, you have to do what we say!" another one of them blurted.

"Easy, my obese friend, we can meet halfway around the table," Edelweiss stood, attempting to pick up the pile of mucosal fruit on the damp napkin.

"You don't seem to have been briefed on why you are here, which is really unsurprising if you ask me," another said, with an obvious tone of authority. The simple act of such verbal control began to bring the focus back for the others.

"Me?" Edelweiss asked, stopping in mid-fruit-pyramid-hoist.

"Yes, you. Do you know why you are here?"

"Oh man, well," she sank into the plastic chair and slumped her breasts on the tabletop in such a way that they nearly became free range. Three of the seven shifted nervously and cleared their throats. "I do know that this is not my last cycle, but definitely not close to my first. I mean, I've done a little bit of self-regression and I can go back pretty far, you know, I was helping hide slaves on the Underground Railroad. I dealt with some European settlers, you know, defending my rightful land as a native—at one point I died from a fungal infection from one of them, of course," Edelweiss sniffed a tear away.

"Native Americans weren't wiped out by fungal infections."

"I can see my work is not yet done," Edelweiss straightened. "I shall have to call upon She Who Flies With Starlings yet again."

"Starlings weren't even introduced to the US until after the Europeans were colonizing, the Indians could not have known what they were."

"We're getting totally off track here. Edelweiss, are you talking about past lives?"

"Of course. You asked me why I was here, I was getting around to that. So far in this life a lot of what I have to learn is not just compassion, I mean, that was one of the early ones, right? Now my lesson is controlling my anger. I'm using anger creatively. I've already figured out that it's about being an activist."

"How did you get to this room, you dumb shit? You can't have come here alone, so how did you get here?"

"Hey, speaking of anger!" she teased. "Just joshing, I came here with my sister-friend Honey."

Someone in the room hissed viciously; someone spastically squeezed a packet of cream cheese until it burst in a solid, constipated ejaculation; someone briefly choked when sucking in before taking a bite of a powdered doughnut; and one other person sloshed a patter of diet soda onto the table top.

Edelweiss, oblivious, continued. "We came here, for the protest. This meeting of the minds," she tapped her forehead.

"Edelweiss Santucci, you were brought here to be experimented upon. We and you are to take very large doses of re'em to try and determine if we can see further into the future, or possibly see other oracles," this was punctuated with disgusted noises around the room. "Since no one has been able to do any of these things before. You have been hand-selected to be a catalyst, so to speak. The image that we all home in on." The speaker stopped and gulped in rage. "You are the strongest one."

Edelweiss was still for such a long moment that the seven feared she had not understood. Startling them, bad enough to make at least two scream, Edelweiss promptly leapt from her chair, arms held high in a victory salute. "I knew it!" She stood with her arms poised in the air for a frozen moment. "I knew it! Espress-Kno™ has known all along about me! You've just been saving me for something more important!"

"It's more complicated."

Edelweiss hugged herself in a lurid display of self-love. "Everything happens for a reason," she was happily saying to herself over and over. "Everything. Everything happens for a reason."

"That's a depressing thought."

"Right, like people get eaten by bloatsharks because they deserve it."

"Of course they do, they're stupid to be near the coast. It's like, evolve, dork."

The group turned to Edelweiss, waiting for the calculated little bomb's fallout to settle. Indeed, Edelweiss faltered, almost imperceptibly, in her chanting, visibly reflecting back on a complicated emotion now lost. She failed to locate it and went into a spat of ohming instead.

One of the seven heaved a frustrated flap of their arms, the sound muffled by layers of insulatory fat. "Let's get this goddamn show on the road."

"What's your hurry?"

"We're out of jerky-filled pretzels."

6.

Aikiko Ellison paused over her open duffel bag, fingers plucking absently at her dry lips. "What am I forgetting?"

"You have clothesh?"

"Yes," she said. "Two gowns, lots of underwear and socks."

The rat shivered, eyes extending from his head. "It'sh cold there."

Aikiko gave a start. "I almost forgot!" she crowed, and sprinted from the bedroom. A moment later she was back clutching a bundle of individually wrapped string cheeses. "These will have to do. They are the only cheese that is safe warm, otherwise," she revealed a handful of energy bars. "Health food."

Emmett squirmed. "Yesh, shtring sheesh, good shtring cheesh, but no oat bar for Emmett, okay?"

"Emmett, you've put on plenty of winter fat."

The rat began to compulsively lick his short glossy fur. "Oh, Emmett," she said, kneeling next to the futon. "Don't take it like that. I don't think you're overweight."

"I'm not overweight," he said and scrubbed his face in a blur of speed. He froze then, for a fraction of a second, then his whiskers began their tell-tale blurring. "Oh, Kundalini ish awake!"

Aikiko dropped to the floor even further, expectantly. The transmissions from the Hound and the troll had ceased for nearly thirty minutes, but Emmett had reassured her that they were not dead. Kundalini was still there, but quiet. When pressed to clarify he had likened the sensation to sleeping.

Emmett moaned. "Oh, ish horrible."

"What is?"

"They hare travelling fasht, in the darknesh, and the thing is so angry! It'sh right there!"

Aikiko made a hopeful motion. "That's good, right? Their plan is working."

"Your plan."

"Wait a minute," Aikiko sat back on her heels. "I didn't make it up. I saw them succeeding at it. It was the best way."

"Yesh. It too has many chanshes of failure, though. But you are right, if one wanted to blow up a building, they are doing it right."

"We have to go now."

Emmett slowly came out of his reverie. "Yesh, time to go. Aikiko, it will be cold I shaid."

"I always wear this," she picked at the frills of velvet around her collar. It was a spectacular nightgown, the kind that girls in The Nutcracker wore. "I don't get too cold."

"Not in Gaffney, no, but near Canada? What about your shnoshoot?"

"How do you know about the snowsuit?"

"Shometimesh at night I can't sleep. I look around."

"It was a gift from my mother. I've never worn it." Aikiko felt a stain of guilt spread unexpectedly at her dismissal of such a gift. For some reason, the vaguely judgemental look that her talking rat was giving her shamed her; all the things she had refused over the years, the attention and the goodwill. She felt like she hadn't needed it before, but then, in a rodenty way, the thought formed in her mind: it wasn't about needing gifts of adoration, it was about accepting them. She had never bothered. Before she realized what she was doing, she stripped the midnight colored velvet over her head, pulled the box still adorned with tatters of Christmas wrap from the closet and unfolded the snowsuit. It zipped up tightly, a snug fit, and crinkled and hissed when she moved.

"I like it," Emmett said.

Aikiko looked down at the new shapes of her encased legs and gave an experimental bend. "Me too."

7.

A person in a white environmental suit (the kind that doesn't seem sturdy enough to offer any protection against anything except when used inside a sterile white room) egressed into the conference room. The suit was wheeling a cart.

"About goddamn time."

"I know, like, did you have to make the re'em yourself or something?"

The person in the environmental suit, who was also wearing a white particle mask, narrowed his eyes threateningly. The cart, an aseptic little number in stainless steel, was silent as it rolled. The cart supported a scale, an opaque milk-colored box, and a corked beaker of clear liquid. On a lower shelf was an indeterminate object, looking something of a lovechild cross between a tiny microwave, a diminutive vacuum, and a hookah. It had a deadly seriousness about it, a sleekness that was not visually pleasing, but some aesthetic reserved exclusively for laboratory equipment.

"What's this shit?" One of the seven asked. There was not a single cardboard-encased ampoule on the cart. "Where's our re'em?"

Edelweiss was in the early stages of crawling over the tabletop to get a look at the cart. Galloway came in at that moment and stood patiently next to her chair, resting a hand on her shoulder. "Ms. Santucci?"

"Yes?"

"I'm sorry to disturb you," Galloway said, uselessly, as she paid him zero attention. "But would you please sign here, here, and here?" He extended a voluminous stack of paper and a pen to her.

Edelweiss glanced at the first page. "What is it?"

"Some legal business. Re'em is sort of, well, quasi-legal, right? And you're not an employee of Espress-Kno™. Signing this will make you one."

"Whoa! That's awesome! Give me that pen."

"Here you go."

"What does 'hereby' mean?"

"It's like, 'formally'."

"What does 'absolve' mean?"

"Ms. Santucci, Edelweiss, the sooner you sign the paper the sooner we can begin. If you want to go over the paperwork, I'd be glad to break with you in another room while everyone waited."

Edelweiss flinched. The room was already full of hostility. "Oh no, that's not necessary," Edelweiss said, and signed in five random places throughout the document.

"Thank you. Christopher here, our tech, will get you started."

All stares slammed mercilessly into the man in the baggy white suit. He was going through the elaborate motions of pouring, measuring, and tuning the machine, which occasionally let out a piercing series of shrieks, as though it was going to detonate. Christopher laid his hands on the white box, took a deep breath, and then began to finagle the lid off. The dual attempts to keep the box steady and forcibly remove the lid made him shake with effort. It prematurely and disappointingly let go, and everyone in the room leaned forward, fascinated. It became clear then that it was not the plastic of the box that was opaque, but its contents. The box was packed solid with pure, government grade re'em.

"What are you doing with that?" One of the seven asked breathlessly when Christopher began to measure a massive portion onto the scale.

"I'm measuring a dosage out."

"You dumbass, that's fifty doses. Where's Galloway?"

"I am aware this is a large dose, though it's not quite fifty. It's being loaded into the nebulizer where it will be flashed with ether and then humidified into a water vapor. And then you will inhale it."

"What?"

"Wait just a minute!"

"What you're talking about is *freebasing!* Isn't it?"

"Freebasing the hugest dose of re'em I've ever taken!"

When the re'em was delivered to its compartment inside the machine, he finally addressed them. "Yes, it is a particularly massive dose. But it's not freebasing. I was under the impression that you all had been informed that you were taking superdoses today."

"We have been," Edelweiss said.

"Great," Christopher said, and went back to adjusting dials on the machine and writing something down on a tablet of paper. "Who's ready?"

"Mememememe!" came a strangled hissing. Everyone stared at Edelweiss as she writhed and raised a shuddering, waving hand, muscles straining in her neck in an attempt to limit the volume of her exuberance.

Christopher wheeled the cart around the table, took eight plastic mouthpieces from sealed packages, and fit them over the end of eight accordioned plastic tubes. After giving each of the seven and Edelweiss one, he addressed the room. "Put your mouth around the mouthpiece and do not inhale. When I tell you to exhale, exhale all of the air in your lungs. Do not inhale still. Do you understand? I promise I won't forget you. Just when you think I've forgotten to tell you to inhale, I will tell you to inhale. Inhale slowly, like you are manually filling your lungs, filling every little single crevice, from the very bottom to the very top. I'll tell you if you are going too fast. Inhale until you can't anymore. Any questions?"

"Yes." It was Edelweiss.

"What is it?"

"If I feel like I haven't had enough, can we have a second round, or is that not okay?"

8.

Ever wonder why soccer moms that drive SUVs, chatting viciously into cellular phones and running stoplights are always so runway slender? A little Hollywood diet secret: rage. The calories burned by physically restraining a perpetual state of fury burns more calories than licking the fat-free yogurt container clean, applying fake tanner and spanking the spawn combined.

Unfortunately, the quantity of rage required for Regina Carey to slim down, even just to a manageable cinema-seat svelte, would have necessitated 768 days of consecutive rage. Such a supreme effort would have a side effect of the most spectacular, fistular, herniated stomach ulcer of all time—which would also be slimming, but had the downside of hospital copays.

Occasionally and fortuitously, Regina Carey was instead subjected to brief bursts of intense rage, so intense in fact that they nearly burnt out the fuse on her pancreas due to its unprecedented funneling-off of fat. But there are no awards given to bodily organs that perform above and beyond the call of duty.

"I can go higher than you, if I have to," Regina was gritting into her telephone, whitish bookends of frothed spittle forming at the corners of her mouth. The calorie count was under way.

"You sure can, Regina, I am simply informing you that if you are wrong about another Level One, you're up for your second review in six months. That's a career-killer, Regina, honest-to-dog." There was a tisking sigh from the other end. "Perhaps this job is too hard on you? There are other positions within Espress-Kno™ available."

"I was not wrong about the first Level One, dickweed!"

"Now, now, Miss Carey, I've got your review papers here in front of me. I quote, 'Employee found responsible for falsity on reported Level One, in conjunction with Employee signature on statement of understanding regarding the Espress-Kno™ Lexicon of Comprehensive Re'em Analyzation Techniques, edition 17.426.C. Specifically section 47q: Undeclarable Destruction Events'—"

"I was there, you goddamn piece of shit, I know what they decided. Fine, you know what? You win. I withdraw my Level One on this. I was mistaken. Happy?"

"Regina, what makes you think this is at all about my happiness? I am concerned for the people of America, the honest citizens that need your accuracy."

"Bullshit. I'm hanging up."

"I have to report this."

Regina Carey almost instantaneously sweated the rest of the way through her aged high school polo shirt (*Go Prairie Voles!*). She shook so violently with ire that her teeth chattered. Jerking, suddenly, in an attempt to abort the cardiac arrest in progress, she ripped the phone cord free from the wall with a sound like a miniature cork popping. Many minutes later, when the tingling had gone away and her color evened out, Regina began to nurse hungrily at a fistful of gummy worms. She closed her eyes in an attempt to remember the image as perfectly as she could: it was very dark, but there was a vehicle, with only its brake lights visible; there was a rapid flutter of alternate paths, but one remained clearer, longer; the location unrecognizable, no matter how many threads she followed, but there it was, this nauseating, calm moment before everything goes to shit, a vehicle careening in the darkness, an impressive gate or wall approaching, floodlights popping on in an audibly completed circuit of several thousand watts and—

CHAPTER SEVENTEEN

1.

—and the manic, rustling assemblage of creepy space-suited men trained in the art of military-grade sedation foam emerged like aborigines. One sleepy tower guard's gun locked up in an attempt to fire at the oncoming vehicle, and another realized, just then, that he was so opposed to killing another human being that he didn't even want to fire off into the night air for fear that a small child was skipping happily through the borderlands of Canada somewhere, right at that moment, conceivably within range of his bullets.

"Ready!" The Captain Reverend called back, and not as a question. "Bail starboard!"

During a scant moment of blankness, Hewey forgot utterly which direction they had previously agreed to bail from the van, and thus, was unable to clarify with himself if it was business as usual (the Captain Reverend's starboard, Hewey's port) or if plans had changed and all was opposite. Facing this moment of occluded truth, Hewey hauled his ripping and straining muscles back for one last time against the fishing rod and its awful catch, and then let go. He watched the rod fly up and away into the darkness, hoping the bloatshark just received a snootful of carbon-fiber fishing pole. He reached back for a final reassuring love-pat on the scabrous head of his beloved friend's dog head, and dove headlong into the forty-mile-per-hour ferns at the roadside.

As he fell, the endorphin release triggered by his muscles relaxing, finally, after an hour of intense strain. It didn't last. He hit the ground feet-first, which previously seemed like the intelligent way to go, but as his ankles fractured, one of them badly, and his trick knee was jammed up into itself like a ball of paper crushing, he wondered if maybe that hadn't been such a good idea. Each passing fraction of a second of white, excruciating pain was enough time to curse himself. He bellowed into the musty embankment, and by the grace of the only things he believed in, in the damp green and brown havens, he was granted a moment of clarity. He raised his head.

The van was busy colliding with the gate, the guards diving away in apparent slow-motion, guns drawn. Hewey noted the flying, skeletal ankles of the Captain Reverend spinning off into the undergrowth, and then

there

(Old Clootie)

badness

itself, hurling into the rear of the crashing van, the sound of it's tons of meat crushing against metal like the sound of a hundred bodies being tossed from a low-flying aircraft, and a tail lashing hard enough to liquefy a guard's torso in one brutal bludgeon.

Hewey pulled the flare gun from his waistband where, Lady bless it, it had not fired prematurely. As the bloatshark thrashed to extricate himself from the van carcass, the troll raised the barrel and fired.

Hewey watched, his face encrusted with pine needles and millipedes, as the flare spun out and away to the right of the shark, its trajectory taking it nearly two meters too far to the side.

And then, just then, to Hewey and nearly a dozen humans' bafflement, the bloatshark jackknifed in a blur of speed, jaws extending nearly a foot outside its maw, nictating membranes sucking in the eyes in what could be the species' only awkward-looking gesture, and snatched the flare clean from its flight path.

Hesitating, the bloatshark turned back to the gate to momentarily snap at a panicked foam-sprayer. Hewey stared down at the tiny human flare gun, unsure if he could reload it. And then he heard the noise.

The shark jerked in the air, snapping at an invisible foe.

There was a moment where the bloatshark just drifted down a bit, lowering a foot at a time like a feather in a still room, its jaws working up and down so slowly that Hewey wasn't sure it was really even moving.

The bloatshark inexplicably puffed then, like a marshmallow in a microwave, and then sucked back in quickly, and then
and then
it detonated.

2.

What the sordid and suspicious-looking inhabitants of the bullet-bus station saw was a rather disheveled half-Japanese girl in a blue and pink snowsuit gasp suddenly, a sort of combination inhale and scream, and the subsequent falling of said half-Japanese girl to her knees.

What Aikiko Ellison and her rat Emmett saw, though, was a blinding light and a sensation of such displacement, such violence, that Aikiko was barely able to keep from urinating on herself. Emmett was not so capable.

Aikiko was acutely aware of a claustrophobic rain-dampness—this was no flower-picking, spinning in circles happy summer shower feeling. This was a thirty pounds of gear, ammo-belt slung over one shoulder, boots filling up with bloody mud slurry, screams of your dying kin-sisters tropical storm kind of feeling.

She was, needless to say, feeling hopelessly betrayed and more than a little despairing. And that was when the explosions began, and an inoffensive memory of chrysanthemum perfume.

Except these explosions were happening now. The sensations weren't unexpected, but for some reason, being forewarned did not lessen the experiences' intensity. Aikiko found herself thinking of the time when she was in middle school and she had been punched in the stomach: she had seen it coming, but as she leaned over in the aftermath, struggling for breath and salivating uncontrollably, she had marveled at how it hadn't mattered. It would've been like preparing to be hungry.

This, as the filthy linoleum slid into focus, was much like then. Aikiko let out an expired adrenaline sigh.

"Hey, you okay?"

Aikiko could not bring herself to look at the person speaking.

"Maybe she feels a great disturbance in the force," someone said, and there was much hoarse laughter.

"What ish *a great dishturbansh is the forsh?*" Emmett whispered.

"I'll tell you later," Aikiko said, and shakily stood, lifted her duffel bag and approached the hazy plastic shield at the counter.

"Yes?" the attendant yapped, and Aikiko was pleased to find that the woman looked remarkably like a Yorkshire Terrier.

"Ticket to Seattle, please."

"First available is tomorrow afternoon, if you wanna catch the big transfer through Dallas."

Aikiko shook her head. "No. Straight through from here. In ten minutes."

The attendant gave a dry enthused sound. "Oh honey, you wish. There ain't no room, you'll have to wait until tomorrow."

"I'll take a standby for now, if it's all the same to you."

The attendant shrugged, gave a pointed glance at the packed waiting room to prove Aikiko's insanity, and typed in the information. A mild commotion rose behind Aikiko.

As the attendant turned to look, someone boredly announced, "Call the damn 911s already," but everyone looked pretty unmotivated considering that there was a raggedy elderly man laid out across the grimy floor, face blue and fingers convulsing. Aikiko didn't have to check his luggage tags to know his destination.

"Now can I have his seat?"

"Don't see why not."

3.

Meanwhile, eight people were sucking off a nebulizer of vaporized re'em. As each of the eight in turn gave great, embarrassing fellatial efforts, they became distant and sweaty. Each closed their eyes, not so much to cut back on confusing visuals, but to create an artificial pocket of personal space-time.

The mumbling began.

A coordinated event started without obvious prompting, with Edelweiss giving outwardly incoherent cues, verbal breadcrumbs, for the others to follow. They paced each other in turn, playing an ultra-private game of hot potato.

"Carry-on luggage."

"Limited weight."

"Proven."

"Reduction of weight calibration?"

"Confirm."

"Confirmation here."

"Confirmation."

"Mark that."

Except something important was different, this time. These seasoned time-spelunkers, these temporal mediums, were struggling for control. Years of experience had not prepared them for this—if anything the monotony had made them soft. This was not a re'emination, the thought went around. This was something dangerous.

The one who reached for the pen to record the phrase "carry-on luggage" for later reference became lost in an ever-widening fractal of everything the pen had ever been a part of, a dizzying panorama of petroleum manufacture, shipping companies, cardboard conglomerates and office supply clerks. Only, instead of this being a thread previously available only under concentration and an extending set of cross-references, it appeared at once, effortlessly and complete. And it didn't end. The fractal expanded exponentially, an infinite series of alternatives took the place of each previous one, a handful a second, hundreds a minute. It accelerated.

"Mayonnaise!" Edelweiss shouted.

"Sandwich Nog!"

"'The Dessert Mayonnaise!'"

"Mark?"

"Gah–"

This was forty seconds after inhalation.

Behind the one-way mirror of the conference room, technicians struggled to keep up. The verbalizations of the eight oracles under monitor became compressed wordlettes.

"Nif!"

"Suh–"

"K-k-ka–"

"Foot!"

Galloway began to panic. "This isn't working," he told the stenographer, who had no time to respond to him. The audio engineer shook her head and said: "Your minutes person hasn't written anything down. They're falling apart."

"She," Galloway was taking a guess on the gender, "can't, obviously. She's totally overloaded."

"Do we clear for a thorazine abort?"

"Status, please?" the nebulizer technician, Christopher, asked via intercom from the conference room.

"We are go!" Galloway snapped. He addressed the darkened room of technicians. "No, no thorazine. That was nearly three thousand dollars worth of re'em. I have to have some kind of data to show for it."

"Oh, three thousand dollars is nothing."

"Ah, guys, this is interesting," the biorhythms guy said.

Galloway swung to look. "What is it?"

"Well, they're equalizing at an extraordinary rate. Look here," he tapped a monitor.

"Tell me what I'm looking at. What do you mean equalizing?"

"Okay, most people's core rhythms begin to equalize when in physical proximity to someone else, as in, if you put an angry person right next to a happy person—sight unseen, mind you—before long the angry person will show signs of physically becoming happier, and the happy person angrier. Think of it as physiological thermodynamics."

"Okay, wonderful. Pheromones, right?"

"We don't know for sure, but we think sometimes, yes, pheromones. But what we're seeing here," he pointed again to a series of peaks and valleys on a graph, changing in such fits of speed that the graphics program was having a hard time rendering it, "is beyond. This is officially abnormal."

Galloway looked through the one-way and then at the technician. "Why do I care? I mean, it's not like we can use that, can we?"

"Jim, it's not just heart and respiration that is equalizing. It's brain activity. I think they are synching up on every level."

"Is that good?"

"It implies telepathy, for starters."

"Ah."

"What the f–" the tech began, brow creased at a sudden spike across the board, but he was interrupted by a subsonic concussion.

Every electronic unit blipped off and then back on a fraction of a second before manuals leapt from shelves in lemming throes, coffee cups sloshed and Galloway, as the only one standing, was thrown to the floor. A red klaxon mounted above the door went into nervous oscillation.

"What the hell was that?"

"I don't know, but look!" the biorhythms tech was practically hugging his monitor.

The vital signs for each of the eight were identical.

"Hey, guys?" Tech Christopher asked in a surprised lilt. He was pacing around the table, particle mask sucking in and out rapidly. He had barely saved the nebulizer and the re'em in the tremor, but that was not what had made him call out.

The eight oracles were twitching sharply in unison, eyes fluttering in perfect symmetry, and mouths uttered noise fragments in eerie stereo. Galloway realized that what he thought were his eyes swimming, was, in fact, a tidal undulation of the eight subjects. The movement wasn't entirely synched, he saw, but was instead a rich and subtle pattern. He was sure, as he stared at it, that if their movement could be traced it would leave behind a growing Spirograph blossom.

The phone chirped.

The audio engineer snatched up the receiver while struggling to right thick technical manuals and move electronics away from pooled coffee. "Yes? Uh-huh. You're kidding. That's impossible! Okay, no, we're fine. Okay, but—" she lifted the handset away from her head and gave it a look. "They hung up."

"What is it?"

"There was an explosion," she said incredulously. "*A bloatshark.* At the gate. We're not to leave this room unless escorted by a guard."

"No way."

"It appears way."

"But how could that be? Don't we, not to mention the government, do nothing but make sure things like this don't happen?"

"A fluke I guess."

"True. You can't hit everything all the time. Stuff gets through."

"What's the fucking use then?"

"I dunno, do you want your paycheck or not?"

4.

Neville Manowicz, CEO of Espress-Kno™ and E Industries, widely misattributed as the Antichrist, was taking a bubble bath.

Before you laugh at him, know this: the tub was a Titan XT-4000, a La Flowa series nine-footer with 36 directional Accuwhip whirlpool jets. It had a bath-mounted touch-pad to adjust speed, pulsation, heat, and current. When the bather was done and the tub drained, the in-tub drying cycle rendered the necessity for towels a thing of the past. It had a chrome swan faucet. With the marble trim, it cost more than most cars.

The explosion forty miles away gave a gentle shimmy to his windows, but since the incident met only three out of five emergency-only at-home contact parameters, he was not disturbed.

5.

For the average observer, it was not immediately obvious that Hewey the troll was, in fact, descended from a very long line of powerful, influential trolls. If trolls believed in royalty, Hewey would certainly have been some sort of Duke-in-law. It was worth knowing that trolls did not believe in aristocracy, as they were about four times more reasonable than any human and thus the concept of oligarchy seemed spastic at best.

So it would be romantic to think that Hewey's miraculous escape from death and physics-defying survival of a bloatshark explosion was due, somehow, to royal blood, but romanticism is so rarely accurate.

Hewey was at that moment struggling to regain consciousness, which from his point of view was a lot like losing all linear sense while reading an exciting part of a book because you accidentally turned two pages instead of just one. He had a fairly clear memory of leaping from a moving vehicle, and a supernaturally clear memory of damaging some of his bones, but how that got him where he was just didn't make sense. He rose gingerly and blinked pine needles and sandy humus from his eyes. He put his hands to his ears to block out the piercing siren that was bugging the shit out of him, but when he did that, it got louder.

Gobhole, he thought.

Hewey scrambled around, trying to feel for the net that he remembered being on his back, but it wasn't there. It was dark, where he was, and he remembered that there had been floodlights at some point, but there weren't any right then. Hewey crawled a little to the side, reaching his arms out in sweeping motions as he went, hoping to feel for the Gobhole, waiting for his night vision to kick in, only to be singed by a merry little fire devil. He blinked madly at the dozens twirling vortexes of flame between him and the barely recognizable shape of his rental van, propped atop the burned out hulk of what had been a guard post. Over the treetops, beyond the guard post, was the coral glow of electric lighting. Hewey flopped to the ground, utterly drained of motivation since he couldn't quite remember why he was here, in this dark and burning forest. The trees above him clutched small lit patches like the Yule trees his family had in the winter, the ones with the cozy candles he and his brothers lashed to the branches with wire. Ripe persimmon-colored fairy lights drifted up and away and died in the night.

Hewey became aware of burning pinpoints in his flesh and felt for one of them. His hand came back sticky with blood. The ringing in his ears had scaled back a tad; when he coughed he could hear himself as though he were coughing in a room down a hall.

"Gobhole?"

Hewey sat up again, his head swimming in the beginning throes of what was going to be a fucking prize-winner of a headache, and felt the damaged pulp of his knee. It wasn't getting better any time soon. His ankles, though, he was pleased to find, were not as bad as he had originally thought—not so fractured that they wouldn't bear his weight.

"Gobhole," he rasped, hoping what sounded nasal and distant to him was enunciated enough for the Hound to hear. "C'mon, mate, where are you?"

Hewey set back down in the brush, trying to catch his bearings. This wasn't where he started. He must have been thrown. Thrown by what? he asked himself, shying away from the beginnings of a memory. He crawled along, his night eyes finally taking up some of the slack, the world clarifying into sections of fire-lit forest and star-lit forest. "Mate?" he called. He paused, not sure what he was looking at.

Dangling from some low branches was the blackened crisp of fishing net. Hewey crawled forward rapidly, gasping as his bad knee hit an exposed gnarl of root, hands sweeping side to side through the foliage and dead detritus in panicked swaths. His hands collided with something.

"Oh bloody hell, lad, oh lad," Hewey crooned as he lifted the hot, chubby mass free of the leaves, horrified to really look. It was the Hound, all right. He gently scraped the debris away and found Kundalini's head. His eyes were closed, but the mass was intact. One of his catfish tentacles was torn off, the meaty little stub already crusted black with blood. His rudimentary ears-buds were okay, and Hewey cradled his friend, checking the body over. There were many nicks and tears, some of them bad enough to flash white fat under the skin. Nothing was bleeding freely, so the troll reasoned that the wounds were mostly superficial.

Hewey's hand shook as he laid it on the Hound's ribcage, and for an eon, he was sure there was no respiration. Hewey's throat caught and he sobbed once, thick snot plugging his nose and stinging tears pushing open tear ducts that hadn't been used in years. He drew in a shuddering breath, forced himself to focus, and felt, as though through a bolt of heavy wet tweed, the Hound's muscles contract for one shallow breath. And then another.

Hewey opened his leather vest and placed the dog inside, tearing off a length of leather lanyard from the lapel and threading it through the buttonholes, lacing the dog in. He heaved himself up, an inch at a time, and briefly feared he would fail after all as a wave of nausea overtook him. After he had stood long enough with most of his weight on the better leg and vomited once, smartly, he lurched forward.

He remembered then, while he held the Hound, remembered the pregnant way the bloatshark had detonated, though he hadn't been able to see the mushroom cloud that made a crater of the forest on both sides of the decimated guard post. Hewey looked up at the trees that had been blasted nude and half-broken in the night, the crackling of fires and unmistakable smears of shark grease. He came across a corpse in the road, its flesh charred back into a lumpy bipedal sprawl, still clutching a once-polished metal nozzle of some dreaded weapon. Hewey nudged the steaming form with his toe.

"Captain!" he called. A hot, putrid wind swept through the blast zone. *"Reverend!?"*

Hewey trudged along, glad that his legs had started to go numb, but careful not to cause further damage. With one hand he cradled the bulge at his belly.

"I'm all damp!" came an angry voice from the forest. Hewey peered into the bushes, sure that only the Captain Reverend could be that cantankerous about having gotten dew on him after surviving a bloatshark explosion.

"You're okay?" Hewey said. He could still hardly hear himself.

"Speak up!" the Captain Reverend screamed.

Hewey was having trouble hearing the Captain Reverend, so he moved into the forest until he found the old bastard, sprawled out in the ferns, half of his face sooty and a bright red streak coming from the ear.

Hewey leaned against a tree and looked about in the darkness, spotting at least one other limp body that could feasibly regain consciousness soon. "I have to go," he told the Reverend. "You should get away. Get out to a main road."

"I can't go with you!" the Captain Reverend screamed. "I'll have to get away from here! Meet up with you later!"

Hewey blinked, thinking he hadn't made himself clear. "I think I only have a few minutes to get in. That's what the girl told me."

"Where's the dog?"

Hewey patted his stomach. "Hurt."

"I'm hungry too. Shoulda had a sammich before we left."

Hewey nodded into the silent forest. "Be safe," he told the old man, and began to move through the night, relieved that the troll DNA still knew what to do: turning the creaking of the evergreen pine into whispers of luck, changing the temperature fluctuations, the nocturnal creatures and the density of the undergrowth into stop and go signs, into secret markers only he could see. Hewey saw where the men in the rubber suits retracted their foam hoses from camouflaged hatches in the ground, and moved invisibly past motion alarms. He smelled the electrical hum of a massive generator over a rise in the forest, and felt the movement of people yards and yards away, beginning their approach to the site of the explosion. They'd have guns, Hewey knew, and he was angry enough now that he didn't care, but he had the Gobhole with him, and that necessitated discretion.

He stood still, leaning awkwardly near a tree in such a matter that hurt his legs, but it was this troll stealth that made him fade into the trees when the men ran by, shouting about there being some sort of emergency at the gate. They'd be looking for intruders soon.

"You're supposed to be awake to help me, mate," Hewey whispered to the mass at his abdomen.

Kundalini remained gently curled there, unconscious.

6.

Though the techs responsible were professionals, each of them, after a time, began to list from their typing and look away from their recording monitors, with the exception of the biorhythms guy, who, glassy-eyed, caressed his monitor and made low, happy noises.

The nebulizer tech had sat down at a spare chair and gone slack, awed to be seeing what he was and terrified that he was going to have to be disappeared later.

Galloway leaned against the two-way mirror, both hands flat against the surface and his forehead and nose between, leaving his nostrils to make twin contrails of condensation below. "They are telepathic now, aren't they?"

"Yes," the biorhythms guy's voice broke.

The eight oracles wove in supernatural synchronicity, far outdistancing any experimental dance troupe that ever existed. They were milliseconds off from each other—not just mimicking each other, but adding to the movements and passing them along—a hand alighting as though for a taxi here, with a ripple of hands alighting after it, the movement changing to a delicate stroke, then to a come-hither, and so on around the table a dozen times. Each incomplete motion and gesture continued with the next oracle, eyes fluttering and rolling in a manner that looked painful, and through it all, *the murmuring*. To Galloway it was like being in a train station or other cavernous room with poor acoustics, some place where voices, once free of their hosts, became originless, and then clustered together in a human noise not unlike that of many birds together. Sections of noise would begin to sound like something familiar, the noise repeated perhaps a hundred times in round-robin, altering a little as it went, but no one could make sense of it. The audio tech was recording and testing the vocals simultaneously, hissing that the noises were identical, right down to the little peaks and jags the sound waves made on her sonographic analyzer. Galloway didn't even hear the tech's baffled jabbering after a while, instead retreating into a state of awe.

"The re'em is already showing signs of being metabolized," someone said.

"How long before they begin to regain consciousness?" Galloway asked. The query left a moist fog across the glass.

"They're quite conscious according to their brainwaves, so it's hard to tell. They could be permanently damaged."

Galloway gently pushed away from the glass. "You think they're brain damaged?"

"Could be, there's no way to tell until later. Shit, some people get permanent damage from as little as a week of insomnia. Can't regulate their emotions afterwards, their little switchboard that controls all those chemical balances gets fried. But the oracles were already so saturated with re'em we could've gotten high from licking them, so who knows."

"I am noting a lessening of the audio synch-up," the woman in the headphones said. "I'm going to guess that they are sobering up."

Galloway turned to the room. "But they've only taken the re'em fifteen minutes ago. It takes hours to metabolize."

"We don't understand this any more than you do," one of the techs said. "Besides, 'sobering up' doesn't mean 'sober'. It means dropping down to a comprehensible level."

"Right." Galloway watched as the oracles swayed in a bizarre oscillation, each of them moving their torsos around from the hips, arms sweeping out in florid patterns before them. He stiffened when he realized that one of them was holding a pen.

"What's going on?" Galloway demanded and scrambled for the intercom, saying into it: "What are they doing, are they writing?"

Christopher leaned over the table, careful to avoid touching the oracles. It appeared that the group's undulations were, in fact, an effort have one of their group write. The pen touched the table top in wide loops, swirling in circles, dipping down and up in a mad dervish attempt.

"I can't make it out yet, I think it's writing," Christopher said to the room. He stood still for a shocked moment, and then ran around to the other side of the table. "God, you've got to get a look at this," he said, excited. "It's the strangest writing I've ever seen. Can we get a camera in here? A hand-held? I can't make it out."

One of the techs in the room with Galloway grabbed a black case and then made for the door.

"Hey!" Galloway said. "If there's some drama happening outside, the guards won't let you in the room with the oracles. I'll go," he took the case and stepped outside. Two MP-5s clicked blackly at him. "I need to get this camera into the conference room," he told the guards.

"You're under room lock-down until we have the all clear," a guard said tonelessly.

Jimmy, momentarily offended that the sentence had not ended in 'sir,' twisted his face into a sneer. "Okay. Then you hand them this camera."

The guards flicked looks at each other. "We can't leave our post."

"The room is right there," Galloway said, practically able to touch the door from where he was standing. "Just hand this camera to the tech standing inside the door and you will have furthered science as we know it."

"We can't do that sir."

Galloway set the camera on the floor, acutely aware of the gun muzzles following him as he bent over, and then reached for his back pocket.

"Sir! Get your hands where we can see them!"

Jimmy held his hands up, his wallet in one of them. "I'm just going into my wallet," he said, exaggerating the motions of unfolding his bill-fold. He pulled out two ten-dollar bills and held them forth. "Put the camera in that room and I'll give you twenty dollars."

For a few seconds, the guards did nothing but stare at his hand. Just before Galloway put them back into his wallet, one of the guards reached forward with black-gloved hand and removed the bills.

"Okay," one of the guards said, and picked up the camera and opened the door of the conference room. He glanced up into the room as he set the case on the floor and his jaw dropped.

"I can have you killed for seeing that," Jimmy admonished.

The guard shut the door and returned back next to the other guard. "Sir, please step back into your room."

"Certainly," Jimmy said, smiling.

"Hey, ten of that is mine," the unmoving guard spoke up.

"But you didn't do anything."

"We're a team," the first guard whined, and Jimmy stepped back into the room.

What the nebulizer technician and, now, the very small entirety of scientific community in the observation booth saw was this: on the tabletop, in thin, anemic ball-point blue were thousands of whorls of loops, an ultramarine thread-pile of them. The wet ink glistened under the florescent tubes, and the hollow rasping of pen on laminate made an oscillating, repetitive noise. This, and the buoyant waving and flickering of fourteen arms mimicking the one with the pen made for some very difficult reading. Galloway put his face closer to the glowing closed-circuit monitor and his proximity to deciphering it made him ill with anticipation.

"Is it coming through okay?" Christopher asked over the intercom, doing a bang-up job of holding the camera steady.

"Oh, you're doing fine," Galloway said sadly. "It just doesn't make any sense."

One of the other techs snorted. "You can't tell me that's not a letter 'g' over on the left there."

"It certainly looks like a letter 'g,'" Galloway admitted, "But are we to assume it means anything, then? Haven't you ever seen that alphabet made from photographs of strange patterns on butterfly wings?"

"No."

"Well, for every letter of the alphabet there's a butterfly out there with a totally random coincidental shape on its wing, you know, a, b, c,—"

"I know what the alphabet is."

The sound tech cleared her throat. "Do they have the same for Japanese? A butterfly coincidence for every kanji? Or is it just an American miracle?"

Galloway sighed and stood at the two-way mirror. The oracles were slowing down. He turned back to the monitor and gasped.

e galactic mu

"What is it?" someone asked, squinting at the monitor.

"Step back from it!" Galloway said. Everyone in the room scrambled back as far from the monitor as they could get and stared. Someone tilted their head from side to side like a dog.

"'e galactic mu'?" Galloway asked.

"That doesn't make any sense."

"It doesn't say that, it doesn't say anything. We're all tired."

"Why can't it say that?" Galloway demanded.

"Why are you so excited that it might say 'e galactic mu'? It's nonsense, it doesn't mean anything. They're cracking."

"You don't know that," Galloway swiveled around to look at the oracles. He was aware that his voice had taken on a frantic pitch. "Just because we don't immediately understand it doesn't mean its nonsense."

7.

Hewey had never done anything so therapeutic in his life. He could sense that dawn wasn't far off, just before the first hoarse, sleepy bluejay screamed, and laid low to the outskirts of the manicured Espress-Kno™

lawns in absolute confidence. The air was that frigid, loamy clean that produced a deep, excruciating ice-cream headache if inhaled through the nose. The outer realm of the Earth's atmosphere felt exactly 50,000 feet above Hewey. Despite his injuries and the frighteningly wounded Gobhole, he felt more like a troll than he'd felt since a trip to the ancestral caves in Scandinavia. His troll-logic (which he'd come to realize had been occluded by an anemic film of human-logic as of late) soothed his nerves with simple algebraic certainty. His injuries were not life threatening. Leaving now would invalidate everything that they had worked for so far. When the quest was absolutely and finally declared untenable (by Hewey, obviously) then he'd feel no regrets about leaving with the alternate mission accomplished—the one about remaining alive. And, he reminded himself, he'd fought a bloatshark and won. A slow smile spread across his face like yellow lichen across granite.

Hewey hoped that Aikiko knew what she was doing, or telling him to do, anyway. The trick, she'd said, was not to get taken in by the outer guards (who were occasionally well-trained and itching for glory), but to get down to the underground parking levels (where the guards were older employees that'd gone soft and slow with disuse).

It wasn't widely known (and even less widely understood) that trolls, though giant and unpleasant looking, could be practically invisible. It wasn't anything external so much as it was the troll's natural ability to capitalize on just not wanting to be seen. They put off such a strong animal desire to *not be seen* that the other creature's defense mechanisms reacted by *not alerting their consciousness that they'd seen anything*. It didn't always work, but it often did, and that was something.

When he began to make a move he exuded this feeling, taking care not to become angry or threatening, as those emotions inevitably caused smaller creatures to panic. He instead moved with the most intense *intent* that he could muster, and like a blush spreading, he felt it working.

Hewey moved past the first set of guards just outside the entrance to the underground-parking garage on his right. One of the men turned his head, a look of mild curiosity on his face, the classic "I've heard a noise" look that mankind and squirrels alike adopt. When the guard's subconscious survival skills made the call to not see Hewey, the man turned back to the other guard and initiated a conversation about the merits of whole versus jellied cranberry sauce. Hewey continued unnoticed.

The dilemma that soon presented itself was thus: when Hewey had descended several levels into the garage, passing within range of a series of observant but fond-of-their-lives guards, he paused to readjust the gobhole. He was fairly sure he was imagining it, but the Hound appeared to be regaining some color, and he was definitely sure that the Hound flinched away from the cold when he opened the vest. Hewey proceeded to the Level E lot and crouched behind a concrete balustrade, releasing his obfuscation as he went. When he'd sufficiently hid the Hound at his belly, he called out, "Eh, mates, you awake?"

"Whosthere?" came a terrified shriek. Hewey caught sight of the two overweight guards scrambling to bring their guns to the ready. One was already at the walkie-talkie, which Hewey tisked at warningly. He called again, "I'm hiding in this lot, see, but I'm afraid you chaps have me surrounded. I am now frightened, for I have no weapons." Hewey did everything he could to keep his voice from growing flat and sarcastic, but failed.

"We do?" One of the guards said.

"Oh yeah. If I surrender to ye, will there be no shooting?"

"Yes?"

"I'm warning you chaps, I'm a bit of a looker. Promise me you don't have your fingers on your triggers."

He used a nice shiny black car to watch a reflection of the men whispering to each other in amazement. Both of them surreptitiously removed their fingers from the trigger wells of their guns. When they'd done this and both tried to yell to him to show himself at the same time, Hewey rose slowly, hands rising first and knees grinding and popping with avalanche sound effects as he stood. He gasped at the pain in his knee, vision swimming a little.

"Freeze!"

"Consider me frozen."

"Shut up!"

"Done and done."

"What weapons are you carrying!"

"None, still."

The guards conferred with each other for a while, the tips of their guns dropping to the ground while they did. Hewey couldn't believe his excellent luck. It was like getting kidnapped by the Tweedles.

"You'll have to come in with us, ah, Mister," one of them men said sternly, though was clearly unsure how to force Hewey to do so. Their handcuffs were useless. "You walk first?"

"Please don't hurt me," Hewey dipped, bowing, and stepped before the men, up to the looming, gaily painted entrance to Level E.

8.

Down the line, many storytellers have tried to tell what those super-dosed oracles were experiencing, but if you had any memory of the sixties or seventies whatsoever, it wouldn't be an enjoyable story. Only so many adjectives involving colors and the way light moves can be strung together before the mind counters by thinking of roast beef. Indeed, there is no real way to help someone else visualize any astral planes or alternative universes without giving them Aunt Moonbeam's special "tea," so I won't try. I will say this, if there is one person whom definitely would not help further humanity by glimpsing the inner light and possibly even our future as a species, then that person is Edelweiss Santucci.

I'm not fond of sloughing off morals on people, but I'll do it for you: enlightenment is wasted on believers.

Edelweiss, though not the smartest nut to fall from the tree, was actually starting to get a good idea of what was going on. She wasn't inclined to try and comprehend what she was experiencing—the experience just went straight to where it was supposed to, with no mental filing required. It was likely, actually, that poor cognitive skills had been in fact acting like a buffer, like a dense layer of biodegradable packing peanuts. As chaos and intensity buffeted around her in screaming jets, she remained encased in a safe shell.

It was with a certain sadness that she felt the seven others slipping away from the back of her mind, and not so much in simple presence, but in sanity. She mentally extended her hands countless times, pulling them back, pushing them in safe directions, but she was getting tired. They were going further and further from her reach.

Edelweiss experienced the futures of mankind like dynasties playing out, deaths and births, constructions and collapses. When these tales reached into the billions, all performing before her as a montage of humanity, she began to slow. She was exhausted all at once, and to her fright, she had no idea where—or when—she was. The images that she swam in were utterly alien, and yet dually familiar, since she had an implicit awareness of how they came to be. This was the future, she reminded herself. But *when, when*?

Edelweiss clenched her jaw so hard her vision swung temporarily to black. *There were such crowds, cheering in sincere joy, and dressed in utterly bizarre styles. Projected recordings of the orbital-built faster-than-light drive accelerating away from the Earth were emblazoned across the sky. Pictures of its crew were more recognizable than any actor's. And there, again, as Edelweiss watched the FTL drive ship blast away, there on it's side the clear text that read* e galactic mu. And she somehow knew, *in that way of re'em that she would never grow tired of,* that e galactic mu meant *"the great universal peace"* in Omni, Earth's newest language.

"E galactic mu," Edelweiss said, in her mind whispering the phrase's translation back half a millennia, the great universal peace. The crew set out, together, on to some indeterminate and unfathomable future, to see *everything else in the universe!*

"e galactic mu," she said again, tears of happiness streaming down her face in hot rivulets. "e galactic mu."

9.

Hewey thought he may have cracked the guard's heads together too hard, but they looked like they had decent health care. There were more guards, of course, but nothing that Hewey couldn't handle. To be certain, a few of them were wily and one had actually fired his weapon (into his own foot, but scary just the same), but all in all, Hewey was a bit surprised at how not-tightly sealed the institution was. He had been harboring a nagging worry that there would be some kind of nasty little door that only opened with a special key-card, or a robot on crab-legs that shot spinning wheels of sleeping-gas canisters, but no. All one needed to get past a guard without knocking their head into something hard was a small plastic card with their own picture on it. Hewey could have made one at a copy shop before he'd arrived.

"Live and learn," he told the Gobhole, and felt a ginger kick in response.

Hewey rounded another corner and came face to face with a guard exiting a bathroom. They stared at each other. Hewey reached out and gripped the guard's shoulder in a friendly, nerve-pinching grip. "Where are the test oracles being held?"

The guard's face was slowly going waxy. "Just, just down the hall."

"Are guards there?"

"Yes!"

"Can you radio them now and tell them that the intruder is in here with you?"

"Yes?"

"Go ahead and do that now, mate."

The guard dropped to the ground, tongue extended (one of the most amazing things about the human body is that when the blood can't come up to the head, it brings the head down to the blood) and pulled his walkie-talkie free. "This is Smith—the intruder is here!" He flinched up at Hewey. "Like that?"

"Yes, that's grand. Now tell them to come help you."

"Help!"

Two guards promptly came trotting from a neighboring corridor, guns neither raised nor with bullets loaded in the chambers, and had their heads smacked together by Hewey, who stood in wait. Hewey turned back to Smith, still sitting on the ground. "Don't move or I'll crack your head." Smith nodded.

10.

Aikiko leapt from the bullet-bus and collected her things, breaking into a brisk trot within a minute of having officially arrived in Birch Bay,

Washington. It was in the pre-light dawn that she called a taxi and waited briefly in the bracing chill.

"Where to?" The driver said when he arrived.

"Shorebeach Cove, the Espress-Kno™ headquarters."

"Uh, I don't know where that is."

"For a fifty you don't?"

"I mean I do, I just ain't waiting for you."

"Fine, drive."

11.

Galloway slumped against the glass, listening to the sound of half a dozen precision machines recording his failure. He asked again, his voice barely above a whisper, "Anything correlating?" After a long pause, the bio-rhythms guy said, "No, the link has been lost."

"Are they coming down?"

"They're officially down, sir."

Galloway watched Edelweiss mutter to herself, tears coursing down her cheeks. The other seven seemed less in control of their bodies. He wearily began to mentally recheck the paperwork he'd done for the overdose inquiry.

In the middle of his selfish reverie, Galloway was fairly sure that he had heard the guards outside the door speaking to someone. He thought he heard one of them raise their voices, but then there was nothing. He felt a wave of irritation for the guards, for their uneducated smugness, for everyone at the facilities lack of rights to be there. Did they work as hard as he did? No. Did they get full medical and dental and regular raises just as he did? Yes. Where was the justice in that?

As this went through his mind he watched thoughtfully as a seven or eight-foot tall person with an enormous potbelly strode into the oracle's room and glared about balefully, the person focusing on Christopher's rigid figure.

"That's a troll," Galloway said. No one seemed to hear him.

He watched as Christopher raised his hands in calm defense, gesturing mildly around the room as though to show that there was nothing worth fighting over. The troll strode over to Edelweiss and hoisted her roughly, without resistance, to his shoulder.

"There's a troll," Galloway said with insistence. He placed he hands on the glass and began to pound. "Troll! There's a troll in there!"

But the troll was gone with terrifying speed, and Galloway shuddered and flinched away from their door, sure that the troll was coming after them next. Except nothing happened.

The biorhythms guy became excited. "Subject eight is down! Subject eight has flatlined!"

The room erupted into action.

After a few panicked seconds Galloway screamed so loudly that his throat tore: "Subject eight hasn't flatlined, a troll just took her!" just as Christopher said over the intercom, "Uh, an intruder has just forcibly removed the chick with the dreadlocks."

Despite the obviously critical nature of the situation, no one moved for quite some time.

12.

If you can bring yourself to imagine such a thing as a squirrel filled with helium, I invite you to do so now. Now, imagine this fantastic creature moving through a forest in the most amber-sweet moment of dawn, not a single pine needle broken in it's passing, not one harsh thought to bring it heavily back to the earth. The forest smells like fresh tomatoes and near-frozen lettuce, a perfect, sweet, watery fragrance unduplicated by any mortal hand.

Hewey was that helium-squirrel, bobbing gently around the ferns and bracken, though he was half again the height and weight of most men, his legs alighting on mounds of moss and deep, spongy loam so quickly that they didn't have a chance to depress. A windless forest air swept past his face, soothing him, waking the small dog at his chest. Hewey held a hand on each of his friends, keeping them safe, as he broke though the forest's presence and found himself on a neglected asphalt road. He looked one way, into the dim mist, and then back, to an idling taxi, its exhaust fogging the morning air.

Hewey slid Edelweiss into the back seat, laying her curled up in a vain attempt to keep from bonking her head, and smiled at the face that he knew would be there behind the passenger window, without ever having seen it before. Edelweiss ceased being comatose long enough to vomit a milky foam onto the floormat.

"Hi," Aikiko said, rolling the window down.

"Morning," Hewey said. "Well."

"I'll see you soon?"

"Yeah. See you soon." At Aikiko's smile he carefully shut the taxi door and tapped Aikiko's window before turning and lumbering back into the aloe-colored evergreen shade. When the last echo of the engine evaporated, Hewey sighed in misery and relief.

EPILOGUE

"Coffee! STAT!"

The girl at the ShantyShak was so startled that she dropped her magazine and slapped her hands over her mouth. "Oh my god!" she breathed into her cupped palm, staring at the vision before her as though a demon had become corporeal.

"But—you've been—you've been missing for nearly *three months!*" she finally managed to say.

The Captain Reverend was so dirty that his skin and his clothes had taken on the same patina of damp sand, a sort of rich-looking buckskin. Twigs and massive snarls of bracken hung from his beard and hair, and there appeared to be a live fern coiling gracefully from near his jacket collar. Where a rock-hard scab formed along the side of his head had recently fallen away, there was a slightly clean spot and a little crushed and delicate ear-stump, now pink with exertion and cold.

As he went to reach into his pocket, the side of his pants tore with a distant sound, like a mummy's sigh. The Captain Reverend stood looking back and forth between the gaping hole in his pants and the tired, dead organ of the pocket in his hands.

"You goddamn mammyrammer piece of shit," he whispered to it incredulously. "Do you see this?" he said much louder, looking at the girl. "Do you see this? I PAID ALMOST *SEVEN DOLLARS* FOR THESE PANTS!"

At his last shout, the girl gave a strangled scream.

"Coffee!" The Captain Reverend called, throwing back his head. When the girl had rushed to get a cup of coffee to him, and he'd fished out enough pennies, and after he'd put in all the cream and sugar the coffee would hold, he wandered back to his still-beached boat, as though nothing had ever happened.

#

dear mom,
for me re-hab was inlitening, but 4 the wrong resons. i
am so much smarter then that! the more they tell me i
am using reem as a cruch im like how can bonding with
eternty be pointles? this group is so wack i cant beleve it.
why make maditory "drug re-hab" for people havnt got any
problem? well my six months r up, so i am comng back to
gaffny for a while.
u cant put a price on life mom!! i kno u kno that. i cant
rember how i got to the re-hab but the nurse sez it was unon-
omus. i didnt turn myself in!!! i am so tuched by espres-knos
gift. what other corprate entity wuld consult me, a outside
sorse, 4 such a importent thing? i don't kno. my life has a
new meening. i wrote them a card to say thanx but they
didn't get it cuz i havnt herd back. i think the clinic wuz
keepng my leters!!!
i luv u and i will see u soon,
edelweiss

#

You can't put a price on life, she told anyone who would listen and many who tried not to (the first time she said this, coincidentally, was at almost the exact same moment that it was decided to not send a corporate assassin after her due to an unexpected budgetary shortfall during an end-of-the-year fiscal audit).

The first thing Edelweiss did, outside of the clinic, was to get a tattoo of a leaf on the back of her neck. She sketched out a sort of messy maple-leaf for the tattoo artist, who had winked and said he knew what she wanted. It represented the new one that she had turned over. She couldn't see the tattoo unless she had a friendly stranger help lift her dreadlocks while she was standing between two mirrors. Since this situation generally presented itself in the form of a wall-mounted mirror and a hand mirror, it always took some time to position herself between the two and find the back of her neck in the reflection. Every time she saw it she'd get excited and jiggle out of position again (much to the benefit of the friendly stranger). But Edelweiss hardly ever forgot it was there, and she hardly ever forgot what it meant: since Espress-Kno™ had helped her see how much the world needed competent, green-party oracles, she was marked to repay the favor.

Jiffy-Re'em™, that most questionable of corporate rip-offs, the Espress-Kno™ of the blue-collar worker, of the Great South (now with oracles in SoCal and Florida), called for Edelweiss' guidance! She'd shivered in revulsion at their signature "One Stop" re'eminations, the dreaded "Drive-Thru", promoting CO_2 and other poisonous gasses by the ton. And the bars on the windows! What kind of close customer care was that? She didn't even want to think about their ridiculous "No Shirt/No Shoes/No Service" signs again, since it took her hours to get over her proletariat indignation at such a violation of personal boundaries.

Oh yes, she thought as she rode the city bus to the yang side of the tracks. That backwards perversion, *how dare they turn something like Espress-Kno™ into some common money-making machine*! She was going to show them what it meant to be a free person. She was going to work at Jiffy-Re'em and work there until the world was a better place, or die trying. And she wasn't going to take no for an answer. If it was the last thing she did. She swore on her mother's grave. Well, when her mother died, she'd swear on it.

#

"Miss Carey, we'd like you to meet the rest of your new group. This is, um, Tony—"

"No, I'm Tony!"

"Yes, yes, Tony, I'm sorry, this lighting is very bad, I can hardly see anyone. Eh, I'm gonna let you seven introduce yourselves instead, how about that."

"There's nothing wrong with the lighting, Galloway."

"Right, but you see, I wear these contacts," he lied. "They are bad in certain lighting. They're special contacts. New."

Regina turned to glare at the seven. Twelve eyes stared back. Another two were squinting down a straw into the bottom of a thaw-it-yourself milkshake, scraping diligently at what sounded like an empty cup.

"Hi," she said.

"Pussy," someone said very, very softly.

"Oh, fuck this," Regina spat, and turned to make for the door. Jimmy Galloway grabbed at her arm and pulled away his hand as though it were burned. He tried not to gag at the sticky, fragrant sweat that clung to his flesh where he had touched her.

"Miss Carey," he pleaded. "Miss Carey, *offer them what you have in the bag.*" He said this last part in such a low whisper that she almost hadn't heard him.

"Why?"

"Do it, please, your job is contingent on this meeting going well today. Just try?"

Regina sighed and turned back to the Seven. She was holding a grocery bag that she'd had yet to look in to, so she walked it over to a small table and began to unpack. "Okay, I've got here—oh, nice, those new Alpine Snax in SwissCheeze flavor, I didn't even know these had gotten to market yet."

"They haven't," Galloway said. "But, we here at Espress-Kno™ thought you'd like to try them. We pulled some strings."

"What else?" Someone begged.

Regina went back to the bag. "We got a tub of Congeal-O in Creamed-Chai-Parfait flavor, a bag of Saltitos in Down South flavor—"

"Wait, 'Down South', what flavor is that?"

Regina squinted at the package. "It says, 'with natural and artificial Cajun flavorings.'"

"Aw-right! Pass those over!"

"What else, what else!"

Galloway, forgotten, backed slowly to the doorway, smiling despite—or perhaps because of—the lack of oxygen he was receiving from breathing as shallowly as he had been. As he slipped from the room he already couldn't be sure which one was Regina and which were the original seven.

#

In a small city park kept tidy not out of civil pride, but in an attempt to discourage the quiescent transient and the drifts of used syringes, a couple sat. They were a nice couple, prone to smiling at passers by without any trace of indulgent infatuation for humanity or otherwise. They had a dog, presumably owing to the overabundance of love they had for one another, since young couples like these so often had pets, the surplus affection otherwise just evaporating off into the atmosphere, unused.

But maybe, if you were to really look, you'd notice that they hardly ever touched each other, this couple, or gazed deeply and searchingly at one another. They didn't even really have much of a conversation—they made noises back and forth, one word at a time, occasionally a sentence. And most curious of all was their dog; it was a scarred, tubby little thing, its skin showing through its short matte fur. It was a pathetic beast, quite disfigured to most eyes. Only the couple knew that the Hound had looked pretty much the same, even before the accident.

But one wouldn't have gotten too far in observing the couple without noticing that one of them was over seven feet tall and built to the same general standards as a Sherman tank. After seeing him, the comparative oddity of his companion, a half-Japanese girl in lederhosen, failed to register as out of the ordinary, nor the rodent hiding in her hair.

Couple or not, the pair and their dog had the look of the well-traveled and rough-worn, the kind of folks that knew when to stop and throw the ball around for a lumpy dog in a tidy park.

POST-EPILOGUE

When the intrepid crew of the FTL drive ship *e galactic mu* left the calm orbit of Earth, they knew there would be no reunions. There is and will never be one word to describe those souls, they that haven't any ties to Earth, but they can identify themselves without a moment to consider. The question was made up by a child, and still holds as the most discerning test for future cosmonauts: if a benevolent alien species contacted you right now and said, "You can come with us and experience the galaxy, but you must come now and cannot tell anyone what you've done. Your family and friends will assume you met with an ill fate, and believe that for the rest of their lives. Will you come?" Well, will you?

If you had to think about it, it's too late.

The crew of the *e galactic mu* had only each other, and that was perfect. It suited their purposes, each of them. They didn't much consider that if they returned, they'd be heroes, because what a Catch-22 that would be; they'd gotten there, on that FTL vessel out, because the world had finally gotten together and done something, as one. They were the phoenix of humanity, a flaming beast born from the lows of one damp rock ball called Earth.

The only strange thing was that the farseers couldn't see past the FTL field. An interesting discovery, that the power of foresight was probably going only around ninety-eight percent of the speed of light; something for the scientists to muck around with, anyway.

Imagine their surprise when everything went awry.

Years into the journey, when the *e galactic mu's* quantum computer began to recognize star formations, the crew became frightened. The computer was obviously malfunctioning significantly, so they couldn't trust its

FTL judgments. What were they to do but drift and wait till space-fever struck and things turned nasty and cannibal? But man, it was uncanny how similar those starfields were.

By the time Earth was actually close enough to recognize, they had it figured. All one-hundred-twelve members of the crew feebly drew air into their lungs, their chests constricted, their bio-monitors tripping alerts at each of the med-cubicles.

Science has proven that the heart, under extreme emotional distress, can break.

It seemed so obvious, in retrospect, that the universe was dough-nut-shaped. What hadn't been obvious is how this failure, this really final frontier, would affect the Earth. Like the evening after Christmas, when all of the presents have been unwrapped, all of the rare and satisfying foods have been eaten, after the red-cheeked young and old have run along, there was nothing. Nothing left at all.

It would be a waste to try and describe to you the destruction that followed. Just know that you could not have made it through. Hardly anyone could.

Will.

***

There are three people that made *e galactic mu* possible: Starr Wall, Jay Williams, and Mike Peterson. Four if you count myself. But that would be weird, I suppose, to thank myself. I wouldn't thank myself—it was a miserable experience and I'm still upset with myself for putting me through it.

My parents, Starr and Jay, took me to the library and helped me check out my 30-item limit every weekend of my childhood, and in later years would spend money they didn't have so I could keep up with whatever Piers Anthony and Mercedes Lackey were cranking out. Give me a break, I was like 11. But they didn't question it, bless them, and let me blunder my way through to the good stuff.

Because Mike Peterson gave me the advice of writing to a single person, *e galactic mu* owes more to him than anyone else. If he laughed, then it was funny. If he turned pages faster, then it was paced right. If he recognized himself as Captain Reverend, then it was maybe a little too transparent. His enthusiasm pushed me through the 100-page blues, and his tenacity alone is responsible for converting my manuscript into a book. Any mistakes herein are his.

Finally, I offer a deep and nerdy bow to William Gibson, whose *Neuromancer* kept me up one night at age 16 and totally and completely obliterated what I thought science fiction was. I thought it was a once-in-a-lifetime night, but I was young and immature and had not yet discovered Neal Stephenson, Elizabeth Hand, Peter Watts, Geoff Ryman and several dozen other authors who have continuously updated my software.

***

SUNDAY WILLIAMS lives in Olympia, WA with her man and her delightfully gassy Boston Terrier.

    e galactic mu is Sunday's first novel.

www.ingramcontent.com/pod-product-compliance
Lightning Source LLC
Chambersburg PA
CBHW060356260626
47160CB00006B/2328